note from the author

NOUGHTS & CROSSES wasn't so much a book I wanted to write as a book I needed to write. It was born of a number of factors, including – but not limited to – a need to deal with a number of events from my past, a desire to tackle the subject of racism head on, and the burning anger I felt regarding the death of Stephen Lawrence and the subsequent mishandling of the police inquiry into his death.

Though these things provided the impetus for sitting in front of my computer for a year to write this novel, I was determined not to put anything down on paper that didn't first and foremost serve the story of Callum and Sephy. That meant an awful lot got left out!

Callum and Sephy and the idea for the book marinated in my head for at least two years before I wrote a single word. I always write detailed biographies for all the major characters in my books. This is to ensure that my characters become real people to me before I start writing, but with Callum and Sephy I took extra care to really get to know them, inside out and backwards. That way, I felt I'd know how they would react in any situation.

I usually write quite a detailed outline of my plot before I get to work, but with NOUGHTS & CROSSES I deliberately didn't. I knew my story arc was going to be about the lives of Callum, Sephy and their families, and I knew the path I wanted them to take, but that was it. So I sat down to write and within a chapter, the characters had taken over. Now, this sounds slightly bonkers to anyone who is not a writer and who has never been through it, but when an author writes, the characters really do take on a life of their own. And if they don't, they should! I wanted Callum and Sephy to take certain paths through the story, but they pulled me down others. Events happened to them in the writing of the novel which I had never planned – at least, not consciously.

That said, Callum had to cope with certain events which were lifted directly from my own childhood and teenage years – events like enduring his history lesson, or being challenged for being in a first class carriage on a train. All this made **NOUGHTS & CROSSES** the most painful, personal, challenging, cathartic and satisfying book I'd written to date. There were times when I had to force myself to continue writing, times when my writing dredged up bitter memories I'd buried deep inside and thought were forgotten.

And – confession time – when I was writing the ending of this book, I was in tears, which at the time I considered totally barking! There I was as the author, and the characters had become so real, such friends to me, that I felt their pain as if it were my own.

I wasn't sure how **NOUGHTS & CROSSES** would be received; whether it would sink without trace, be mercilessly panned, or find any kind of audience. And, quite frankly, that wasn't a consideration. I knew I was writing a book that would make some adults very uncomfortable (and it did!) because I was dealing with racism, terrorism, the class system and the artificial divides we always seem to put between ourselves and others. But it was a risk I was willing to take.

NOUGHTS & CROSSES was quite simply a book I had to write, a story I had to tell.

I hope you enjoy it.

malorie blackman

NOUGHTS & CROSSES

www.malorieblackman.co.uk

NOUGHTS & CROSSES

Includes the explosive short story,

CALLUM

malorie
blackman

CORGI

NOUGHTS & CROSSES
A CORGI BOOK 978 0 552 55570 8

First published in Great Britain by Doubleday,
an imprint of Random House Children's Publishers UK
A Random House Group Company

Doubleday edition published 2001
Corgi edition published 2002
Reissued 2006
This edition published 2012

25

Penguin Random House is committed to a sustainable future for
our business, our readers and our planet. This book is made from
Forest Stewardship Council® certified paper.

MIX
Paper from
responsible sources
FSC® C018179

Random House Children's Publishers UK,
61–63 Uxbridge Road, London W5 5SA

www.**randomhousechildrens**.co.uk
www.**totallyrandombooks**.co.uk
www.**randomhouse**.co.uk

Addresses for companies within The Random House Group Limited
can be found at: www.randomhouse.co.uk/offices.htm

THE RANDOM HOUSE GROUP Limited Reg. No. 954009

A CIP catalogue record for this book is available from the British Library.

Printed and bound in Great Britain by Clays Ltd, St Ives plc

'This must be the most original book I've ever read.
It's intelligent, emotional and imaginatively wicked . . .
I insist on calling it a work of art'
Benjamin Zephaniah

'An inspired take on Romeo and Juliet . . .
Unforgettable' **Independent**

'Epic . . . Dramatic, moving and brave'
Guardian

Malorie Blackman is acknowledged as one of today's most imaginative and convincing writers for young readers. *Noughts & Crosses* has won several prizes, including the Red House Children's Book Award and the Fantastic Fiction Award, has been adapted for the stage by the Royal Shakespeare Company, and is soon to be a graphic novel. Malorie has also been shortlisted for the Carnegie Medal.

In 2005 Malorie was honoured with the Eleanor Farjeon Award in recognition of her contribution to the world of children's books, and in 2008 she received an OBE for her services to children's literature. She has been described by *The Times* as 'a bit of a national treasure'.

This book is dedicated with love to my husband, Neil,
And to our daughter, Elizabeth

THE McGREGOR FAMILY

THE HADLEY FAMILY

Ryan ——— Margaret
(Meggie)

Jude   Lynette   Callum

Kamal ——— Jasmine

Persephone   Minerva
(Sephy)   (Minny)

That's just the way it is.
Some things will never change.
That's just the way it is.
But don't you believe them.

Bruce Hornsby and the Range

'Honestly, Mrs Hadley,' said Meggie McGregor, wiping her eyes. 'That sense of humour of yours will be the death of me yet!'

Jasmine Hadley allowed herself a rare giggle. 'The things I tell you, Meggie. It's lucky we're such good friends!'

Meggie's smile wavered only slightly. She looked out across the vast lawn at Callum and Sephy. Her son and her employer's daughter. They were good friends playing together. *Real* good friends. No barriers. No boundaries. Not yet anyway. It was a typical early summer's day, light and bright and, in the Hadley household anyway, not a cloud in their sky.

'Excuse me, Mrs Hadley.' Sarah Pike, Mrs Hadley's secretary, approached from the house. She had shoulder-length straw-coloured hair and timid green eyes which appeared permanently startled. 'I'm sorry to disturb you but your husband has just arrived. He's in the study.'

'Kamal is here?' Mrs Hadley was astounded. 'Thank you, Sarah.' She turned to Meggie. 'His fourth visit home in as many months! We're honoured!'

Meggie smiled sympathetically, making sure to keep

her mouth well and truly shut. No way was she going to get in the middle of another inevitable squabble between Kamal Hadley and his wife. Mrs Hadley stood up and made her way into the house.

'So, Sarah, how is Mr Hadley?' Meggie lowered her voice to ask. 'Is he in a good mood, d'you think?'

Sarah shook her head. 'He looks about ready to blow a fuse.'

'Why?'

'No idea.'

Meggie digested this news in silence.

'I'd better get back to work,' Sarah sighed.

'Would you like something to drink?' Meggie pointed to the jug of ginger beer on the patio table.

'No, thanks. I don't want to get into trouble . . .' With obvious trepidation, Sarah went back into the house.

What was she afraid of? Meggie sighed. No matter how hard she tried, Sarah insisted on keeping her distance. Meggie turned back to watch the children. Life was so simple for them. Their biggest worry was what they'd get for their birthdays. Their biggest grumble was the time they had to go to bed. Maybe things would be different for them . . . Better. Meggie forced herself to believe that things would be better for the children, otherwise what was the point of it all?

On those rare occasions when she had a moment to herself, she couldn't help but play 'what if' games. Not the big 'what if's that her husband sometimes liked to indulge in, like, 'What if a virus wiped out every single Cross and not a single nought?' or 'What if there was a revolution and all the Crosses were overthrown? Killed.

Wiped off the face of the planet.' No, Meggie McGregor didn't believe in wasting her time on big, global fantasies. Her dreams were more specific, more unattainable than that. Her dreams were all around one subject. What if Callum and Sephy . . .? What if Sephy and Callum . . .?

Meggie felt a peculiar, burning sensation on the back of her neck. She turned to find Mr Hadley standing on the patio, watching her with the strangest expression on his face.

'Is everything all right, Mr Hadley?'

'No. But I'll survive,' Mr Hadley moved forward to the patio table to stand over Meggie. 'You were deep in thought there. Penny for them?'

Flustered by his presence, Meggie began, 'I was just thinking about my son and your daughter. Wouldn't it be nice if . . ?' Appalled, she bit back the rest of the sentence, but it was too late.

'What would be nice?' Mr Hadley prompted, silkily.

'If they could . . . could always stay as they are now.' At Mr Hadley's raised eyebrows, Meggie rushed on. 'At this age, I mean. They're so wonderful at this age – children, I mean. So . . . so . . .'

'Yes, indeed.'

Pause.

Kamal Hadley sat down. Mrs Hadley emerged from the kitchen to lean against the door frame. She had a strange, wary expression on her face. Meggie felt nervous. She started to get to her feet.

'I understand you had a wonderful time yesterday.' Mr Hadley smiled at Meggie.

'A . . . a wonderful time?'

'Yesterday evening?' Mr Hadley prompted.

'Yes. It was quite quiet really . . .' Meggie replied, confused. She looked from Mr to Mrs Hadley and back again. Mrs Hadley was watching her intently. What was going on? The temperature in the garden had dropped by several degrees and despite his smiles, Mr Hadley was obviously furious at something – or someone. Meggie swallowed hard. Had she done something wrong? She didn't think so, but God only knew that being around Crosses was like walking on eggshells.

'So what did you do?' Mr Hadley prompted.

'P-pardon?'

'Last night?' Mr Hadley's smile was very friendly. Too friendly.

'I . . . we stayed home and watched telly,' Meggie said slowly.

'It's nice to have a relaxing evening at home with your own family,' Mr Hadley agreed.

Meggie nodded. What did he expect her to say to that? *What was going on?* Mr Hadley stood up, his smile now a thing of the past. He walked over to his wife. They both stood just watching each other as the seconds ticked by. Mrs Hadley began to straighten up. Without warning, Mr Hadley slapped his wife full across the face. The force of the blow sent Mrs Hadley's head snapping backwards to strike against the door frame.

Meggie was on her feet in a second, her horrified gasp audible, her hand out in silent protest. Kamal Hadley gave his wife a look of such contempt and loathing that Mrs Hadley flinched back from it. Without a word passing between them, Mr Hadley went back into the house.

Meggie was at Mrs Hadley's side in an instant.

'Are you OK?' Meggie's hand went out to examine the side of Mrs Hadley's face.

Mrs Hadley knocked her hand away. With a puzzled frown, Meggie tried again. The same thing happened.

'Leave me alone,' Mrs Hadley hissed at her. 'When I needed your help, you didn't give it.'

'I . . . what . . ?' And only then did Meggie realize what she'd done. Mrs Hadley had obviously used Meggie as an alibi for the previous night and Meggie had been too slow to pick up on what Kamal Hadley had really been asking her.

Meggie's hand dropped back to her side. 'I think I should get back to work . . .'

'Yes, I think that would be best.' Mrs Hadley's look was venomous before she turned and walked back into the house.

Meggie turned around. Callum and Sephy were still playing at the other end of the vast garden, oblivious to everything that had just happened. She stood and watched them, trying to capture for herself some small part of their pure joy in each other. She needed something good to hold on to. But even the distant sound of their laughter couldn't dampen down the deep sense of foreboding creeping through her. What would happen now?

That night, Meggie sat at the table sewing patches over the patches in Jude's school trousers.

'Meggie, I'm sure you're worrying about nothing,' Ryan, her husband sighed.

'Ryan, you didn't see the look on her face. I did.'

Meggie bit off the thread and picked up another patch. Jude's school trousers were more patch than original material.

The phone started to ring. Meggie picked it up before the first ring had even died away.

'Hello?'

'Meggie McGregor?'

'That's right.' Meggie's sewing fell unheeded to her feet.

'It's Sarah Pike here . . .'

Meggie couldn't help but notice the apology already in her voice. 'How are you, Sarah?'

'Fine, er . . . OK. Look, I've got some bad news . . .'

Meggie nodded slowly. 'I'm listening.'

Sarah gave an embarrassed cough before she continued. 'Mrs Hadley has asked me to inform you that . . . that your services at the Hadley household will no longer be required. She will pay you four weeks' wages in lieu of proper notice, plus give you a good reference.'

Meggie's blood turned to ice water in her veins. Whatever else she'd been expecting, it wasn't this. Heaven only knew it wasn't this.

'She's . . . she's really sacking me?'

'I'm sorry.'

'I see.'

'I'm really sorry,' Sarah's voice dropped to a whisper. 'Between you and me, I think it's grossly unfair.'

From one nought to another . . .

'It's OK, Sarah. It's not your fault.' Meggie replied.

She looked across at Ryan. His expression grew harder and tighter by degrees. Let him get upset. Let him be angry. All she could feel was . . . nothing. A nothing that went way beyond the numbness enveloping every part of her body.

'Sorry, Meggie,' Sarah said again.

'That's OK. Thanks for letting me know. Bye, Sarah.'

'Bye.'

Meggie put down the phone. The clock on the TV counted out the silent moments that passed. 'That's the end of Jude's education,' she sighed at last.

'But we promised him we'd pay for him to carry on at school,' Ryan said, aghast.

'Pay with what?' Meggie rounded on her husband. 'The leaves off the trees? The hairs off our legs? What?'

'We'll find a way . . .'

'How? We're barely managing to survive as it was. What will we do without my wages coming in? Jude will have to forget about school. He'll have to go out to work.'

'You'll get another job,' Ryan tried.

'Not with another Cross family I won't. D'you really think Mrs Hadley will stand idly by whilst I get another job with one of her friends?'

There was dawning horror on Ryan's face as he realized what his wife meant.

'Yes, exactly,' Meggie sighed.

She stood up and moved to sit next to her husband on the old sofa in front of the fire. Ryan put his arm around her. They sat in silence for a long, long time.

'Ryan, we're in trouble,' Meggie said at last.

'I know,' Ryan replied.

Meggie jumped to her feet, her expression hard and

determined. 'I'm going to see her.'

'What're you talking about?' Ryan frowned.

'I've worked for that woman for fourteen years, ever since she was pregnant with her daughter Minerva. Seeing me is the very least she can do.'

'I don't think that's a good idea . . .' Ryan's frown deepened.

'Ryan, I need to get my job back. And if I have to beg, then so be it,' Meggie insisted, pulling on her coat. Her expression was now so hard, it might've been carved in granite.

'No, Meggie . . .'

'I don't like it any more than you do, but we have no choice.' Meggie didn't wait for any further argument. She headed out of the door.

Ryan watched his wife leave the house. No good would come of this. He could feel it.

Two hours later, Meggie was back.

And that was the night that Lynette disappeared . . .

THREE YEARS LATER . . .

Callum And Sephy

one. Sephy

I wriggled my toes, enjoying the feel of the warm sand trickling like fine baby powder between them. Digging my feet even deeper into the dry, yellow-white sand, I tilted back my head. It was such a beautiful August afternoon. Nothing bad could ever happen on a day like today. And what made it even better was the fact that I could share it − something rare and special in itself, as I knew only too well. I turned to the boy next to me, my face about to split wide open from the smile on it.

'Can I kiss you?'

My smile faded. I stared at my best friend. 'Pardon?'

'Can I kiss you?'

'What on earth for?'

'Just to see what it's like,' Callum replied.

Yeuk! I mean, *yeuk*!! I wrinkled up my nose − I couldn't help it. Kissing! Why on earth would Callum want to do anything so . . . so feeble?

'Do you really want to?' I asked.

Callum shrugged. 'Yeah, I do.'

'Oh, all right then.' I wrinkled up my nose again at the prospect. 'But make it fast!'

Callum turned to kneel beside me. I turned my head up towards his, watching with growing curiosity to see what he'd do next. I tilted my head to the left. So did he. I tilted my head to the right. Callum did the same. He was moving his head like he was my reflection or something. I put my hands on Callum's face to keep it still and dead centre.

'D'you want me to tilt my head to the left or the right?' I asked, impatiently.

'Er . . . which way do girls usually tilt their heads when they're being kissed?' asked Callum.

'Does it matter? Besides, how should I know?' I frowned. 'Have I ever kissed a boy before?'

'Tilt your head to the left then.'

'My left or your left?'

'Er . . . your left.'

I did as asked. 'Hurry up, before I get a crick in my neck.'

Callum licked his lips before his face moved slowly closer towards mine.

'Oh no you don't,' I drew back. 'Wipe your lips first.'

'Why?'

'You just licked them.'

'Oh! OK!' Callum wiped his mouth with the back of his hand.

I moved forward to resume my original position. Keeping my lips tight together, I wondered what I should do with them. Purse them so that they stuck out slightly? Or should I smile to make them seem wider and more appealing? I'd only ever practised kissing with my pillow. This was a lot different – and seemed just as silly!

'Hurry up!' I urged.

I kept my eyes wide open as I watched Callum's face

move down towards mine. Callum's grey eyes were open too. I was going cross-eyed trying to keep my focus on his face. And then his lips were touching mine. How funny! I'd expected Callum's lips to be hard and dry and scaly like a lizard's skin. But they weren't. They were soft. Callum closed his eyes. After a moment, I did the same. Our lips were still touching. Callum's mouth opened, making mine open at the same time. Callum's breath mingled with mine and felt warm and sweet. And then without warning his tongue was touching mine.

'Yeuk!' I drew back immediately and stuck my tongue out, wiping it with my hand. 'What did you do that for?'

'It wasn't that bad, was it?'

'I don't want your tongue on mine.' I shook my head.

'Why not?'

' 'Cause . . .' I shuddered at the thought of it, '. . . our spit will mix up.'

'So? It's meant to.'

I considered this.

'Well?'

'OK! OK!' I frowned, adding. 'The things I do for you! Let's try it again.'

Callum smiled at me, the familiar twinkle in his eyes. That's the thing about Callum – he looks at me a certain way and I'm never quite sure if he's laughing at me. Before I could change my mind, Callum's lips were already on mine – and just as soft and gentle as before. His tongue flicked into my mouth again. After a brief moment of thinking *ugh*! I found that it wasn't too bad. In fact it was actually quite nice in a gross-to-think-about-but-OK-to-do sort of way. I closed my eyes and began to return Callum's kiss. His tongue licked over mine. It was warm and wet but it didn't make me want to heave. And then my tongue did the same to him. I began to feel a little strange. My heart was beginning to thump in a peculiar, hiccupy way that made me feel like I was racing down a roller-coaster, roaring out of control. Someone was tying knots with my insides. I pulled away.

'That's enough.'

'Sorry.' Callum sat back.

'Why're you apologizing?' I frowned. 'Didn't you like it?'

Callum shrugged. 'It was OK.'

I was annoyed. I didn't know why, but I couldn't help it. 'Have you kissed any other girls besides me?'

'No.'

'Any Cross girls?'

'No.'

'Any nought girls?'

'No means no.' Callum huffed with exasperation.

'So why did you want to kiss me?'

'We're friends, aren't we?' Callum shrugged.

I relaxed into a smile. 'Of course we are.'

'And if you can't kiss your friends then who can you kiss?' Callum smiled.

I turned back to the sea. It shone like a shattered mirror, each fragment reflecting and dazzling. It never ceased to amaze me just how beautiful the sand and the sea and the gentle breeze on my face could be. My family's private beach was my favourite place in the whole world. Kilometres of coastline that was all ours, with just a couple of signs declaring that it was private property and some old wooden fencing at each end, through which Callum and I had made a gap. And I was here with my favourite person. I turned to look at Callum. He was looking at me, the strangest expression on his face.

'What's the matter?'

'Nothing.'

'What're you thinking?' I asked.

'About you and me.'

'What about us?'

Callum turned to look out over the sea. 'Sometimes I wish there was just you and me and no-one else in the whole world.'

'We'd drive each other crazy, wouldn't we?' I teased.

At first I thought that Callum wasn't going to answer.

'Sephy, d'you ever dream of just . . . escaping? Hopping on the first boat or plane you come across and just letting it take you away.' There was no mistaking the wistfully wishful note in Callum's voice. 'I do . . .'

'Where would you go?'

'That's just the point,' Callum said with sudden bitterness. 'This place is like the whole world and the whole world is like this place. So where could I go?'

'This place isn't so bad, is it?' I asked, gently.

'Depends on your point of view,' Callum replied. 'You're on the inside, Sephy. I'm not.'

I couldn't think of an answer to that, so I didn't reply. We both sat in silence for a while longer.

'Wherever you went, I'd go with you,' I decided. 'Though you'd soon get bored with me.'

Callum sighed. A long, heartfelt sigh which immediately

made me feel like I'd failed some test I hadn't even known I was taking.

'We'd better get on with it,' he said at last. 'What's the lesson for today, teacher?'

Disappointment raced through me. But then, what did I expect? '*Sephy, I could never be bored of you, with you, around you. You're exciting, scintillating, overwhelming company!*' Yeah, right! Dream on, Sephy!!

'So what're we doing today?' Callum's voice was tinged with impatience.

'OK! OK!' I said, exasperated. Honestly! The sun was too warm and the sea was too blue to do any schoolwork. 'Callum you've already passed the entrance exam. Why do we still have to do this?'

'I don't want to give any of the teachers an excuse to kick me out.'

'You haven't even started school yet and already you're talking about being kicked out?' I was puzzled. Why was he so cynical about my school? 'You've got nothing to worry about. You're in now. The school accepted you.'

'Being in and being accepted are two different things.' Callum shrugged. 'Besides, I want to learn as much as I can so I don't look like a complete dunce.'

I sat up suddenly. 'I've just had a thought. Maybe you'll be in my class. Oh, I do hope so,' I said eagerly. 'Wouldn't that be great?'

'You think so?'

I tried — and failed, I think — to keep the hurt out of my voice. 'Don't you?'

Callum looked at me and smiled. 'You shouldn't answer a question with a question,' he teased.

'Why not?' I forced myself to smile back.

Taking me by surprise, Callum pushed me over onto the sand. Indignant, I scrambled up to kneel in front of him.

'D'you mind?' I huffed.

'No. Not at all.' Callum smirked.

We looked at each other and burst out laughing. I stopped laughing first.

'Callum, wouldn't . . . wouldn't you like to be in my class . . ?'

Callum couldn't meet my eyes. 'It's a bit . . . humiliating for us noughts to be stuck in the baby class.'

'What d'you mean? I'm not a baby.' I jumped to my feet, scowling down at him.

'Jeez, Sephy, I'm fifteen, for heaven's sake! In six months' time I'll be sixteen and they're still sticking me in with twelve- and thirteen-year-olds. How would you like to be in a class with kids at least a year younger than you?' Callum asked.

'I . . . well . . .' I sat back down.

'Exactly!'

'I'm fourteen in three weeks,' I said, unwilling to let it drop.

'That's not the point, and you know it.'

'But the school explained why. You're all at least a year behind and . . .'

'And whose fault is that?' Callum said with erupting bitterness. 'Until a few years ago we were only allowed to be educated up to the age of fourteen – and in noughts-only schools at that, which don't have a quarter of the money or resources that your schools have.'

I had no answer.

'Sorry. I didn't mean to bite your head off.'

'You didn't.' I said. 'Are any of your friends from your old school going to join you at Heathcrofts?'

'No. None of them got in,' Callum replied. 'I wouldn't've got in either if you hadn't helped me.'

He made it sound like an accusation. I wanted to say sorry and I had no idea why.

Callum sighed. 'Come on, we'd better get to work . . .'

'OK.' I turned and dug into my bag for my school books. 'What d'you want to do first? Maths or History?'

'Maths. I like Maths.'

'Yeuk!' I shook my head. How could anyone in their right mind like Maths?! Languages were my favourite subjects, followed by Human Biology and Sociology and Chemistry. Maths fought with Physics for the subject I liked the least. 'Right then. Maths it is.' I wrinkled my nose. 'I'll tell you what I've been revising over the last week and then you can explain it to me!'

Callum laughed. 'You should get into Maths. It's the universal language.'

'Says who?'

'Says anyone with any sense. Look at how many different languages are spoken on our planet. The only thing that doesn't change, no matter what the language, is Maths. And it's probably the same on other planets too.'

'Pardon?'

'That's probably how we'll talk to aliens from other planets when they get here or when we get to them. We'll use Maths.'

I stared at Callum. Sometimes when I talked to him, the seventeen months between us seemed to stretch to seventy years. 'Are . . . are you winding me up?'

Callum's smile was no answer.

'Stop it! You're giving me a headache.' I frowned. 'Can we just get on with the Maths in my book and forget about chatting with aliens for a while?'

'OK,' Callum said at last. 'But Sephy, you should think above and beyond just us. You should free your mind and think about other cultures and other planets and oh, I don't know, just think about the future.'

'I've got plenty of time to think about the future when I'm tons older and don't have much future left, thank you very much. And my mind is quite free enough.'

'Is it?' Callum asked slowly. 'There's more to life than just us noughts and you Crosses.'

My stomach jerked. Callum's words hurt. Why did they hurt? 'Don't say that . . .'

'Don't say what?'

'*Us* noughts and *you* Crosses.' I shook my head. 'It makes it sound like . . . like you're in one place and I'm in another, with a huge, great wall between us.'

Callum looked out across the sea. 'Maybe we are in different places . . .'

'No, we aren't. Not if we don't want to be, we aren't.' I willed Callum to look at me.

'I wish it was that simple.'

'It is.'

'Maybe from where you're sitting.' At last Callum turned towards me, but his expression stemmed the words I was about to say. And then, just like that, his expression cleared and his easy smile was back. 'You're very young, Sephy.'

'I'm only a year and a bit younger than you, so don't start talking down to me.' I fumed. 'I get enough of that at home.'

'OK! OK! Sorry!' Callum raised his hand in a placatory manner. 'Now then, how about some Maths?'

Still annoyed, I opened my school study book. Callum shuffled closer until his arm and mine were touching. His skin was warm, almost hot – or was it mine? It was hard to tell. I handed him the book and watched as the pages on polygons instantly caught and held his attention.

Callum was the one person in the world I could tell anything and everything to without having to think twice about it. So why did I now feel so . . . out of step? Like he was leaving me behind? He suddenly seemed so much older, not just in years but in the things he knew and had experienced. His eyes were a lot older than fifteen. My eyes were different – they reflected my exact age, less than one month away from my fourteenth birthday. Not a day less and certainly not a day more. I didn't want things to change between us – ever. But at that moment I felt as if I might as well stand on the beach and command the sea never to move again.

'How does this bit work?' Callum asked, pointing to an interior angle of a regular octagon.

I shook my head, telling myself not to be so silly. Nothing would ever come between me and Callum. I wouldn't let it. Neither would Callum. He needed our friendship just as much as I did.

Needed . . . That was a strange way to put it. Why had

I thought of it that way? As a friendship both of us needed? That didn't make any sense at all. I had friends at school. And a huge, extended family with cousins and aunts and uncles, and plenty of great whatevers and great-great whatevers to send Christmas and birthday cards to. But it wasn't the same as Callum and me. Callum glanced up impatiently. I smiled at him. After a brief puzzled look, he smiled back.

'It works like this,' I began and we both looked down at the book as I began to explain.

'We'd better be getting back – before your mum has every police officer in the country searching for you,' Callum said at last.

'Suppose so.' I picked up my sandals and rose to my feet. Then I had a brilliant idea. 'Why don't we go back to yours? I haven't been to your house in ages and I could always phone up Mother once I'm there and . . .'

'Better not,' Callum said, shaking his head. He'd started shaking his head the moment the suggestion had left my mouth. He picked up my bag and slung it over his shoulder.

I frowned at Callum. 'We used to be in and out of each other's houses all the time . . .'

'Used to be. Let's leave it for a while – OK?'

'How come I never go to your house any more? Aren't I welcome?'

' 'Course you are. But the beach is better,' Callum shrugged and set off.

'Is it because of Lynette? 'Cause if it is, I really don't mind about your sister being . . . being . . .' My voice trailed off at Callum's furious expression.

'Being what?' Callum prompted, fiercely.

'Nothing,' I shrugged. 'Sorry.'

'This has nothing to do with Lynette,' Callum snapped.

I immediately shut up. I seemed to have an acute case of foot-in-mouth disease today. We walked back in silence. Up the stone steps, worn to satin smoothness by the procession of centuries of feet and along the cliff side, heading further and further inland, away from the sea. I looked across the open grassland towards the house which dominated the view for kilometres around. My parents' country house. Seven bedrooms and five reception rooms for four people. What a waste. Four people in such a vast house – four lonely peas rolling about in a can. We were still some distance from it but it rose like an all-seeing giant above us. I pretended I didn't see Callum flinch at the sight of it. Is it any wonder I preferred the laughter of his house to the dignified silence of my own? We walked on for wordless minutes until Callum's steps slowed and stopped altogether.

'What's wrong?' I asked.

'It's just . . .' Callum turned to face me. 'It doesn't matter. Give me a hug?'

Why was Callum in such a touchy-feely mood this afternoon? After a moment's hesitation, I decided not to ask. Callum looked different. What I'd thought of as a permanent teasing sparkle in his eyes when he looked at me was gone without a trace. His eyes were storm-grey and just as troubled. He ran his fingers over his short-cut, chestnut brown hair in a gesture that seemed almost nervous. I opened my arms and stepped towards Callum.

I wrapped my arms around him, my head on his shoulder. He was holding me, squeezing me too tightly but I didn't say a word. I held my breath so it wouldn't hurt so much. Just when I thought I'd have to gasp or protest, Callum suddenly let me go.

'I can't go any further,' Callum said.

'Just up to the rose garden.'

'Not today.' Callum shook his head. 'I have to go.' He handed back my bag.

'I am going to see you tomorrow after school, aren't I? In our usual place?'

Callum shrugged. He was already walking away.

'Callum, wait! What's the ma . . ?'

But Callum was running now — faster and faster. I watched my best friend tear away from me, his hands over his ears. What was going on? I carried on walking up to the house, my head bent as I tried to figure it out.

'PERSEPHONE! INSIDE! NOW!'

My head snapped up at the sound of my mother's voice. Mother came hurtling down the steps, her expression dour and fierce — as always. She'd obviously not had as many glasses of wine today as she normally did, otherwise she wouldn't be in such a bad mood. I turned back to where Callum had been, but he was already out of sight — which was just as well. Mother grabbed my arm with bony fingers that bit like pincers.

'I have been calling you for the last half an hour.'

'You should've called louder then. I was down on the beach.'

'Don't be cheeky. I told you not to wander off today.' Mother started dragging me up the stairs behind her.

'Ouch!' I banged my shin against one of the stone steps where I'd been too slow to pick up my feet. I tried to bend to rub my bruised skin but Mother was still dragging me.

'Let go. Stop pulling me. I'm not luggage.' I pulled my arm out of Mother's grasp.

'Get in the house now.'

'Where's the fire?' I glared at Mother as I rubbed my arm.

'You're not to leave the house for the rest of the day.' Mother entered the house. I had no choice but to follow.

'Why not?'

' 'Cause I said so.'

'What's the . . ?'

'And stop asking so many questions.'

I scowled at Mother but she was oblivious – as always. To her, my dirty looks were water off a duck's feathers. The warm, wonderful afternoon was excluded from our house with the closing of the front door. Mother was one of those 'refined' women who could make the quiet closing of a door as forceful as a slam. Every time Mother looked at me, I could feel her wishing that I was more ladylike, like my scabby big sister, Minerva. I called her Minnie for short when I wanted to annoy her, because she hated it so much. I called her Minnie all the time. She loved our house as much as I hated it. She called it 'grand'. To me it was like a bad museum – all cold floors and marble pillars and carved stonework which glossy magazines loved to photograph but which no-one with half a gram of sense would ever want to live in.

Thank God for Callum. I hugged the knowledge of

how I'd spent my day to myself with a secret smile. Callum had kissed me. Wow!

Callum had actually *kissed* me!

Wowee! *Zowee!*

My smile slowly faded as a unbidden thought crept into my head. There was just one thing that stopped my day from being entirely perfect. If only Callum and I didn't have to sneak and creep around.

If only Callum wasn't a nought.

two. Callum

'I live in a palace with golden walls and silver turrets and marble floors . . .' I opened my eyes and looked at my house. My heart sank. I closed my eyes again. 'I live in a mansion with mullion windows and leaded light casements and a swimming pool and stables in the acres and acres of grounds.' I opened one eye. It still hadn't worked. 'I live in a three up, two down house with a lock on the front door and a little garden where we grow veggies.' I opened both eyes. It never worked. I hesitated outside my house – if you could call it that. Every time I came back from Sephy's, I flinched at the sight of the shack that was meant to be my home. Why couldn't my family live in a house like Sephy's? Why didn't any nought I knew of live in a house like Sephy's? Looking at our rundown hovel, I could feel the usual burning, churning sensation begin to rise up inside me. My stomach tightened, my eyes began to narrow . . . So I forced myself to look away. Forced myself to look around at the oak and beech and chestnut trees that lined our street, lifting their branches up to the sky. I watched a solitary cloud slowdance above me, watched a swallow dart and soar without a care in the world.

'Come on . . . you can do this . . . do this . . . do this . . .' I closed my eyes and took a deep breath. Steeling myself, I pushed open the front door and walked inside.

'Where've you been, Callum? I was worried sick.'

Mum launched in before I'd even closed the door behind me. There was no hall or passageway with rooms leading off it like in Sephy's house. As soon as you opened our front door, there was our living room with its fifth-hand threadbare nylon carpet and its seventh-hand cloth sofa. The only thing in the room that was worth a damn was the oaken table. Years before, Dad had cut it and shaped it and carved the dragon's leaf pattern into it, put it together and polished it himself. A lot of love and work had gone into that table. Sephy's mother had once tried to buy it but Mum and Dad wouldn't part with it.

'Well? I'm waiting, Callum. Where were you?' Mum repeated.

I sat down at my place around the table and looked away from Mum. Dad wasn't bothered about me – or anything else, for that matter. He was totally focused on his food. Jude, my seventeen-year-old brother, grinned knowingly at me. He's a really irritating toad. I looked away from him as well.

'He was with his dagger friend.' Jude smirked.

I scowled at him. 'What dagger friend? If you don't know what you're talking about you should shut your mouth.' *Don't you call my best friend that . . . Say that again and I'll knock you flat . . .*

Jude could see what I was thinking because his smirk broadened. 'What should I call her then? Your dagger what?'

He never called them Crosses. They were always *daggers*.

'Why don't you go and get stuffed?!'

'Callum, son, don't talk to your brother like . . .' Dad didn't get any further.

'Callum, were you with *her* again?' Mum's eyes took on a fierce, bitter gleam.

'No, Mum. I went for a walk, that's all.'

'That had better be all.' Mum banged down the dinner pan. Pasta sloshed over the sides and onto the table. Seconds later, Jude had whipped up the overspill and it was in his mouth!

Astounded seconds ticked past as everyone at the table stared at Jude. He even had Lynette's attention – and that was saying something. Not much brought my sister out of her mysterious world.

'How come the only time you move faster than greased lightning is when food is involved?' Mum said, her lips twitching somewhere between disgust and amusement.

'It's called incentive, Mum,' Jude grinned.

Amusement won. Mum started to laugh. 'I'll give you incentive, my lad!'

And for once I was grateful to Jude for drawing attention away from what I'd been doing all afternoon. I glanced around the table. Already Lynette was turning away, her head bowed as always, her attention on her lap – as always.

'Hi, Lynny . . .' I spoke softly to my big sister. She looked up and gave me the briefest of smiles before returning her gaze to her lap.

My sister looks like me – the same brown hair, eyes the same shade of grey. Jude's got black hair and brown eyes and looks like Mum. Lynny and I don't look like Mum or Dad particularly. Maybe that's part of the reason why we've always been close. Closer than Jude and I. She was the one who looked after me when Mum had to work and couldn't take me with her. But now she can't even look after herself. She's a bit simple. She looks her age, twenty, but her mind is outside time. She's away with the fairies as my grandma used to say. She wasn't always that way. Three years ago something happened which changed her. An accident. And just like that the sister I knew was gone. Now she doesn't go out, doesn't talk much, doesn't think much as far as I can tell. She just *is*. She stays lost in the middle of her own world somewhere. We can't get in and she doesn't come out. Not often anyway, and certainly not for any length of time. But her mind takes her to somewhere kind, I think, to judge by the peaceful, serene look on her face most of the time. Sometimes I wondered if it was worth losing your marbles to find that kind of peace. Sometimes I envied her.

'So where have you been all this time?' Mum resumed her previous conversation.

And I'd thought I'd got away with it. I should've guessed that Mum wouldn't let the matter rest. Once she gets a bee in her knickers . . .

'Just walking, I told you.'

'Hhmmm . . .' Mum's eyes narrowed but she turned around and headed back to the cooker for the mince. I breathed an outward sigh of relief. Mum was obviously tired because for once she'd chosen to believe me.

Lynette gave me one of her secret smiles. She turned to spoon pasta onto her plate as Mum returned with the pan of mince.

'Ready for school tomorrow, Callum?' Dad said warmly, seemingly oblivious to the instant tension rising up around the table like razor wire.

'Ready as I'll ever be, Dad,' I muttered, pouring myself a glass of milk from the dinner jug so that I wouldn't have to look at anyone.

'It'll be tough, son, but at least it's a start. My son is going to Heathcroft High School. Imagine that!' Dad took a deep breath, his chest actually puffing up with pride as he smiled at me.

'I still think he's making a big mistake . . .' Mum sniffed.

'Well, I don't.' Dad's smile vanished as he turned to Mum.

'He doesn't need to go to their schools. We noughts should have our own schools with the same opportunities that the Crosses enjoy,' Mum retorted. 'We don't need to mix with them.'

'What's wrong with mixing?' I asked, surprised.

'It doesn't work,' Mum replied at once. 'As long as the schools are run by Crosses, we'll always be treated as second-class, second-best nothings. We should look after and educate our own, not wait for the Crosses to do it for us.'

'You never used to believe that,' said Dad.

'I'm not as naïve as I used to be – if that's what you mean,' Mum replied.

I opened my mouth to speak but the words wouldn't come. They were just a jumble in my head. If a Cross had said that to me, I'd be accusing them of all sorts. It seemed to me we'd practised segregation for centuries now and that hadn't worked either. What would satisfy all the noughts and the Crosses who felt the same as Mum? Separate countries? Separate planets? How far away was far enough? What was it about the differences in others that scared some people so much?

'Meggie, if our boy is going to get anywhere in this life, he has to go to their schools and learn to play the game by their rules. He just has to be better at it, that's all.'

'That's all?'

'Don't you want something more for your son than we ever had?' Dad asked, annoyed.

'How can you ask me that? If you think . . .'

'I'm sure everything will be fine, Mum. Don't worry,' I interrupted.

Mum clamped her lips together, her expression thunderous. She stood up and went over to the fridge. I could tell from the way she took out the water bottle and slammed the fridge door shut that she wasn't happy. My going to school was the only thing I'd ever heard my parents argue about. Mum twisted the top off the bottle and tipped it so that it was directly over the yellow painted pottery jug she'd made a few weeks back. Water gushed out, rising up in the jug to slosh over the sides and down onto the work surface, but she didn't alter the angle of the bottle.

'You'll soon think you're too good for us.' Jude punched me on the arm for good measure. 'Just don't go getting too big for your boots!'

'Of course he won't. And you'll be on your best behaviour at Heathcroft, won't you?' Dad beamed. 'You'll be representing all of us noughts at the school.'

Why did I have to represent all noughts? Why couldn't I just represent myself?

'You must show them they're wrong about us. Show them we're just as good as they are,' Dad continued.

'He doesn't need to go to their stuck-up school to show them that.' Mum came back to the table, slamming the water jug down on the plastic tablecloth.

Milk and water, water and milk – that was all we ever had with our dinner. Unless we were extra short of money, in which case it was just water. I lifted my glass of milk to my mouth and closed my eyes. I could almost smell the orange juice Sephy's family nearly always had at their dinner table. Chardonnay for her mother and a claret for her dad and a choice of fizzy water, fruit juice – usually orange – and/or fizzy ginger beer for Sephy and her sister, Minerva. No bottled tap water for them. I remembered years ago when Sephy had snuck me my first taste of orange juice. It was icy-cold and oh, so sweet and I held each sip in my mouth until it became warm because I was so loath to swallow. I wanted the orange juice to last – but of course it hadn't. Sephy snuck me orange juice as often as she could after that. She couldn't understand why I loved it so much. I think she still can't.

I took a sip of my drink. My juice had too obviously passed through a cow first! I guess I didn't have enough imagination to turn milk into orange juice.

'He'll soon be as stuck-up as them.' Jude prodded me in the same place where he'd just punched me, turning his finger this way and that to make sure that it really hurt.

I put down my glass and glared at Jude.

'Come on then . . .' Jude whispered for my ears only.

I carefully placed my hands on my lap, my fingers interlocked.

'What's the matter? Am I embarrassing you?' Jude teased maliciously.

Beneath the table, my fingertips were beginning to go numb, I was pressing them together so hard. Ever since I'd passed the exam and got into Heathcroft, Jude had become totally unbearable. He spent every waking moment trying to goad me into hitting out at him. So far I'd managed to resist the intense temptation – but only just. I had sense enough to know that if Jude and I got into a fight, he'd wipe the floor with me. I hated it here so much. Oh, to get away. Far away. Even if I couldn't get up and physically leave the table, I had to get out of here before . . . before I exploded.

Sephy . . . Sephy and the beach . . . and Maths . . . and our kiss. I smiled as I remembered her insisting that I wipe my mouth before our first kiss. She did make me laugh.

That's right, Callum. Just drift away. Out of the house . . . back to the beach . . . back to Sephy . . .

She did make me laugh . . .

'You're not listening to a single word, are you?' Mum's rasp cut through my reverie.

'I was listening,' I denied.

'What did I just say then?'

'My new uniform is over my chair and I'm to get up extra early and have a wash before putting them on. My writing books are in the school bag under my bed,' I repeated.

'You heard me. That doesn't mean you were listening!' Mum replied.

I smiled. 'What's the difference?'

'My reaction!' Mum said at once. Smiling reluctantly, she sat down. The atmosphere wasn't perfect, but at least it was better than it had threatened to be less than five minutes ago.

'A son of mine at Heathcroft School.' Dad shook his head, his spoon poised before his lips. 'Imagine that!'

'Shut up and eat your food, fool!' Mum snapped.

Dad looked at her and burst out laughing. Everyone else joined in – except Lynette.

I spooned pasta and mince into my mouth, smiling as I chewed. To tell the truth, I was looking forward to school tomorrow. I was actually going to secondary school. I could make something of myself, do something with my life. Once I had a proper education behind me, no-one could turn around and say, 'You're not smart enough or good enough'. No-one. I was on my way UP! And with a proper education behind me, nothing could stand between Sephy and me. Nothing.

three. Sephy

I moved the cursor over to SHUT DOWN and clicked, yawning as I waited for my PC to switch off. It seemed to be taking for ever tonight. At last, there was a clunk and the screen went black. I pressed the button to switch off my monitor and switched off the loudspeakers. Now for a quick drink and then bed. First day of school tomorrow. I groaned at the thought. School! I'd see all my friends again and we'd have the usual conversations, about the places we'd visited, the films we'd seen, the parties we'd posed at – and before long it would be like we'd never been away from school at all. The same old faces, the same old teachers, the same old, same old! But that wasn't strictly true, was it? At least tomorrow would be a bit different from the start of every other new term. Four noughts, including Callum, were starting at my school. Maybe he'd even be in my class. And if he wasn't we were bound to share some lessons together. *My best friend was going to attend my very own school*. That one thought alone was enough to make me grin like a silly idiot!

'Please God, let Callum be in my class,' I whispered.

I walked out of my room and headed along the landing. Callum in my class . . . That would be so great! I was looking forward to showing him the playing fields and the swimming pool, the gym and the music rooms, the dining hall and the science labs. And I'd introduce him to all my friends. Once they got to know him, they'd think he was as great as I did. It was going to be wonderful.

I crept down the stairs. As thirsty as I was, I didn't relish the prospect of running into Mother. She was so miserable. I couldn't understand it. I could still remember when Mother had been all smiles and hugs and jokes – but that was long ago and far away now. About three years ago. Since then, there had been a complete change. Her sense of humour had grown old and died before the rest of her and these days her lips were turned down in a frown that was permanently carved into her skin.

I shook my head. If that's what growing old was about then I never wanted to grow old. At least Dad was still fun – when he was around, which wasn't often. Every adult I met for the first time loved to tell me how great my dad was – how he was so smart, so funny, so handsome, how he was destined to go all the way to the top. I'd've liked to discover those things about my dad for myself. A man with oily hands and a sweaty smell who came to Mother and Dad's last dinner party had spent his entire time with me talking about how Dad would be Prime Minister one day and how I must be so proud of him. I mean, that man could've won a gold medal at the International Games for being the most boring person in the world. Why on earth would I care about Dad becoming the Prime Minister? I saw little enough of him as it was. If he became Prime Minister I'd have to watch the telly just to remember what he looked like.

'Those bleeding heart liberals in the Pangaean Economic Community make sick! They said we in this country had to open our schools to noughts, so we did. They said we had to open our doors to recruiting noughts into our police and armed forces, so we did. And they're still not satisfied. And as for the Liberation Militia, I thought letting a few blankers into our schools would spike their guns . . .'

I froze on the bottom step at the sound of Dad's bitterly angry voice.

'It wasn't enough. Now the Liberation Militia have had one of their demands met, they don't see why they can't have a few more. And then it'll be a few more after that.' Another voice – Dad had a guest.

'Over my cold and rotting body! I knew granting even one of the Pangaean EC's demands was a mistake. God spare us from liberals and blankers!'

I winced at the venom in Dad's voice. And I'd never heard him refer to noughts as blankers before. *Blankers* . . . What a horrible word! A nasty word. My friend Callum wasn't a blanker. He wasn't . . .

'The Liberation Militia are growing impatient with the rate of change in this country. They want . . .'

'And just who are "they"?' Dad demanded. 'Who's the head of the Liberation Militia?'

'I don't know, sir. It's been a slow business working my way up the ranks and the Liberation Militia are very careful. Each military group is divided into different cells or units, with multiple drop-off points if they want to communicate with others in the Militia. It's very hard to find out who's in charge.'

'I don't want excuses. Just do it. That's what I'm paying you for. I'm not going to lose my place in the government because of some terrorist rabble-rousers.'

'They call themselves Freedom Fighters,' Dad's guest stated.

'I don't care if they call themselves descendants of the angel Shaka, they're scum and I want them wiped out. All of them.'

Silence.

'I'll keep working on it.'

Dad's derisive snort was the only reply the other man got.

'Sir, about these meetings . . . they're becoming more and more dangerous. We should find a safer way to communicate.'

'I still want these face-to-face meetings at least once a month.'

'But it's not safe,' the man with Dad protested. 'I'm putting my life on the line every time . . .'

'I don't want to hear it. You can e-mail me or phone as often as you like but I want to see you at least once a month. Is that understood?' Dad snapped.

At first I thought the other man wasn't going to answer. But at last he said, 'Yes, sir.'

I tiptoed closer to the drawing room. Who was Dad talking to? I could only hear their voices.

'Blankers going to my daughter's school . . .' I could almost hear Dad shaking his head. 'If my plan doesn't work, it'll take a miracle to get re-elected next year. I'll be crucified.'

'There are only three or four going to Heathcroft, aren't there?' the other man asked.

'That's three or four more than I thought would pass

the entrance exam,' Dad said with disgust. 'If I'd thought any of them stood a chance of passing the test, I would never have amended the education bill in the first place.'

Every word was like a poison dart. An icy shiver shot through me and it was like my heart was being ripped apart. I was so . . . so *hurt*. Dad . . . My dad . . .

'Less than two dozen noughts are going to Cross schools nationwide. That's not so many, surely?' the other man pointed out.

'When I want your point of view, I'll buy it,' Dad dismissed.

Did he even know that Callum was one of the noughts going to my school? Did he even care? I doubted it. I took another tentative step forward. I glanced across the hall. Dad's reflection was clearly visible in the long hall mirror opposite the drawing room. I could only see the back of Dad's guest reflected in the mirror as he had his back to the door, but I was more than a little stunned to see it was a nought. He had blond hair, tied back in a pony-tail and he was wearing a stained sheepskin coat and big brown boots with a silver-coloured chain above the heel of each one. I couldn't remember the last time I'd seen a nought in our house, except in the kitchen, or cleaning. Why was he here? Who was he? It didn't make any sense. Nothing they were saying made any sense.

I took another step forward, my eyes still focused on the mirror across from the drawing room – which was my mistake. I tripped over the telephone cord making the phone drag slightly across the table. It wasn't much of a noise. But it was enough. Dad looked around and saw me via the hall mirror just as I could see him. His guest turned around.

'Sephy, go to bed – NOW.'

Dad didn't even wait for me to leave before he slammed the drawing-room door shut. I'd barely gathered my scattered wits when the door opened again and Dad marched out alone, slamming the door shut behind him.

'What did you see?' he demanded as he strode over to me.

'P-pardon?'

'What did you see?' Dad grasped my shoulders. A drop of spit came out of his mouth and landed on my cheek but I didn't wipe it away.

'N-nothing.'

'What did you hear?'

'Nothing, Dad. I just came down for a drink. I'm thirsty.'

Dad's eyes blazed with rage as he scowled at me. He looked like he wanted to hit me.

'I didn't see or hear anything. Honest.'

Long moments passed before Dad's grip on my shoulders slowly slackened off. His contorted face relaxed.

'C-can I get my drink now?'

'Go on then. Just hurry up.'

I walked off towards the kitchen even though I wasn't thirsty any more. My heart was slamming against my ribs and my blood was roaring in my ears. I knew without turning around that Dad was still watching me. Once I reached the kitchen, I poured myself a glass of water and headed back up to my bedroom. I was out of Dad's sight in the kitchen but I still went at a 'normal' pace, as if somehow he could see me through the walls. I left the kitchen and started to head upstairs, my glass of water in my hand.

'Princess, wait . . .' Dad called me back.

I turned my head.

'I'm sorry I bit your head off.' Dad forced a smile as he came up the stairs behind me. 'I've been a bit . . . edgy all day.'

'That's OK,' I whispered.

'You're still my princess, aren't you?' asked Dad, hugging me.

I nodded, trying to get past the lump in my throat. Trying not to spill my water.

'Off you go to bed then.'

I carried on walking up the stairs, my pace carefully careless. And Dad stood in the hall, watching my every move.

four. Callum

I tipped everything out of my school bag and onto my bottom bunk-bed − for the umpteenth time. Ruler, pencil-case, pens, pencils, exercise book, calculator. I went through the list Heathcroft High had sent to my mum and dad. I had everything they'd specified and yet it still felt as if there was something missing, as if it wasn't enough. I took the corner of my bed sheet and rubbed it over the calculator again. No amount of polishing would ever make this dinosaur calculator look brand new. I rubbed my hand over my tired eyes.

'Don't be so ungrateful. At least you've got a calculator.' *Just keep telling yourself that, Callum . . .*

Slowly, carefully, I started packing all my school stuff back into my bag.

I'm lucky . . I'm lucky . . . I'm lucky . . . I'm going to school . . .

I played that one thought over and over again in my head, scared to let it go in case of what might happen. Someone knocked at my door. It was either Mum or Lynette. Jude didn't knock, he just barged straight in and Dad never came into our room. If he wanted to talk to me, he always called me out on to the landing. I hoped it was Lynette.

Mum popped her head around the door. 'Can I come in?'

I shrugged, placing my calculator on top of the other stuff in my bag. Mum came into the room, carefully shutting the door behind her. I could guess what was about to come next. She sat on my bed, picked up my school bag and immediately emptied everything out. Very carefully, Mum started packing all my stuff back. Moments passed before she spoke. 'I just wanted to say that whatever happens tomorrow, well done for getting into Heathcroft High.'

That I hadn't expected. I stared at her.

'What d'you mean, whatever happens tomorrow?'

'Nothing.' Mum's smile wobbled before disappearing altogether. 'It's just that . . . that I want you to be happy.'

'I am happy.' I frowned.

'I don't want to see you . . . upset. I don't want you to get hurt.'

What on earth was she talking about? 'Mum, I'm only going to school. I'm not going into the army!'

Mum's attempt at a smile was back. 'I know. But I think you and your father are underestimating how much of a . . . challenge it's going to be. I don't want to see you upset. Besides which . . . well, we've heard some rumours . . .'

'What kind of rumours?'

'Some of the Crosses aren't happy about noughts going to their schools. We've heard rumours that some of them are determined to cause trouble. So, no matter what happens, don't let yourself be provoked into lashing out. Don't give them a reason to kick you out.'

'Is that what you've been worrying about?'

Mum didn't reply.

'Don't worry,' I told her. 'I've got into Heathcroft now and nothing, not even dynamite, is going to get me out again.'

'Good for you.' Mum stroked my cheek. I brushed her hand away. I mean, *please!*

'Too old for that?' Mum teased.

'Much too old,' I replied.

'Too old for a kiss goodnight?'

I was just about to give Mum my honest opinion when the look on her face halted the words on my lips. I realized that the kiss wasn't for my benefit, it was for hers.

'Go on then. If you must,' I grumbled, offering her my cheek.

Silence. I turned to see why the dreaded kiss hadn't been delivered but the moment I looked at Mum she burst out laughing.

'What's so funny?' I frowned.

'You are, my darling.' Mum put me in a bear hug and kissed my cheek like she was trying to burrow her lips into it. Jeez!

'Make sure you set your alarm so you've got plenty of time for a wash before school.' Mum stood up and headed for the door.

'I'm not going to bed yet, Mum. I'm coming downstairs for a while to watch telly.'

'Just for a little while. You've got school tomorrow.' Mum wagged her finger. Her hand dropped to her side and she smiled. *'You've got school tomorrow* . . . I like the sound of that!'

'So do I!'

Mum headed downstairs with me following close behind her. Halfway down the stairs, Mum stopped so abruptly that I almost collided with her.

'Cal?'

'Yes, Mum?'

'You . . . you mustn't think I'm not proud of you, 'cause I am.'

'I know, Mum,' I said.

Mum carried on walking downstairs. I thought about what she'd just said. The funny thing was, until she said it, I didn't think she was proud of me. In fact, part of me still suspected that Mum would've rather I'd failed the Heathcroft High entrance exam. But I hadn't. I'd passed. And no-one could take that away from me. *I'd passed.*

We walked into the downstairs room. Lynette and Dad sat on the sofa. Jude sat at the dinner table poring over what looked like a map – not that I was particularly interested. Mum sat down next to Dad and I sat next to Lynette. It was a squash but a cosy squash.

I looked at my sister. 'You OK?'

Lynette nodded. Then a slow-burning frown spread out over her face. And *that* look was back in her eyes. My heart plunged down to my shoes and bounced back up again.

Please, Lynette. Not tonight . . . not now . . .

'Lynny, d'you remember my seventh birthday?' I began desperately. 'You took me to see my first film at the cinema. There was just you and me and you got annoyed with me because I wouldn't take my eyes off the screen, not for a second. D'you remember you told me that I could blink because the screen wasn't about to vanish. Lynny . . ?'

'Why am I here?' My sister's troubled grey eyes narrowed. 'I shouldn't be here. I'm not one of you. I'm a Cross.'

My stomach lurched, like I was in a lift which had suddenly plunged down at least fifty storeys in about five seconds flat. Every time I convinced myself that Lynette was getting better, she'd get that look on her face . . . She'd stare at us like we were all strangers and she'd insist she was one of them.

'What're you talking about. You're a nought,' Jude said with scorn. 'Look at your skin. You're as white as the rest of us. Whiter.'

'No, I'm not.'

'Jude, that's enough,' said Dad.

'No, it's not. I'm fed up with this. Keeping Lynette in this house so she won't embarrass us by telling everyone she's a Cross. She's barking mad, that's what she is. And Callum's just as bad. He thinks he's better than us and as good as the Crosses, even if he doesn't say it.'

'You don't know what you're talking about,' I hissed.

'No? I've seen you looking up at this house when you've come back from your dagger friend. I've seen you hating it and hating us and hating yourself because you weren't born one of them,' Jude spewed out. 'I'm the only one of the three of us who knows what he is and accepts it.'

'Now listen here, you brainless . . .'

Jude sprang out of his chair, but only a couple of seconds before I did.

'Come on then, if you reckon you're hard enough,' Jude challenged.

I stepped forward but Dad got between the two of us before I could do little more than clench my fists.

'See?' Lynette's small, puzzled voice rang out as clear as a bell. 'I don't behave like that. I can't be a nought. I just can't.'

All the fight went out of me. Slowly, I sat back down again.

'Listen, Lynette . . .' Mum began.

'Look at my skin,' Lynette spoke as if Mum hadn't. 'Such a beautiful colour. So dark and rich and wonderful. I'm so lucky. I'm a Cross – closer to God . . .' Lynette looked around at all of us and smiled. A broad, beaming, genuinely happy smile that lit every line and crease of her face and squeezed my heart.

'Stupid cow,' Jude muttered.

'That's enough!' Dad shouted at him.

Jude sat, a sullen, brooding look on his face. Lynette looked down at her hands stroking one over the other. I looked too. All I could see were pale white hands, blue veins clearly visible through the almost translucent skin. She looked up at me and smiled. I smiled back. Forced it really, but at least I tried.

'Don't you think I'm beautiful, Callum?' Lynette whispered.

'Yes,' I replied truthfully. 'Very.'

five. Sephy

I looked out of the car window, watching the trees and fields and sky melt and merge into each other in a passing blur. The first day of term. I sat up straighter, a smile of pure happiness creeping across my face. Callum . . . He alone made the first day of term new and exciting and different.

'OK back there, Miss Sephy?'

'Fine thanks, Harry.' I directed my smile at our nought driver. He was watching me via the driver's interior mirror.

'Nervous?'

I laughed. 'Are you kidding?'

'I guess not,' Harry replied ruefully.

'Harry, could you drop me . . ?'

'Off around the corner from school.' Harry finished for me.

'If that's OK.'

'Well, it'll have to be – won't it?' Harry shook his head. 'If your mother finds out . . .'

'She won't.'

'I still don't see . . .'

I sighed. During term-time, Harry and I had this conversation at least three times a week.

'Harry, you know how I get teased if my friends see you driving me. I get all kinds of comments about having feet which are too precious to touch the pavement or I get asked when I'm going to have my wings fitted and all sorts. I'm not in the mood to be teased – not on my first day back.'

'I know but . . .'

'Please?'

'Oh, all right then.'

'Thanks, Harry.'

'If I get into trouble . . .'

'You won't. I promise,' I smiled.

Harry turned into Cherry Wood Grove, a couple of streets away from Heathcroft, my school. I hopped out, dragging my school bag off the white leather seat.

'See you later.'

'Yes, Miss Sephy.'

I waited until Harry had driven off and was out of sight before taking a step. He'd caught me out like that before

– pretending to drive off and then doubling back when my back was turned. As I ambled along, I heard a strange, rumbling sound – like someone playing a radio really loudly, but far enough away so that I couldn't make out exactly what was being said. As I approached the corner, shouts like an angry wave rolled up towards me. But even that couldn't prepare me for what was about to happen next. I turned the corner and . . .

And.

At the far end of the road, there was a huge crowd outside my school. And they were shouting and chanting. I froze for a moment, then started to walk towards them. Then I started to run. What on earth was going on? It didn't take me long to find out.

'NO BLANKERS IN OUR SCHOOL. NO BLANKERS IN OUR SCHOOL.'

The slogan was shouted out over and over again. Callum and three other noughts were surrounded by police officers who were trying to push their way through the crowd to get to the school entrance. More police stood in an arm-linked line trying to push the crowd of Crosses back into two orderly groups. I ran faster, but the closer I got, the less I could see. I pushed and elbowed my way through the crowd.

'Callum! CALLUM!'

'NO BLANKERS IN OUR SCHOOL . . .'

The police officers were still trying to push through the crowds of adults and Heathcroft pupils who in turn were determined not to let them pass.

'BLANKERS OUT . . .'

I forced my way up the steps to the school entrance

ahead of the crowd and the police, watching as the police battled to hold back the crowd, watching as Callum and the others looked neither to the right nor the left but straight ahead without even blinking.

'NO BLANKERS IN OUR SCHOOL . . .'

I spotted Julianna and Adam and Ezra in the crowd, all of whom were my good friends. But worst of all I saw my own sister Minnie in the crowd. And she was shouting just as hard as all the others.

'NO BLANKERS IN OUR SCHOOL . . .'

There was a roaring in my head which matched the roaring all around me. I was in the middle of chaos. Callum and the other noughts tried to make their way up the steps to the school entrance. The crowd surged forward at that, the palpable wave of their anger hitting me almost like a punch. Suddenly a cry went up. Callum's head dipped down, followed by the heads of the police officers.

'One of them is hurt!'

Callum . . . it wasn't Callum, was it?

'A blanker's hurt.'

The news spread through the crowd like a virulent disease.

'HOORAY!' Spontaneous cheers filled the air. The police lines trying to hold the crowds back were knocked to the ground as the crowd rushed forward like air into a vacuum. I was on the very top step looking down at it all. And I've never felt such fist-clenching, teeth-gritting fury. A policewoman stepped to one side and I saw Callum squatting down by a nought girl who looked like she was in a bad way. Blood trickled from her forehead and her eyes were closed.

Mr Corsa, the headmaster, emerged from behind me. He stared at the crowd – the *mob* before him – looking shocked and ashen.

'Mr Corsa, we have to help that girl,' I pointed. 'She's hurt.'

Mr Corsa didn't move, even when I repeated what I'd just said. I was caught up in a hurricane, with all the noise and madness whirling round me until my head was about to explode.

'Stop it! Just stop it!'

Nothing.

'STOP IT! YOU'RE ALL BEHAVING LIKE ANIMALS!' I shouted so hard my throat immediately began to hurt. 'WORSE THAN ANIMALS – LIKE BLANKERS!'

The sounds of the crowd slowly died away. 'Just look at you,' I continued. 'Stop it.' I glanced down at Callum. He was staring at me, the strangest expression on his face.

Callum, don't look at me like that. I didn't mean you. I'd never mean you. It was just for the others, to get them to stop, to get them to help. I didn't mean you . . .

six. Callum

She didn't say that. She couldn't have. Not Sephy. I'm going to wake up in a moment. Wake up from this chaos, this nightmare. Wake up and laugh – or bawl – at the tricks my mind's playing. She didn't say that . . .

But she did . . .

I'm not a blanker. I may be a nought but I'm worth more than nothing. I'm not a blanker. A waste of time and space. A zero. I'm not a blanker. I'M NOT A BLANKER.

Sephy . . .

seven. Sephy

The waves lapped up onto the beach. It was a lovely autumn evening, a beautiful end to a lousy day. I couldn't remember when I'd felt so miserable, so wretched. Callum was sitting right next to me but he might as well have been sitting on the moon.

'Aren't you going to say anything?' At first I thought he wasn't going to answer.

'What would you like me to say?'

'I said I'm sorry,' I tried again.

'I know.'

I watched Callum's profile – unreadable and implacable. And it was my fault. I understood that much, even if I didn't quite understand what I'd done.

'It's just a word, Callum.'

'Just a word . . .' Callum repeated slowly.

'Sticks and stones, Callum. It's one word, that's all,' I pleaded.

'Sephy, if you'd slapped me or punched me or even stabbed me, sooner or later it would've stopped hurting. Sooner or later. But I'll never forget what you called me, Sephy. Never. Not if I live to be five hundred.'

I wiped my cheeks but the tears still came. 'I didn't mean it. I didn't mean you. I was . . . I was trying to help.'

Callum looked at me then and the expression on his face made my tears flow faster. 'Sephy . . .'

'Please. I'm so sorry.' I dreaded to hear what he was going to say next.

'Sephy, maybe we shouldn't see so much of each other any more . . .'

'Callum, no. I said I was sorry.'

'And that makes everything all right, does it?'

'No, it doesn't. Not even close. But don't do this. You're my best friend. I don't know what I'd do without you.'

Callum turned away. I held my breath.

'You must promise me something,' he said softly.

'Anything.'

'You must promise me that you'll never *ever* use that word again.'

Why couldn't he understand that I hadn't been talking about *him*? It was just a word. A word Dad had used. But it was a word that had hurt my best friend. A word that was now hurting me so very, very much. I hadn't fully realized just how powerful words could be before this. Whoever came up with the saying 'sticks and stones may break my bones but words will never hurt me' was talking out of his or her armpit.

'Promise me,' Callum insisted.

'I promise.'

We both turned to look out across the sea then. I knew I should go home. I was so late for dinner it was almost breakfast-time. Mother would go ballistic. But I wasn't going to leave first. I didn't want to get up. So I didn't. I shivered, even though the evening wasn't cold.

Callum took off his jacket and put it around my shoulders. It smelt of soap, and chips – and him. I hugged it tighter around me.

'What about you?' I asked.

'What about me?' he replied.

'Aren't you going to get cold?'

'I'll survive.'

I moved in closer and put my head on his shoulder. His body stiffened and for a moment I thought he was going to move away, but then he relaxed and though he didn't hug me the way he usually did, he didn't shrug me off either. One word . . . one word had caused all this trouble between us. If I lived to be five million, I would never, ever say that horrible word again. Ever. The sun was beginning to set now, burning the sky pink and orange. We sat and watched in silence.

'I've been thinking it over and . . . well, we can still be together outside school but I don't think you should talk to me when we're in school,' Callum said.

I was more than stunned. 'Why on earth not?'

'I don't want you to lose any of your friends because of me. I know how much they mean to you.'

'You're my friend too.'

'Not when we're both at school I'm not,' Callum told me.

'But that's just silly.'

'Is it?'

My mouth opened and closed like a drowning fish, but what could I say? Callum stood up.

'I have to go home now. You coming?'

I shook my head.

'Your mum will hit the roof and then the nearest orbiting satellite!'

'It's Monday. She's visiting friends,' I told him.

'What about your dad?'

'You know he's never home during the week. He's at our town house.'

'And Minerva?'

'I don't know. Probably with her boyfriend. Don't worry about me, Callum. I'll stay here for a little while longer.'

'Not for too long, OK?'

'OK.' I handed back his jacket.

Almost reluctantly, he took it. Then he walked away. I watched, willing him to turn around, to turn back. But he didn't. It was as if I was outside myself, watching the two of us. More and more I was beginning to feel like a spectator in my own life. I had to make a choice. I had to decide what kind of friend Callum was going to be to me. But what surprised – and upset me – was that I even had to think about it.

eight. Callum

'D'you know what time it is?' Mum ranted the moment I set foot through the door. She and I rarely had any other conversation.

'Sorry,' I mumbled.

'Your dinner's in the oven – dried out and not fit for eating by now.'

'It'll be fine, Mum.'

'So where have you been until ten o'clock at night?' Dad surprised me by asking. He didn't usually nag me about coming home late. That was Mum's department.

'Well?' he prompted when I didn't answer.

What did he want me to say? *'Well, I said goodbye to Sephy at the beach almost two hours ago, but then I hid in the shadows and followed her home to make sure she got back OK. Then it took me over an hour to walk home.'* Yeah, right! That little snippet of truth would go down like a lead balloon.

'I was just out walking. I had a lot to think about.' And that part at least was the truth.

'Are you OK, son?' Dad asked. 'I went down to Heathcroft as soon as I heard what was going on, but the police wouldn't let me in.'

'Why not?'

'I had no official business on the premises – unquote.'

Dad couldn't mask the bitterness in his voice.

'Those rotten, stinking . . .'

'Jude, not at the dinner table please,' Mum admonished.

Glancing at Jude, I saw he had enough anger in him for everyone else around. He was scowling at me like I was the one who'd had Dad kept off the school premises.

'So how was school? How were your lessons, son?' Dad asked quietly.

The honest answer or the acceptable one?

'I was OK, Dad,' I fibbed. 'Once we got into school it was all right.'

Except that the teachers had totally ignored us, and the Crosses had used any excuse to bump into us and knock our books on the floor, and even the noughts serving in the food hall had made sure they served everyone else in the queue before us. 'It was fine.'

'You're in there now, Callum. Don't let any dagger swine drive you out – you understand?'

'I understand.'

'Excuse me.' Mum rounded on Dad. 'But when I say I don't want swearing at the dinner table, that applies to everyone – including you.'

'Sorry, love,' Dad said ruefully, winking conspiratorially at us into the bargain.

'You were on the telly,' Jude told me. 'So was your "friend". The whole world heard what she said . . .'

'She didn't mean it like that.' The words slipped out before I could stop them. Big mistake.

'She didn't mean it?' Jude scoffed. 'Have you lost your mind? How can you not mean to say something like that?

She meant it all right.'

'That family are all the same.' Mum sniffed. 'I see Miss Sephy is growing up to be just like her mother.'

I had to bite my lip at that. I knew better than to argue.

'You're better off out of that house,' Dad told Mum vehemently.

'You don't have to tell me twice,' Mum agreed at once. 'I miss the money but I wouldn't go back for all the stars in space. Anyone who can put up with that stuck-up cow Mrs Hadley is a better person than me.'

'You were friends once . . .' I reminded her, spooning some totally dried out mashed potato into my mouth.

'Friends? We were never friends,' Mum snorted. 'She patronised me and I put up with it 'cause I needed a job – that's all.'

That wasn't how I remembered it. A few years ago and a lifetime away, Mum and Mrs Hadley had been really close. Mum was Minerva's, then Sephy's, nanny and a general mother's helper from the time Minerva was born. In fact, I was closer to Sephy than I'd ever been to anyone, even my own sister Lynette who was my best friend in this house. I remembered when I was a toddler and Sephy was just a baby – I'd helped to bathe her and change her nappy. And when she got older, we played hide-and-seek and catch and tag in the Hadley grounds, whilst Mum and sometimes Mrs Hadley watched us and chatted and laughed. I still don't know what happened to change all that. One week Mrs Hadley and Mum were like best friends and the next week, Mum and I were no longer welcome anywhere near the Hadley house. That was over three years ago now.

I still sometimes wondered how Mrs Hadley expected Sephy and I to go from being so close to not seeing each other at all? Sephy told her it was impossible. I told my mum the same thing. Neither of them listened. But it didn't matter. Sephy and I still saw each other at least every other day and we'd never stop. We'd promised each other. The most sacred of promises – an oath sealed with our blood. We just couldn't tell anyone about it, that's all. We had our own world, our own secret place on the beach where no-one went and where no-one would ever find us – not if they didn't know where to look. It was a small space, tiny really, but it was *ours*.

'Shush, everyone. The news is on,' Dad admonished.

I held my breath.

What happened at Heathcroft wasn't the first item of news at least. The first item was about the Liberation Militia.

'Today Kamal Hadley, Home Office Minister, declared that there would be no hiding place, no safe haven for those noughts misguided enough to join the Liberation Militia.' The newscaster's face disappeared to be replaced by that of Sephy's dad outside the Houses of Parliament. His face seemed to fill the whole screen.

'Isn't it true, Mr Hadley, that your government's decision to allow selected noughts in our schools was as a direct result of pressure from the Liberation Militia?'

'Not at all,' Sephy's dad immediately denied. 'This government does not allow itself to be blackmailed by an illegal terrorist group. We acted on a P.E.C. directive that this government had been on the verge of implementing anyway.'

My dad snorted at that.

'Our decision to allow the crème-de-la-crème of nought youth to join our educational institutions makes sound social and economic sense. In a civilized society, equality of education for those noughts with sufficient aptitude . . .'

I tuned out at that. Sephy's dad hadn't changed since the last time I'd spoken to him which was yonks ago now. He never used one word where twenty patronizing ones would do. I didn't like him much. Correction! Pompous twit! I didn't like him at all. I didn't like any of Sephy's family. They were all the same. Minerva was a snob. Her mum was a bitch and her dad was a git. They all looked at us noughts through their nostrils.

'The Liberation Militia are misguided terrorists and we will leave no stone unturned in our efforts to bring them to justice . . .' Sephy's dad was still at it. I was about to mentally switch off again, but then Jude did something that brought me out of my daydream.

'Long live the Liberation Militia!' My brother punched the air, his fingers locked in a fist so tight that I reckoned it would surely hurt to straighten them again.

'Too right, son.' Dad and Jude exchanged a knowing look, before they both turned back to the telly. I frowned at them, then turned to look at Mum. She immediately glanced away. I looked back at Jude and Dad. There was something going on. Something to do with the Liberation Militia and my brother and my dad. I didn't mind that. What I did mind was that I was being excluded.

'There have been unconfirmed reports that the car bomb found outside the International Trade Centre last month was the work of the Liberation Militia,' the news-caster continued. 'What attempts are being made to find those responsible?'

'I can tell you that our highest priority is to find those responsible and bring them to swift and irrevocable justice. Political terrorism which results in the death or serious injury of even one Cross always has been and always will be a capital crime. Those found guilty will suffer the death sentence, no two ways about it . . .'

Blah! Blah! Blah! Sephy's dad droned on for at least another minute, not letting the newscaster get a word in edgeways, sideways or any other ways. I tuned out again, waiting for him to finish, hoping he wouldn't.

nine. Sephy

'Sephy, your dad's on the telly.' Mother opened my bed-room door to tell me.

I mean, big deal! Mother still thought I was five, bouncing up and down with excitement at the sight of my daddy on the TV.

'Sephy!'

'Yes, Mother. I'm watching.' I pressed my TV remote control to switch it on. Anything for a quiet life! I got the right channel first time. How lucky!

'. . . is misguided to say the least.' Dad didn't look too

pleased. 'Minister Pelango is very young and doesn't realize that the rate of change in our society needs to be slow and steady . . .'

'Any slower and we'd be going backwards,' Minister Pelango interjected.

Dad didn't looked too pleased at that either, though it made me smile.

'We call ourselves civilized, yet noughts have more rights in other P.E.C. countries than they do here,' Pelango continued.

'And in plenty of other countries they have a lot less,' Dad snapped back.

'And that makes the way we treat them right, does it?'

'If our ruling party politics don't gel with Mr Pelango's beliefs, then maybe he should do the honourable thing and resign his seat on the government,' Dad said silkily.

'No chance!' came the immediate reply. 'Too many people in this government live in the past. It's my duty to drag them into the present or none of us – noughts or Crosses – will have a decent future.'

Mum left my room. The click of my bedroom door closing was immediately followed by the press of another TV channel button. I didn't care which one. Any other channel would do. I'd grown up with politics, politics, politics being rammed down my throat. I wasn't interested in being caught up in it in any manner, shape or form. Why couldn't Mother understand that?

ten. Callum

When at last Kamal Hadley had stopped dribbling on, Heathcroft School appeared on the telly. Of course, they didn't bother showing the fact that the police officers who were meant to be guarding us were letting the crowd get to us to poke and pinch and punch. Somehow the camera was never in the right place to show that the whole back of my jacket was awash with Cross spit. Surprise! Surprise! There wasn't even a hint of any of that.

'The noughts admitted to Heathcroft High School met with some hostility today . . .' the news reporter began.

Some hostility? This reporter's middle name was obviously 'Euphy', short for Euphemism!

'Police officers were drafted in to keep the peace as it was feared that nought extremists might try to take advantage of the volatile situation . . .' the newscaster continued.

Jude started muttering under his breath and to be honest, I didn't blame him. Even I was disgusted at that and I had a much longer fuse than my brother. Lynette took hold of my hand. She smiled at me and I could feel the anger seeping out of my body. Only Lynette and Sephy could do that – make all the rage that sometimes threatened to blow up inside me just fade to nothing. But sometimes . . . sometimes I got so angry that I scared even myself.

The image on the screen cut from Shania falling over to Sephy shouting at the crowd. The TV camera zoomed in for a close-up. The newscaster announced as a voiceover, 'Persephone Hadley, daughter of Kamal Hadley, had a hand in stopping the fracas . . .'

'I'm going up to my room. I've got homework.' I leapt to my feet.

I was too late. Those words spilt out of the telly before I could leave. I knew what to expect, what she was going to say, and it still made me wince. I left the room before anyone could say a word to me, but I knew my entire family was watching me leave. Closing the door quietly behind me, I leaned against it and took a deep breath.

Sephy . . .

'They are all the same,' I heard Jude scoff. 'Crosses and noughts will never live in peace, let alone be friends and Callum's just fooling himself if he thinks that Cross girl cares one clipped toenail about him. When push comes to shove she'll dump him so fast his body will turn pear-shaped!'

'You and I may know that, but he doesn't,' Dad surprised me by saying.

'Well, the sooner he learns it, the better,' Mum sighed.

'And are you going to be the one that tells him?' Dad asked. ' 'Cause I'm not.'

'There's not one of those Crosses that can be trusted,' Jude declared.

No-one disagreed.

'Someone should tell Callum the truth. Otherwise he's

going to get hurt,' Jude continued.

'Are you volunteering?' asked Dad.

'I will, if I have to,' replied Jude.

'No! No, I'll do it,' Mum said. 'I'll do it.'

'When?'

'When I get round to it. Now back off, both of you,' Mum snapped.

I couldn't listen to any more. I went upstairs, my shoulders slumped, my head hanging down. For the first time ever, I wondered if maybe my family was right and I was wrong.

eleven. Sephy

It was time for History. I hate History. It's a total waste of time. There was only one good thing about it. Callum was down to take History as well. My friend Claire tried to sit next to me.

'Er . . . Claire, could you sit somewhere else today. I'm saving this seat for someone.'

'Who?'

'Someone.'

Claire gave me a scathing look. 'Be like that then.' And she flounced off without a backwards glance. I sighed and watched the door eagerly. Callum and the other noughts were the last ones to come in. Others barged past them and Callum let them get away with it. I wouldn't have.

I smiled at Callum and indicated the seat next to me. Callum looked at me, then looked away and sat next to another nought. Others in the class looked from me to him and back again. My face burned with humiliation. How could he show me up like that? How could he? I know what he'd said the previous evening, but I wanted to show him I didn't care who knew we were friends. It didn't bother me one little bit. So why would Callum turn his back on me like that?

Mr Jason entered the room and launched into the lesson before he'd even shut the door. And within the space of two minutes it was clear he was in a foul mood – even worse than usual. Nobody could do anything right, especially the noughts.

'Who can tell me one of the significant events of the year 146 BC?' Mr Jason asked tersely.

146 BC! I mean, who cared?!! I decided to wind down and sleep with my eyes open until the lesson was over. Callum bent down to get something out of his bag. From my position I couldn't see what. CRACK! Mr Jason smacked a big heavy History textbook down on Callum's desk.

'What's the matter, boy?' Mr Jason asked. 'Too poor to even pay attention?'

Callum didn't answer. Some in the class tittered. A few didn't. Mr Jason was being a real pig and when he walked past me, I glared at him to let him know exactly what I thought about the way he was carrying on. That put his back up as well. I got told off twice in less than thirty minutes. But I didn't care. Mr Jason wasn't important. I had other things on my mind – like how to prove to Callum that I really didn't care if people knew he was my friend. In fact, I was proud of it. But how to do it . . ? And then it came to me! Eureka! The perfect solution. If only this lesson would hurry up and finish. All I could think about was lunch-time. I was desperate to be one of the first to get to the food hall. When at last the buzzer sounded, I was the first out of my chair. Trying to be the first out of the room, I barged past my teacher.

'Er, d'you mind?'

'Sorry, sir,' I tried to carry on moving past him. Big mistake!

'As you're in such a tearing hurry you can wait until last to leave the classroom.'

'But, sir . . .'

Mr Jason raised a warning hand. 'Any arguments and you'll be lucky to get lunch at all.'

I shut up. Mr Jason was a real, ill-tempered, ill-mannered slug. And he had to toil hard to work his way up to that. So I waited whilst everyone else grinned smugly at me as they strolled past. I was late getting to the food hall when today of all days I wanted to be one of the first. Callum and the other noughts already had their food and were sitting down by the time I walked through the food-hall doors. All the noughts were sitting at a table by themselves, just like yesterday.

I lined up in the food queue. I wasn't going to do anything out of the ordinary, so why was my heart bumping in such a strange way? I collected my chicken and mushroom pie with the usual over-boiled trimmings, my jam tart with over-sweet custard and my carton of milk and, taking a deep breath, I headed for Callum's table. Callum and the other noughts glanced up as I approached their table, only to look away again almost immediately.

'D'you mind if I join you?'

They all looked so shocked, it wasn't even funny. The other noughts continued to look stunned, but Callum's expression turned. I sat down before he could say no and before I could bottle out.

'What d'you think you're doing?' he snapped.

'Eating my lunch,' I replied before cutting into my pie. I tried to smile at the other three noughts but they instantly returned to eating their food.

'Hi. I'm Sephy Hadley.' I thrust my hand under the nose of the nought girl I was sitting next to. She had a dark brown plaster on her forehead which stuck out on her pale white skin like a throbbing thumb. 'Welcome to Heathcroft.'

She looked at my hand like it was about to bite her. Wiping her own hand on her tunic, she then took mine and shook it slowly.

'I'm Shania,' she said softly.

'That's a pretty name. What does it mean?' I asked.

Shania shrugged. 'It doesn't mean anything.'

'My mother told me my name means "serene night",' I laughed. 'But Callum will tell you I'm anything but serene!'

Shania smiled at me. It was tentative and brief but at least it was genuine – whilst it lasted.

'How's your head?' I asked, pointing at the plaster.

'It's OK. It'll take more than a stone step to dent my head.'

I smiled. 'That plaster's a bit noticeable.'

'They don't sell pink plasters. Only dark brown ones.'
Shania shrugged.

My eyes widened at that. I'd never really thought about
it before, but she was right. I'd never seen any pink plasters. Plasters were the colour of us Crosses, not the
noughts.

'Sephy, just what d'you think you're doing?' Mrs
Bawden, the deputy headmistress, appeared from
nowhere to scowl down at me.

'Pardon?'

'What're you doing?'

'I'm eating my lunch.' I frowned.

'Don't be facetious.'

'I'm not. I'm eating my lunch.'

'Get back to your own table – at once.' Mrs Bawden
looked like she was about to erupt kittens.

I looked around. I was now the centre of attention –
the very last thing I'd wanted.

'B–but I'm sitting h–here,' I stammered.

'Get back to your own table – NOW!'

What table? I didn't have my own table. And then it
dawned on me exactly what Mrs Bawden meant. She
wasn't talking about me getting back to my own table.
She was talking about me getting back to my own kind. I
glanced around. Callum and the others weren't looking at
me. Everyone else was. They weren't.

'I'm sitting with my friend, Callum,' I whispered. I
could hardly hear my own voice so I have no idea how
Mrs Bawden heard me – but she did. She grabbed my arm
and pulled me out of my chair. I was still holding on to
my tray, and everything on it went flying.

'Persephone Hadley, you will come with me.' Mrs Bawden yanked me away from the table and dragged me across the food hall. I tried to twist away from her, but she had a grip like a python on steroids. I turned my head this way and that. Wasn't anyone going to do anything? Not from the look at it. I twisted sharply to look at Callum. He was watching but the moment I caught his eye, he looked away. I stopped struggling after that. I straightened up and followed Mrs Bawden to the headmaster's office.

Callum had turned away from me. I didn't care about the rest, but I cared about that. He'd turned away ... Well, I was slow getting the message, but I'd finally got it. God knows, I'd finally got it.

twelve. Callum

I had to get out of there. I left my lunch half-eaten and walked out of the food hall without saying a word to any of the others.

I had to get out of there.

I walked out of the food hall and out of the building and out of the school, my steps growing ever faster and more frantic – until by the time I was out of the school gates, I was running. Running until my back ached and my feet hurt and my heart was ready to burst and still I kept running. I ran all the way out of the town and down to the beach. I collapsed onto the cool sand, my body bathed in sweat. I lay on my stomach and punched the sand. And again, and again. Until I was pounding it with both fists. Until my knuckles were red raw and bleeding.

And I wished more than anything else in the world that the sand beneath my fists was Sephy's face.

thirteen. Sephy

I spotted our Mercedes in its usual place, just outside the main school building. As I approached it, a strange man got out and opened one of the back doors for me. He had mousy-brown hair which lay flat and lank against his head, and ice-light, ghost-like blue eyes.

'Who are you?'

'Karl, your new driver.'

'Where's Harry?' I asked, climbing into the car.

'He decided to move on.'

'Without telling me?'

Karl shrugged and slammed the door shut. I watched him sit behind the wheel and start the car, a frown digging deep into my face.

'Where did he move on to?'

'I don't know, Miss.'

'Why did he want to leave?'

'I don't know that either.'

'Where does Harry live?'

'Why, Miss Sephy?'

'I'd like to send him a Good Luck card.'

'If you give it to me, Miss, I'll make sure he gets it.'

Karl's eyes and mine met in the internal driver's mirror. 'OK,' I said at last. What else could I say?

Harry wouldn't go away and leave me, not without saying goodbye first. I knew he wouldn't – just as surely as I knew my own name. Something horrible then occurred to me.

'You . . . you r-really are my new driver, aren't you?'

'Of course, Miss Sephy. Your mother employed me this morning. I can show you my ID card if you'd like.' Karl's smile flitted fleetingly across his face.

'No, that's OK,' I said. I sat back in my seat and clipped up my seat-belt.

We drove off. I saw some others, pointing to me and whispering or laughing or both as our car went past. My sitting at the noughts table had spread around the school like a bad dose of the flu. And I knew I hadn't heard the end of it. Mr Corsa threatened that he was going to send a letter home to my mum and e-mail my dad. No doubt a protest to the Queen was in the offing too. And I wouldn't have minded any of that if Callum hadn't turned his back on me. But he had. And I was never going to forget it. He had looked away from me like . . . like he didn't know me. Like I was nothing. Maybe Mother was right, after all. Maybe Crosses and noughts could never be friends. Maybe there was too much difference between us.

Did I really believe that?

I didn't know what I believed any more.

fourteen. Callum

I don't know how long I sat there, watching the sun burn into the sky as it set, watching the night grow steadily more secretive. Why had my life suddenly become so complicated? For the last year all I could think about, or even dream about, was going to school. Sephy's school. I was so busy concentrating on getting into Heathcroft that I hadn't given much thought to what I'd do when I actually got there. I hadn't really thought about what it would be like to be so . . . unwanted. And what was the point anyway? It wasn't as if I'd get a decent job after it. No Cross would ever employ me for more than the most mundane, menial job, so why bother? But I wanted to learn. A yawning hole deep inside me was begging to be filled up with words and thoughts and ideas and facts and fictions. But if I did that, what would I do with the rest of my life? What would I be? How could I ever be truly happy knowing that I could do so much more, *be* so much more, than I would ever be allowed?

I was trying so hard to understand how and why things were the way they were. The Crosses were meant to be closer to God. The Good Book said so. The son of God was dark-skinned like them, had eyes like them, had hair like them. The Good Book said so. But the Good Book said a lot of things. Like 'love thy neighbour', and 'do unto others as you would have them do unto you'. If nothing else, wasn't the whole message of the Good Book to live and let live? So how could the Crosses call themselves 'God's chosen' and still treat us the way they did? OK, we weren't their slaves any more, but Dad said the name had changed but nothing else. Dad didn't believe in the Good Book. Neither did Mum. They said it'd been written and translated by Crosses, so it was bound to be biased in their favour. But the truth was the truth, wasn't it? Noughts . . . Even the word was negative. Nothing. Nil. Zero. Nonentities. It wasn't a name we'd chosen for ourselves. It was a name we'd been given. But why?

'I DON'T UNDERSTAND . . .' The words erupted from me in an angry rush, heading for the sky and beyond.

I sat there for I don't know how long, furious thoughts darting around my head like bluebottles, my head aching, my chest hurting. Until I suddenly snapped out of it with a jolt. Someone was watching me. I turned sharply and a shock like static electricity zapped through my body. Sephy was further up the beach, standing perfectly still as the wind whipped around her, making her jacket and skirt billow out. We were about seven metres apart – or seven million light years, depending on how you looked at it. Then Sephy turned around and started to walk away.

'Sephy, wait.' I jumped to my feet and sprinted after her.

She carried on walking.

'Sephy, please. Wait.' I caught up with her and pulled her around to face me. She pulled away from my grasp like I was contaminated.

'Yes?'

'Don't be like that?' I pleaded.

'Like what?'

I glared at her. 'Aren't you going to stay?'

'I don't think so.'

'Why not?'

At first, I thought she wasn't going to answer.

'I don't stay where I'm not wanted.' Sephy turned around again. I ran to stand in front of her.

'I did it for your own good.'

A strange expression flitted across her face. 'Did you? Was it my good or your own you were thinking about?'

'Maybe a bit of both,' I admitted.

'Maybe a lot of one and none of the other,' Sephy contradicted.

'I'm sorry – OK?'

'So am I. I'll see you, Callum.' Sephy tried to walk around me again, but I moved directly into her path. Fear tore at my insides. If she left now, that would be the end. Funny how a few hours ago, that'd been exactly what I was wishing for.

'Sephy, wait!'

'For what?'

'H–how about if you and I go up to Celebration Wood this Saturday? We could have a picnic.'

Sephy's eyes lit up although she tried her best to hide it. I breathed an inward sigh of relief although I was careful not to show it.

'Celebration Wood . . ?'

'Yeah. Just you and me.'

'Are you sure you won't be ashamed to be seen with me?' Sephy asked.

'Don't be ridiculous.'

Sephy regarded me. 'What time shall I meet you?' she said at last.

'How about ten-thirty at the train station? I'll meet you on the platform.'

'OK.' Sephy turned away.

'Where're you going?' I asked.

'Home.'

'Why don't you stay a while?'

'I don't want to disturb you.'

'Sephy, get off it,' I snapped.

'Get off what? You're a snob, Callum. And I never realized it until today,' Sephy snapped back, just as angry. 'I thought you were better than that, above all that nonsense. But you're just like anyone else. "Crosses and noughts shouldn't be seen together. Crosses and noughts shouldn't be friends. Crosses and noughts shouldn't even live on the same planet together".'

'That's rubbish!' I fumed. 'I don't believe any of that, you know I don't.'

'Do I?' Sephy tilted her head to one side as she continued to scrutinize me. 'Well, if you're not a snob, you're a hypocrite, which is even worse. I'm OK to talk to as long as no-one can see us, as long as no-one knows.'

'Don't talk to me like that . . .'

'Why? Does the truth hurt?' asked Sephy. 'Which one is it, Callum? Are you a snob or a hypocrite?'

'Get lost, Sephy.'

'With pleasure.'

And this time, when Sephy walked away I didn't try to stop her. I just watched her leave.

fifteen. Sephy

There's a proverb which says, 'Be careful what you wish for, because you might get it!' I never really knew what that meant – until now. All those months helping Callum with his work so he'd pass the Heathcroft entrance exam. All those nights wishing on every blazing star that Callum would pass so we could go to the same school together, be in the same class together even. And now it'd all come true.

And it was horrible. Everything was going wrong.

I sighed, then sighed again. I couldn't hide in this toilet cubicle for ever. And who was I hiding from anyway? I was hiding from all those people who'd been pointing and whispering as I walked past them in the school corridor – but mainly from Callum. After what had happened the previous evening, I was afraid to face him. I was so afraid he wouldn't be my friend any more. So if I didn't see him, I could pretend that nothing between us had changed. But I couldn't sit on the toilet lid for ever. The bell rang for the end of break-time. I stood up and took a deep breath.

'OK . . . Here goes . . .' I muttered to myself.

I drew back the bolt and opened the cubicle door. I was just stepping out of the cubicle when it happened. Lola, Joanne and Dionne from Mrs Watson's class in the year above mine, pushed me back into the cubicle and crowded in after me.

'We want to have a word with you,' Lola began.

'And it has to be in here, does it?' I asked.

Joanne shoved me so hard, I had to put out my hand to stop myself from toppling over.

'We heard about what you did yesterday . . .' Joanne said.

'I did a lot of things yesterday.' My heart began to thump in my chest, but I wasn't about to give these three the satisfaction of knowing I was scared.

'In the food hall,' Joanne continued. 'You sat on the blankers table.'

'What's it to you?' I asked.

Lola slapped my face. Shocked, my hand flew to my stinging cheek. It wasn't that she'd slapped me particularly hard, it was just that no-one had ever hit me before. Not even Minerva, my sister.

'I don't care if your dad is God Almighty himself,' Lola told me. 'Stick to your own kind. If you sit with the blankers again, everyone in this school will treat you like one of them.'

'You need to wake up and check which side you're on,' added Joanne.

'Why d'you want to be around them anyway?' Dionne piped up. 'They smell funny and they eat peculiar foods and everyone knows that none of them are keen to make friends with soap and water.'

'What a load of rubbish!' The words tumbled out of my mouth before I could stop them. 'Callum has a wash every day and he doesn't smell. None of them do.'

Dionne, Jo and Lola all looked at each other.

Lola pushed me down so I ended up sitting down on the toilet lid looking up at them.

Any second now the door will open and someone will come in . . . Callum will come in and stop them. He'll pull them off me and sort them out. Any second now . . .

I tried to get to my feet but Lola pushed me down again and kept her hand on my shoulder, her fingers biting into my skin.

'We're only going to say this once,' Lola told me icily. 'Choose who your friends are very carefully. If you don't stay away from those blankers, you'll find you don't have a single friend left in this school.'

'Why d'you hate them so much?' I asked, bewildered. 'I bet none of you has even spoken to a nought before.'

'Of course we have,' Joanne piped up. 'I've spoken to blankers lots of times – when they serve us in shops and restaurants . . .'

'And there are some working in our own food hall . . .'

'Yeah, that's right. And besides we don't need to speak to them. We see them on the news practically every other day. Everyone knows they all belong to the Liberation Militia and all they do is cause trouble and commit crimes and stuff like that . . .'

I stared at them, astounded. They can't really be serious, I thought. But they could obviously read what I was thinking all over my face.

'The news doesn't lie,' Lola told me huffily.

'The news lies all the time. They tell us what they think we want to hear,' I said. Callum had told me that and at the time I didn't fully understand what he meant. But I did now.

'Who told you that?' Joanne's eyes narrowed. 'Your dad?'

'I bet it was one of her blanker friends,' Lola said with scorn. 'They're blank by name and blank by nature.'

'What d'you mean?' I asked.

'Blank, white faces with not a hint of colour in them. Blank minds which can't hold a single original thought. Blank, blank, blank,' Lola recited. 'That's why they serve us and not the other way around.'

'You ought to sell that horse manure worldwide. It's quality stuff. You'd make a fortune!' I sprung up. 'Noughts are people, just like us. You're the ones who are stupid and ignorant and . . .'

Lola gave me another slap around my face for that, but this time I was ready for it. Win or lose they weren't going to get away with it. I made a fist, drew it back and punched Lola in the stomach. She doubled over with an 'Oof!' I struck out with my elbows and my fists and my feet all at the same time, trying to make as many of my blows count before they could react. I had the element of surprise on my side, but not for long. Joanne and Lola each grabbed a flailing arm whilst Dionne straightened up to glare down at me. Dionne was the best fighter in her year and everyone knew it. But if she was expecting me to beg or cry, she'd have a long wait. She gave me a slow smile of satisfaction.

'Blanker-lover . . . You've had this coming for a long time,' she said softly.

And then she let me have it.

THE TURNING

sixteen. Callum

'Callum, wait.'

It was the end of another lousy school day where the most obvious lesson I'd learnt was how much the Crosses despised and resented us. I tried to tell myself that only a few Crosses had bashed into me; it wasn't all of them by any means, but that didn't help much. I mean, it wasn't exactly as if any of the other Crosses had tried to stop it either.

'Callum, hold on. WAIT!'

I turned and watched Shania race towards me, her school bag slapping up and down against her side.

'What's the matter?'

'Have you heard?' Shania puffed.

'Heard what?'

'About Sephy?'

'What about Sephy?'

'She's been beaten up,' Shania said with relish. 'She was found crying in the girls' toilets, the ones next to the library.'

My heart stopped. I swear it did. Just for a second, but it did stop. I stared at Shania. I couldn't have said a word then if my life had depended on it.

'Serve her right!' Shania said with glee. 'Coming over

to our table and acting like the big "I am".'

'She didn't. It wasn't like that.' Was that really my voice, so hollow and cold?

'Of course it was. She wanted to lord it over us, a little kid like that sitting at our table. Well, we didn't have to teach her a thing or two; her own kind did it for us.'

I shook my head. 'What're you talking about?'

'Just 'cause her dad's in the government, that Sephy Hadley thought she'd play Lady Magnanimous and sit with us. I bet she went and scrubbed her hand after I shook it.' Shania sniffed.

'W-where is she now?'

'They sent for her mum but no-one knew where she was so the chauffeur came to pick her up instead. Her mum was probably having her nails . . .'

I didn't bother to listen to any more. I walked away whilst Shania was in mid-sentence.

'Hey, Callum. Wait for me. D'you fancy an ice-cream at the . . ?'

I started to run until my legs were moving so quickly, my feet scarcely touched the ground. I ran and ran and I didn't stop until I was at the Hadley's. I pressed on the bell and kept my finger on it for the fifteen or twenty seconds it took for someone to open the front door.

'Yes?' Sarah Pike, Mrs Hadley's secretary, opened the door and glared at me with angry suspicion.

'I want to see Sephy – please.'

'I'm afraid the doctor said she's not to be disturbed.' Sarah tried to shut the door in my face. I stuck my foot in the door.

'I want to see Sephy. Is she all right?'

'She's badly bruised and very upset. The doctor has advised that she be kept at home for the rest of the week.'

'What happened? Why . . ?' I didn't get any further.

'Who is it, Sarah?' At the sound of Mrs Hadley's voice, Sarah almost broke my foot in her haste to shut the door. I pushed back and Sarah had to spring back to stop the door from walloping the side of her head. Mrs Hadley stopped on the stairs when she saw me. She recognized me at once.

'You're the McGregor boy, aren't you?'

'That's right, Mrs Hadley.' She didn't have to say that. She knew who I was all right.

'What can I do for you?' Her voice dripped with frost.

'I just heard what happened. I'd like to see Sephy, please.'

'Don't you think you've done enough.' At my blank expression, Mrs Hadley went on, 'I believe my daughter was beaten up for sitting at your lunch table yesterday. You must be so proud of yourself.'

I shook my head. The words wouldn't come. I tried to think of something, anything to say – but what?

'And as I understand it, you turned your back on her and told her to go away,' said Mrs Hadley. 'Is that right?'

Mrs Hadley didn't understand. No-one understood. Not even Sephy. 'Should I have let her sit at our table for longer then? I knew this was going to happen. That's why I didn't want her sitting with us. That's the only reason.'

'So you say.' Mrs Hadley turned around and started to go back up the stairs.

'If I'd welcomed her on to our table with open arms,

you'd have been the first to condemn her and me as well,' I shouted after her.

'Sarah, see this . . . boy out. And make sure he doesn't set foot in my house again.' Mrs Hadley issued her orders without even turning around. She just carried on walking up the stairs in her ladylike, unhurried fashion.

'Please let me see Sephy,' I begged her.

'You're going to have to go now,' Sarah told me apologetically.

'Please . . .'

'I'm sorry.' Sarah gently but firmly kicked my foot back and shut the door.

I rubbed a weary hand over my face which was dripping with perspiration. No-one understood. No-one.

Least of all – me.

seventeen. Sephy

There was absolutely nothing on the telly. What a choice! Silly cartoons, a brainless quiz game, the news or a war film. With a sigh I plumped for the news. I looked at the screen without really watching it. The newsreader finished the story of a banker who'd been sent to prison for fraud and was now talking about three nought robbers who'd smashed in the front of an exclusive jewellery store and made off on motorbikes with gems and jewellery and watches worth close to a million. Why was it that when noughts committed criminal acts, the fact that they were noughts was always pointed out? The banker was a Cross. The newsreader didn't even mention it.

'Who did it?'

I turned to face my sister, Minnie.

'Who was it, Sephy?' she repeated. 'Who beat you up? 'Cause whoever it was, I'll kill them.'

I shook my head, switching off the telly before turning away. *Go away, Minnie*, I thought.

Her outrage was comforting, if more than a little surprising. But all I wanted was to be left alone. There were about three eyelashes over each eye that didn't hurt. The rest of my body ached like blazes. And the last thing I wanted to do was open my sore, bruised lips to speak.

'How many of them were there?'

I held up three fingers.

'Would you recognize them if you saw them again?'

I shrugged.

'Would you?'

'I don't know. Maybe. Go away.' I was talking like my mouth was full of stones – and sharp, jagged ones at that.

'No-one thumps my sister and gets away with it. No-one.'

'Well, they did, and they have.'

'I'll find out who did this and when I do – they'll be really, *really* sorry.' And the look in my sister's eyes told me that she was serious. Deadly serious. For the first time since the three pigs had started laying into me, I felt almost good. Minnie had never been on my side like this before. It was almost – but not quite – worth it if it meant Minnie and I would grow closer . . .

'No-one touches a Hadley. No-one,' Minnie stormed. 'If they think they can get to you with no comeback, then it won't be long before someone tries it on with me. I won't have that.'

My tentative bubble of well-being was well and truly burst.

'Go away, Minnie. Now!' I shouted, the words slurred and blurred as they left my mouth. But even if the words were practically incomprehensible, the look on my face obviously wasn't. Minnie stood up and slammed out of my bedroom without another word.

I closed my eyes, trying to find something to focus on besides the bruises all over my body. Callum . . . Even thinking of him didn't bring me the comfort it usually did. No-one cared. Not about *me* – not about who I really was and what I thought and felt inside. What was it about me that made everyone turn away? Even my best friend had turned his back on me. I knew I was feeling well and truly sorry for myself, but I couldn't help it. I had no-one now. I had nothing.

Ruddy noughts . . . This was all their fault. If it hadn't been for them . . . And as for Lola and the others. I was going to get them, if it was the very last thing I did. I was going to get them – and good. I opened my eyes and stared out into nothing but hate. Minnie and I had a lot more in common than I'd ever imagined. And I wasn't sorry either.

eighteen. Callum

Maths! This was something I could do! Something in this world I could make sense of. Mrs Paxton had already taken me to one side and told me that I would probably be moving to the top Maths stream for my own year after the Crossmas holidays. Mrs Paxton was one of the few Cross teachers who didn't treat me like poo she wanted to scrape off her shoes. And she'd offered me extra lunch-time or early-morning tuition if I wanted it. I was on the last question of my sheet on simultaneous equations when a strange ripple swept through the classroom. I looked up.

Sephy.

My heart bounced about like it was pinging on elastic. Sephy was back. A whole five days without seeing her. A whole five days with no word from her. She looked OK. Maybe one cheek was a little puffy but otherwise just the same as before. Except for her eyes. She looked every-where but directly at me.

'Welcome back, Persephone,' smiled Mrs Paxton.

'Thank you.' Sephy's smile was fleeting.

'Take a seat.' Already Mrs Paxton was turning back to the whiteboard.

Sephy looked around, as did everyone else. The only free seat was next to me. Sephy looked at me, then immediately looked away again. Her gaze swept around the room. I bent my head. Another ripple spread round the room. Mrs Paxton turned around.

'Is something wrong, Persephone?'

'There's nowhere for me to sit, Mrs Paxton,' Sephy said quietly.

'There's a seat next to Callum. Er . . . that's quite enough noise from the rest of you. Get on with your work,' Mrs Paxton called out against the rising tide of voices.

'But Mrs Bawden said I wasn't to sit with any of the noughts . . .'

'Mrs Bawden meant at lunch-time,' Mrs Paxton declared. 'There's only one spare seat left in the class and unless you'd rather sit on the floor, I suggest you use it.'

Dragging her feet, Sephy came and sat down next to me, drawing her chair away as she did so. And she didn't look at me once. Inside, my guts were melting.

'OK, who's finished the first equation?' Mrs Paxton said.

A few hands went up. Mine stayed down. I wanted to look at Sephy but I didn't dare.

Clasp my hands together. Bow my head. Close my eyes.

I know . . . I know noughts aren't really supposed to believe in you or pray to you because you're really the God of the Crosses, but please, please don't let anything or anyone come between me and Sephy. I'm begging you. Please. If you're up there.

nineteen. Sephy

Jeez! Time moved like a petrified glacier. That sounded like something Callum would say. I smiled, but it died almost immediately. Something Callum would say – when he used to talk to me. When he used to be my friend. Mrs Paxton was blathering on about simultaneous equations like they were the best thing since computers were invented. And every word was flying zip-zap straight over my head! When was the bell going to sound? Come on . . . Come on . . . At last!

I didn't even take time to gather up my books. I just swept the whole lot into my school bag.

'Sephy, wait.'

I hovered in between sitting and standing, looking like a hen trying to hatch an egg. Slowly, I sat back down.

'How are you? Are you OK now?'

'Yes, thank you.' I still couldn't look at him. I went to stand up again. Callum's hand on my forearm stopped me. He immediately removed it. He couldn't even bear to touch me.

'I'm glad,' he whispered.

'Are you?' I turned to him. 'You could've fooled me.'

'What does that mean?'

My hands itched to knock the bewildered look off his

face. Just who did Callum think he was fooling? I glanced around the room. Others were listening intently even though they were trying to pretend they weren't. I lowered my voice so only Callum would hear what I was going to say. And I was determined it'd be the last thing I ever said to him.

'Don't pretend you were worried about me,' I told him. 'You didn't come to see me once. You didn't even send me a Get Well Soon card.'

Callum's face cleared. He leaned forward, also aware of our audience. 'I came to see you every day. Every single day,' he whispered. 'Your mum gave orders that I wasn't to be let in. I stood outside your gates every afternoon after school. Ask your mum . . . no, ask her secretary Sarah if you don't believe me.'

Silence.

'You came to see me?'

'Every day?'

'Really?'

'Ask Sarah . . .'

I didn't need to ask Sarah.

'Sephy, wild horses couldn't have kept me away.'

We regarded each other, our expressions equally sombre.

'I have to go now.' I stood up. We were attracting way too much attention. Callum stood up too.

'Look, meet me in our special place after dinner tonight. We can't talk here.'

I turned to walk away.

'Sephy, if you're not there, I'll understand,' Callum whispered.

She wasn't going to show. Why should she after everything she'd been through? After I'd let her down? Be
truthful. What I did in the food hall wasn't for Sephy's
own good or even my own. It was because I was scared.
Scared of standing out, scared of being invisible. Scared of
seeming too big, scared of being too small. Scared of
being with Sephy, scared of being away from her. No
jokes, no prevarications, no sarcasm, no lies. Just scared
scared scared.

God only knew how tired I was of being afraid all the
time. When was it going to stop?

'Hello, Callum.'

Sephy's voice behind me had me whipping around to
face her.

'Hi. Hello. How are you?'

'Fine.' She turned to look out over the sea. 'Isn't it a
lovely evening?'

'Is it? I hadn't noticed.' My gaze followed hers. She was
right. It was beautiful. The sky was on fire and the waves
broke relentlessly silver and white on the rocky beach.
But I turned away from it. I had other things on my mind.

'Persephone, you have to believe me. I did come to
visit you, I swear . . .'

'I know you did.' Sephy smiled at me.

I frowned. 'You spoke to Sarah?'

'Didn't have to.' Sephy shrugged.

'I don't understand. Why didn't you talk to Sarah?'

'Because I believed you.'

I looked at Sephy carefully then and realized that the old Sephy, *my* Sephy, was back. Relief whirled through me on angel's wings. Such relief that my body actually shook with it.

'Besides, it sounds like just the sort of thing my mother would do,' Sephy sniffed.

I wanted to ask her what and where and how, but I couldn't. I didn't want to push my luck. We stood for a while, just being. But the need to explain by way of apology gnawed away at me, eating a bigger hole in my insides with each passing moment.

'I'm sorry I missed our trip to Celebration Park last Saturday,' Sephy sighed. 'I was looking forward to that.'

'Never mind. We've been there before and we'll go again.' I shrugged.

Pause.

'Sephy, do you remember the last time we went to Celebration Park?'

Sephy frowned. 'When we had our summer picnic?'

I nodded.

'Yeah, of course I remember. What about it?'

'What d'you remember?' I asked.

Sephy shrugged. 'We travelled up by train. We went to the park, found a secluded spot, had our picnic, played silly games, came home – the end of a lovely day.'

'Is that how you remember it?'

'Of course. Why?'

I studied Sephy, wondering if she was telling the truth. Or was it simply a case of the truth as she saw it, where her vision wasn't and never would be the same as mine. A lovely day . . . Was that really all she remembered? How strange. My memory of the day was slightly different . . .

THE PICNIC

twenty-one. Sephy

We had a wonderful day together, the day we went to Celebration Park. I'd lied and told Mother that I was spending the day with Helena's family. I knew Mother wouldn't check. Helena's family were almost as rich as us and in my mother's mind that meant that I couldn't be lying. I mean, why would I lie about spending the day with one of the richest but most boring girls in my class? In my class? In the northern hemisphere more like. Helena's family were 'like us' – as Mother was fond of saying. I could spend as much time with her as I liked.

So I'd lied. And met Callum at the train station instead. The park was wonderful. The whole day was just brilliant.

Except for the train journey . . .

twenty-two. Callum

I hadn't been sure if Sephy was going to show. But then I was never sure – and she *always* did turn up. And every time she did show, I'd tell myself, 'See! You should have more faith in her.' And then I'd answer myself, 'Next time. Next time I will.'

But next time always found me wondering if this would be the day that Sephy wouldn't be able to make it. Unfair as it was, I wondered each time if today was the day that Sephy was going to let me down.

'Penny for them.' Sephy's voice sounded in my ears at the exact same time as her bony, pointy fingers prodded me in my kidneys, making me jump.

'Jeez, Sephy. I do wish you wouldn't do that.'

'You love it!' Sephy's grin was huge as she walked around me.

'No, I don't actually.'

'I see you're in one of your sunshine moods.'

I took a deep breath and smiled. It wasn't me, it was my doubts snapping at her. And she was here now. She was here.

twenty-three. Sephy

One of these days, Callum's going to forget himself and actually look pleased to see me.

I just won't hold my breath whilst I'm waiting, that's all.

'There's your ticket.' I handed it over to Callum. I'd raided my bank account to get enough to buy two first-class tickets. I could've asked Mother for the money, or Sarah, but then they would've wanted to know exactly why I wanted it. No, this was much better. It made the day 'ours' somehow, because the money was mine and nothing to do with my mother or anyone else. I smiled. 'This day is going to be perfect.'

I could feel it in my water.

twenty-four. Callum

The train journey from hell, that's what it was. A journey which ruined the rest of the day as far as I was concerned. We were on our way to Celebration Park. There were only three more stops to go – when they got on. Police officers on a routine inspection. Two of them, boredom plastered over their faces.

'ID passes please. ID passes please.'

Sephy looked surprised. I wasn't. We both dug out our ID cards as they made their way up the first-class train carriage. I watched the cursory glances they gave the ID passes of all the Crosses in the carriage. I was the only nought. Would they stop and ask me lots of questions? Huh! Is pig poo smelly?

An officer of trim build and sporting a pencil-thin moustache stood right in front of me. He looked at me then took my ID pass without a word.

'Name?' he snapped out.

What's the matter? Can't you read?

'Callum McGregor.'

'Age?'

'Fifteen.'

Can't read numbers either, huh? That's too bad.

'Where are you going?'

None of your business.

'Celebration Park.'

'Why?'

To cut my toenails.

'Picnic.'

'Where d'you live?'

On the moon.

'Meadowview.' Meadowview by euphemistic name only. Rubbishshackview would've been more appropriate. The officer looked from my ID card to my face and back again. My thumbprint was on the card. Was he going to break out a magnifying glass and ask me to hold out my right hand so he could compare the imprint on the card to my print? It wouldn't've surprised me.

'You're a long way from home, boy.'

I bit down on the inside of my bottom lip, not trusting myself to speak. Both officious officials stood in front of me now. There was barely enough room to get a paper-clip between their legs and my knees. I sighed.

Ladies and gentlemen, for your delectation and delight, another performance of 'You're a nought and don't you ever forget it, blanker boy.'

'Let me see your ticket.'

I handed it over.

'Where did you get the money to buy this kind of ticket?'

I looked up at them, but didn't speak. What was there to say? They had the scent of blood in their nostrils and I didn't stand a chance, no matter what I said or did. So why bother?

'I asked you a question,' Moustaches reminded me.

As if I'd forgotten.

'Did you buy this ticket?' Moustache's accomplice asked.

The truth or prevarication? What was Sephy thinking? I couldn't see her. The no-brain brothers were in the way. If only I could see her face.

'I asked you a question, boy. Did you buy this ticket?'

'No, I didn't,' I replied.

'Come with us, please.'

Time to get my posterior pummelled. Time to get my derrière dealt with. Time to get my bum bounced right off the train.

How dare a nought sit in first class? It's outrageous. It's a scandal. It's disgusting. Disinfect that seat at once.

'Officer, he's with me. I bought the tickets.' Sephy was on her feet. 'Is there a problem?'

'And you are?'

'Persephone Hadley. My dad's the Home Office Minister, Kamal Hadley. Callum is my friend,' Sephy said firmly.

'He is?'

'Yes, he is.' Sephy's voice had a steely tone to it that I'd never heard before. Not from her anyway.

'I see,' said Moustaches.

'I can give you my father's private phone number. I'm sure he'll sort all this out in a moment. Or you'll be able to talk to Juno Ayelette, his personal secretary.'

Careful, Sephy. I'm tripping over all those names you're dropping.

'So is there a problem, Officer?' repeated Sephy.

Sniff! Sniff! Was I imagining things or was there the definite hint of a threat in the air? And I wasn't the only one to smell it. Moustaches handed back my ID pass.

'Would you like to see my ID as well?' Sephy held out her pass.

'That won't be necessary, Miss Hadley.' Moustaches almost bowed.

'I really don't mind.' Sephy thrust it under Moustaches' nose.

'That won't be necessary,' Moustaches repeated, looking straight at Sephy. He didn't even glance at her ID card.

Sephy sat back down again. 'Well, if you're sure.'

She turned to look out of the window. Moustaches was effectively dismissed. Sephy's mother would've been proud. Moustaches glared at me like it was my fault. He'd been humiliated, and by a child no less, and he wanted to take it out on someone. Sephy was off-limits, and now, so was I. He was burning to re-establish his authority but he couldn't. Not with us anyway. Moustaches and his colleague moved off down the carriage. Sephy turned to me and winked.

'You OK?' she asked.

'Fine,' I lied. 'Wasn't that fun?'

'Not so as you'd notice.' Sephy's gaze returned to the passing scenery. 'But I'm not going to let them or anyone else ruin my day. Celebration Park, here we come!'

I turned to look out of the window. I didn't want to look at Sephy. Not yet. I didn't want to blame her for the way the police treated me and every other nought I knew. I didn't want to hold her responsible for the way security guards and store detectives followed me around every time I entered a department store. And I'd stopped going into bookshops and toy shops and gift shops when I realized that no matter where I went in them, all eyes were upon me. After all, it was one of those well-known Cross-initiated facts that we noughts didn't pay for anything when there was the chance of stealing it instead. I didn't want to resent Sephy for the way my education was automatically assumed to be less important than hers. I didn't want to hate her because she was a Cross and different to me. So I carried on looking out of the window, pushing the knot of loathing deeper inside me. Deeper and deeper. The way I always did.

No, I didn't want to look at Sephy. Not yet. *Not yet.*

BREAKDOWN

twenty-five. Sephy

'You're thinking about those police officers on the train, aren't you?' I asked.

Callum didn't even bother to deny it. But then why should he? In his shoes, they would've annoyed me as well.

Annoyed . . . Come on, Sephy, be honest. You were a lot more than just 'annoyed'. And they weren't even picking on you.

'Why did you want me to remember our trip to Celebration Park?' I asked.

Callum shrugged, then smiled. 'Because it was a good day. A day we had all to ourselves once we got to the park.'

That wasn't true. He'd wanted to say something about our train journey to Celebration Park and my mother not letting him in to see me. Somehow, he felt one was connected with the other. I'm not completely stupid. I'm not as naïve as I used to be either. I'm finally growing up. I wanted Callum to tell me what he was really thinking, what he was really feeling, but part of me was afraid, I admit it. So I nodded noncommittally instead. It didn't matter what I said to Callum or anyone else; my main memory of that day was of the police officers and how they'd treated Callum and how I'd burned with resentment for him and how I'd been ashamed of them. And myself. I'd felt ashamed of myself a lot recently, and, if I'm honest, part of me resented Callum for it. I didn't want to feel guilty for just being, but that's how he was beginning to make me feel.

Suddenly all I had were questions. How come in all the early black-and-white films, the nought men were always ignorant drunkards or womanisers or both? And the women were always near-brainless servants? Noughts used to be our slaves but slavery was abolished a long time ago. Why were noughts never in the news unless it was bad news? Why couldn't I stop looking at each stranger I passed and wondering about their lives?

I'd started watching people – noughts and Crosses. Their faces, their body language, the way they spoke to their 'own' kind. The way they spoke to others who weren't the same. And there were so many differences, they swamped the similarities. Noughts relaxed around each other in a way they rarely did around Crosses. And Crosses were constantly on their guard when near noughts. Bags got clutched tighter, footsteps quickened, voices grew brisker and brusquer. All our lives criss-crossing but never really touching. A world full of strangers living with all that *fear*. Nothing was a given any more. Not my life. Not theirs. Nothing.

I can't remember when our lives had become so complicated. A few years ago . . . or maybe even a few months ago, life had been so easy. But the ache in my chest told me like words couldn't that those days were over.

'It *was* a good day, wasn't it?' Callum smiled.

It took me a second to catch up. 'Yes, it was.'

The truth, but not the whole truth and nothing but.

Say it, Callum. Whatever it is, say it. I can take it. At least, I'll try . . .

But he didn't. The silence dragged between us and the moment passed.

'It'll be winter soon,' I sighed.

Winter always made it harder for me to leave the house and meet Callum. Mother accepted my many trips to the beach because as far as she was concerned, I was a dreamer and the beach was where I did my dreaming. Unlike the town house, our country place had minimum security so I could pretty much come and go as I pleased – within reason. And going down to the beach in winter was beyond reason as far as Mother was concerned. To be honest, walking down to the beach in the dark wasn't my most favourite thing. Dusk and the air heavy with silence and long shadows made me . . . nervous.

'Who pummelled you?'

'Pardon?'

'Who beat you up?' Callum repeated.

'Everyone's asking me that,' I sighed. 'Can't we just let it rest?'

'You don't want them to get away with it, do you?'

' 'Course not. But there's not a lot I can do about it. Sure, I was going to tell the headmaster about them and get them expelled or put drawing-pins in their shoes or jump out at them when they were each alone. I was going to do all those things, but they're not worth it. It happened and now it's over, and I just want to forget about it.'

'Tell me who did it and then you can,' Callum said.

I frowned. 'You're not going to do anything stupid, are you?'

''Course not. I'd just like to know who did this to you.'

'Lola, Joanne and Dionne in Mrs Watson's class.' I said at last. 'But it's over now. OK?'

'OK.'

'Callum . . .'

'I was just curious. Besides, what could I do? They're Crosses and I'm a lowly nought.' Callum tugged on his forelock before bowing low.

'Stop it . . .'

'Stop what?'

'Callum, it's me. Sephy. I'm not your enemy.'

'I never said . . .'

I took Callum's face in my hands. 'Look at me, Callum.'

Only when I felt his whole body relax did I remove my hands from his face.

'Sorry,' he said at last.

'So am I,' I told him. 'So am I.'

twenty-six. Callum

When I got home, the house was in uproar – and for once it had nothing to do with me. Lynette was having one of her 'turns' and Jude was letting it wind him up, as usual. When I stepped through the front door and heard him shouting at her, I thought, 'Same old, same old!'

But I was wrong.

For the first time ever, Lynette was shouting back at him. My sister and Jude were squaring up to each other, with Dad in the middle of them, desperately trying to keep them apart. And Jude's lip was bleeding . . .

'You're nothing but a git, and a vulgar git at that,' Lynette screamed at the top of her lungs.

'At least I don't delude myself,' Jude shot back at her.

'And what's that supposed to mean?' asked Lynette.

'Jude, don't. Lynette, please.' Dad wasn't getting very far.

I looked around for Mum, knowing as I did so that she must be out. There was no way she'd have let things get this far. Dad was there, being his usual feeble self.

'Dad, what's going on?' I asked, pulling on his arm.

Dad turned to shrug me off and that was all the space Jude needed. He lashed out at Lynette. She hit him straight back. Seconds later, Dad was between them, again pushing them apart. I hadn't seen Lynette and Jude fight since before my sister's mind had shut down.

'Look at you! You think you're too good to even breathe the same air as us,' Jude hissed. 'Well, I've got news for you, sis. When the daggers look at you, they see someone who's just as white as me, for all your airs and graces.'

Daggers again. Every other sentence out of his mouth these days seemed to be 'ruddy daggers this' and 'ruddy daggers that'.

'I'm not like you. I'm . . . I'm different. I'm brown. Look at my dark skin. Look . . .'

Pushing past Dad, Jude grabbed Lynette's hands and pulled her to the cracked wall-mirror behind the sofa. He pulled her back against him, his cheek against her cheek. Lynette instantly tried to pull away but Jude wouldn't let her.

'See that!' Jude roared. 'You're the same as me. As white as me. Who d'you think you are? I'm sick and tired of being looked down on by you. You're the most pathetic person I know. If you hate what you are, do something about it. Just die or something! And if there is a God, you'll come back as one of those ruddy daggers you love so much, and then I can stop feeling guilty about hating you.'

Jude pushed Lynette away from him. She stumbled and fell, arms outstretched against the mirror.

'Dad, do something,' I shouted at him.

'Jude, that's enough. More than enough,' said Dad.

'It's not even close.' Jude turned on him, nostrils flaring. 'It's time she heard the truth from someone and who else is going to tell her? You? The spineless wonder? Mum won't say a word because Lynette is her favourite and the only person Callum cares about is his dagger friend Persephone. So who else is going to show Lynette how it really is?'

'And who are you to show anyone how it really is?' I challenged. 'You're always so sure you're right, aren't you? You make me sick. Lynette isn't the only one here who can't stand you.'

Jude stared at me. Without warning he let out a howl like an animal in pain and charged at me. I had time to do little more than take a step back before Jude's head smashed into my stomach and he knocked me to the ground, knocking all the wind out of me. Dazed, I wondered why his fists weren't laying into me until I realized that crashing to the ground had knocked the wind out of him as well. I pushed him up and backwards, drawing up my legs at the same time to knee him in the back. He groaned but didn't get off me. He drew back his fist. I crossed my arms in front of me, getting in his way so he couldn't hit my face.

The next thing I knew, Jude was being pulled off me.

'What the hell is the matter with you?' Dad shouted at Jude, his face almost puce with anger.

I leapt to my feet ready to do battle. Jude tried to turn back to me but Dad wasn't having it.

'Don't turn your back on me when I'm talking to you,' Dad raged.

'Oh, get lost, Dad.' Jude was already turning away from him.

Dad did something that stunned both of us. He spun Jude around and slapped him across the face. Mum was handy with a slipper whenever we gave her cheek but Dad had never so much as raised his voice to any of us before, let alone hit us.

'Don't you ever, *ever* talk to me like that again as long as you live.' Dad's voice was quiet and all the more menacing for it. 'I'm too old and I've had to contend with too much crap in my life to put up with disrespect in my own house. You have no idea what your sister's been through, so how dare you judge her?'

'W-what's she been through?' Jude sniffed, rubbing his face. It was like he was no longer seventeen years old but seven.

'Three years ago, Lynette and her boyfriend were attacked. By our own. Three or four nought men.' Dad's voice rasped with contempt. 'D'you remember when your mum lost her job so you had to leave school, and around the same time, Lynette was away from home for a while?'

'You said she'd gone to stay with Aunt Amanda.' The horrified words crept out of my mouth. 'You said Aunt Amanda was ill and Lynny had volunteered to look after her.'

'Your mum and I said what we had to say. Those men almost beat Lynette's boy to death and they beat Lynette so badly she was in hospital for over two weeks. She begged us not to tell you what had really happened.'

'I didn't know . . .' Jude breathed.

'And d'you know why Lynette was attacked?' Dad carried on as if Jude hadn't spoken. 'Because her boyfriend was a Cross. Your sister was beaten and l-left for dead because she was dating a Cross. And she didn't even tell us. She was afraid of what we'd all say. So is it any wonder that she can't bear to think of herself as one of us any more? Is it any wonder she can't even leave this house any more? Her mind hasn't been right since 'cause she's still hurting. So leave her alone. D'you hear me? D'YOU HEAR ME?'

Jude nodded. I nodded, even though Dad wasn't talking directly to me. I turned to look at Lynette. My sister, Lynette.

'Dad, she's bleeding.' I pointed.

Dad was by her side in a second. Lynette's palms were bleeding where she'd banged them into the cracked mirror. Lynette was staring down at the crimson patches on her hands as if she'd never seen her own blood before. She looked up to stare at her reflection in the mirror, as if she'd never seen her face before either.

'Where's Jed, Daddy?' Lynette whispered.

'Jed?' Dad looked stricken. 'Honey, Jed went away a long, long time ago. Let me clean up your hands.'

Lynette pulled her hands out of Dad's grasp. She turned them this way and that, before she slowly raised her head to look at Dad. That faraway, peaceful expression she always wore was dead and gone.

'Where am I?'

'At home.' Dad's smile was as fake as plastic. 'You're safe now. I'm here. I'll look after you.'

'Where's Jed?' Lynette looked around the room.

'Listen, honey, Jed and his family moved away a long time ago. They've gone. He's gone . . .'

'Not a long time ago . . . Yesterday . . . Last week . . .' Lynette's voice was barely above a whisper.

'Darling, it was years ago,' Dad persisted.

'I'm . . . I'm seventeen?'

'No, love. You're twenty. Twenty last April.' Dad swallowed hard. 'Come on, let me . . .'

'I thought I was seventeen. Eighteen . . .' Lynette buried her face in her hands, smearing her cheeks with blood. 'I don't know what I thought.'

'Lynette, please . . .'

'Lynette, I didn't know.' Jude stretched out his hand towards Lynette. She slapped it away.

'Keep your hands away from me,' she said with vehemence.

Jude's hand fell to his side. 'My nought hands, you mean?'

Silence. Lynette looked down at her hands again.

'Your hands are the same as mine. The same as *theirs*.' And Lynette turned and ran up to her room before any of us could say another word.

Dad and Jude regarded each other and, never before had I seen either of them look so . . . lost. Looking at them made my eyes begin to sting and water but I stared and didn't blink, waiting for the feeling to, if not die, then at least lessen to the extent where I wouldn't make a complete fool of myself. I turned so Dad and Jude wouldn't see my expression and caught sight of myself in the mirror.

My face was the reflection of Dad and Jude. My expression was theirs. My thoughts and feelings and hates and fears were all theirs, just as theirs were mine, and though I like to think I'm quick and on the ball, I hadn't even realized. Until now.

twenty-seven. Sephy

I stood in the doorway, watching Mother sip at her glass of white wine. I realized with a start that I had to think back a long way to remember seeing her without a glass of Chardonnay in her hand.

'Mother, can I have a party for my fourteenth birthday?'

Mother looked up from her magazine. That's all she ever did, read and drink, spend time in the gym or the pool and drink, shop and drink. And the only things she ever read were those glossy magazines with impossibly beautiful women on the cover and inside. Women with polished mahogany skin who looked like they'd never had a pimple in their lives – nor a decent meal either come to that. Women with teeth which shone like fresh snow in sunshine.

Something else struck me. I'd never seen a nought in any of my mother's magazines. Not one. No white or pink faces anywhere. In fact, there'd actually been something on the news at the beginning of the year when the first nought model was featured in one of the high fashion magazines. I couldn't see what all the fuss was about at the time. To be honest, I still couldn't.

'A party, eh?' Mother's voice brought me back to the

here and now. 'I don't see why not.'

And that was it! I was so surprised, I couldn't speak. I'd expected far more of an argument!

'After all, your teenage years don't last very long. You should make sure you enjoy every moment of them,' Mother smiled.

I wondered how many glasses of wine it had taken to bring on this good mood. And even though I knew I was being uncharitable, I still resented the glass in her hand for making Mother happy where my sister Minnie and I couldn't.

'Where would you like to have it?' Mother continued.

'Couldn't we have it here, in our house?'

'I suppose so.' Mother shrugged. 'We could take on some extra help for the day to help out. D'you want an entertainer or a magician?'

'Mother, I'll be fourteen.'

Mother raised her eyebrows. 'So?'

'So I'll have an entertainer!' I smiled.

Mother smiled back. One of our rare moments of connection.

'So how many guests d'you think you'll have?' asked Mother.

'Everyone in my class. And some of my cousins. And my other friends from ballet school and riding. About forty odd, I suppose.'

'Fine. Run along and talk to Sarah. Get her to sort it out.' Mother's nose was already back in her magazine.

I might've guessed Mother wouldn't want to get her hands dirty. And with a personal secretary and chauffeur and maids and servants, why should she? But I would've loved it if she'd been interested enough to even ask me what I wanted as a birthday present. Oh, I got birthday and Crossmas presents from Mother and Dad. It's just that they never bought them. They never even chose them. Mother's secretary Sarah had very good taste. But each one of her selected presents sat at the back of my wardrobe or at the back of a drawer or under my bed, unused. And no-one ever asked me if I liked my presents. No-one ever even asked why they never saw them again after the day they were given. The presents didn't matter. Maybe because I didn't either. Only one person cared if I lived or died. He'd done so much for me in the past and now it was my turn to do something for him.

I had a little surprise for Mother and everyone else. A surprise that would ensure that my birthday party was talked about and remembered for ages to come. I hugged my secret to me. I would get into awful trouble but I didn't care. I really didn't. I'd had enough of this attitude of 'live and let live – but not in my neighbourhood'. It wasn't that I thought I was better than everyone else or anything, but someone had to start somewhere, show them all what hypocrites they were.

So why not now?

And why not me?

twenty-eight. Callum

'Ryan, this isn't the way to change things. Alex Luther, for instance . . .'

'Alex Luther, my left buttock!'

'Ryan, language!' Mum told him off.

'Meggie, get real!' Dad said impatiently. 'Alex Luther is barely living, just about breathing proof that trying to change the way it is by using peaceful methods doesn't work. That blanker has been in prison more times than any eight prison governors I know.'

'Don't call him that,' Mum said furiously. 'It's bad enough when ignorant Crosses call us blankers without us calling ourselves by the same name.'

'We name it, we claim it,' said Dad.

'Nonsense! We use it, Crosses think they can too. Besides, that's not my point. Alex Luther is a great man . . .'

'I'm not saying he isn't, but the General is making more of an impact than Alex Luther.'

'And if my granny had wheels she'd be a wagon!' Mum snorted.

'What's your point? The General is . . .'

'A warmonger!' Mum's tone made it very clear what she thought of the General, the anonymous head of the

Liberation Militia. 'Killing and maiming always make more of an impression than peaceful protests and sit-ins and passive resistance, but that doesn't make it right.'

'The General . . .'

'I don't want to hear one more word about the General. You talk about him as if he were God's brother or something.'

'As head of the L.M., he's the next best thing . . .' Dad replied.

In response, Mum used a series of words I'd never heard her say before. I left her and Dad arguing about the General versus Alex Luther and crept down the stairs. Weren't the two of them ever going to sleep? I'd already been waiting half an hour for them to give up and shut up. How many times had they had the same argument? No-one ever won. It just made them mad at each other. What was the point?

I glanced up at the clock in our living room. Two-thirty in the morning. Earlier, Sephy had left her usual message that she wanted to talk to me urgently. We had a secret signal. She'd phone three times, each time letting the phone ring twice before calling off. That way she didn't have to talk to anyone or let my mum and dad or Jude know that she was phoning. Of course the phone ringing then stopping drove Mum and Dad nuts but the trick was not to do it too often. If I needed to get hold of her urgently, I did the same thing, although it was more tricky phoning during the day because one of Sephy's house servants usually picked it up pretty quickly. Once I heard the signal, I knew Sephy would phone me between two-thirty and three in the morning – whenever it was safe for her to sneak out of her room and use one of the phones in her house. When I phoned her with our signal, we'd usually meet in her rose garden around the same time of night. So here I was, hovering over our one and only phone like a vulture, waiting for the first brrrr to sound so that I could pick it up before it disturbed everyone else in the house.

Quarter to three came and went, as did three o'clock. At five past three I decided that Sephy was obviously not going to call me. Maybe it'd just been too difficult to get to a phone. I was heading up the stairs when the first trill sounded. I've never moved so fast. But even then a full brrrrr rang out before I could pick up the receiver.

'Callum?'

'Shush!' I whispered. I anxiously looked up the darkened stairs, listening intently for the sound of a bedroom door opening. Moments passed. Nothing.

'Sephy?'

'Sorry I'm late, but Mum came down ten minutes ago and she's only just gone back upstairs.'

'That's OK.'

Sephy's voice barely made it to a whisper, the same as mine. I was standing in our living room talking to my best friend in the pitch dark. It made it feel adventurous and illicit somehow.

'Callum . . .'

'I'm glad you phoned.' I got in first. 'What lessons do we have tomorrow?'

'Double Maths, then History. English, P.E., I.T. and Music in the afternoon. Where's your timetable?'

'I left it at school,' I replied softly. And then something

Sephy had said sunk in. 'Oh no, not History!'

'What's wrong with History?'

'Mr Jason,' I said grimly. 'He's going to use the lesson to stick it to me the way he always does.'

'What're you talking about?'

'If you don't know then I can't tell you,' I said.

Silence stretched between us.

'You still there, Sephy?'

'Yes, I'm still here,' Sephy replied.

'So why did you want to talk to me?' I asked. 'What was so urgent?'

'What're you doing on the twenty-seventh of September, that's two weeks on Saturday?'

I frowned into the darkness. 'Nothing as far as I know. Why?'

'D'you want to meet up for my birthday?'

'Sure. But your birthday's on the twenty-third, isn't it?'

'Yeah, but I'm having a birthday party at the house on the twenty-seventh. You can come round.'

I'd obviously misheard her. 'Round to your house?'

'That's right.'

'I see.'

'See what?'

'You want me to come round to your house?'

'That's what I said, isn't it?'

'I see.'

'Stop saying that.'

What else did she want me to say? Why was she inviting me to her house when her mum would take one look at me and have me carried from the building? What was the point? What was she up to?

'You're sure you want me to come over?' I asked.

'I'm positive. Will you?'

'Does your mum know you're inviting me?' At first I thought Sephy wasn't going to answer.

'No,' she said at last.

'But you are going to tell her?'

' 'Course.'

'Before or after I turn up at your party?'

'Don't be so ruddy smart!' Sephy snapped, which more than answered my question. 'So are you coming?'

'If you want me to,' I said slowly.

'I do. I'll give you all the details after school tomorrow. OK?'

'OK.'

'Bye, Callum.'

I put down the phone, getting it right first time now that my eyes were accustomed to the dark. Sephy wanted me at her birthday party, knowing it would cause nothing but trouble.

What was she up to? There was only one reason I could think of, but if I was right, it would mean that Sephy didn't think of me the way I thought of her. If I was right, it would prove that to Sephy I was a nought first and everything else came afterwards.

twenty-nine. Sephy

I couldn't get to sleep. I turned to the left, then turned to the right, I lay on my stomach, then lay on my back. I'd've stood on my head if it would've done any good. I just couldn't get to sleep. What had seemed like a good idea at the time was now growing fungus all over it and beginning to smell. I wanted Callum at my birthday party. Hell, if things were different, he'd be the first on my invite list.

But things weren't different.

I lay on my stomach and punched my pillow. Why was nothing ever simple?

thirty. Callum

'The purpose of today's history lesson is to show you all how famous scientists, inventors, arts and media celebrities and other people of note are all people, just like you and me.'

'But we already know that, sir,' Sade said. 'I mean, what else would they be?'

I'd been wondering that myself.

'When we think of great explorers or inventors or actors or anything else, it's sometimes very easy to think of them as "out there" – somewhere above and beyond us. I want all of you to realize that they're just like you and me, that we too can aspire to greatness. Anyone in this room can be a scientist or an astronaut or anything they want to be if they work hard and are determined.' Mr Jason looked directly at me when he said that, the familiar look of contempt on his face. What was it about me that rubbed him up the wrong way? Was it just my colour he despised so much? I couldn't help being white, any more than he could help being black. I mean, he wasn't even that black anyway. He was more beige than brown, and a very light beige at that, so he had nothing to gloat about. I smiled secretly to myself as I remembered the saying Dad was always spouting: '*If you're black, that's where it's at. If you're brown, stick around. If you're white, say goodnight.*'

When you got right down to it, Mr Jason had less cause to look down on me than Mrs Paxton who was dark, dark brown, but she was totally different. She treated me like a real person. She didn't see me as just a colour – first, last and always. I liked her. She was like an oasis in this scorching hot desert.

'Now then, can anyone tell me who invented automatic traffic signals which led to the traffic lights we use today, and he also invented a type of gas mask used by soldiers during World War One?'

Everyone sat silent. Slowly, I put my hand up. Mr Jason saw my hand but looked around for someone else to ask. Everyone else's hands stayed down.

'Yes, Callum?' Mr Jason asked reluctantly.

'Garrett Morgan, sir.'

'Correct. What about this one, class? Who pioneered blood banks?'

Once again, no hands went up – except mine.

'Yes, Callum?' Mr Jason's voice was now tinged with sarcasm.

'Dr Charles Drew,' I replied.

'And I suppose you also know who was the first person to perform open heart surgery?'

'Dr Daniel Hale Williams.'

'The first man to reach the North Pole?'

'Matthew Henson.'

All eyes were upon me now. Mr Jason gave me one of the filthiest looks I've ever had in my life.

'The saying "The Real McCoy" is named after?'

'Elijah J. McCoy,' I replied.

Mr Jason drew himself up to his full height. 'Why don't I just sit down and you can teach this lesson?'

What did he want from me? He was asking questions that I knew the answers to. Was I supposed to just sit there and pretend to be ignorant?

'Can anyone tell me what all these scientists and pioneers really had in common?' Mr Jason asked.

A few more hands went up at that. Mr Jason wasn't the only one who was relieved – not that I was going to answer any more questions anyway.

'Yes, Harriet?' said Mr Jason.

'They're all men?' Harriet replied.

'Our examples are, but there have been plenty of women pioneers and scientists and achievers as well,' Mr Jason smiled. 'So can anyone tell me what else all the people mentioned have in common?'

There were a couple more guesses after that – like, 'They're all dead,' 'They all won the Nobel prize', 'They all made a lot of money from what they did' – but none of them were right. And it was so obvious. At last, I couldn't stand it any longer. My hand crept up.

'Ah! I wondered if we were going to hear from you again.' Mr Jason directed more of a smirk than a smile in my direction. 'So what's the answer then, Callum?'

'They were all Crosses,' I replied.

Mr Jason's smirk grew so wide I'm surprised he didn't swallow his ears. 'Correct! Well done!' He started moving round the class. My face burned pink then scarlet as every eye in the class turned on me.

'Throughout history, from the time our ancestors in Cafrique sailed to other lands and acquired knowledge of gunpowder, writing, weapon-making, the arts and so on, we have been the dominant race on Earth. We have been the explorers, the ones to move entire backward civilizations onwards . . .'

I couldn't let him get away with that. My hand shot up again.

'Yes, Callum?'

'Sir, I read somewhere that noughts have made a significant contribution to the way we live today too . . .'

'Oh yes? Like how?' Mr Jason folded his arms across his chest as he waited for my answer.

'Well, for example, Matthew Henson was *joint* first to the North Pole. Robert E. Peary was with him.'

'Robert who?'

'Robert Peary. He was co-discoverer of the geographic North Pole.'

'How come I've never heard of him then?' Mr Jason challenged.

'Because all the history books are written by Crosses and you never write about anyone else except your own. Noughts have done lots of significant things, but I bet no-one in this class knows . . .'

'That's quite enough.' Mr Jason cut me off in mid-tirade.

'But, sir . . .'

'How dare you spread these pathetic lies about nought scientists and inventors?' Mr Jason's hands were clenched at his side now and he glared at me furiously.

'They're not lies,' I protested.

'Who's been filling your head with all this nonsense?'

'It's not nonsense. My dad told me.'

'And where did your dad get it from?'

'I . . . I . . .' My voice trailed away.

'Exactly!' said Mr Jason. 'Now go and stand outside the headmaster's room. And don't come back into this room until you've got all that nonsense out of your head and you're ready to accept my teaching.'

I grabbed my bag and jumped to my feet, knocking my chair over in the process. I turned and glared at Sephy. Her gaze dropped away from mine almost at once. Not bothering to pick up my chair, I slammed out of the room. I knew that little act of defiance would probably get me in even more trouble. But as I marched down the corridor towards Mr Costa's room, I was so livid I was shaking. It wasn't nonsense. It wasn't lies. It was the truth. Centuries ago, Crosses had moved across northern and eastern Pangaea from the south, acquiring along the way the know-how to make the guns and weapons that made everyone else bow down to them. But that didn't mean that what they did was right. We noughts had been their slaves for so long, and even though slavery had been formally abolished over half a century ago, I didn't see that we were much better off. We were only just beginning to be let into their schools. The number of noughts in positions of authority in the country could be counted on the fingers of one hand – without including the thumb! It wasn't right. *It wasn't fair.*

And though I knew that nowhere was it written that life was meant to be fair, it still made my blood bubble to think about it. Why should I feel grateful to any of them just because they'd let me into one of their precious schools? What was the point? Maybe Mum and Jude were right. Maybe this was a complete waste of my time?

My steps slowed as I approached the school secretary's room. Was I meant to stand in the corridor or go into the secretary's office and wait outside the headmaster's door. After dithering about for a few moments, I decided that Mr Jason probably wanted me to stand where I could get into the maximum amount of trouble. That meant standing right outside Mr Costa's door. I peered in through the glass in the secretary's door. She wasn't there. That was something at any rate. I went in, carefully shutting the door behind me. I reckoned I'd slammed enough doors that morning. I'd taken two steps into the office when quiet but angry voices floated out past Mr Costa's slightly ajar door to meet me.

'And I'm telling you that something needs to be done.' It was Mrs Paxton's voice. 'How much longer are you going to let this situation continue?'

'If the blankers are finding it tough here, then maybe they should go elsewhere,' came Mr Costa's reply.

I froze, not even breathing as I waited to hear what was said next.

'Mr Costa, the *noughts*,' Mrs Paxton stressed the word, 'are being constantly picked on. It's only a matter of time before one of them retaliates.'

'Not in my school, they won't,' Mr Costa snapped back.

'All I'm saying is, it's up to us to lead from the front. If we teachers make it clear that such behaviour won't be tolerated, then our students will have to follow our example.'

'Mrs Paxton, are you really that naïve? Noughts are treated in this school exactly the same way as they're treated outside . . .'

'Then it's up to us to make this school a haven, a sanctuary for Crosses and noughts. A place where we provide equality of education, equality of opportunity and equality of treatment.'

'Oh, really. You're making mountains out of gnat bites,' Mr Costa dismissed.

'Better to over-estimate the problems than ignore them altogether.' Mrs Paxton was annoyed and making no attempts to hide it.

'Enough! No-one wanted them here in the first place.'

'I did,' Mrs Paxton shot back. 'And so did some of the other teachers and the government and . . .'

'The government did as the Pangaean Economic Community ordered. They were afraid of sanctions and that was the only reason they did it.'

'The reason doesn't matter. The point is, they did it. We'll reap what we sow, you mark my words. The noughts are here now and if we don't act soon, this whole scheme will fail.' Pause. 'Or is that the point?'

Mrs Paxton was fighting a losing battle and she didn't even know it. I couldn't bear to listen to any more. I turned and tiptoed out, careful to shut the door behind me without making a sound. Less than a minute later, Mrs Paxton came striding out of the secretary's office. She stopped abruptly when she saw me.

'Callum, what're you doing out here?' Mrs Paxton frowned. 'Callum?'

'Mr Jason sent me out of the class, miss.'

'Why?'

I bit my lip. My gaze dropped away from hers.

'Why, Callum?'

'We . . . we had an argument . . .'

Mrs Paxton waited for me to continue.

'. . . about history.'

'Oh yes?'

'It's not fair, Mrs Paxton. I've read thousands of history books and not one of them mentions us noughts, except to say how the Crosses fought against us and won. I thought history was supposed to be the truth.'

'Ah!' Mrs Paxton nodded. 'And you expressed your views to Mr Jason?'

I nodded.

'I see.'

'Callum, sometimes it's better to leave certain things unsaid . . .'

'But that's what everyone does . . Nearly everyone does,' I amended. 'And things that go unsaid soon get forgotten. That's why us noughts aren't in any of the history books and we never will be unless we write them ourselves. Mr Jason didn't like it when I said that us noughts have done things too. But then Mr Jason doesn't like anything I do or say. He hates me.'

'Nonsense. Mr Jason just doesn't want to see you fail. And being hard on you is his way of trying to . . .' Mrs Paxton sought for the appropriate thing to say, 'to toughen you up.'

'Yeah, right.' I didn't even try to keep the derisive scepticism out of my voice.

Mrs Paxton placed a hand under my chin to raise my head so that I had to look directly at her. 'Callum, a change of policy at this school and all schools was long overdue. Believe me, Mr Jason doesn't want to see you fail any more than I do. We don't want to see any of the noughts fail.'

'And he told you this, did he?'

Mrs Paxton's hand dropped to her side. 'He didn't have to.'

'Yeah, right.' I dismissed immediately.

Mrs Paxton looked thoughtful for a few moments. 'Callum, I'm going to tell you something in the strictest confidence. I'm going to trust you. D'you understand?'

I didn't, but I nodded anyway.

'Mr Jason isn't against you. And d'you know why?'

'No . . .'

'Because his mother was a nought.'

thirty-one. Sephy

'Don't treat me like this, Kamal. I won't stand for it.'

'Then go and have another bottle or eight of wine. That's about all you're good for these days.'

I winced at Dad's tone of voice, so utterly contemptuous and he made no attempt to hide or disguise it. Minnie sat on the stair above mine as we listened to one of our parents' rare arguments. Rare because Dad was never at home. Rare because on the very few occasions that Dad *was* home, Mother was usually too out of it to notice or too refined to start an argument. We'd just finished our dinner in the family room and both Minnie and I had been sent upstairs by Mother to do our homework. That alone was enough to tip us off that something was going on. Mother never told us to do our homework unless she wanted to get us out of the way.

'So you're not even going to deny it?' Mother asked.

'Why should I? It's about time you and I faced the truth. Past time in fact.'

'Kamal, what've I done to deserve this? I've always

been a good wife to you. A good mother to our children.'

'Oh yes,' Dad agreed. And if possible his tone grew even more sneering. 'You've been an excellent mother to *all* my children.'

I turned to give my sister a puzzled look. She was looking straight ahead. What did Dad mean by that?

'I did my best.' Mother sounded like she was starting to cry.

'Your best? Your best isn't up to much.'

'Was I supposed to let you bring your bastard into our house?' Mother shouted.

'Oh no! The great Jasmine Adeyebe-Hadley bring up her husband's child as her own? That would never do. I mean, God forbid that you should chip a nail or dirty one of your designer gowns looking after my son.'

'I should have let you bring your son into our house, I know that now,' Mother said. 'But when you told me, I was hurt. I made a mistake.'

'So did I, when I married you,' Dad shot back. 'You wanted to punish me for my son who was born before you and I ever met and that's what you spent years doing. Don't blame me if I've finally decided enough is enough.'

Dad had a son? Minnie and I had a *brother*. I turned to my sister. She was looking at me, her eyes narrowed. We had a brother . . .

'Kamal, I want . . . I was hoping that maybe we could start again,' Mother began hesitantly. 'Just you and me. We could go away somewhere and . . .

'Oh, Jasmine, don't be ridiculous,' Dad interrupted. 'It's over. Just accept the fact. Besides, look at you . . . You've really let yourself go.'

I gasped at that – and I wasn't the only one.

'You're a cruel man,' Mother cried.

'And you're a drunk,' said Dad. 'And worse than that, you're a boring drunk.'

Minnie stood up and headed upstairs. I didn't blame her. I knew I should do the same. Stop listening. Walk away. Just go, before I ended up hating both my parents – but I stayed put. Like a fool, I stayed put.

'If it wasn't for me you wouldn't be Deputy Prime Minister. You'd be nowhere.' Mother's voice trembled as she spoke.

'Oh please! Don't pretend you did it for me because we both know that you did it for yourself, then the kids, then our neighbours and your friends. What I wanted, what I *needed*, came a long way down your list.'

'I didn't hear you protest when my parties got you known by all the right people, started you moving in all the right circles.'

'No, I didn't complain,' Dad admitted. 'But you got just as much out of it as I did.'

'And now you're going to walk out on me and your children for that . . . that . . .' Mother's voice dripped with bitterness.

'Her name is Grace,' Dad interrupted harshly. 'And I'm not walking out on you now. I left a long time ago; you just refused to believe it. You and the children will get everything you need. You'll be well provided for. And I want regular access to my girls. I love them too much to let you poison their minds against me. But after the next election, I'm going to make it officially known that you and I are no longer together.'

'You won't get away with this. I'll . . . I'll divorce you,' Mother threatened. 'I'll tell all the newspapers . . .'

'You'll divorce me?' Dad actually laughed. I flinched, sticking my fingers in my ears, only to take them out again at once. 'Jasmine, the day you divorce me will be the happiest day of my life.'

'You can't afford the scandal of a divorce in your position. A position I helped you to get.'

'If I had a penny for every time you've said that, I'd be the richest man on the planet,' Dad replied.

Dad's footsteps sounded on the parquet floor. I jumped to my feet and darted upstairs, not stopping until I'd reached my bedroom. I leaned against the door and closed my eyes. I didn't cry. I wasn't even close to crying. I grabbed my jacket from over my chair and ran downstairs, heading out of the door before anyone could stop me. I needed to clear my head and our house wasn't the place to do it. I ran and ran, through the rose garden, across the wasteland, towards the beach. Maybe if I ran fast enough my thoughts would click into some sort of order.

Dad had found someone else. He was leaving. And I had an older brother, older than Minnie. Nothing in my life was a fact. There was nothing to cling on to, nothing to anchor myself to. I just whirled around and around and . . .

Callum . . .

Callum was already there – in our place. In our space. I ran along the beach the moment I saw him and plonked myself down beside him. Callum put his arm around my shoulders. We sat in silence, whilst I tried to straighten out my thoughts. I looked at his face which was in profile. But

I could see enough to realize there was something bothering him, something that was making him sad.

'I'm sorry about Mr Jason,' I said at last. 'I finally got what you were talking about in today's lesson.'

'Don't apologize for him,' Callum frowned. 'It's not your place to apologize for every moronic cretin in the world.'

'Only the moronic Cross cretins?' I asked with a brief smile.

'Not even those.' Callum smiled back. 'I'll tell you what, you don't apologize for every Cross who's an idiot and I won't apologize for every nought who's the same. Agreed?'

'It's a deal.' Callum and I shook hands.

Come on! Best to get it over with! I told myself. Taking a deep breath, I said, 'Callum, I've got a confession to make. About my birthday party.'

He became very still the moment the words left my mouth. 'Oh yes?' he prompted, his arm dropping away from my shoulders.

'It's just that . . . I wanted you there, but for mostly the wrong reasons.'

'Which were?'

'I wanted to upset Mum and my so-called friends,' I told him. 'I wanted to hit back at all of them.'

'I see.'

'No, you don't,' I said. 'I'm telling you now because I'm taking back my invite.'

'Why?'

'Because . . . because,' I said, hoping Callum would get my ridiculous attempt at an explanation.

He secret-smiled at me, saying dryly. 'Thank you.'

'You're welcome! We'll do something else for my birthday – OK?'

'OK.'

'Growing up is hard work,' I sighed again.

'And it's going to get harder,' Callum warned, his voice suddenly grim.

I looked at him and opened my mouth to ask what he meant. But I closed my mouth without saying a word. I was too afraid of the answer.

thirty-two. Callum

It was late at night, past eleven, as I lay on top of my bed, trying to make sense of what Mrs Paxton had told me. *Mr Jason's mother was a nought . . .* I was missing something somewhere. Mrs Paxton had been so sure that Mr Jason was on my side and yet every time he looked at me . . .

He hated me.

I was sure of it. I was *almost* sure of it. Maybe I was just being paranoid. Maybe I was just being a coward, assuming that every Cross was my enemy so that if it turned out to be the case I could say 'I told you so!' But Mrs Paxton wasn't my enemy. And Sephy certainly wasn't. I rubbed my hands over my forehead. My thoughts were spinning round so much they were giving me a splitting headache. I wasn't sure of anything any more.

Someone knocked on my door. I sat up.

'Who is it?'

'Lynny,' said my sister. 'Can I come in?'

''Course.'

Lynette came into the room, quietly shutting the door behind her.

'You OK?' I asked.

'No,' Lynny shook her head. 'You?'

'The same. But I'll survive.'

Lynny gave me a strange look at that. But then she smiled and the peculiar expression on her face vanished without trace. Since Lynny's and Jude's fight, neither of them had spoken to the other. Not one word. My sister sat down at the foot of my bed. She started picking at the loose threads on my duvet cover. I wasn't sure what to say, so I said nothing.

'How's school?'

'It's OK. I'm learning a lot.' And wasn't that the truth!

Lynny must've picked up on my tone of voice because she looked up and smiled dryly. 'Tough going, huh?'

'The toughest.'

'Reckon you'll stick with it?'

'I'm in now. Wild horses couldn't drag me out,' I said belligerently.

Lynny smiled, her face full of admiration. 'How d'you do it, Callum?'

'Do what?'

'Keep going?'

I shrugged. 'I don't know.'

'Yes, you do,' Lynny challenged, which kind of made me start.

I smiled at her total conviction that I knew what I was doing. 'I guess, I keep going because I know what I want.'

'Which is?'

'To be someone. To make a difference.'

Lynny looked at me and frowned. 'What if you can't do both?'

'Huh?'

'If you can only have one, which one means more to you? Being someone or making a difference?'

My smile was broad as I looked at her. I couldn't help it.

'What's so funny?' Lynny asked.

'Nothing. It's just that you and me talking like this, it reminds me of the old days,' I told her. 'We used to have debates about anything and everything. I've missed our talks.'

Lynny smiled back at me, her smile waning as she said, 'You haven't answered my question, and don't try to wriggle out of it! Which one means more – being someone or making a difference?'

'I don't know. Being someone, I guess. Having a large house and money in the bank and not having to work and being respected wherever I go. When I'm educated and I've got my own business, there won't be a single person in the world who'll be able to look down on me – nought or Cross.'

Lynny considered me carefully. 'Being someone, eh? I would've put money on you choosing the other one!'

'Well, what's the point of making a difference if you've

got nothing to show for it, if there's not even any money in it?' I asked.

Lynny shrugged. She had a strange expression on her face, like she was sad for me.

'What about you? What keeps you going?' I asked.

Lynette smiled, a strange, mysterious smile as her thoughts turned in on themselves and I was totally excluded.

'Lynny?' I prompted, uncertainly.

My sister stood up and headed for the door. I thought that was the end of the conversation but she turned to me, just before she left the room.

'D'you wanna know what kept me going, Cal?' Lynny sighed. 'Being bonkers! I miss being insane . . .'

'Lynny, don't say that.' I leapt up. 'You were never insane.'

'No? Then why do I feel so empty now. I know I was living in a fantasy world before, but at least . . . at least I was somewhere. Now I'm nowhere.'

'That's not true . . .'

'Isn't it?'

'Lynny, you are all right, aren't you?' But even as I asked the question, I knew the answer.

'I'm fine. I just need to sort myself out.' Lynny sighed deeply. 'Callum, doesn't any of this ever strike you as – pointless?'

'What d'you mean?'

'Just what I said. Our being here – it works from the Crosses' point of view, but what about our own? Because if this is all there is, we might as well be robots. We might as well not exist at all.'

'Things will get better, Lynny,' I tried.

'D'you really believe that?'

'Yeah. I mean, I'm at Heathcroft High, aren't I? A few years ago that would've been impossible. Unthinkable.'

'But none of their universities will take you.'

I shook my head. 'You don't know that. By the time I'm ready to leave school they might.'

'And then what?'

'I'll get a good job. And I'll be on my way up.'

'Doing what?'

My frown deepened as I glared at my sister. 'You sound just like Mum.'

'Sorry. I didn't mean to.' Lynny turned around to leave the room. 'Just remember, Callum,' she said, her back towards me, 'when you're floating up and up in your bubble, that bubbles have a habit of bursting. The higher you climb, the further you have to fall.'

Lynette left the room, without bothering to shut my door. I stood up and walked over to do it myself, still annoyed with her. Of all people my sister should not just understand my dreams but cheer them. Let down didn't even begin to describe how I felt. I was just about to slam my door shut when I caught sight of Lynny's face as she closed her own bedroom door behind her. She was hurting inside. Hurting badly and close to tears. I stepped out onto the landing, wincing as my bare feet struck a nail not flush with the greying, warped floorboards. By the time I'd rubbed my toe and looked up again, Lynny had gone.

thirty-three. Sephy

'Minnie, can I come in?'

'If you must,' my sister said grudgingly.

I walked into her room, only to stop short when I saw my sister's face. She'd been *crying*. I'd never seen my sister cry before. Ever.

'Minnie, are you . . ?' I didn't finish my question. I already knew the answer and besides, asking it would only have cheesed her off.

'How many times do I have to tell you not to call me Minnie?' my sister snapped. 'My name is Minerva. M-I-N-E-R-V-A! Minerva!'

'Yes, Minnie,' I said.

Minnie looked at me and smiled reluctantly. 'What d'you want, frog face?' she asked.

I sat down on the chair in front of her dressing table. 'I think Mother and Dad are going to get a divorce.'

'That won't happen,' said Minnie.

'How can you be so sure?'

' 'Cause Dad's been threatening Mother with a divorce for years – and it hasn't happened yet.' Minnie shrugged.

I thought for a moment. 'But it was Mother who threatened it this time, not Dad.'

Minnie's head snapped up at that. She stared at me.

'D'you think they might then?' I whispered.

Minnie shrugged and looked away again.

'And what about our brother?' I asked.

'He's not our brother. He's just our dad's son.' Minnie stood up and walked over to her window. 'And what about him?'

'How do we find him?'

'We don't.' Minnie looked at me like I'd lost my marbles.

'But don't you want to know who he is? What he looks like? Aren't you curious?'

'Of course not. I wasn't curious about him three years ago when I found out about him, so why should I be curious now?'

'Three years ago!' I said, aghast. 'You knew we had a brother three years ago? Why didn't you tell me?'

'Why would I do that?' Minnie frowned. 'What good would that have done? Dad had a fling before he met Mother and had a son. That's all I know or want to know.'

I stared at my sister. It was like we were having two different conversations. She couldn't see my point of view and I certainly couldn't see hers.

'Minnie, don't you even want to know our brother's name?'

'Stop calling him our brother. And no, I don't.'

'Well, I do. I'm going to ask Dad and . . .'

Minnie flew across the room and pulled me off my chair in about two seconds flat. 'You'll do no such thing, d'you hear?'

'But Minnie . . .'

'How d'you think Mother'd feel if you started asking about Dad's son? She's unhappy enough without you making it worse.'

'OK! OK!' Minnie let go of my arms. I immediately rubbed them to try to get the circulation going again.

'Is that why she's so unhappy? Because of . . . Dad's son?' I asked.

Minnie regarded me, considering her answer very carefully before she spoke. 'That's part of the reason.'

'And the other part?'

'She had an affair a while ago and . . .'

'*Mother?*' My eyes were open so wide they must surely plop onto my cheeks. 'Mother had an affair?'

'Don't sound so surprised.' Minnie smiled at my expression. 'I think she only did it to make Dad sit up and take a bit more notice.'

'Did it work?'

'What d'you think?' Minnie said, scornfully. 'If anything it drove them further apart. And then Mum felt even more alone. She hasn't got any friends, you know.'

'What're you talking about? She's got friends dripping out of cupboards,' I scoffed.

'Not close ones. Not real friends that she can tell anything and everything to.'

'She's probably driven them all away with her funny moods,' I sniffed. 'One moment she's pushing me away or acting as if I don't exist and the next she wants to know about every minute of my day. If I didn't have to live in the same house as her I wouldn't put up with her either.'

'She's lonely,' said Minnie.

'Why doesn't she just go out and make some new friends then?' I asked.

Minnie smiled, one of her superior smiles that instantly ruffled my feathers. 'You're very young, Sephy.'

'Don't be patronizing,' I fumed.

'I'm not. I'm just stating a fact. And d'you know what I wish for you?'

'What?' I asked, expecting something unpleasant.

'That you never grow older.'

thirty-four. Callum

Well, Callum, this is it. Are you going to do it or not? Are you going to stand up for yourself? You've had more than half a term of this . . . this crap. Speak. Say something. Don't be such a wimp. DO IT!

'Excuse me, Mr Jason. May I have a word with you?'

'As long as it's a short, fast word,' Mr Jason replied without bothering to look up from fastening his bag.

I looked around, waiting for the last person to leave the classroom.

'Well?' Mr Jason snapped, as he headed for the door.

'Why . . . why did I get a C-minus for my mid-term grade when I got twenty-seven marks out of thirty in your last test and came first?'

'Your grade reflects other things besides how well you did in the test.'

'Like what?'

'Like your coursework and homework to date, not to mention your attitude.'

'I've never got less than nine out of ten for my homework.'

Mr Jason stopped in his tracks, just beside the door. I finally had his full attention. 'Are you questioning my judgement? Because that's exactly what I mean when I say your attitude leaves a lot to be desired.'

'I'd just like to know your reasons, that's all.'

'I gave you the grade you deserved – no more, no less.'

'Adotey got a B when my work so far this term has been getting better marks than his and I got five more in the test.'

'If you don't like the way I've graded you, you can always appeal,' Mr Jason challenged.

But I was ready for that one. 'OK, I will.'

I went to move past him but he slammed the door shut before I could leave.

'I see you've chosen this particular time to make a fool of yourself, McGregor. Your grade will not be altered, I can promise you that.'

I regarded him, Mrs Paxton's words still ringing in my ears.

'Why d'you hate me so much?' My words tumbled out in angry frustration. 'If anything you should be on my side.'

Mr Jason drew himself up to his full height, his eyes giving me frostbite. 'What're you talking about, boy?'

'You're half-nought so I don't understand . . .'

Mr Jason's bag dropped to the floor, forgotten. He gripped my shoulders and started shaking me. 'Who told you that . . . that lie?'

'I . . . no-one. I just thought . . . You're lighter than Mrs Paxton and all the others so I just thought . . .'

Mr Jason released me as suddenly as he'd grabbed me. 'How dare you? *How dare you?* Who else have you said this to?'

'No-one.'

'No-one?'

'I swear.'

'Every time I look at you, I thank God I'm not one of you. D'you hear me? I thank God.'

'Y-yes, sir . . .'

Mr Jason picked up his bag and marched out of the classroom. I didn't realize it until he was out of sight, but I was shaking. Actually, physically shaking.

But at least that question was answered.

thirty-five. Sephy

Mr Jason strode down the corridor with a face like a cold rice pudding. The man was *seriously* ticked off. I only noticed because I was looking at the faces of every male that passed me, wondering if this boy looked like my brother, or if that boy had the same eyes, the same nose, the same mouth as my brother. I'd been at it all day. I'd been at it ever since I'd heard I had a brother. *My brother.* I turned the corner and saw Callum standing in the doorway of our classroom. I was ready to tell him my news now. Quickly checking up and down the corridor to make sure we were alone, I said, 'Callum, guess what? You'll never believe what I found out from eavesdropping on Mother and Dad . . .'

'Not now, Sephy.'

'But Callum, this is important . . .'

'Sephy, I said not now. Can't you think of anyone else but yourself for a change?' Callum snapped.

And he strode off, in the opposite direction to Mr Jason. But not before I realized that the expression on his face mirrored that of Mr Jason. Exactly.

thirty-six. Callum

We were all sitting down for dinner and not one of us spoke. No-one had anything to say. Lynny kept her head bowed and concentrated on her plate of sausages and chips. Jude had the same sour, sullen look on his face that he'd worn since he and Lynny had had their fight. Dad's face was sad. Mum threw down her knife and fork, the clatter making us all jump.

'Goodness me! What's the matter with everyone?'

'Meggie . . .'

'Don't Meggie me.' Mum frowned at Dad. 'There's been a funny atmosphere in this house for a while now. What's going on?'

'I'm going for a walk.' Lynny sprang out of her chair.

'Lynny?' Mum wasn't the only one who was surprised. This was the first time Lynny had shown the slightest interest in leaving the house by herself since I don't know when.

'It's OK, Mum. I'll only be gone for a little while.'

'Where're you going?' asked Mum.

Lynny smiled gently. 'Mum, I'm a big girl now. Stop worrying.'

'Want some company?' I asked.

Lynny shook her head. She turned abruptly and headed upstairs.

'I thought you were going for a walk?' Mum called after her.

'I want to do something first,' Lynny called back.

I carried on eating my dinner for the want of something better to do.

'I'm going now. I'll see you all later,' said Lynny, when she finally came downstairs again.

And she grabbed her wraparound jacket and headed out of the door with all of us watching her. Lynny turned round. Mum half stood up, but then she sat down again, never taking her eyes off my sister.

'Bye, everyone,' Lynny smiled softly, the saddest, loneliest smile I've ever seen. And then she shut the door behind her and was gone.

'Ryan, I want to know exactly what's going on – and don't say it's nothing. That won't work this time. One of you had better start talking – and fast.'

Jude lowered his head. I looked at Jude. Dad looked at Mum.

'Meggie, it was when you last went to visit your sister,' Dad said at last.

'I'm listening,' Mum prompted sombrely.

And, as Dad told her exactly what had happened, we waited for the storm to hit.

Mum sat glaring at each of us in turn. I knew she was still doing it, even though I didn't dare look at her. After a lot of shouting, she'd spent the last three and whatever hours staring and glaring and scowling, until I don't know about the others, but I felt like a withered worm, twisting for her contemptuous inspection.

'Ryan, where's my daughter?' asked Mum for the umpteenth time.

Dad didn't answer. He couldn't. He just continued to hang his head.

'Jude and Lynette fighting . . . Ryan, I can't believe you let it happen. You are the most ineffectual useless man it's ever been my misfortune to come across,' Mum said with deep reproach.

'It's not Dad's fault, Mum,' Jude tried.

'And you can shut right up.' Mum turned on him like a cornered rat. 'I'm sick to the back teeth of this belief you have, that you and your opinions are always right and everyone else is wrong. You've been picking on your sister and goading her for months now.'

'Well, you've been doing the same to me, so that makes us about even,' Jude shot back bitterly.

'I've been picking on you – as you call it – because you're not doing anything with your life. You could work with your dad in the lumberyard or do an apprenticeship with Old Man Tony but . . .'

'Old Man Tony is always bombed off his trolley! Light a match in front of his mouth and the whole street would go up in flames. And I don't want to work in his ruddy bakery!' Jude shouted. 'If I get into that, I'll never get out again. I'll be covered with flour and baking bread till the day I die.'

'It's an honest job.'

'I don't want an honest job!'

'You don't know what you want,' Mum dismissed with a snort.

'Yes, I do. I want to go to school.' The words came out in a rush.

I stared at Jude. Since when had he wanted to go back to school? He'd always scorned me for having my nose in book after book. When I'd been studying for the Heathcroft High entrance exam, every word, every syllable he'd directed my way had dripped with sarcasm and contempt.

'Jude, we've been through this before,' Mum sighed her impatience. 'We didn't have the money to keep you in school. I lost my job – remember?'

'But you found the money for Callum to go to school,' said Jude. 'Every bit of care and attention in this house goes to Lynette and Callum. When is it my turn?'

'Boy, stop talking nonsense,' Mum snapped. 'You're

our son and we love you – just the same as the others – but at this precise moment I don't like any of you very much.'

'Then I won't inflict my presence on you any longer.' Jude sprang to his feet and headed for the front door.

'Jude . . .' Mum was also on her feet and moving forward.

Jude threw open the front door, but was halted in his tracks by the presence of two police officers, framed by the darkness outside. One of the officers had his arm raised, ready to knock on the door. They seemed as startled to see us as we were to see them. The officer in front was obviously the one in charge. A police sergeant, I think he was. A thin, reedy man whose uniform looked at least a size too big for him. The constable was almost the exact opposite. He was built like a brick outhouse. What he lacked in height, he made up for in width. Both of them were Crosses of course. Nought police officers were as rare as blue snow.

'Mr McGregor?' The senior police officer looked around the room. Dad stood up slowly.

'Lynette . . .' Mum whispered. Her trembling hand blindly sought and found the back of the sofa, her eyes never leaving the officers.

'May we come in?'

Dad's nod was brief. 'Please.'

They stepped into our living room, carefully shutting the door behind them.

'I'm Sergeant Collins and this is Constable Darkeagle,' said the senior policeman.

'Officers?' Dad prompted when no-one in the room

spoke. We were all wound so tautly that platitudes just made our torture worse.

'I'm so sorry, sir, ma'am. I'm afraid I've got some bad news.'

The officers had pitying, embarrassed looks on their faces. Dad swallowed hard, his expression carved in granite.

'What's happened?' he asked quietly.

Mum's grip on the sofa tightened, her knuckles whitening. I stared at the officers, telling myself that no matter what they said, it wouldn't, *it couldn't* be as bad as the thoughts racing through my head.

But it was.

'You have a daughter called Lynette McGregor?'

Dad nodded.

'I'm terribly sorry, sir, but there's been an accident – a tragic accident. I'm afraid she walked right into the path of an oncoming bus. Er . . . witnesses said she seemed to be in a world of her own. Maybe she had things on her mind?'

No-one answered his question. I don't think he expected an answer because he went on almost immediately.

'It was no-one's fault. If it's any consolation, she was killed instantly. She didn't suffer. I'm so sorry.'

No-one spoke. I kept my eyes on the officer, the bearer of the bad news. I couldn't have looked at any other member of my family then if my life had depended on it.

It was all my fault.

That's how it felt. I remembered her staring at herself in the cracked living-room mirror, her hands bloody where she'd cut herself on the rough glass. Only a few days ago. Only a lifetime ago. Lynette . . .

'Your daughter is in the morgue of the local hospital if you wish to see her . . .'

'NO!' Mum let out a sudden howl like a wounded animal and sunk to her knees.

Dad was at her side at once. Jude took a step forward then stopped. The two police officers looked away, unwilling to be spectators at Mum's grief. I stood like a statue, frozen and mute. The seconds ticked past. Dad hugged Mum to him, rocking her. Mum didn't speak and she didn't cry. She didn't make another sound. Her eyes were closed as she let Dad rock her. Sergeant Collins stepped forward, a card in his hand.

'This is my number. If you need anything, anything at all, just phone me. I've written the number of a bereavement service on the back of the card in case you want to use it.'

Dad took the card. 'That's very kind of you, Officer. Thank you.' His voice shook as he took the card.

'I'm so sorry,' Sergeant Collins said one more time before ushering the constable out of the front door.

At the click of the closing door, I sank down onto the sofa. Lynette entered my head and filled my thoughts and spun around me and danced through me until it felt like she was swallowing me up. Jude stood quite still, looking utterly lost. Mum opened her eyes slowly. She pulled herself away from Dad, who reluctantly let her go, before turning to face us. A solitary tear trickled down her cheek.

'You must all be so proud of yourselves,' she said. 'I hope you're happy now.'

'Meggie, that's not fair,' Dad began. 'The officer said it was an accident.'

Mum looked at each of us in turn. 'Was it? Or did she have her mind on what you all said to her?' Then Mum buried her head in her hands, murmuring, 'My baby . . . my baby . . .'

And we could do nothing but stand and watch – all of us together, each of us utterly alone.

thirty-seven. Sephy

I flicked from channel to channel to channel, searching for something to watch. Looking for something to occupy my time. Nothing on that channel. Nothing on that channel either.

'For goodness' sake!' Minnie snatched the remote control out of my hand and threw it across the room.

'What's biting you?' I asked.

'Doesn't anything ever bother you?' Minnie asked, shaking her head.

'Lots of things bother me,' I frowned.

'But nothing that you actually lose any sleep over, eh?'

'What're you talking about?'

'Mother and Dad are splitting up. It's actually going to happen. Doesn't that mean anything to you?'

'It means a lot to me,' I protested. 'Dad's got someone else. Mother's drowning her sorrows even worse than before and you lash out at me all the time because I'm an easy target. But there's not a single thing I can do about any of it, is there?'

Minnie gave me a look that would've felled a giant redwood, before she marched out of the room. I stood up and hunted for the remote. I mean, jeez! Was it my fault?

What did she want from me, for goodness sake? If I could've done something about Mother and Dad then I would've. But one person, especially someone like me, never made a difference to a ruddy thing. At last I found the remote and sat back down on the sofa, growing more angry with each passing second. Minnie drove me nuts with her constant moods and her sulky behaviour. In fact, if she thought . . .

'Sephy, phone for an ambulance. Quick!'

I've never moved so fast in my life. I took the stairs, two and three at a time, following the sound of Minnie's voice. I ran into Minnie's bedroom but it was empty. I dashed into Mother's bedroom across the landing and stopped suddenly like I'd hit an invisible brick wall. Mum was slumped on the floor, a tablet bottle by her side with a few scattered pills on the carpet. A very few pills. Minnie cradled Mum's head on her lap, frantically stroking her hair and calling her name.

'An ambulance. Now!' Minnie screamed at me.

I ran along the landing to the phone, shock freezing my eyes wide open. Mother had tried to kill herself.

My mother had tried to kill herself . . .

thirty-eight. Callum

There was something wrong with me. I didn't cry. I couldn't. I sat on my bed and stared into nothing and I couldn't cry. I lay on my back with my hands behind my head – and nothing. I lay on my stomach, burying my face into my pillow, waiting for the tears to start. But they didn't. My sister was dead and I couldn't feel a thing. My head still buried in my pillow, I clenched my fists and stuck them under it so I wouldn't do something silly like punch the wall or the headboard. My fingers brushed against something cold and smooth. I sat up and lifted up my pillow. There was an envelope with *Callum* written on it in my sister's neat, tiny writing. Shock, hot and electric, shot through me. I picked it up. The letter dropped to the floor. I stared down at it, unable to believe my eyes.

'Lynny?' I whispered, confused.

I looked around, expecting to see her standing in my bedroom doorway, smiling at me, 'Gotcha!' all over her face. But the room was empty. What should I do? I bent down and picked up the letter between two trembling fingers. I was desperate to know what it said, but at the same time, I was terrified. Count to three and then do it. I got to two, then tore open the letter. My heart hammering, I began to read.

Dear Callum,

This is a very hard letter to write but I wanted you of all people to know the truth. By now, if I'm very lucky and God is very good, I won't be around any more. I'm tired and I want out, it's as simple as that. I've tried to think of the best way to do this and I think walking in front of a bus or a tram or a train is the easiest. A car is too hit and miss! See! My sense of humour has come back, along with my sanity. The return of my sanity, I can stand. It's the return to reality that I can't cope with.

I'll try to make it look like an accident so that I don't shame Mum and Dad but I wanted you to know the truth. I'm not ashamed of who I am any more, but I don't want to live in a world where what I am isn't good enough, where nothing I do will ever be good enough because I'm a nought and I always will be and nothing will ever change that. I hope you and Sephy have more luck than Jed and me — if that's what you want. Take care of yourself. And whatever life throws at you, be strong. Be strong for both of us.

All my love,
Lynette

Lynny . .

I stared down at the letter in my hand. The words blurred and swam before me. I didn't have to read it a second or a third time. Once was more than enough. Crumpling the letter in my hand, I squeezed it smaller and smaller. I squeezed it like my heart was being squeezed. I sat perfectly still, for a minute, an hour, I don't know how long. Long enough for the pain in my throat to subside. Long enough for my eyes to stop smarting. And only when I could trust myself not to hurt so much, only then did I move. I tore the letter into a hundred pieces and let them fall to the floor like paper rain.

For the first time in my life I hated my sister. Hated her. She'd given in. She'd given up on life and left me to live it for the both of us. *All my love* . . . Was that all love did for you? Made you give up and give in? Left you open to pain and hurt? If it was, I swore that nothing would ever make me do the same as her.

Nothing.

thirty-nine. Sephy

Minnie and I sat together, her arm around my shoulder.

'Minerva . . ?'

'Shush!' Minnie whispered. 'Mother will be all right. You'll see. She'll be fine.'

I looked up and down the carpeted corridor. The place looked more like a hotel than a hospital. Did they really know what they were doing? And where was Mother? They'd only let us in the ambulance because Minnie had insisted and kept her hand in Mother's all the time. And the moment we arrived, Minnie and I had been ushered to a waiting area whilst Mother was put on a trolley and wheeled off somewhere else. The minutes ticked, ticked, ticked by – and still nothing. No word, no nurses, no doctors, nothing.

I looked down at my twisting hands in my lap.

Please, God . . . Please . . .

'Minerva? Persephone? Ah, there you are,' Juno Ayelette, Dad's personal secretary, marched along the corridor towards us.

Minnie sprung to her feet. Following her lead, I did the same.

'It's a shame you two didn't have your wits about you,' Juno told us.

Puzzled, I looked from Juno to Minnie, who was just as baffled as I was.

'You should've phoned me first rather than phoned for an ambulance on a landline. The story is already out that your mother took an overdose because your dad has found someone else.' Juno frowned. 'This is going to take some fancy footwork on my part.'

I shook my head, convinced that my mind was playing tricks. Surely I'd heard that wrong? I must've. No-one could be so thoughtless. So heartless.

'Mother tried to commit suicide . . .' Minnie whispered.

'Of course she didn't,' Juno scoffed, taking out her mobile phone. 'Anyone who tries to commit suicide takes a lot more than four sleeping tablets. She was just trying to get attention and sympathy.' She pressed a series of numbers on her phone.

I turned to my sister. 'Minnie, what . . ?'

'Hi, Sanchez?' Juno's voice cut across my own. 'Listen. We need to call in a few favours. I'm at the hospital and . . . yes, of course she's fine . . . it's nothing at all, I promise you, but we need to spread the word that it was an accident, nothing more . . . Yes . . . Yes . . .'

Minnie snatched the phone out of Juno's hand and threw it to the ground before grinding it under the heel of her boot. I stared at my sister, my heart racing, my eyes alight with new found admiration.

'How dare you . . ?' Juno began.

'You can go to hell,' Minnie screamed at her.

'You're a spoilt brat, Minerva Hadley.'

'And you're an insensitive cow!' And with that my sister marched off towards the casualty department.

I smirked at Juno before I ran to catch up with my sister. She glanced my way, her expression grim.

'Electric, Minerva. Just electric!' I told her.

And whilst she didn't smile, the grim expression on her face softened.

Slightly.

forty. Callum

It was the day of Lynette's funeral – a week after her 'accident'. A week of no school, no tears, no nothing. I'd gone for a late morning walk down to the beach. Alone. I stood on the sand, wearing my one and only formal blue suit and watched the waves lap back and forth, wondering why they did that. What was the point – if there was one? Did anything in this world have a point or was Lynette right? At last I walked home. Alone.

Only to find our house filled to overflowing with people. Friends, family, neighbours, strangers. I hadn't expected all these people. I couldn't cope with them. A quiet funeral, Dad had said. It looked like we had every nought in Meadowview struggling to get into our living room. I stood in a corner and watched for a while. Friends and strangers alike fought to be the first to say how sorry they were and spout on about 'tragic accidents' and 'wasted lives'. So many people had come to pay their last respects that our front and back yards were both full – never mind the house. The level of noise from all the chatter was incessant. I reckoned it wouldn't be long before I'd have to escape somewhere for some peace and quiet or I'd explode. Jude was with some of his friends, the now permanently sombre expression on his face. He wasn't saying much, but he was drinking. Lager, I think it was. And from the way he was swaying on his feet, it obviously wasn't his first. Well, if he wanted to be stupid, then I for one wasn't going to stop him. Let him make a fool of himself, for all I cared. The whole world could go to hell for all I cared.

What would Lynny have made of all this fuss? She'd probably have been as bewildered by it as I was. And what would Mum and Dad and Jude say if they found out that Lynny's 'accident' was anything but? Stupid question. I knew what they'd say, how they'd feel. So they would never know. I'd burnt the torn-up bits of Lynny's letter. No-one but me knew what had really happened. And I vowed that it would stay that way. I owed Mum and Dad that much. Especially Mum.

The noise around me was relentless. I rubbed my already throbbing temples. Had Mum and Dad really invited all these people? Where was Dad anyway? I hadn't seen him for a while. Nor Mum for that matter. I moved around the room as best I could, shaking hands and nodding my thanks at all the 'I'm so sorry's bombarding me from every direction. Just when I thought I'd have to duck out of there or burst, I finally saw Dad. He was huddled in a corner with two other men. One had untidy, wavy-blond hair tied back in a pony-tail and he wore a trim moustache. The other had dark chestnut-brown hair and the kind of tan that must've been paid for. He looked almost mixed race – lucky beggar. How I wished I could afford the treatment to make my skin permanently darker.

I started to walk towards them but the intense, solemn look on all their faces halted my steps. I watched, concentrating hard on trying to read their lips. Even though I'd never done it before, it was as if I'd somehow convinced myself that all I had to do was focus, to be the best lip-reader in the world. Well, the best nought lip-reader at any rate.

Dad wasn't saying much. He nodded, then nodded again. A word here, a nod there, that's all he did. It seemed to be enough for the two men though because as the conversation went on they began to smile and pat Dad on the back. Then one of them pressed something into Dad's hand. Dad didn't look at it, but immediately stuffed it into his jacket pocket. Out of the corner of my eye, I saw Mum enter the room. She looked around for Dad. She saw him and immediately starting making her way through the crowd in Dad's direction. Then she stopped. She'd noticed who Dad was with. Fury flashed across her face. She pushed towards them even more vigorously then. I was so busy watching Mum watching Dad that I wasn't aware of the silence sweeping through the room until it had reached and passed me. Looking around, I saw that every eye was on something going on behind me. No-one spoke. No-one moved. I turned, wondering what could've happened to cause such a reaction.

Seeing her was like a boxer's punch to my stomach. I was actually winded and breathless.

Sephy . . .

What was she doing here? Was she mad? Stillness rippled out from her, like the ripples when a stone is thrown into a pond. Sephy walked towards me, looking straight at me, but she didn't say a word. Then her gaze swept past me, her face set as she walked on by. I turned as did everyone else to see what she was going to do. She walked up to my mum who was only a couple of steps away from my dad by now.

'Mr and Mrs McGregor, I just wanted to come and see you to say how sorry I am about Lynette. I know what you're going through. My mother . . . I know . . .' Sephy's voice trailed off. She would've had to have the hide of a rhino not to pick up on the atmosphere in the room. 'I hope I'm not intruding or anything . . . I just wanted to say . . . I'm sorry . . .'

Mum was the first to recover. 'You're not intruding, Miss Hadley.' She stepped forward. 'Thank you for coming. Can I get you a drink?'

Sephy looked around at all the people staring at her,

most of the faces now suspicious and hostile. 'No, I don't think I should stay.'

'Nonsense. You've come this far, you can't leave without a drink. Can she, Ryan?' Mum spoke directly to Dad.

Dad was alone in the corner of the room. The two men he'd been talking to had vanished – seemingly into thin air. But it didn't matter. Sephy had all of Dad's attention. He was glaring at her like she was some kind of disgusting fungus he'd found growing in his navel. It was exactly like the look Mrs Hadley shot at me when I went to see Sephy after she'd been beaten up. *Exactly* like it.

'Ryan?' Mum's stern voice had Dad raising his head to look at her.

'Hello, Miss Hadley,' Dad managed to spit out.

'I'll go.'

'Sephy . . .' I stepped forward but Jude got in first.

'Yes, go!' he said furiously. 'Who told you to come here in the first place? You and your false sympathy aren't wanted.'

'Jude, that's enough,' Mum told him firmly.

'If she cares so much, where was she for the last three years when Lynette was out of her head and we didn't have two beans to rub together, never mind the money to get Lynny the help she needed? Where was this dagger when you got fired, Mum, and I had to drop out of school? Where was she when Harry over there got the boot?' Jude pointed to a man by the door. 'And all because she wanted to behave like a brat even though she knew it would get him into trouble.'

Sephy was staring at this guy, Harry, who was glaring right back at her. I'd never seen him before in my life. What did he have to do with Sephy?

'Our new chauffeur told me you'd decided to quit.' Sephy's voice was little more than a whisper but in the stillness of the room it was enough for everyone to hear.

'I got fired because you were left alone to face the riot at your school,' Harry called bitterly across the room. 'I begged you to stay in the car but you didn't want to – remember? When your face was plastered all over the TV screen and I was nowhere to be seen, your mother kicked me out so fast I'll have the imprint of her foot on my backside 'til the day I die.'

Whispered comments full of anger and antagonism swept around the room.

Sephy shook her head, shocked. 'I didn't know. I swear I didn't know.'

'Didn't take the trouble to find out either.' Harry turned away in disgust.

'You and others like you have brought us nothing but grief.' Jude pushed Sephy hard against her shoulder. Some of the others in the room gasped at his audacity. Shoving a Cross like that was just asking for trouble, but Jude was way past caring. 'And then you have the nerve to come over here . . .'

'Mrs McGregor, Mr McGregor . . .' Sephy appealed to them for help.

'Persephone, I think it's best you should leave,' Dad told her directly.

'But I haven't done anything . . .' said Sephy, bewildered.

'That's right, you haven't,' Dad agreed, pointedly. 'You come here in your fancy dress which cost more than I make in a year and we're supposed to smile and cheer? Is that how it's meant to work?'

'No . . .' Sephy whispered.

'Just go away,' Jude hissed at her. 'Go on, get lost before I do something I'll regret.'

Sephy looked around. Her eyes met mine. I tried to step forward but some woman behind me grabbed my arm and pulled me back.

'Let her go. Noughts and Crosses don't mix, boy,' the woman whispered to me.

Sephy shook her head and darted from the room. I could see only too well the shimmer in her eyes as she ran past me. Even though the room was full to capacity, a pathway opened up for her like Angel Shaka's parting of the Sea.

'You had no right to do that, Jude.' Mum waited until Sephy had gone before rounding on my brother.

'Oh yes he did,' Dad answered before Jude could open his mouth. 'She wasn't wanted here. Jude only told her the truth.'

Mum wasn't the only one to stare at Dad. Where had all that come from? I'd thought Dad's motto was to live and let live. When had that changed? When Lynny died . . ? Or maybe it was there all the time and I'd just chosen not to see it.

'Ryan . . ?' Mum said.

Around us, people started talking again – nervous, embarrassed chatter. I reached Mum's side at the same time as Dad.

He stopped and looked straight at Mum, a cold, hard expression on his face I'd never seen before. 'Meggie,' he said. 'My ineffectual days are over.'

Then he moved past her. Mum turned to stare after him. I watched Dad's retreating back. There was something about him, the way he walked, the way he talked . . . Something in his voice scared me. Scared the living daylights out of me.

forty-one. Sephy

It'd only been three years since Callum's mum had worked for mine. Three short years. Three years had passed like three minutes to me, but walking into Callum's house had been like walking into a room full of strangers. I remembered Callum's mum and dad so clearly but my memory of them was nothing like the reality. They hadn't wanted me there. Not one of them had. With everything that'd happened to my mother, I wanted to show them that I really did care, that I understood. Minnie and I could've so easily been in the same boat as Callum, no matter what Juno said.

Each move I made in Callum's direction just seemed to pave my way faster to hell.

forty-two. Callum

I went and sat down beside Sephy on the beach. Neither of us spoke. I was getting sand on my one good suit but I didn't care. I was past caring.

'I didn't mean any harm, Callum,' Sephy said at last.

'I know but . . .'

'But it wasn't the best idea I've ever had in my life,' Sephy sighed.

'Not as such – no,' I said.

'I can't seem to do anything right at the moment,' Sephy said at last. There wasn't a trace of self-pity in her voice, just the merest hint of sadness. 'I am sorry about your sister, Callum. I just wanted to show how much. I thought sending a card would be a bit . . . a bit . . .'

'Impersonal?'

'Exactly,' Sephy sighed again. 'It was just a spur of the moment thing to walk over to your house. I thought it'd make a difference somehow.'

I didn't know what to say to that, so I said nothing.

'This is growing up, isn't it?' Sephy asked.

'I think it is,' I nodded.

'Would you put your arm round me please?'

I hesitated.

Sephy sighed. 'If you'd rather not.'

'No, it's not that.'

Sephy gave me one of her looks.

'I just . . . never mind.' I put my arm around her. She put her head on my shoulder. And we both sat and watched the waves foam up on the beach and the shadows lengthen.

THE SPLIT

forty-three. Sephy

Minnie and I walked along the corridor towards Mother's private room. It'd been two weeks since Mother's accident. Karl, our chauffeur, brought us to see Mother each evening and although Mother was physically better, her behaviour was really making me worry. The mother I'd got used to over the last few years had disappeared, and in her place . . .

'Minerva! Persephone! I'm so glad to see you. I've missed you both so much. Come and give me a hug.'

Minnie and I glanced at each other before doing as we'd been asked. Mother hugged Minnie, then gave me a bear hug which left me breathless.

'I love both of you so much,' she told us, her voice trembling with emotion. 'You know that, don't you?'

Minnie nodded, embarrassed.

'We love you too, Mother,' I said, feeling very uncomfortable. I wasn't used to Mother saying such things. Jeez! I wasn't used to Mother saying much of anything.

'I know you love me.' Mother pulled me to her to kiss both my cheeks. It was only by a supreme effort that I didn't wipe my face the moment she released me.

'You're the only ones who care whether I live or die,' Mother continued. The gratitude in her voice made me feel incredibly uncomfortable – and guilty. Had Dad been to see her yet?

'Your friends would visit you too, if you told them you were in here,' Minnie pointed out.

'NO! No. I don't want anyone . . . No. I'll see them when I leave.'

'When will that be?'

'When I'm all better,' Mother announced brightly. Too brightly. Minnie and I exchanged another look.

'Are you coming to see me tomorrow?' Mother asked.

'Yes, of course,' Minnie said.

'Do me a favour? Could you bring me my make-up bag? I feel naked without my make-up.'

'OK, Mother,' Minnie said, quietly.

Mother was still smiling, a frantic almost manic look on her face. 'Oh, and a bottle of champagne – to celebrate my lucky escape,' Mother laughed.

'Champagne?'

'Yes, of course. Or failing that, some white wine will do.'

'Mother, I don't think that's a good idea . . .'

'Just do as you're told.' The first crack appeared in Mother's mask. She plastered it over with a broad smile. 'Sorry, love. I'm a bit on edge. If you don't help me Minnie, no-one else will. Y-your father hasn't even been to see me. Not a phone call. Not so much as a Get Well Soon card.' An even wider smile than before. 'So I'm celebrating. Today is the first day of the rest of my life. So bring me what I asked for – OK, sweetie?'

'OK, Mother.'

'Good girl.'

'I love you, Minerva.'

'Yes, Mother.'

'My two best girls.' Mother leaned back with a smile. Her smile faded into a look of such intense sadness that I could hardly bear to look at her. 'Here's a little life lesson for my two best girls. Never make a mistake because it will never be forgiven. Or forgotten. Never put a foot out and you'll never put a foot wrong.'

'I don't understand, Mother,' Minerva frowned.

'I made a mistake once.' Mother's eyes were closed now and her voice was faraway and dreamy. 'I did something I shouldn't've. But I was lonely. Your father was never at home and I was so tired of being alone. But he found out. I made a mistake you see. And I've never stopped paying for it.'

'Mother, it doesn't . . .'

'So don't be like me.' Mother opened her eyes and smiled brightly. 'Be perfect. My perfect little girls. I love you so much.'

I bent down, untying my shoelace so that I could tie it up again. A single tear splashed down onto my shoe. But Mother didn't see it.

So that was OK.

forty-four. Callum

'I'm going out.' Mum pulled on her jacket as she spoke.

'Where?' Dad stood up from the table where he'd been poring over some kind of map with Jude.

'For a walk.' The front door was now open.

'Meggie, how much longer are you going to carry on like this?' said Dad.

'Like what?' asked Mum, her back to us.

Jude and I exchanged a glance. Lynette's funeral was over three months ago now and Dad wasn't the only one who'd changed. Most nights Mum had taken to going for long walks, returning long after I'd gone to bed and was meant to be asleep. Crossmas had come and gone in our house without much cheer. The new year had started and here we all were, occupying opposite ends of the compass.

Dad sighed, exasperated. 'Meggie, why won't you talk to us? To me?'

Mum turned, her eyes ablaze. 'Will you give that up?' she asked, pointing to the long map spread out all over our table.

'No.'

'Then we have nothing to say to each other.'

'Meggie . . .'

Mum headed out of the door, slamming it shut behind her.

'What's going on, Dad?' I asked.

Dad was still staring at the front door. I doubt if he even heard me. I tried to move closer to the table but Jude rolled up the map before I had a chance to take a good look at it. I did see enough of it this time though to realize that it wasn't just a map; it was a blueprint.

'Come on, Jude, we've got work to do,' Dad said grimly.

'Where're you going, Dad?' I asked.

'Out.'

'Out where?' I asked.

'To a meeting.'

'What meeting?'

'None of your business,' Dad replied tersely, pulling on his coat.

'Where is it?'

'That's none of your business either.'

Jude ran a large elastic band around the now rolled up blueprint and went to join Dad. He put the blueprint down by his feet and put on his jacket which was hanging on a hook by the door. There was no way he was going to let that blueprint out of his sight. I regarded both Jude and Dad, standing together at the front door looking in every way like father and son – and I felt totally excluded.

'How come Jude gets to go with you and I don't?'

'Because you're not old enough,' said Dad.

Jude snorted and muttered something under his breath. At Dad's warning look he shut up. What were both of them up to? A house of secrets, that's what my home had become. Mum had withdrawn to a place where none of us were able to reach her. And on top of that, Jude and Dad were doing something where I wasn't wanted.

And I missed Lynette so much.

She never said very much and goodness knows she never did much but it was like she was the glue that kept our family together and now that she was gone we were each floating further and further away from one another.

Something else to hate my sister for.

'Please let me come with you,' I pleaded.

I didn't know where Mum was and I didn't want to be on my own. I needed to belong somewhere, to something, to someone.

'No way,' Jude shot out before Dad could open his mouth.

'I won't be any trouble.'

'Yeah, right!' Jude scoffed.

Dad walked over to me and placed a hand on my shoulder. 'Callum, where we're going you can't follow.'

'Why not? If Jude's old enough to belong to the Liberation Militia then so am I.'

'What?' Dad spun around. 'Jude, you stupid boy. What've you been saying? You know we're not meant . . .'

'I didn't say anything, Dad. I swear,' Jude denied vehemently.

'Jude didn't tell me,' I said.

'Then who did?' Dad asked brusquely.

'No-one. I worked it out for myself. I'm not stupid,' I told him. 'So can I come with you now?'

'No way. We're going to a Liberation Militia meeting

and you're too young. Besides, if you were seen it'd be the end of your school career. Is that what you want?'

'I don't care. I'm just wasting my time at Heathcroft and everyone knows it.' I shrugged away from Dad's hand. 'Colin's dropped out and Shania's been expelled for no reason and everyone's taking bets on how much longer Amu and I are going to be there. Besides, I was thinking of leaving anyway.'

'Over my dead body,' Dad flared up at once. 'You are going to school and you'll stay at school until you're eighteen and then you'll go on to university. Do I make myself clear?'

I looked away from him, my lips firmly together.

'Callum, I asked you a question.' Dad grabbed my chin and forced my face around till I had no choice but to look directly at him. 'You will not leave school without any qualifications. Understand?'

'Yeah, OK.' I mumbled.

Dad headed for the door, beckoning to Jude as he did so.

'And don't bother blabbing to your dagger friend about us being in the Liberation Militia,' Jude hissed at me. 'Not unless you want to put a noose around our necks.'

Both Dad and Jude left the house without a backward glance and once again I was alone.

forty-five. Sephy

Minnie was reading one of those 'ten ways to get your man' women's magazines that are incredibly, tediously boring! But Minnie's sixteen – two years older than me – so I guessed it was only a matter of time before I started reading that stuff too. Right now though, I had other things on my mind. I licked my lips, nervously.

'Minnie, what are we going to do?'

'What d'you mean?'

My sister was being either really thick or really evasive.

'Mother. Her drinking's getting worse,' I said.

'She's just smoothing out the rough edges,' Minnie smiled wryly as she answered with Mother's often repeated line, trotted out whenever we tried to bring up the subject of her drinking.

'Any smoother and she won't have to walk places, she'll just roll,' I frowned.

'You tell her that,' Minnie challenged.

My sister was no use at all. I huffed impatiently so she'd get the message, but her nose was already back in her magazine. Mum'd been at home for a while now and she was steadily getting worse. She spent a lot of time in her room. And when she did emerge it was always to smother us with kisses and tell us how much she loved us before she made her way to the wine cellar or the kitchen. Funny how she always reeked of expensive perfume as she smothered us with hugs and kisses. It was a close-run thing to say which was the most overpowering – her perfume or her kisses. Or maybe her attempts to prove to us that she wasn't drinking any more. She wasn't fooling anyone.

Because it was so obvious. She was growing more and more out of it. Sadder and lonelier – and worse.

And there wasn't a single thing I could do about it.

forty-six. Callum

Saturday. It was eighteen days and five months after Lynette's death. Funny I should think of it that way. The days before the months. My sixteenth birthday in February had come and gone, with a card and a book signed from both Mum and Dad, but bought and wrapped by Mum. It hadn't been much of a birthday. No-one had felt like celebrating. And sitting round the table cutting the birthday cake had been a silent affair – because Lynny wasn't there. The winter had come and gone and spring had arrived – and nothing had changed. Funny that not a single day passed without me thinking about Lynette. When she was here, she so often just seemed to fade into the background, like something that's always there but you never really think about. Like air. But now that she was gone . . .

Lynette's secret still hung heavily over me, like a shroud. No-one knew the truth about her death except me. And with each passing day, the longing to tell someone grew stronger. There was Sephy, but each time I tried to tell her the truth about my sister, the words just wouldn't come. It felt like I was being disloyal to not just Lynette but my whole family by wanting to tell Sephy and no-one else. On the spur of the moment, I headed for the phone and used our signal to phone Sephy's house. Within five minutes she was phoning me back.

'Hello you,' I said.

'Hello yourself,' Sephy replied.

'So what're you up to today then?' I asked. I had to keep my voice down because Mum and Dad were upstairs. Jude was out – as per usual – so I was taking this opportunity to use the phone. I was hoping Sephy wouldn't have anything planned so that we could spend this Saturday together.

'I'm going shopping! With Mother!' Sephy wailed.

'Poor you.' I had to struggle to keep myself from laughing out loud at Sephy's tone of voice. She hated shopping at the best of times. And as for shopping with her mum, that must be her idea of hell on earth.

'It's not funny!' Sephy snapped.

'Of course not,' I soothed.

Sephy gave a very undignified snort down the phone. 'You're laughing at me again.'

'As if.'

'What're you going to be doing with the rest of the day then?' Sephy asked me.

'I thought I might go to the park, or maybe the beach. Maybe I'll do both. I haven't decided yet.'

'That's right, rub it in.'

'Just think of all that lovely money you're going to spend,' I told her.

'Mother's going to spend it, not me. She's decided she needs some spending therapy,' Sephy replied.

'Well, if you can't get out of it, get into it!'

'I'd much rather be with you,' Sephy admitted.

There it was again, that familiar twist in my stomach whenever she said things like that to me.

'Hello?' Sephy said, uncertainly.

'I'm still here. Maybe we can meet up later this afternoon?' I suggested.

Sephy sighed. 'I doubt it. Mum wants to buy me some dresses and update my school uniform and she wants to buy herself an evening dress and some shoes. Just the shoes by themselves will take three or four hours at least.'

'Why? Has your mother got duck's feet or something?'

'No, just a duck's taste in shoes. I swear, Callum, it's going to be *torture*!'

'I might see you at the shopping centre actually. I've got to get some things for school,' I said.

'Like what?'

'Pens, rulers and I was thinking of buying myself a new calculator.'

'I'll keep my eyes open for you,' Sephy said. 'Maybe I'll see you at the café? You can stop me from going completely insane!'

'If I miss you at the centre, how about getting together this evening then? We could have a late picnic on the beach. Around six o'clock?'

'I'll try but I can't guarantee anything,' Sephy said.

'Fair enough.'

'Saturday in the Dundale Shopping Centre,' Sephy groaned. 'Just shoot me now and put me out of my misery!'

Laughing, I said bye and put the phone down. And then I thought of Lynette again – and the laughter stopped.

forty-seven. Sephy

'D'you like these shoes?'

'Yes, Mother. They're really nice,' I smiled.

'But those burgundy ones with the thin straps were better, weren't they?'

'What burgundy ones?'

'The ones we tried in Roberts & Miller,' Mum replied.

That was four shoe shops ago.

'Well, I really like these ones,' I tried.

'I think I'll go back to Roberts & Miller and try on those burgundy ones just once more.'

Aaaarrrrrgggggghhhhhhh!

forty-eight. Callum

Lunch was over, without too much grief – for once. Jude had come home from heaven only knew where so we'd all eaten together – which made a change. Mum indulged in small talk, telling us all about what our neighbours and relatives and friends were up to, whilst Jude was his usual effervescent, scintillating self and didn't say one word. No-one was particularly bothered that I didn't have much to say either. Before I'd swallowed my last mouthful, my knife and fork clattered onto my plate and I jumped up. Grabbing my jacket off the back of the sofa, I headed for the door.

'Where're you going?' Mum asked with a smile.

'The shopping centre.'

Jude leapt up like a scalded cat. 'Oh no you're not.'

I frowned at him. 'I'll go where I ruddy like. Since when is it any of your business where I go?'

'Callum, you don't want to go there. Not today,' Jude said, nervously.

'Jude?' Mum stood up slowly.

A tense, watchful atmosphere entered the room like chilling fog.

'Why shouldn't I go?' I asked my brother.

He didn't answer.

'What's going on?' I persisted.

I turned to Mum. She was staring at Jude, a stunned look on her face. From her expression, she was obviously well ahead of me.

'Don't go there, Callum,' Jude told me, pointedly.

'But . . .' And only then did I click.

The Liberation Militia were planning something at the Dundale. Something Jude knew about. Something my brother didn't want me anywhere near. And then I remembered.

'Sephy's at the shopping centre,' I said, horror-stricken.

'Callum . . .' Jude began.

I didn't wait to hear any more. I ran out of the house, leaving the front door wide open as I raced for the shopping centre.

forty-nine. Sephy

Mother was driving me nuts! In our five long, *long* hours together, I'd bitten my tongue so many times it'd swollen up to the size of a football and was choking me. If she asked me for my opinion on one more pair of shoes, I couldn't be held responsible for my actions. I sipped my orange juice, grateful for the short but welcome break away from her. She'd gone back to the car park to pack away her various purchases. She was enjoying herself. I'm glad one of us was!

'Sephy! Thank God! You have to get out of here.'

'Callum!' I beamed. 'Where did you spring from?'

'Never mind that. You've got to leave this place now.'

'But I haven't finished my drink . . .'

'Never mind your ruddy drink. You have to leave –
NOW!'

I looked at Callum then, really looked at him. He was
scared. No . . . he was terrified.

'What's going on?'

'Don't argue. Out!' Callum told me grimly. 'Come on.'

Callum dragged me out of my seat and towards the café
door.

'Excuse me, love, but is this boy troubling you?' a
stranger asked as I was dragged past his table.

'No! No, he's a friend of mine,' I called back. 'He
wants to show me something . . .'

Callum dragged me out of the café and along the concourse and then every alarm in the world went off, at least
that's what it sounded like.

'What's going on?' I asked, looking around.

'Move it. Come on.'

And we were running towards the nearest exit. Others
around us were looking around and frowning, wondering
what was going on. Maybe they saw Callum and I racing
for the nearest exit, maybe we started it. I don't know.
But it seemed like moments later, everyone was shouting
and racing for the exits. We were amongst the first ones
out of the Dundale. We stumbled out into the spring sunshine and still Callum had hold of my hand and was
pulling me after him.

'Where're we going?' I asked breathlessly.

'Run. Come on,' Callum puffed from beside me. 'I thought I'd never find you. It took me almost half an hour to find you. Move.'

'Callum, I'm getting a stitch,' I protested.

'Tough. We've got to keep going.'

'Callum, enough!' I pulled my hand out of his. 'You're . . .'

Then there was a flash like the very air was alight, followed a fraction of a second later by the most colossal boom. I was blown off my feet and into the air like a dry leaf in a high wind. And even from where we were, I could feel an intense heat on my back. I landed flat on my face, my arms outstretched. There was a strange ringing sound in my ears and it wouldn't stop. For I don't know how long, I lay in a daze. Was I dead? Was this what it felt like to die? I closed my eyes tight and covered my ears, trying to block out the incessant ringing sound – only it was inside my head, not outside. I swallowed hard and my ears popped, and the ringing stopped. Twisting around, I turned to see what on earth had happened. Billowing smoke shot out of the shopping centre. For a moment it was eerily quiet, like the end of the world. I wondered panic-stricken if the explosion had deafened me. And then I heard screaming and sirens and all hell was let loose.

I turned to Callum, who lay stunned beside me.

'Are you OK?' You're not hurt?' Callum asked anxiously, running his hands up and down my back and arms.

'Y-you *knew* that was going to happen . . .' I realized,

aghast. 'You didn't . . . Tell me you didn't . . .' I shook my head. No, that was preposterous. Callum had nothing to do with whatever that explosion was. It must've been a bomb. But Callum didn't do that. He wouldn't. He *couldn't*.

But he *knew*.

'Mother! Oh my God!' I jumped to my feet and raced towards the car park across the street from the shopping centre.

I was almost across the street when I remembered Callum. I turned around.

But he was gone.

fifty. Callum

I'd barely got the key in the lock before the front door was flung open and Mum pounced on me.

'Where've you been? You look terrible. Are you all right? Where's Jude? Isn't he with you?'

'I thought he was here,' I said wearily, closing the front door behind me.

'No, he left almost as soon as you did,' said Mum. 'What happened?'

'Didn't you hear?' I asked, astonished.

'Hear what?'

She should've heard the explosion from here. But then

again, maybe not. Our house was right across town from the shopping centre.

'It hasn't been on the telly?' I turned to the TV, perplexed. The news wasn't on, just a rerun of some ridiculous detective programme where practically every low life in it was a nought. I recognized this episode. A cop was chasing a nought scumbag who'd shot and killed his partner.

'Callum, talk to me. What happened?'

'Mum . . .'

'We interrupt this programme to bring you a news-flash,' a voice suddenly declared.

My head whipped up. The telly's most popular news-reader appeared, his expression grim. My heart began to thump in a crazy way that made me feel physically sick.

'Please don't let it be something bad about us noughts,' Mum breathed.

'Just under thirty minutes ago, a bomb exploded at the world-famous Dundale Shopping Centre. At least seven people are known to have been killed outright with scores more wounded. Casualties are being taken by ground and air ambulances to the local hospitals. All hospitals in the immediate area have been put on full alert. A warning was received from the nought group calling itself the Liberation Militia only five minutes before the bomb actually exploded.'

'That's a lie,' Jude said.

Mum and I turned as one to see Jude standing in the doorway with Dad beside him. We turned back to the TV screen as Dad shut the front door.

The newsreader's face was replaced by a TV camera at the scene. It swung around this way and that, filming the carnage of people lying on the ground, windows shattered, blood on the concourse. There was no voice-over to accompany it. No voice echoing sorrow at the devastation. No voice filled with indignation. No sound at all. Just silence.

Which made it worse.

The camera focused on one woman sitting on the ground, rocking back and forth, blood running down her forehead and into her eyes. On to the next atrocity. The camera moved in a jerky fashion as if the person holding the camera was shaking, trembling, which he or she probably was. A child knelt by a man's side. The child was crying. The man was still. The camera was only on them for a second or two, but it was enough.

The Prime Minister appeared on the screen, his expression angry and forbidding.

'If the Liberation Militia think this cowardly, barbaric act of terrorism is going to win over the vast population of this country to their way of thinking, then they are very much mistaken. All they've done is strengthen our resolve not to give in to such "people" or tactics.'

'Dad . . .' Jude whispered.

'Shush.' Dad focused on the telly and nothing else.

The newscaster's face re-appeared. 'A senior police officer on the scene believes that the bomb was planted in a café bin inside the shopping centre but stated that it was too early to speculate. He did promise however that the perpetrators of this crime would be brought to swift justice. There will be more information about this in our main news bulletin after the current programme. Once again, a bomb has gone off in the Dundale Shopping

Centre, killing at least seven people.'

The detective programme returned just as the cop gave a flying tackle and brought the killer nought to the ground.

'Dad? What happened? You said . . .'

'Shush, boy,' Dad admonished, looking at Mum.

Mum used the remote to switch off the telly. Then she turned to look directly at Dad. 'I'm going to ask you something, Ryan, and I want your solemn promise that you're going to tell me the truth.'

'Not now, Meggie.' Dad headed for the stairs. Mum instantly moved to block his way.

'Yes, *now*. Did you or Jude plant that bomb?'

'I don't know what you're talking about.'

'Damn it, Ryan, don't treat me like a cretin. Promise me you had nothing to do with this business.'

Dad didn't speak. He regarded Mum, defiance in every bitter twist and turn of his expression. 'What I did or didn't do is none of your business,' Dad said at last.

I'd never heard Dad speak to Mum like that before. The pinched, angry look on Mum's face was an indication she'd never heard that tone of voice from Dad either. Mum and Dad regarded each other, their expressions setting harder and harder. They were standing perfectly still and moving further and further apart. Mum deliberately turned her back on Dad to face Jude.

'Jude, did you plant that bomb? NO! Don't look at your father. I asked you a question – now answer it.'

'We . . .'

'Jude, keep your mouth shut, d'you hear?' Dad ordered grimly.

'Jude, I'm still your mother,' Mum said very, very quietly. 'Answer me please.'

Desperately, Jude looked from Mum to Dad and back again.

'Jude . . ?' said Mum.

'We had to, Mum. Our cell was ordered to do it. Some of us set it up last night, but they said they'd phone through with the warning an hour before it went off. I swear they did. They said that everyone would be evacuated in plenty of time.' The verbal waterfall tumbled from Jude's mouth.

'You killed, you *murdered* all those people . . .' Mum whispered, appalled.

'Dad said they would phone through with a warning. That's what he said. I don't understand.' Jude turned bewildered eyes towards Dad.

Mum's whole body was shaking, heaving. Her lips clamped together as she struggled to stop herself from retching.

'Meggie . . .' Dad's mask slipped for the first time that evening. He looked so forlorn. He touched Mum's arm. She spun around and slapped his face so hard, there was a crack as her fingers bent right back.

'You murdering, lying . . . You promised me there'd never be anything like this. You promised you'd only be involved in the background, in planning. You *promised*.'

'I didn't have any choice. Once you're in, they've got you – and you have to do as you're told.'

'You don't. You could've said no. You *should*'ve said no.'

'I was protecting you, Meggie. And our sons. I had no choice.'

'Protecting us from what? From something you inflicted on us in the first place?' Mum dismissed.

'Who d'you think I'm doing all this for?' Dad cried.

'I know exactly who you're doing all this for. But she's dead, Ryan – and murdering innocent people won't bring her back.'

'You've got it wrong, Meggie.' Dad shook his head.

'Have I? I warned you, Ryan. I begged you not to involve Jude in all this.' Mum cradled her now-limp right hand in her left. One of her fingers was bent back on itself in a definite V-shape.

'I'm sorry . . .' Dad began. But if anything that just made things worse.

'Sorry? *Sorry?* Say that to the families of all those people you murdered,' Mum yelled at him. 'How could you? I can't bear to look at you.'

Dad straightened up. His eyes flint-like again. The mask was back – with a vengeance. 'At least now the Crosses will know we mean business.'

'All those people killed and maimed and that's all you have to say about it?' Mum's voice dropped to a strange hush.

'They were legitimate targets,' said Dad.

Mum stared at Dad like she'd never seen him before. Silence. She turned away, wearily. 'In that case we have nothing more to say to each other. Jude, could you take me to the hospital please? I think I've broken one of my fingers.'

'I'll take you,' Dad insisted.

'I don't want you anywhere near me. Don't you ever come near me again,' Mum hissed. 'Come on, Jude.'

Jude looked at Dad, unsure of what to do. Dad nodded and turned away. Jude took Mum by her left arm and led her out of the house. Only when the door shut, did Dad let go. Closing his eyes, he wrapped his arms around himself and bent his head, almost like he was praying. Except I knew he couldn't be because Dad doesn't believe in God. He began to tremble like Old Man Tony when he's got the DTs.

'Dear Lord, please . . .' Dad began. But then he opened his eyes and saw me watching him. He started with surprise. A second or two passed before I saw recognition on his face. In everything that had happened, I'd been completely forgotten. By everyone.

'I'll . . . I'll just go and see if Jude and Mum n-need my help,' I stammered.

It wasn't that I wanted to be with them so much. I just needed to get away, to be somewhere else. Dad didn't try to stop me. I grabbed my jacket and headed out, shaking as the door shut behind me. The evening air was warm and welcome on my skin. Was I going to try and catch up with Mum or Jude or just run and run and keep going – for ever and ever, amen? I looked left, then right. My conscience made up my mind for me. I followed after Mum and Jude.

fifty-one. Sephy

If only I could stop my mind from spinning. If only I could shut out everyone and everything for just a few hours. Just long enough to get some sleep, so that I could think clearly afterwards. But I couldn't switch off.

After two fruitless hours of tossing and turning and counting everything from sheep to ring-tailed lemurs, I gave in and sat up, as wide awake as I'd ever been. I glanced at the silver clock on my bedside table – a fourteenth birthday present a few months ago from my father. A present he'd probably never even seen. It was still quite early. I'd gone to bed early, mainly because Mother had insisted, but even the regular beat of the second hand counting away time couldn't lull me off to sleep tonight.

Thank goodness Mother was OK. She was still packing away her shopping when the explosion went off. Glass from the centre was everywhere, scattered across most of the car park. And Mother was in a mad panic, screaming out my name over and over. The moment she saw me, she rushed towards me and gave me a hug which lifted me right off my feet. But we were OK – which is more than could be said for a lot of poor people still caught inside the Dundale when the bomb went off.

'We should see if we can help,' I'd said.

'No way. We're leaving now. At once,' Mother insisted.

And no amount of arguing on my part could change her mind. She wanted to put as much space between us and the Dundale Centre as fast as possible. I wasn't sure about the wisdom of her driving us home but we'd managed to get back home OK. Mother then insisted on checking me over properly but apart from a bruise on my forehead and a couple of grazes on my knees and hands I was fine – outside.

Inside, I couldn't get it out of my head that Callum had known about the bomb. He'd probably saved my life. But I almost wished he hadn't. Almost.

With a sigh I got up and headed downstairs to the kitchen. There had to be something I could do to help me get to sleep. A glass of warm milk perhaps. Mother was in her room and Minnie was away, spending the weekend with her best friend.

The kitchen was dark and silent and strangely comforting. I got myself a glass from one of the cupboards and headed for the fridge. The moment I opened it, I was instantly flooded with light.

What to drink? Warm milk or cold orange juice? In the fridge door was a half-full bottle of Chardonnay. I took out the bottle and swirled around the golden liquid. My mother lived in this bottle – and others like it. She was probably upstairs now, drinking to forget today's events. Drinking to forget a lot of things. After a moment's hesitation, I poured myself just enough to cover the bottom of the glass. The first sip almost made me gag. It tasted like refined vinegar. What did Mother see in this stuff? I took another sip. After all, there had to be something to it if Mother liked it so much. Another sip. Then another. And another. I poured out a bit more, half a glassful this time. I drank slowly but steadily. By the time I'd finished, Chardonnay didn't taste quite so bad. And it made me feel funny, pleasant inside. Sort of warm and squishy. Pouring out a whole glassful, I headed back to my bedroom. I sat up in bed, sipping at my wine, feeling very grown-up as I let it wash over me and through me and into me. My head started to sway from the inside out. Backwards and forwards, rocking me gently.

At last, I put down the empty glass and curled up in bed. This time I didn't even have to think about trying to sleep. This time I left the world behind the moment my head touched the pillow.

And I slept like a log.

fifty-two. Callum

Mercy Hospital was a sad joke. The rundown accident and emergency department was busting at the seams, and then some. It looked like many of the people there were nought casualties from the shopping centre. The walking, walk-in wounded. There were people crying, shouting, one woman was screaming at regular five-second intervals and no-one was taking the least notice of her. The air smelt of strong, cheap disinfectant. It was so strong I could almost taste it as it caught at the back of my throat, but it still couldn't quite mask the nastier smells of vomit and blood and urine it was trying to disguise. The whole place reeked of barely organized chaos. All the nurses were noughts and all but one of the doctors. I wondered what a Cross doctor was doing at a nought hospital. Building his stairway to heaven no doubt. I looked at my brother. He'd been involved in all this chaos and carnage around us. How did it make him feel to see the result of his handiwork? But he wasn't looking around. He was looking down at the ground, like his gaze was permanently stuck there.

'Are you all right, Mum?'

'I'll survive.'

Mum sat on one of the rock-hard benches, her face rigid and set as she cradled her purple-blue, swollen finger. It looked awful. I kept stealing glances at Mum, wondering why she wasn't crying. It must've hurt like blazes.

'Are you sure you're OK, Mum,' Jude asked, looking up at last.

'Yes.'

Ten seconds later. 'Are you all right, Mum?'

I wasn't surprised when she finally barked at him, 'No, I'm not all right, Jude. I've broken my finger, it hurts like hell and I'm sick of your stupid questions. So just shut up, OK?'

Everyone around us turned to look. Jude lowered his head, his cheeks flaming.

Mum looked at Jude's bent head and sighed. 'Look, I'm

sorry, love . . .' She carefully removed her good hand from underneath her bad and tried to put it on Jude's shoulder. Jude shrugged her off.

'Jude, I'm mad at your dad and I'm taking it out on you. I'm sorry. OK?' Mum put her hand on Jude's shoulder again. This time he didn't try to remove it.

'OK?' Mum said softly.

Jude shrugged and nodded at the same time.

'Callum, go and get yourself a drink or something,' said Mum.

'Why?'

'I want to talk to your brother in private. I have something to tell him.'

'Mum, please . . .' Jude began.

'This has nothing to do with the L.M.,' Mum told him. 'This is about you and me.'

'Can't I stay?' I asked.

'No. Do as you're told,' Mum ordered.

I walked over to the vending machine on the other side of the waiting room, but I wasn't thirsty. Besides which, I didn't have any money. Besides which, it was out of order anyway. It looked like someone had given it a good kicking – or tried to at any rate. I leaned against it, watching Mum speak earnestly to Jude.

Then even from where I was standing, I saw all the colour drain from Jude's face as he stared at Mum. He leapt up, profoundly shocked. Mum pulled him back down to sit next to her and carried on talking. She leaned forward towards Jude, speaking rapidly with an animation and urgency that showed she was telling Jude something serious. Very serious. I straightened up as I watched them, wondering what on earth was going on. Jude started shaking his head, slowly at first, then more and more quickly. Whatever Mum was telling him, he didn't like it. He didn't believe it. Or maybe he didn't want to believe it. I couldn't stand it any longer. I started walking back to them. By the time I reached them, Jude was looking straight ahead, his face pale, his eyes almost feverishly bright.

'Mum?'

'Sit down, Callum.'

I sat down next to my brother. Mum put her hand on Jude's shoulder. He turned to look at her, still stunned.

'Jude, darling, I . . .'

'Excuse me.' Jude jumped up and headed for the exit without a backwards glance.

'Where's he going?' I asked.

'I don't know,' Mum replied unhappily.

'Is he coming back?'

'I don't know.'

'Why's he upset?'

'Not now, Callum. OK?'

It wasn't, but I let it drop. Almost half an hour later, Jude came back. He sat down in his original place without saying a word.

'Are you OK, love?' Mum asked, gently.

Jude gave her a look like nothing I've ever seen before. Full of hurt and love and anger. Mum actually blushed and turned away. Seconds later, Jude did the same. It was obvious, neither of them was going to tell me what was going on. The minutes crawled by as we all sat in stony silence.

'Mrs Margaret McGregor?' A nurse finally called out from outside the room next to the reception desk.

Mum stood up slowly, doing her best to protect her finger.

'Mrs Margaret . . .'

'She's here,' I called out. 'She's just coming.'

Mum tried to stand up. I attempted to help her but it was hard going.

'Are you trying to melt into that chair or are you going to get up and help?' I snapped at my brother.

In a daze, Jude stood up. We steadied Mum between us and all walked into the nurse's little cubby-hole.

'My mum needs to see a doctor,' I said when we'd barely got our feet into the room.

'All patients are assessed here first before they see a doctor,' the nurse informed us.

'That's fine,' Mum said, casting a warning look at me.

The nurse shut the door behind us as Mum and Jude sat down. I stood up behind him. The nurse headed back to her chair stating, 'I'm Nurse Carter. I'll be your primary nurse whilst you're at the hospital.'

'Good. Fine.' Mum nodded.

'Formalities first, I'm afraid. Before we can administer any kind of medical care, I'll need to see your ID cards.'

'Sorry?' Mum frowned.

'It's the new government ruling. All patient IDs have to be checked and registered. I think it's their way of trying to stop benefit swindles.'

'I beg your pardon?' Mum's frown deepened. 'I'm not even on benefits.'

'It doesn't matter. This hospital and every other nought

hospital in the country gets a certain amount of money per patient we treat. The government are claiming that some hospitals have been trying to abuse the system. So the government's foolproof plan,' the sneer in Nurse Carter's voice made it only to clear what she thought of this so-called 'foolproof' plan, 'is to check each patient's ID card photo and fingerprint, so that patients can't hop around from hospital to hospital getting sickness certificates and hospitals can't lie about the numbers of patients they treat. That's the theory anyway.'

'And if I refuse to hand over my ID card?' Mum asked.

'Then we can't treat you,' Nurse Carter shrugged, regretfully.

'I don't think I have it. I left it at home.'

Nurse Carter sighed. 'Then I'll need the ID cards of at least two other people who can vouch for you.'

'I resent this. I'm not trying to defraud anyone,' Mum fumed.

'I know. And no-one here is accusing you of anything of the kind. But unfortunately we have no choice.'

Mum lifted up her hand. Although her palm was facing down and the back of her hand upwards, Mum's index finger was a V pointing up at the yellowing ceiling.

'Why don't you just chop off my finger and hold it to ransom until I can prove I'm who I say I am?'

'That won't be necessary,' the nurse smiled. She turned her gaze on Jude and me. 'These are your sons?'

'Yes,' Mum answered brusquely.

'They're fine boys.'

'I think so.' Mum allowed herself a faint trace of pride as she looked straight at Jude. 'Very fine boys.'

As Jude blushed, I ruffled his hair.

'Get off,' he scowled at my grinning face.

'Which one's the oldest?'

Mum paused for only a moment as she remembered Lynette. 'Jude here,' she supplied before my brother could. 'And this is Callum, my youngest.'

'OK, Jude,' Nurse Carter smiled. 'May I see your ID card?'

Jude dug into his jacket pocket and pulled it out. I did the same. Nurse Carter swiped them through something attached to her computer. It looked a bit like a machine for checking credit cards.

'What's that for?' Jude asked.

'All done.' The nurse handed Jude's ID back to him. She held out her hand to give back mine.

'What is that?' I asked. I hadn't failed to notice that she hadn't answered Jude's question.

'It just stores your ID details and thumbprints on our hospital database.'

'I don't want my sons' fingerprints stored,' Mum leapt to her feet, her face pale. 'Wipe it off – NOW.'

'Don't worry, Mrs McGregor. As soon as you're able to bring your ID card, your sons' details will be deleted.'

'You're sure?' Mum said slowly, sitting back down.

'Positive. That's standard hospital procedure.' Nurse Carter looked from Mum to Jude and I and back again. She was trying – and failing – to keep the curiosity out of her expression.

Jude looked down at his hands. And then I realized what was going on. So much for my so-called intelligence. I hadn't realized until now why Mum had panicked at the thought of Jude's prints being on file somewhere. Today was obviously my day for being incredibly slow on the uptake.

Nurse Carter lifted Mum's right hand by the wrist. 'How did you do this anyway?'

'It was an accident,' Mum mumbled. 'I hit something I shouldn't've.'

Nurse Carter gave Mum a considering look. 'I see,' was all she said.

The nurse examined Mum's hand very carefully, turning it this way and that as gently as she could. But even at her gentlest, the nurse still made beads of sweat break out over Mum's forehead and brought a pained shimmer to her eyes.

'Well, you've definitely dislocated something in there!' Nurse Carter said at last.

I mean – duh! We knew that already. And the look Mum gave the nurse said as much.

'Yes, I know! But it never hurts to get a second opinion on these things! You'll need an X-ray and then we'll get a doctor to sort you out. OK?'

Mum nodded.

We had to wait an hour before one of the only two X-ray rooms in the entire hospital became available. And then we had to wait another forty-five minutes before a doctor came to see us. The doctor finally gave Mum two injections at the base of her finger to numb any pain she might feel whilst he reset her bone, but he wriggled the needle around so much each time, that poor Mum was almost biting a chunk out of her lip by the time he'd finished. He prodded it a few times.

'Does that hurt?' the doctor asked.

'No.'

'You're sure.'

'Of course I'm sure. I'm hardly going to say no otherwise, am I?'

The doctor acknowledged Mum had a point with a nod of his head. He carefully manipulated her finger, feeling along it on both sides before giving it a hard tug. Jude and I winced and I for one closed my eyes. He should've given us some warning. I didn't realize he was going to just yank it.

'Did that hurt?' he asked, immediately.

Mum shook her head. 'The injections did,' she said. 'That didn't.'

'Good,' the doctor smiled. He took a bandage out of his pocket and started binding Mum's index finger to her middle finger. 'You'll need to keep this out of water and bandaged for the next three weeks.'

'Three weeks! I can't keep my fingers bandaged up for that long. I'm a housemaid. How can I clean anything with my fingers like this?'

'You either keep them bandaged for three weeks or you can forget about being able to use them at all,' the doctor warned. 'You must give your finger a chance to heal.'

'But, Doctor . . .'

'I mean it, Mrs McGregor. If you don't take my advice, you'll regret it.'

Mum scowled at him, but she got the message.

'You OK, now Mum?' I asked as we left our curtained cubicle.

'I'll live.' Mum's voice was clipped with worry. She headed straight back to Nurse Carter's station. Using her left hand, she knocked on the door – three smart taps that signalled business. The door opened almost immediately.

'I'll be back first thing tomorrow morning with my ID and I'm going to trust you to delete my sons' ID info from your database,' Mum said.

'Which son?' Nurse Carter asked.

'Both of them,' Mum declared.

'Don't worry,' Nurse Carter smiled gently. 'It's as good as done already. You have nothing to worry about.'

Mum visibly relaxed. 'Good. Good! Thanks for all your help.'

'My pleasure.' Nurse Carter shut the door as Mum turned to leave.

Moments later we were out of A&E – thank goodness – and on our way home. It was a good forty-minute walk back home, but the early April night wasn't too chilly. I looked up and made a wish on the first star I saw – something Sephy had taught me. The same wish made on every star I saw.

'Is your finger still OK?' Jude asked Mum.

'Yes. The injections haven't worn off yet.' Mum smiled.

They walked side by side back home, with me trailing behind them.

Our IDs were on the hospital database. Why did that worry me so much?

Don't be silly, I told myself. *You're agonizing over nothing.*

How did the saying go? If you go looking for trouble, you will surely find it.

fifty-three. Sephy

I limit myself to a glass a night, just enough to warm me up and chill me out. Waking up the following morning after my first night's drinking had taught me not to overdo it. Each minute sound, each tiny movement had set off a series of massive explosions in my head like nothing I'd ever experienced before – and I never wanted to go through that again either. All things in moderation. I'm not a drunk, not like Mother. I just drink because . . . Well, because.

I don't like the taste of this stuff particularly. And God knows it still gives me the worst morning headaches I've ever had in my life. But it makes me feel OK when I'm drinking it. Kind of warm and careless. It smooths out the rough edges – as Mother says. I don't mind so much about Mother any more. I don't even mind so much about Callum. A couple of drinks and I don't mind about anything.

Isn't that cool?

fifty-four. Callum

Mum went back and had our information deleted off the hospital database but she's still not happy. The slightest noise outside, the lightest knock at the door and we have to scrape her off the ceiling.

'Why don't you just walk around with an "I am guilty!" sign wrapped around you?' Dad snapped.

I winced the moment he said it, as did Mum.

'I'm sorry, Meggie,' Dad sighed.

Mum turned and walked away from him, without saying a word. Dad slammed out of the house. Jude turned up the telly volume, even though it was fine as it was before. I bent my head and carried on with my homework.

But we couldn't go on like that.

We were all sitting down for Sunday lunch of mince and spaghetti when Mum suddenly threw down her fork.

'Ryan, I want you out of this house,' Mum declared.

The floor beneath my chair disappeared and I started free falling.

'W-what?' Dad frowned.

'I want you out of this house by morning. I've thought about it and this is the only way,' said Mum. 'It's too late for you and me, but it's not too late for Jude. I'm not going to let you drag a noose around his neck. I love him too much to let you do that.'

'I love him too,' Dad stared at her.

'I don't like the way you show it,' Mum told him. 'So you must leave.'

'I'm damned if I'll leave my own house,' Dad declared.

'You will if you love any of us as much as you say you do,' Mum said.

I looked from Dad to Mum and back again, horrified. I wasn't the only one at the table who knew that Mum meant every word.

'You've never understood why I'm doing this,' Dad said bitterly. 'I want something more for my sons. Something better.'

'And the end justifies the means?'

'Yes. In this case it does. Especially when the daggers haven't left us with any other option.'

'I'm not arguing with you, Ryan. Just pack your b-bags and leave. OK?'

'No, it's not OK,' Dad shouted, making us all jump.

'If Dad leaves, then so do I,' Jude piped up.

'No, you won't,' Mum and Dad spoke in unison.

Jude looked at Dad, bewildered. 'But you can't stop me from belonging to the Liberation Militia. I'm not going to bow out now.'

'Jude . . .' Mum said, intensely hurt.

'Mum, for the first time in my life I'm doing something I totally believe in. I can actually do some good, make a difference.'

Make a difference . . .

'I'm sorry if that upsets you but sending Dad away

won't change my mind. I'll just go with him, that's all.'

'And if I don't take you?' Dad asked.

'Then I'll find somewhere else to stay. But I'm not giving up the L.M. I'm not.'

'Then you can both leave,' Mum said, stonily. 'And I'll do whatever I have to do to protect Callum. If I can only save one of my children then so be it.'

They all started shouting and screaming at each other at that. I stood up and headed for the door. I had to get out of there. Fast. They were all too busy hating each other to notice me. I slipped out of the front door and ran.

fifty-five. Sephy

'Hi Callum, old friend! Old buddy! Old pal! How are you on this glorious day? Isn't it a beautiful Sunday? The birds are singing. Not over here, but somewhere they must be singing, don't you think? Don't you think, old buddy? Old pal?' I burst out laughing.

Callum had a very strange look on his face as he watched me. He wasn't laughing though. Why wasn't he laughing? I tried to stop, but the look on his face made me laugh even harder. He leaned forward and sniffed at my breath. The look on his face made me laugh until my eyes began to water.

And the next thing I knew, Callum had me by the

shoulders and was shaking me like a country dog shakes a rabbit.

'S–s–stop i–it . . .'

'What the hell d'you think you're doing?' Callum shouted at me.

The look on his face scared me. Actually scared me. I'd never seen him so furiously angry before. 'L–let go . . .'

Callum let go of me almost before the words were out of my mouth. I stumbled backwards and fell in a heap. I tried to scramble to my feet but the beach was swaying. If the beach would just stop swaying for two seconds . . .

'Look at you, Sephy,' Callum said, his voice ringing with disgust. 'You're drunk as a skunk.'

'I am not. I've had just one glass of cider today, that's all. Or maybe two,' I giggled, adding conspiratorially. 'It would've been wine, but I don't want Mother to get suspicious . . .'

'How could you be so *stupid*?' Callum roared. I wished he'd stop. He was making my head hurt. 'You want to end up like your mother?'

'Don't be ridiculous.' I finally managed to get to my feet, but the whole world was rocking beneath them.

'I'm not. I can't stand your mother but at least she had a reason to start. What's your excuse? Not enough attention? Daddy's allowance not big enough? Mummy not giving you enough love? Bed not wide enough? Bedroom carpet not plush enough?'

'Stop it . . .' I was sobering up fast. Callum was being *horrible*. 'Don't stand there and judge me. How dare you?'

'If you behave like a complete moron, don't bleat when that's how others treat you.'

'I'm not a moron.'

'No, you're worse. You're a drunk. A lush. An alcy.'

I covered my ears. 'Don't say that. That's enough . . .'

'Is it? Come on then. I'm waiting to hear your reasons. I'm all ears.'

'You wouldn't understand.'

'Try me.'

'I'm tired, OK,' I shouted at him, shouted for the whole world to hear.

'Tired of what?'

'Of my mother and father, my sister, of you too if you must know. I'm tired of the way you all make me feel. This is it for me, isn't it? Be a good girl, study at school, study at university, get a good job, marry a good man, live a good life and they all lived happily ever after. The whole thing just makes me . . . makes me want to puke. I want something more in my life . . .'

'And you reckon you'll find it in a wine bottle?'

I kicked at the sand beneath my feet. 'I don't know where else to look,' I finally admitted.

'Sephy, don't follow your mother, OK? She's headed for a mental home – or a coffin. Is that really what you want?'

That made me start and no mistake. Was that really where Mother was going? I didn't want her to die like that. *I* didn't want to die like that. I regarded Callum, seeing myself as he must see me. A silly, pathetic child who thought that drinking was a way to grow older faster. A way to stop feeling, 'cause then nothing could hurt me.

'I should be getting back,' I said at last, massaging my throbbing temples.

'Sephy, promise me you won't drink any more.'

'No,' I said at once.

Callum looked so hurt and unhappy, that I couldn't leave it there. I just couldn't.

'But I promise I'll try,' I added.

On the spur of the moment, I leaned forward and kissed Callum on the lips. He moved back.

'Don't want to see what kissing is like any more – huh?' I tried to tease.

'You stink of alcohol,' Callum told me.

My smile vanished. 'D'you know something, Callum? Sometimes you can be just as cruel as my dad is to my mother.'

'Sorry.'

I turned to walk away.

'Sephy, I'm sorry.' Callum pulled me back.

'Just get lost.'

'Not without you.' Callum gave a pathetic attempt at a smile.

'Leave me alone,' I screamed at him, knocking his arm away. 'I should've known you wouldn't understand. I should've realized. Besides, you have other fish to fry now. You're part of the Liberation Militia. You must be so proud of yourselves . . '

'I'm not a member of the L.M. I never have been,' Callum denied harshly.

'How did you know about the bomb at the Dundale then?'

Callum pressed his lips firmly together. I recognized that look, he wasn't going to say a word.

'You should've let me get blown up, Callum. Sometimes . . . sometimes I wish you had . . .'

Callum kissed me then. And it wasn't like the first time we'd kissed either. He wrapped his arms around me and closed his eyes and kissed me. And after a startled moment, I did exactly the same.

And it wasn't bad, either.

But it wasn't enough. Our kiss deepened and his hands began to wander, and so did mine.

And it made things better. But it wasn't enough.

fifty-six. Callum

Of course I admit it. Things went too far. We didn't go all the way. Not *all* the way. But I'd only meant to kiss her to show that I didn't care if she reeked of ruddy cider. I wouldn't even care if her face was covered with puke . . . well, maybe that's going a bit far! But I wanted to show her . . . Anyway. I'm going to have to be more careful. Sephy's just a kid really. We both stopped in time. Not just one of us. I think we both realized we were moving too far too fast.

But now, the thing is, I'm doing my head in thinking about her. Jude would bust a gut if he could read my mind. He'd probably literally do it too. I'm only sixteen and Sephy's not even fifteen yet. In my world the trouble never stops. In hers, it never starts. This drinking nonsense is just her way of getting attention. I mean, it's not even as if she's getting drunk on proper booze. Not whisky or gin or vodka but cider, for goodness' sake! She's bored, that's all it is. I wish she could live half my life. Just half. That'd soon give her something to occupy her time.

Come on, Callum, think of something else or you'll never get any sleep. I wonder what she's doing at this precise moment. Lying in bed thinking of me? I hope so.

Dear God, if you really are out there, somewhere, please find some way for Sephy and I to be together when we're older. For good and all when we're older. Together for ever. Dear God, please. If it's not too much to ask. If you're out there . . .

Callum for goodness' sake, stop daydreaming and get some sleep. You're being totally pathetic. Stop it!

There was no warning. No knock at the door. No warning shouts. Nothing. The first I knew about it was the CRASH when our front door was battered in. Shouts. Calls. A scream. Footsteps charging. Doors banging. More shouts. More footsteps – pound, pound, pound up the stairs. By the time I was fully awake and had swung my legs out of bed, smoke was everywhere. At least I thought it was smoke. I dropped to the floor.

'Jude? JUDE!' I yelled, terrified that my brother was still asleep. I jumped up, looking around for him.

It was only then that I realized it wasn't smoke filling my room, filling the house. The strong smell of garlic caught in the back of my throat and brought instant tears to my eyes. I coughed and coughed, my lungs threatening to explode from my body and my eyes were streaming. *Tear gas.* I struggled to my feet and groped my way to the front door.

'DOWN! GET DOWN!' A voice, no, more than one voice, screamed at me.

I turned in the direction of the voice, only to be pushed to my knees, then down to the ground. My chin hit the hard floor, making me bite down on my tongue. My arms were jerked behind my body. Hands bent back. Cold, hard steel cutting into my wrists. My eyes hurt. My lungs hurt. My tongue hurt. I was pulled to my knees, then yanked up. Pushed and pulled and punched forward. I couldn't see. I closed my burning eyes – and I admit, I was crying by now, trying to clear the tear gas, desperate to stop the pain. My lungs were being filed with sandpaper. Stop breathing. Just stop. But I couldn't. And each breath was strong as ammonia, sharp as a razor.

'JUDE! MUM! DAD!' I called out, only to choke over the words. Only to choke. I couldn't take much more. My body began to seize up, curl in on itself. And suddenly we were out. Out of the house. Out into the cool, night air. I tried to draw a breath. My lungs were being sliced. I gasped. More air – clean, fresh air. Just as I was pushed into the back of a car, I heard my mum crying.

'MUM!' I called. I blinked, and blinked again, looking around, trying to see her. Shapes and shadows swam before me. The car took off. My hands were still hand-cuffed behind my back. My whole body hurt.

And I still didn't know why.

fifty-seven. Sephy

I can't keep doing this, bouncing between Mother and Minnie and school and Callum like a pinball. Everyone's controlling my life except me. And I can feel it's going to get worse, not better. I need to do something. I need . . . I need to get out of here.

But Callum . . .

I don't want to lose him. I don't want to leave him. But I must. Callum's a survivor. I'm not. He'll understand if I explain it to him. I can't think when I'm around him. He confuses me. Around him, all I do is think about him. Sad, but true! Pathetic, but true!

He kissed me tonight. And held me. And ran his hands over my back and my bum and my waist. And pressed me against him. And it felt so strange. Like I belonged right there with him. Except I didn't. I wish I knew why he did it. If only I could read his mind.

Wouldn't it be wonderful if Callum and I . . ?

STOP!

Don't be ridiculous. You're fourteen, for goodness' sake. Sephy, you need to get a life – literally! By the time you're ready to settle down, Callum will probably be married with six kids. Sort yourself out first, your life out second, and your love life out last! As if Callum would be interested in a kid like you anyway?

But he did kiss me . . .

Listen to me, talking to myself. Telling myself off. I'm really losing it. But I need to take my own advice. Get away. Get a life. Start now, before it's too late.

'Mother, I want to go away to school.'

Mother opened her eyes and blinked at me like a stunned owl. 'W-what, sweetie?'

'I want to go away to school. I need to get away from here, from . . . everything.'

'W-where would you go?' Mother struggled to sit up on her bed. Her eyes were vampire red. There was a tell-tale smell in the room. I looked at Mother and it was like looking in a mirror that foretold the future. But only for an instant. The smell was vile, the sight was worse. And the mirror cracked.

'I want to go away to school. A boarding school somewhere . . .'

Callum . . .

'I was thinking maybe Chivers Boarding School 'cause it's not too far away.'

Just far enough away to keep me away from here. Too far for weekend visits in either direction. Far enough away to find something I liked about myself. Far enough away to grow up.

'Only about one hundred and fifty kilometres,' I continued.

Callum . . .

'But . . . what would I do without you?'

I could see from Mother's eyes that our conversation

was finally beginning to sink in.

'You'll have Minnie. And the servants. And all your friends and your parties and . . . everything.' I forced a smile. 'I want to go. Please, Mother?'

'You really want to leave?'

'Yes.'

Mother looked at me. A moment of perfect understanding between us. And it made me so sad. I almost changed my mind then. Almost. But not quite.

'I can see you've made your mind up about this.'

'I have.'

'And when would you want to start?'

'Now. Or in September at the latest.'

'But September's only a few months away.'

'I know.'

Mother looked at me, then lowered her gaze. 'I don't think so, sweetie,' she said, sombrely.

'Mother, I want to go.'

'I don't think it's a good idea,' Mother said, shaking her head.

'For who? You or me?'

'I said no, Sephy.'

I turned and slammed out of her room, grimly satisfied at the muffled wail Mother let out at the noise. I leaned against the wall, trying to figure out what my next move should be. In a moment of pure clarity I realized there was only one thing holding me back. One person stopping me from packing my bags and walking to Chivers right now. I had no idea how I was going to explain my plans to him but I had to. Callum would understand. He'd be on my side once he understood my reasons. Callum and I were like two sides of the same coin.

If Mother thought I was going to let the matter stop and drop here, she had another thought coming. I needed to get away. Get out.

Before it was too late.

fifty-eight. Callum

'Tell me about your brother's involvement with the Liberation Militia.'

'My brother's not in the Liberation Militia,' I denied, the words coming out as little more than a slur. I was so tired. How long had we been doing this? One hour? Twenty?

Two plain-clothed officers sat at the table opposite me. Only one of them was doing the talking though. This was obviously their version of bad cop, silent cop. 'I'll ask you again, which L.M. cell d'you belong to?'

'I don't. I don't. I don't.'

'When did Jude join the Liberation Militia?'

'He didn't – as far as I know.'

'When did your mother join the L.M.?'

'She didn't. She hasn't.'

'You sound very sure.'

'I am.'

'You weren't that sure about your brother.'

'I . . . I am.'

'What L.M. cell does your father belong to?'

'None of them.'

'Come on now. We know all about your family's involvement with the L.M.'

'What d'you need me for then?'

The two officers exchanged a look. I was cheesing them off. Good.

'Corroboration,' said the silent one at last. 'Confirm what we know already and we'll go easy on you.'

'I don't know anything.' I tried to rest my head on my arms on the table but the one who'd done most of the talking pushed my head back up. I sat back in my chair, utterly weary and something else besides. But I wasn't going to show them that.

'Don't mess us about, son.'

'I'm not your son.'

'And I'm not someone you want to make an enemy of,' said the non-talkative officer.

'Whose idea was the Dundale bomb? Your brother's or your father's?'

'You all hate Crosses, don't you?'

'You'd all do whatever it took to annihilate the lot of us. That's true, isn't it?'

'How old were you when you joined the L.M.?'

And on. And on. And round. And round. Question after question. No rest. No peace. No respite. Until my head was spinning giddy and each question echoed with the one before it and the one before that. Until I thought, *So this is what it's like to go crazy . . .*

And what about Mum and Dad and Jude? Where were

they? What were they doing? Why were the police so intent on my brother? I bit down hard on my bottom lip, terrified that I was actually voicing my thoughts, terrified of what I might give way. Think of something else. Think of nothing at all. Think of nothing. And that's when my mind closed down and the world stopped spinning.

I opened my eyes slowly. Please, no more questions. I couldn't take any more questions. I wasn't in the interrogation room any more. I was back in my cell, with Mum sitting on the bed beside me, stroking my hair back off my face.

'Callum? Thank goodness. Are you OK? They didn't hurt you.'

I took my time to sit up, shaking my head as I did so.

'W-where's Dad? Where's Jude?' I asked.

'Your dad's still being questioned and,' Mum took a deep breath, 'I don't know where Jude is. He wasn't in the house when those animals came crashing in.'

'He wasn't? What's going on? What do they want? Why're they going on and on about Jude?'

'They found an empty can of drink near to where the Dundale bomb went off,' Mum said grimly.

'So?'

'So, the can had Jude's prints all over it. So they say. It's a damned lie of course but they reckon they cross-referenced it with the print on his ID card.'

'But how did they get hold of his ID card . . ?' And then I realized.

Mum nodded. 'They scanned in his card when we were at the hospital. I guess they got the information from the computer before the nurse had a chance to delete it – if she ever really did.'

'But Jude didn't . . .' I looked straight at Mum. 'Did he?'

'They're saying he planted the bomb. They're saying w-when they catch him, he'll . . . he'll hang.' And Mum's face dissolved into a stream of tears.

'They won't get him. Once Jude knows they're looking for him . . .' I said, frantically.

'It's just a matter of time.' Mum shook her head. 'We both know that. And they've already issued a reward for information leading to his capture.'

'What kind of reward?'

'Fifty thousand.'

There was nothing to be said at that. Words and tears and prayers were useless. With that kind of money up for grabs it was just a matter of time before Jude was arrested.

'They've probably planted the evidence themselves. They don't have a clue who planted that bomb and they're just looking for a scapegoat.' My voice was barely above a whisper. I couldn't take it all in. They wanted to *hang* my brother. Nothing on this earth would make me believe he'd actually planted that car bomb. He might've been there, but he wouldn't've been the one to put it together and set it to go off. Jude wouldn't do that. He wouldn't. 'If they only want Jude, why're they still questioning Dad?'

'Dad demanded to see them once we knew why they were after Jude,' Mum told me.

'Why? What's Dad doing?'

'I have no idea.' Mum wiped her eyes with the back of

her hand. 'Probably saying the same as you, no doubt. I just hope he's careful.'

I stared at Mum. 'What d'you mean?'

Mum just shook her head. Before I could speak, the cell door clicked open. An officer I hadn't seen yet, opened the door wide. He was a slim man with cutting eyes who looked at us like we were worse than nothing.

'You two can go now.'

'Where's my husband?' Mum asked at once.

'He's being held, after which he'll be formally charged,' the officer told us.

'Charged with what?' I asked.

'My husband has done nothing wrong. Why's he being held?' Mum asked, her voice shaking, but it was hard to tell whether it shook with fear or anger.

'Get your things and leave,' the officer said. 'I haven't got all day.'

'I demand to know why you're holding my husband. I want to see him – now.' Mum exploded.

One look at the officer's furious expression was enough to tell me that there'd be snowball throwing contests in hell before this guy helped us in any way.

'You can leave or you can spend the rest of the night in this cell,' the officer's voice dripped ice. 'It's your choice.'

'May I see my husband please?' Mum forced herself to be civil. But it was too late.

'I'm afraid not. No-one but his lawyer will be allowed to see him until after he's formally charged,' the officer told us.

'What is he going to be charged with?' I asked again, desperate for an answer.

'Political terrorism and seven counts of murder.'

fifty-nine. Sephy

'Come on, Callum! Pick up the phone.'

Nothing doing. It just continued to ring. I glanced down at my watch. Where was everyone? Someone should've picked up the phone by now. It was almost nine o'clock in the morning for goodness' sake!

I put the phone down, trying to swallow down the uneasy feeling in my stomach.

Wait till later, then tell him your news in person. Tell him that come September, you'll be gone.

Will he try to persuade you to stay? Will he even care?

Wait till later and find out.

sixty. Callum

The offices of Stanhope and Rigby were every shade of dingy grey and dirty white imaginable. The waiting-room chairs were more like benches, made from the hardest –

and I do mean *hardest* – oak. The coffee machine had scum marks all over it. And the windows were so dirty it was impossible to make out anything beyond them. This was the fifth solicitor's office offering free legal aid that Mum and I had tried. Once the other solicitors had learned about Dad's case, we'd been shown the door so fast I was beginning to suffer from jet lag. But this office was by far the seediest. I told myself that beggars couldn't be choosers, but it didn't help.

'Mum, let's go,' I said, standing up. 'We can find better solicitors than this.'

'What d'you mean?' Mum frowned.

'Look at this place. I bet even cockroaches avoid this dump.'

'Don't judge by appearances.' A voice from behind made me jump. Mum stood up as I turned around.

A middle-aged man with jet black hair, silvering at the temples, stood in the doorway. He wore a checked shirt and denims and an expression on his face that was harder than titanium nails.

'And you are?' I asked.

'Adam Stanhope,' the man replied.

'This is your company, Mr Stanhope?' Mum asked.

'My father started it. I've carried it on,' he said.

I was impressed with that, for a start. Only one of the other solicitors we'd tried had been a nought. The rest had been Crosses. I knew there were no nought barristers but I hadn't expected to come across a nought solicitor whose father had been a solicitor before him. 'Where's Mr or Ms Rigby then?' I asked, still not sure whether or not I liked this guy.

'Dead. This way please.' Mr Stanhope turned and led the way out of the waiting room.

Mum gave me one of her warning looks as we followed him. We walked behind him, our footsteps not so much clicking as crunching on the cracked lino. Goodness only knew what it was covered with. A thin coating of honey-flavoured cereal from the sticky feel of it. We stopped outside a door which looked like a reinforced toilet cubicle door. Mr Stanhope flung open the door and – wow!

Polished wooden floor, creamy-white walls, mahogany furniture, leather sofa, every thing in the room spelt class with a capital C! I stared at Mr Stanhope, amazed.

'I thought you'd like my office!' Mr Stanhope said dryly. 'Tell me, d'you think this room makes me a better solicitor or a worse one?'

I got the point. 'Why is your waiting room so grotty then?'

'Let's just say that Crosses are shall we say, reassured by its appearance,' said Mr Stanhope. 'It doesn't pay to appear too successful. Please take a seat, both of you.'

I waited until Mum sat down first before doing the same.

'How can I help you, Mrs . . ?'

'Mrs McGregor,' Mum supplied. 'It's about my husband, Ryan. He's being held by the police.'

'Has he been formally arrested?'

'Yes.' Mum lowered her head, before forcing herself to look Mr Stanhope straight in the eye. 'He's been charged with murder and political terrorism.'

'The Dundale bombing,' Mr Stanhope sat back in his chair.

'That's right,' Mum replied. 'But he didn't do it. I know he didn't do it.'

'He told you that, did he?'

'The police won't let me talk to him. I need a lawyer, someone who can get in to see him on my behalf.'

'I see.'

'I don't have much money.'

'I see.'

'I saw in the telephone directory that you do legal aid work?'

If Mr Stanhope leaned any further back his whole body would sink right through the chair. Did he think bad luck was contagious then?

'Can you help us?' Mum asked, a tinge of impatience in her voice.

Mr Stanhope stood up and went to look out of his crystal-clear window. Venetian blinds were positioned to let in optimum light while still keeping the room private. I wondered what he could see. I wished I knew what he was thinking.

'Legal aid wouldn't begin to cover the costs in a case like this,' Mr Stanhope began. 'I can't work for free, Mrs McGregor . . .'

'I'm not asking you to,' Mum replied rapidly. 'I'll pay you whatever it takes. I just want my husband's name cleared.'

Mr Stanhope gave Mum a long hard look before answering. 'I'll go and see your husband first. Then I'll make a decision.'

Mum nodded and stood up.

'But from this moment on, you talk to no-one but me. Understood?'

Mum nodded again.

I stood up and asked, 'Mr Stanhope, are you any good?'

'Pardon?'

'As a lawyer, are you any good?'

'Callum!' Mum admonished.

'No, Mrs McGregor, it's a fair question.' Mr Stanhope turned to me. 'I've won far more cases than I've lost. OK?'

'OK.' I nodded.

We left the office.

Mum and I sat in the police-station waiting room for ages and ages. No-one offered us a coffee. A couple of times we got a 'Can I help you?' from officers entering the station, but that was all. Mr Stanhope had disappeared to talk to Dad and 'review the police case'. They didn't have a case, so what was taking so long? I wanted to see Dad. I wondered where Jude was. I wanted to go home and wake up and find that the last year hadn't happened. I wanted too much.

Mum stared ahead, twisting her thumbs around each other whilst we waited. I was beginning to wonder if Mr Stanhope had just given up and gone home and we'd been forgotten, when he finally made an appearance. And from the look on his face, I could tell right away that it wasn't good news.

'What's the matter? Is he all right?' Mum leapt to her feet. 'What have they done to him?'

'Could both of you come with me please?' Mr Stanhope said grimly.

After exchanging a worried look, Mum and I followed

the lawyer without a word. A police officer held open one of the heavy double-doors which led to the cells.

'Thank you.' Mr Stanhope acknowledged the gesture, as did my mum.

I didn't. The officer walked behind us. When we got to the last cell on the left, we all stood to one side as the officer opened the door. The moment the door was open, Mum flew into the room. I hadn't blinked before Dad and Mum were hugging each other as if they were glued together.

'Ryan, what's going on?' Mum whispered. 'Are you OK? You're not hurt . . ?'

Dad turned to beckon to me. Slowly, I walked over to him, knowing that he was going to hug me too. I wasn't wrong either. I wanted to be hugged by him. I didn't want to let him go because I was so scared. He hadn't done anything. Why was he still being held?

'Mr McGregor, would you like to tell your family what you told me?' Mr Stanhope asked.

'Never mind that,' Dad dismissed. 'Where's Jude? Have they let him go? Is he safe?'

'Jude? The police never had him. He wasn't in the house.' Mum frowned. 'I have no idea where he is.'

Dad stared, then he looked so furiously angry that I found myself taking a step backwards.

'Those bastards! They said they had him. They said Jude was as good as hanged . . .' Dad swallowed hard and turned away from Mum and me. Now he looked like the whole world had descended onto his shoulders.

'Ryan, w-what did you do?' Mum whispered.

Silence.

'Ryan . . ?'

'I signed a confession admitting to all the charges . . .' Dad's voice trailed off.

'What?' Mum breathed. 'Are you crazy?'

'They said they had Jude – and proof he was the bomber. They said someone had to take the blame for the Dundale bomb and it was up to me who took the fall.'

'And you believed them?' Mum asked furiously.

'Meggie, they threatened that you and Callum would also go to prison for conspiracy. It was my life or the lives of my entire family.'

'Did you do it? Did you plant the bomb that killed all those people?'

Dad looked straight at Mum. He didn't even blink. 'No.'

'Then why . . ?'

'I had no choice,' Dad repeated. Anger held his body tense and rigid. He looked like he was about to snap in half.

Mum blinked, totally bemused. 'If you put your hand up to the Dundale murders, you'll hang.'

'I know,' said Dad quietly.

I looked at Mr Stanhope, as if his face could tell me what I couldn't understand on Dad's.

'You want to die?' Mum asked, bewildered.

'Don't be stupid.'

'Mrs McGregor, the moment Detective Inspector Santiago told your husband the identification of the person whose prints were found, your husband confessed to everything. And his dictating and signing of the confession were videotaped. The tape will clearly show his confession was made without duress,' said Mr Stanhope softly.

Dad lowered his head and lowered his voice to match, until it was barely above a hushed whisper. 'Meggie, they found two of Jude's fingerprints on a cola can fragment in the bin where the bomb went off . . .'

'That doesn't prove anything . . .' Mum interrupted, her voice harsh. 'That just means . . .'

'A print was also found on part of the bomb casing that survived the explosion,' Dad cut across her. 'And the prints match . . .'

The world flipped crazily and I started to fall faster and further away from sanity.

Jude was the bomber . . .

That couldn't be right. The Crosses had set him up, framed him. My brother wasn't a bomber. He wouldn't do anything like that. And he certainly wouldn't be stupid enough to leave his fingerprints all over the bomb casing – unless he thought there wouldn't be anything left of the bomb to identify one way or another so why bother to wear gloves? Jude was the bomber . . .

'I told the police the truth.' Dad raised his voice to its normal level. 'I brought the cola from home. I didn't want to risk anyone seeing me if I went into the shops to buy one. That's the only reason it's got Jude's fingerprints on it. He must've handled it and put it back and I didn't realize. And as for the casing, I kept the . . . the necessary equipment around the house. Jude must have handled that as well. He obviously didn't realize what he was touching, he was just curious.' Dad raised his head and spun around, shouting into each corner of the room in turn, 'Jude had nothing to do with this, d'you hear? I'm guilty. No-one else.'

They didn't believe that, did they? No-one in his or her right mind would believe that ridiculous cock-and-bull story.

'Ryan . . .' Tears flowed down Mum's face.

'No, Meggie. I'm guilty. That's the truth and I'm sticking to it. I won't let them put you and Callum in prison for this. Or Jude,' Dad interrupted. He lowered his voice again. 'Just make sure that Jude stays lost so the daggers can't get their hands on him. If they find him, he'll rot in prison.' A tiny, sad smile played over Dad's face, but it was gone in an instant. 'But at least my confession means he won't die.'

sixty-one. Sephy

'Today, Ryan Callum McGregor of 15, Hugo Yard, Meadowview was formally charged with Political Terrorism and seven counts of murder for the bombing outrage at the Dundale Shopping Centre. He has confessed to all charges so the court case against him will be a mere formality. His family consisting of his wife Margaret and two sons, Jude and Callum, are said to be in hiding.'

Every word was an arrow pinning me to my chair.

But he didn't do it. I knew that as surely as I knew my own name. Callum's dad was no more the bomber than I was. Of course, he didn't do it. I had to help. I had to prove that. But how? There had to be some way. Something I could do. What could I do to help him?

Think. Think . . .

'Blanker scumbag!' Minnie hissed from across the room. 'His whole family should swing, not just him.'

'Minerva, I won't have language like that in this house, d'you hear? You don't live in Meadowview.'

'Yes, Mother,' Minnie said, chastened. But it didn't last long. 'And to think we've had him here, in this very house. And his wife actually used to work here. If the press get hold of that little bit of info, they're going to have a field day – and Dad's going to have kittens.'

'What d'you mean?' I asked.

'Oh Sephy, use your brain. If Ryan McGregor gets off, Dad will be accused of favouritism and protecting his own and all sorts, whether or not it has anything to do with him.'

'But the Dundale bomb had nothing to do with Mr McGregor . . .'

'Nonsense. He's confessed, hasn't he?'

I turned to Mother. She looked very thoughtful.

'Mother, they won't really hang him, will they?'

'If he's guilty . . .' Mother shrugged.

'And Callum goes to our school,' Minnie continued. 'Dad's going to get it in the neck for that as well.'

'Callum has absolutely nothing to do with this.'

'An apple never falls far from the tree,' Minnie nodded.

'What a pile of . . .'

'Persephone!' Mother's harsh warning had me biting back the rest of what I wanted to say.

'Even if Ryan McGregor is guilty – which I don't believe for one second – that doesn't mean that Callum . . .'

'Oh, Persephone. Grow up.' The rebuke didn't come from my sister. Mother shook her head at me before she stood up and left the room.

'You haven't a clue about the real world, have you?' Minnie said, her voice dripping with contempt.

'Congratulations! You sound just like Mother,' I took malicious delight in telling her.

Minnie said something incredibly unladylike and flounced out of the room. I smirked at her disappearing back until the door was shut. Then my smile faded. I stared at the closed door, feeling totally alone. What was it about me that made everyone do that? Walk out. Leave. Abandon me. After dismissing me. Why did what I said and did invariably drive everyone away.

Mother. Minnie. Even Callum.

But I was right about this one. Callum's dad wasn't the Dundale bomber.

Mother and Minnie were wrong. And I was going to prove it. I just had to figure out how.

sixty-two. Callum

After only about five minutes of waiting, Mum and I were shown in to Mr Stanhope's plush office. His secretary had told Mum that it was 'urgent' and 'about the case' but that was all she said. Mum and I both had the same question – 'What case?' The last time we'd seen Mr Stanhope, which was three days ago now, he'd told us quite categorically that he wasn't going to take the case.

'Mrs McGregor, Callum, please take a seat.' Mr Stanhope was all smiles from the moment we set foot inside his hallowed walls. One look at his face and my heart began to thump with painfully suppressed hope.

'You have some news?' Mum asked eagerly. 'Are they going to let Ryan go?'

'I'm afraid not.' Mr Stanhope's smile faded slightly, his voice full of regret. 'Your husband still insists that he's guilty.'

And just like that the hope inside was all but snuffed out. Again. Why had he asked us here then?

'I've been trying to get in touch with you at your home address but there's been no reply,' Mr Stanhope told us.

'We're not at our house any more,' Mum glanced at me. 'We're staying with my sister, Charlotte, on the other side of Meadowview.'

'You've been getting hate letters?' Mr Stanhope asked sharply.

'Amongst other things,' I scoffed. Like bricks through the window and death threats.

'Well, I'm happy to tell you that I will now be able to take on your husband's case,' Mr Stanhope told Mum. 'And the really good news is, I've persuaded Kelani Adams QC to take the case – not that she took much persuading.'

'Kelani Adams!' Mum was astounded. And she wasn't the only one. Kelani Adams was not just a nationally renowned but a world-renowned barrister. A Cross barrister. Why would any Cross take on Dad's case? 'I can't afford a lawyer like Kelani Adams.' She shook her head.

'Don't worry about that. That's all taken care of.'

'What does that mean?' I asked, before Mum could.

'It means, it's all taken care of,' Mr Stanhope frowned at me.

Mum and I exchanged a long look.

'I'd appreciate it if you answered my son's question properly,' Mum said.

'An anonymous benefactor has stepped forward with a very generous sum of money, and a promise of however much more is necessary to ensure that your husband gets the fairest trial possible.' Mr McGregor picked his way carefully through the words.

'We don't take charity, Mr Stanhope,' Mum said, tight-lipped.

'It's not charity,' Mr Stanhope shot back. 'I was told to inform you of that in the strongest possible terms.'

'By who?' Mum asked.

'As I said, I received a banker's cheque and a typewritten, unsigned note with certain instructions,' said Mr Stanhope.

'May I see the note?'

'I'm afraid not. One of the conditions on it was that you shouldn't be allowed to see it.'

'I see.'

I'm glad she did, 'cause I sure as hell didn't.

'Mrs McGregor, this is your husband's one and only chance to emerge from this case a free man. I would strongly advise you to take it.'

'Let me get this straight,' Mum said slowly. 'The only reason you're still involved in this case is because someone has paid you to stay involved – is that right?'

'Well, I wouldn't put it quite like that . . .'

'And the only reason Kelani Adams is involved is because she's being paid a great deal of money – is that right?'

'No,' Mr Stanhope said at once. 'The money allowed me to approach the best and she's it. The best does not come cheaply. Once she'd read your husband's file, she was more than prepared to take the case.'

'And I'm meant to be grateful for that, am I?'

'If gratitude is too much to ask, then your acceptance of the situation is all that will be required,' said Mr Stanhope.

Mum turned to me. 'Callum?'

It was hard to be asked for my opinion. Part of me wanted to leave it all down to Mum. Lynette was gone, Jude had disappeared, Dad was in prison and Mum and I were left floundering on our own. I wanted Mum to turn to me and tell me that everything would be OK again. I wanted her to make all the decisions, even the wrong ones. Especially the wrong ones.

'Mum, I think we should do whatever it takes to get Dad out of prison,' I said at last.

'OK then,' Mum said to the solicitor. 'I'll go ahead with whatever you and Ms Adams suggest. But first of all I'd like to speak to my husband as soon as possible.' She looked from me to Mr Stanhope. 'Alone.'

'I'll see what I can do,' came the solicitor's reply.

And all I could do was hope that Mum and I weren't making a big, big mistake. Not just for our sakes – but for Dad's as well.

But for me the most sickeningly humbling thing of all was I knew who had sent the money to Mr Stanhope.

Sephy.

I had no idea how she'd done it. And I had even less idea how I was ever going to thank her, never mind repay her. But I would. I sat in Mr Stanhope's office, on his expensive brown leather chair and swore an oath before God that I would pay her back. If it took me every penny I earned for the rest of my life, I would repay her.

sixty-three. Sephy

I came home from school and got the shock of my life. Dad's suitcases were in our hallway.

'Dad? DAD?'

'I'm in here, Princess.'

I raced into the family room, following Dad's voice like I was tied to it.

I leapt into his arms.

'Dad! I've missed you.'

'I've missed you too.' Dad swung me around – at least he tried to. 'Good grief! What have you been eating?' he exclaimed, dropping me. 'You weigh a ton!'

'Thanks!' I giggled with pure joy. Dad was home. Dad was *back*. 'Are you staying for good?'

'For a while at least,' Dad nodded.

But not in my direction. For the first time I saw that we weren't alone.

Mother was sitting in her rocking-chair, moving slowly backwards and forwards as she watched us.

'What . . . what's going on?' I asked.

'Ask your father. He has all the answers,' Mother replied.

I clicked then. Clicked on and died inside. Dad wasn't back for Mother. He wasn't back for any of us. Ryan

McGregor and politics were the ones who'd brought him home — nothing else.

'You're only here until after the trial, aren't you?' I asked Dad.

'The trial of the century' was what the newspapers and the telly were calling it. They should call it the miracle trial of the millennium if it managed to bring Dad back home.

'It's all up in the air,' Dad smiled, stroking my cheek. 'Nothing's decided.'

I took one look at Mother and I knew that was a lie. At least, she believed it was a lie, which was probably the same thing.

sixty-four. Callum

'Ah, Callum. Come in.'

I was seeing a lot of plush offices this week. First Mr Stanhope, now Mr Costa, our headmaster. It was only the second time I'd been in Mr Costa's office. Crosses seemed to be big on mahogany! And his carpet was like walking on spring grass, soft and bouncy and lush. Mr Costa sat down behind his mahogany desk and leaned back, then leaned forward, his elbows on his table as he tried to figure out which would be the most favourable position. His chair was more like a throne than otherwise, making the headmaster seem even more imposing. The sunshine shone through his crystal-clear windows behind him, making him even darker, like he was a powerful silhouette.

'Sit down please.'

I sat down in one of his squeaky leather chairs.

'Callum, there's no easy way to say this, so I'm going to get right to the point.'

'Yes, sir?'

'Until the matter regarding your father is satisfactorily resolved . . .'

The alarm bells now pealing in my head were deafening.

'The governors and I have decided that it would serve everyone's best interests if you were suspended for a while.'

So that was that. I was out.

'I'm guilty until my dad's proven innocent? Is that the way it works?'

'Callum, I do hope you're going to be reasonable about this.'

'Should I empty my locker now or will the end of the day be soon enough?'

'That's entirely up to you.' Mr Costa folded his arms and sat back in his chair.

'You must be so thrilled,' I told him bitterly. 'Three down, only one more to go.'

'Meaning?'

'Meaning Colin has gone and you couldn't wait to get rid of Shania and now it's my turn.'

'Shania was expelled for gross misconduct,' Mr Costa said haughtily.

'Shania only slapped Gardner Wilson because he hit her

first,' I shouted at him. 'And everyone knows that, including you. How come Shania gets expelled and Gardner gets away with a telling off? Why isn't it gross misconduct when a Cross does it?'

It was the same story up and down the country. In the few schools into which us noughts had been allowed, we were dropping like flies. Expelled, or what the authorities euphemistically called 'excluded', for those things which would get Crosses detention or a severe telling off. The odd Cross or two may even have got suspended once in a while. But they certainly weren't being expelled with anything like the frequency we were.

'I have no intention of justifying school policy to you.' Mr Costa stood up. Our meeting was at an end. 'We'll be happy to review your situation once the dust from all this clears.'

But the dust was never going to clear, was it? And we both knew that.

'Good luck to you, Callum.' Mr Costa held out his hand.

'Yeah, right!' I looked at his hand with disdain.

Good luck to me, as long as it was somewhere else. The further away the better. As far as Mr Costa was concerned, I had already gone. I stood up and marched out of the room. I wanted to slam the door shut behind me, bring it off its hinges, but I wasn't going to give him the satisfaction of saying, 'See! I was right about him. Behaved just as I thought he would.'

And then I thought better of it. I turned back and slammed the door as hard as I could. I only just got my fingers out of the way in time but it was worth it. It was a futile gesture, but it made me feel good.

I strode down the corridor. Mr Costa came thundering out of his room.

'Callum, come here.'

I carried on walking.

'I said, come back here,' Mr Costa called after me, furiously.

I smiled – and carried on walking. I wasn't part of his school any more. I didn't have to do what he said. I wasn't part of the whole Cross way of life. Why should I do what any of them said? Only when I heard Mr Costa slam back into his office did I slow down. My throat had swollen up from the inside out. I was being gutted like a fish wriggling for its life on a slab. I was out of Heathcrofts.

And I was never coming back.

THE TRIAL . . .

sixty-five. Sephy

I hesitated for only a moment. Steeling myself, I knocked on my sister's bedroom door.

'Go away!'

I walked in, darting to my left as a pillow came hurtling towards me.

'Don't your ears work?' Minnie fumed. She was sitting up on her king-size bed, scowling like it was going out of fashion.

I wanted to giggle but I knew that might make her suspicious. Anyway, it would be a cider-induced giggle, not a real one. I wasn't so drunk that I didn't know that much.

'Minnie? I want to ask your advice about something.'

'Oh yes!' My sister raised a sceptical eyebrow. She's very good at that. She's going to be a Mother-clone when she grows up. Just like me, I guess – if I didn't do something about it.

'What would you say if I told you that I'm thinking of going away to school?'

I instantly had her full attention.

'Where?'

'Chivers.'

'The boarding school?'

I nodded.

Minnie looked me up and down until I began to feel really uncomfortable. She asked, 'What does Mother say about it?'

'She said no, but . . .'

'But then she would,' Minnie finished for me.

'So what d'you think?' I repeated.

'I think it's an excellent idea. Which is why I asked Mother the exact same thing a few weeks ago.' Minnie smiled dryly.

'You did!' I was astounded.

'You're not the only one who needs to get out of here.'

I sat down at the foot of Minnie's bed. 'Is it that obvious?'

'Sephy, you and I have never got on, and I'm sorry about that,' Minnie sighed. 'Maybe if we'd been able to count on each other, we'd have done better. Instead we've both tried to get through this on our own.'

'What d'you mean?'

'Come off it, Persephone. You drink to escape, I become more bitchy and spiteful. We each do what we have to do.'

Flames shot through my body. 'I don't drink . . .' I denied.

'Oh?' Minnie scoffed. 'Well, unless you've taken to wearing cider perfume, I'd say you're into booze big time.'

'Cider isn't alcohol.'

Minnie started laughing.

'Not like wine or whisky or something,' I said, furiously.

'And I just like the taste . . . That's the only reason. I'm not a lush.'

Minnie shuffled towards me as I spoke before she put her hand on my shoulder. 'Who're you trying to convince? Me or yourself?'

And then I did the last thing either of us expected. I burst into tears. My sister put her arm around me then, allowing my head to rest on her shoulder – which just made me feel worse.

'Minerva, I've got to get out of here. I've got to, before I explode.'

'Don't worry. I'm working on it with Dad.'

'Yeah, for yourself. But what about me?'

'No, I'm working on Dad for both of us,' said Minnie. 'I keep telling him that we both need to get away from the atmosphere in this house.'

I pulled away from Minnie to ask, 'Are you getting anywhere?'

'I think so. I'm wearing him down.'

'How come you didn't tackle Mother?' I had to ask.

'Because she cares too much,' Minnie replied.

'Whereas Dad doesn't care at all,' I said, bitterly.

'Not true. Dad does care in his own way.'

'Just not as much as he cares about his political career,' I added. 'He only moved back so it'd look good for the McGregor trial. And he's meant to be back but we hardly ever see him.'

'D'you want to see more of him then?' Minnie asked.

I considered. 'Not particularly.'

'Then be careful what you wish for,' Minnie told me.

'Don't worry, Sephy. Come September, you and I will both be out of this madhouse.'

'You're sure?'

'I promise.'

sixty-six. Callum

I sat up high in the packed public gallery. Far below me and to my right, I could see my father. Just the bruised left side of his face. It was only the second time I'd seen him since the police had crashed into our lives. The judge was droning on and on at the jury, telling them what the case was about and what it was not about. Twelve good men and women and true, hanging on the judge's every word. Twelve good Cross men and woman, of course. How else could justice be served? My stomach churned as the clerk of the court finally stood up and faced Dad.

'Ryan Callum McGregor, on the charge of Political Terrorism, how do you plead – Guilty or Not Guilty?'

'DAD, DON'T DO IT!' I couldn't help it. Even as the words left my mouth, I knew I was doing more harm than good but how could I just sit idly by and watch this . . . this farce of a trial.

'Any more outbursts from the public gallery and I will have all members of the public evicted from this court. I hope I've made myself understood,' Judge Anderson threatened.

He was glaring at me – as were all the members of the jury. Mum put a restraining hand over mine. Dad looked up and our eyes met. He looked away again, almost immediately. But not before the image of his battered face had burnt its way into my mind. His split lip and his bruised cheek and his black eye. But there was no condemnation on his face, just a sweeping, intense sadness. The clerk repeated his question.

'On the charge of Political Terrorism, how do you plead? Guilty or Not Guilty?'

Silence.

Silence that went on and on and on.

'The defendant will please answer the question,' Judge Anderson said brusquely.

Dad glanced up at Mum and me again.

'Not guilty!' he said at last.

A collective gasp broke out from every corner of the courtroom. Mum squeezed my hand. Whispers and inaudible comments flew around the room. Dad's lawyer turned around and smiled briefly at us. She was careful to wipe all trace of her smile off her face before she turned back to face the judge.

'You are charged, by means of the afore-mentioned state crime of political terrorism, with the murder of Aysha Pilling,' the clerk continued. 'How d'you plead? Guilty or Not Guilty?'

Dad's reply was stronger this time. 'Not guilty.'

And that was his reply to each of the separate charges read out to him. By the time the clerk had read the seventh murder charge, he had to shout to make himself heard.

So did Dad. 'NOT GUILTY!'

The courtroom erupted. The judge had everyone in the public gallery thrown out of the court, but I didn't care. It was one of the happiest moments of my life.

Not guilty! You tell 'em Dad!

sixty-seven. Sephy

I got the shock of my life. I received a subpoena saying I had to be in court on the following Monday. The subpoena was sent via Mother as I was underage, making her directly responsible for making sure that I turned up on the right day at the right time.

'Why do they want me there?' I said horrified, as I stared down at a whole load of legal jargon that I didn't really understand.

'That's what comes from hanging around noughts,' Minnie told me maliciously.

I was about to tell her where to go, when to my surprise, Mother jumped in before me.

'Minerva, if you kept quiet, you'd at least give the illusion that there's more in your head than just air!' Mother snapped.

Minnie flounced out at that – and good riddance. I turned to smile at Mother but her expression wasn't much better than Minnie's.

'This is exactly why I've always warned you to stay away from that boy – and his whole family,' Mother told me. 'Now our names are going to be dragged into court and through the mud and the newspapers are going to be ecstatic. Your father isn't going to like this one little bit.'

'It's hardly my fault,' I tried to defend myself.

'Then whose fault is it?' Mother snapped. 'Sephy, it's time you learnt that if you lie down with dogs, you're bound to get fleas.'

And she left the room, leaving me to stare after her.

sixty-eight. Callum

'Do you swear to tell the truth, the whole truth and nothing but the truth?'

I looked down at the Good Book under my hand. It was cool, almost cold beneath my fingers. The truth . . . Which version of the truth would this Cross court find acceptable?

'I do,' I replied. Although I spoke quietly, my voice rang out throughout the courtroom. They'd obviously turned my microphone up to maximum. They didn't want to miss a word. And I didn't want to say a word, afraid that one stray syllable would be the death of my dad. I looked around. The judge sat behind a raised platform. The witness box where I stood was next to the judge's platform from where we could both look out over the rest of the court. The prosecution lawyer, a hard-faced man called Shaun Pingule QC, sat glaring at me. Kelani Adams looked straight ahead, barely blinking. She looked like she was in a world of her own. Mind you, this was her world. It sure wasn't mine.

'You may be seated,' Judge Anderson told me.

'No,' I said, adding as an afterthought. 'Thank you. I'd rather stand.'

The judge turned away with just the slightest raising of one shoulder.

Shaun Pingule stood up. I held my breath.

'Could you state your full name for the record, please?'

Nothing to catch me out there. Or was there? Think. Keep your answers short, Callum.

'Callum Ryan McGregor.'

'Do you belong to the Liberation Militia?'

Kelani Adams jumped to her feet. 'I object, Your Honour. Callum McGregor is not on trial here.'

'It goes to witness credibility, Your Honour,' Pingule argued.

'I'll allow it,' the judge replied.

Pingule repeated his question. 'Do you belong to the Liberation Militia?'

'No, I don't,' I replied before the last word had died away.

'So you don't?'

'That's right. I don't.'

'Are you sure about that?'

'Your Honour . . .' Kelani was on her feet again.

'Move on, Mr Pingule,' Judge Anderson directed.

I stole a glance at the jury. Pingule had set me up and no mistake. By asking me the same question over and over, he'd made it out without saying explicitly that I was lying. I could see the suspicion in the faces of the jury already and I'd only been asked one question – admittedly three different ways, but only one question.

'Does your father belong to the Liberation Militia?'

I glanced across to where Dad sat. He was looking straight ahead, somewhere years ahead or years behind. 'No, he doesn't,' I replied.

Had I waited too long to answer? Had the jury been aware of the slight pause before I spoke? I glanced at them again. Two of them were writing something down in their notepads.

'How can you be so sure?'

'Because my father wouldn't hurt a fly.'

'Whereas the Liberation Militia would?' Pingule asked, dryly.

'Objection, Your Honour!'

'Sustained.'

'My dad doesn't belong to the L.M.,' I repeated.

'Callum, what's your opinion of the L.M.?'

'Your Honour, objection . . .'

'Overruled.' The judge didn't even look at Dad's lawyer this time. His eyes were on me.

My opinion of the L.M. . . . ? What should I say to that? I looked around. The noughts in the public gallery waited for me to answer. So did Dad's lawyer. So did the jury. So did Dad . . .

'I . . . any organization which promotes equality between noughts and Crosses is . . .' My mind went blank. I was starting to panic inside. What should I do now? 'Noughts and Crosses should be equal,' I tried again. 'I support anyone who tries to bring that about.'

'I see. And the end justifies the means does it?'

Kelani jumped to her feet again. A yo-yo had nothing on her. 'Your Honour ...'

'Withdrawn,' Pingule said with an airy wave of his hand.

I glanced at the jury. The statement may have been withdrawn but it'd done its work.

'Did your father ever mention belonging to or joining the L.M.?'

'No.'

'Did your brother Jude ever mention belonging to or joining the L.M.?'

'No.'

'So no-one in your family had anything to do with the planting of the bomb at the Dundale Shopping Centre?'

'That's right.'

'And you're sure that no-one in your family knew anything about it?'

'That's correct.' How many more times?

'Including you?'

'Including me,' I agreed, trying to keep the annoyance out of my voice. My sweaty palms told me that I was being led into a trap but I had no idea what it was. My shirt was beginning to stick to my sweaty body. I wanted to wipe my forehead but I thought that would make it look too much like I was lying, so I clenched my fists to keep them by my sides.

'Your Honour, my learned colleague has been asking the same question for the last ten minutes,' Kelani snapped. 'If he has a point, perhaps he could be instructed to get to it some time soon.'

'I have every intention of doing just that.' The prose-cutor's smile was oily to say the least. 'Your Honour, I call into evidence exhibit D19.'

What on earth was D19? I watched as a TV with a massive screen and a VCR were wheeled into the court. As two men set up the equipment opposite the jury, I risked a glance at my dad. He was watching me. And the moment I caught his eye, he almost imperceptibly shook his head. At first I wondered if I'd imagined it, but he continued to look at me, his eyes burning into mine, and I knew I hadn't. I turned to Pingule, wondering what he was up to. And I swear he smirked back at me. One of the court clerks handed him a remote control handset. He turned to the TV. I did the same. If my heart was thump-ing before, it was dive-bombing now. The screen flickered to life. I don't know what I'd been expecting but the Dundale Shopping Centre wasn't it. The video had obviously been made from one of those closed-circuit TV cameras that were dotted all over the centre. And with a gasp of pure horror, it suddenly hit me what was coming.

'Your Honour, this tape has been put together by the police, my office and two independent witnesses from prominent nought groups, to ensure that what we see today is exactly what was taped on the day of the infamous bombing,' Pingule explained.

'Your Honour, I strenuously object,' Kelani began furiously. 'I haven't had a chance to preview these tapes and . . .'

'I only acquired them yesterday evening and I and my colleagues have been working through the night to assemble this footage . . .' Pingule didn't get very far.

'Your Honour, I must insist on being allowed to view the tapes first before they are entered into evidence so that I have a chance to prepare my defence . . .'

'Your Honour, there are precedents to presenting evidence in court not yet seen by the defence. If I can quote . . .'

'No, you may not,' Judge Anderson interrupted. 'I am well aware of the precedents, Mr Pingule. You're not the only one who went to law school.'

'My apologies.'

'Your Honour . . .' Kelani tried to bring the judge back to the subject in hand.

'No, Ms Adams. I'll allow it,' said Judge Anderson. 'I will however allow the court a recess after this witness has been questioned to give you time to prepare your response.'

As Kelani sat down she gave the judge a look that was pure ice. He didn't miss it either. I saw from the slight tightening of his lips that he was less than pleased. I glared at Kelani. How would antagonizing the judge help my father's case?

'Now then, Callum, please could you identify the person running out of Allan and Shepherds Fine Goods store?' asked the prosecutor.

I stared at the screen. Then blinked and swallowed hard. There was no mistake.

'It . . . it's me,' I whispered.

'Could you speak up please?' Pingule said.

'IT'S ME.' I didn't mean to shout, but that's how it came out.

'Can you tell me what you were doing in the Dundale at this time, approximately ten minutes before the bomb went off?'

'I can't remember.'

'Let's see if I can refresh your memory,' said Pingule.

He pointed the remote at the TV and pressed the fast forward button. The time code at the bottom of the video leapt ahead seven minutes before he stopped the tape.

'Is this still you entering the Cuckoo's Egg café?'

I nodded.

'We need a verbal response for the court audio tape,' the judge told me.

'Yes,' I said.

Pingule let the tape play. A few moments later I could be seen leaving the café and pulling Sephy behind me. Although you couldn't hear what was being said, it was obvious that all I wanted to do was get her out of there. The alarm at the shopping centre must've gone off then because Sephy started looking around, puzzled. I pulled her towards the nearest exit and then we both started running. Once we were out of the exit, Pingule fast forwarded for a couple of minutes and, without warning, there was a white flash from the café and the tape went dark.

The silence was damning.

'Do you still insist that neither you nor any member of your family knew anything about the Dundale bomb?' Pingule asked, scathingly.

'Yes.'

'I see. In this film, who are you pulling from the Cuckoo's Egg café?'

'Sephy . . .'

'Persephone Hadley? Kamal Hadley's daughter?'

'Yes.'

'What's your relationship with Persephone Hadley?'

'She . . . she's a friend . . .'

Someone up in the public gallery started to whisper at that.

'Could you tell this court why you were in such a hurry to get Persephone out of there?'

'I . . . er . . . I said I'd meet her and I was late.'

'Really?' Pingule raised a sceptical eyebrow. 'When you found her, why didn't you sit down in the café with her or go for a stroll around the shops? What was the hurry?'

'I was late and I was afraid her mum would appear at any second and . . . and I wanted to show her something.'

'What?' Pingule prompted.

'I can't remember.'

More murmurs from the public gallery.

'With everything that's happened, I can't remember. It was something silly – a car or a plane or something.'

'Indeed?'

'Yes.' I was sweating so much, I was going to have to swim away from the witness box.

'No further questions,' Pingule said, his voice ringing with contempt before he sat down.

I hung my head.

Forgive me, Dad.

I couldn't even look at him. I started to walk down the steps of the witness box.

'Just a moment, Callum.' Kelani's voice brought me back to the present. I looked up. She waved me back into the witness box. I did as directed.

'Could you describe your relationship with Mrs Hadley, Persephone Hadley's mother?' Kelani asked gently.

'Mrs Hadley doesn't like me . . . much.'

'Why d'you say that?'

'She told her secretary not to let me into her house.'

'I see. D'you know why?'

I coughed nervously. 'Sephy . . . Persephone was beaten up at school. Mrs Hadley blamed me.'

'Why? Did you do it?'

'No, of course not,' I said, appalled. 'Some girls from the year above her did it.'

Pingule rose to his feet. 'Your Honour, I fail to see the relevance of this line of questioning . . .'

'Ms Adams?' Judge Andersen prompted.

'I'll come directly to the point, Your Honour,' Kelani smiled. 'Callum, what would you have done if Persephone had been in the café with her mother?'

How should I answer that? Think! Think!

'I . . . would've waited until Sephy was alone before trying to speak to her.'

'But that might've taken a while.'

I faked a nonchalant shrug. 'I wanted to show Sephy what was outside but it wouldn't have been the end of the world if I hadn't. I would've waited until she was alone. I wasn't in a hurry.'

'Thank you, Callum,' Kelani smiled at me. 'That will be all.'

sixty-nine. Sephy

'Miss Hadley, could you tell us what happened when you were in the Cuckoo's Egg café on the day of the bombing?' Mr Pingule, the prosecutor, smiled at me encouragingly, which helped a little. A very little. I hadn't expected to be quite so nervous. I didn't want to be here. The courtroom was too warm and too big. They should've just painted huge eyes all over the floor and the walls and the ceiling and had done with it. And even that would've been far less intimidating than the judge, the lawyers and the jury.

'Take your time, Miss Hadley,' the judge smiled.

I smiled back at him, gratefully. Maybe I could do this. Maybe it wouldn't be so bad after all.

'I was having a drink in the café. Mother . . . my mother had gone back to our car to put away our shopping.'

'Go on,' Mr Pingule prompted gently.

'Well, Callum came in and said we should leave ...'

'Why?'

I swallowed hard. I'd sworn on the Good Book not to lie. But the judge and the jury wouldn't understand the truth. The truth was more than just a spoken sentence. It was a combination of the thoughts and feelings and the history behind them. Was I making excuses? Dressing them up in reasons and justifications and deliberate evasions? Seven people died. No reasoning in the world would ever change that fact, or excuse it.

'Miss Hadley, did Callum give you a reason why you should leave the café?'

'He . . . he wanted to show me something . . . outside . . . I assumed he wanted to show me something outside. I mean . . .' Did I assume it? I must've done. Until the bomb went off.

'What?'

'Pardon?'

'What did he want to show you?' Mr Pingule's smile was wearing a little thin.

'I don't know. I can't remember. I don't think he said.'

'Come now, Miss Hadley . . .'

'He didn't say,' I insisted. 'It was going to be a surprise but . . . but the bomb went off before he could tell me.'

'And that's the truth?'

'Yes.' The truth. But not the whole truth and nothing but. I remembered a saying of my mother's. A wise person tells what she knows, but not *all* she knows. Did that apply in a court of law? Somehow I didn't think so. I watched as Mr Pingule regarded me, a strange look on his face. At last he spoke.

'Miss Hadley, Callum's your friend, isn't he?'

I nodded. 'Yes.'

'And you wouldn't want anything or anyone to hurt him and his family, would you?'

'No.'

'D'you understand that the only way you will hurt him

today is if you don't tell the truth?'

'I know that,' I replied.

'Good. So I'll ask you again,' An edge was beginning to creep into Mr Pingule's voice now. 'Why did Callum want you to leave the Dundale Shopping Centre so urgently?'

'He wanted to show me something outside.' My voice was stronger now.

'I see. Tell me something, Miss Hadley, how would you describe Callum McGregor?'

'Objection, Your Honour. What has Miss Hadley's opinion of her friend Callum have to do with my client, Ryan McGregor?' asked Kelani.

'I'm wondering that myself, Ms Adams,' Judge Anderson nodded. 'Objection sustained.'

'What is your relationship with Callum McGregor?'

'We're friends. Good friends.'

'Perhaps, more than . . . good friends?'

'He's my friend, that's all.'

'Your honour . . .' Kelani got no further

'Very well then,' Mr Pingule was well and truly annoyed now. 'Miss Hadley, do you know who is responsible for the bomb at the Dundale Shopping Centre. Yes or no?'

'Of course not. How could I?' I said, shocked that he'd even asked me.

'Indeed. No further questions.' Mr Pingule sat down.

I didn't know who'd planted that bomb. *I didn't want to know.* And that, more than anything else I'd said or even thought so far in court, was the truth.

seventy. Callum

Now that my evidence was out of the way, I was allowed to watch from the public gallery. I didn't sit with Mum, even though she wanted me to. But how could I? Between the two of us, Sephy and I had pretty much put the noose around Dad's neck. But then Kelani Adams showed why she was a red-hot lawyer. A man called Leo Stoll was called to the stand. I didn't recognize his name or his face when he entered the witness box. He was a middle-aged Cross who was obviously not short of a penny or two. I glanced across at Mum. She had a puzzled, quizzical look on her face. I shrugged. It was no good asking me who he was. I didn't have a clue.

I watched as Leo Stoll was sworn in, then waited with bated breath to see what he had to do with my father. Kelani Adams stood up, and faced the witness.

'Mr Stoll, could you tell the court what you do for a living.'

'I'm a police officer – now retired.' His voice was deep and melodious, like a baritone singer or something.

'You don't look old enough to retire.' I could hear the smile in Kelani's voice, although I couldn't see her face as she had her back to the public gallery.

'I was retired through ill health,' Mr Stoll replied.

'Oh?'

'I was knocked over by a nought joyrider. My hip was completely pulverised. I was offered a desk job but after years spent out in the field,' Mr Stoll shrugged, 'well, I just couldn't face it. So I took early retirement instead.'

'Do you recognize the defendant, Ryan McGregor?'

'Nope. Never seen him before in my life,' Mr Stoll said firmly.

Mr Pingule glanced at Kelani. I reckoned she had one more question before he jumped to his feet, bleating to the judge about the relevance of her questions.

'Mr Stoll, have you ever seen Callum McGregor before?'

'Who?'

My heart plunged down to my feet. Why was she asking him about me? Was that her strategy? To get Dad off by hanging me out to dry?

'Callum McGregor, could you stand up please?'

I hung on to the safety rail and pulled myself upwards. I was burning under the gaze of every eye in the court. This was just as bad as standing in the witness box.

'Oh yes, I've seen him before,' Mr Stoll said, with no hint of hesitation in his voice.

'Where?' Kelani asked.

'On the afternoon that the Dundale bomb went off,' Mr Stoll replied. 'I was having a cup of coffee in the Cuckoo's Egg café. That boy came in and started to drag out a girl who'd been sitting down minding her own business. As she was being dragged out, I asked if she was OK. I may have a dodgy hip but I still know a move or two!'

'Quite! So what happened then?' Kelani prompted.

'The girl said that the boy was a friend of hers and that he was just taking her out to show her something,' said Mr Stoll.

'You're sure that's what she said,' Kelani asked eagerly.

'Positive. Like I said, I used to be a police officer so I've been trained to observe and remember.'

Did Sephy say that? I couldn't even remember. I just remember my desperation to get her out of the Dundale before the whole place was blown to smithereens.

'Did the girl seem particularly scared or worried in any way?' Kelani asked.

'Not at all. She was treating the whole thing like it was a big joke.'

'And how come you survived the bomb blast?'

'I finished my coffee and left less than a minute after the boy up there and his friend.'

'Thank you, Mr Stoll. No more questions.' Kelani Adams sat down.

Spontaneous cheers erupted throughout the court-room. Judge Anderson tried to restore order but it wasn't going to happen. In the end he had to clear the court. But just like that, my story had been corroborated. And by a Cross police officer of all people. If it'd been funny, I would've busted a gut laughing.

seventy-one. Sephy

Every evening I sat glued to the early evening news for any information about Callum's dad's trial. I'd racked my brains to try and come up with some way of helping him. But I'd drawn a complete and utter blank. What could I do? What could just one person do? So I sat and watched like the rest of the country whilst a reporter told us in great detail what had happened that day in court. They occasionally showed Callum and his mum hiding their faces from the cameras as they came out of the court.

The night they showed Callum's house burnt to the ground I went to my bedroom and cried and cried. Luckily, Callum and his mum were staying with relatives but it still hurt to think of what my friend was going through. I wanted to phone but I didn't have Callum's new number. I wanted to visit him but I didn't have his new address. I still went down to the beach once in a while but Callum was never there. I pretended to myself that we just kept missing each other. I'd arrive at five, he'd arrive at six. I'd arrive at six, he'd arrive at seven. But deep down I knew that he'd stopped coming. He had more important things on his mind.

I don't know how Callum's mum managed to get Kelani Adams to defend Callum's dad but I was so glad she had. Even before I'd had to go into the courtroom, I'd heard of Kelani Adams QC and I wasn't really into politics or current affairs or anything like that. According to the reporters on the telly, Kelani was making sure that the trial was as fair as possible – and putting the judge's back up in the process. Good for her!

Ryan Mcgregor just had to be found not guilty. It was only right and proper.

It was only just.

It was only justice.

seventy-two. Callum

Dear Sephy,
  This is a very hard letter for me to write. I keep putting it off and putting it off and this is about the tenth draft.

I scrunched up the paper and threw it in the already overflowing bin. Start again.

Dear Sephy,
  I'm just going to come right out and say this. I don't know how you managed to get all that money together to help my dad but I love you for it. Our lawyer, Kelani Adams, is really on our side, to the extent that the judge has threatened twice to hold her in contempt of court.

I don't know how, but some day, some how, I'll make it up to you. I just want you to know that I'll be for ever . . .

Another sheet of paper scrunched up and thrown in the bin. I folded my arms on the table and rested my head on them. Good or bad, every aspect of my life lay in the hands of others. Kelani Adams, the jury, my so-called education at Heathcroft, even with Sephy. Maybe this was it. Maybe this was all there was or ever would be to my life. I was so sick and tired of being this helpless.

Over the last few months, I'd had a recurring nightmare about being in a cardboard box, no bigger than I was. A normal, simple cardboard box. But no matter how hard I pushed or punched, I just couldn't smash my way out. In fact the more I tried, the harder it became. And in my bad dreams, it was only when my hands were bloody and I was gasping frantically for breath that I realized I wasn't in a box at all. It was a coffin. And once I realized that, I stopped struggling and just waited to die. That's what terrified me the most.

I stopped struggling and waited to die.

seventy-three. Sephy

At last the trial was over. The jury was out, considering its verdict. I was actually flicking from TV station to TV station trying to find any news item that would bring me more up to date. I'd seen the so-called evidence weighed up by numerous experts on any number of news programmes as well as in the papers. And they all thought Callum's dad was guilty. No-one ever came right out and said so. There was a lot of useless talk about the 'balance of probabilities' and the 'pros and cons' of the case and discussions on the evidence. Funny, but I've never been the slightest bit interested in the news before. Now suddenly I couldn't stop watching it. When Minnie started moaning in my ear about watching something else, I went up to my room to watch it in peace and private.

Ryan McGregor wasn't guilty.

So why did I feel like I was the only person in the world – the only Cross in the world – to believe that?

seventy-four. Callum

Mum and I held hands as we waited for the foreman to speak. Hope and hopelessness churned in my stomach like oil and water.

'Foreman of the jury, have you reached a verdict upon which you are all agreed?'

'We have, Your Honour.'

'D'you find the defendant, Ryan Callum McGregor, Guilty or Not Guilty of the crime of Political Terrorism?'

Why was he taking so long to speak? Answer the question . . . What's your answer?

He opened his mouth and said something but I didn't hear. Why couldn't I hear? I shook my head and leaned forward, concentrating hard. Had he spoken? I'm sure he'd said something. I saw his mouth open and close. I licked my dry lips, feeling sick. I looked at Mum. Her expression was carved in granite. Next to Mum a blonde woman buried her face in her hands. The man next to her shook his head in disbelief. Why couldn't I hear anything? Maybe because I didn't want to hear.

'D'you find the defendant Ryan Callum McGregor, Guilty or Not Guilty of the murder of Aysha Pilling?' The clerk's voice rang out like a gunshot.

And I heard the verdict that time. God help me, I heard it.

OX———————————— **THE WAY IT IS . . .**

seventy-five. Sephy

I sat on our garden swing, twisting it this way and that. I didn't actually swing any more – that was kid's stuff. I just . . . twisted. It was hot. Too hot.

'Sephy, what're you doing?' Mother yelled across our garden at me.

Uh-oh! Trouble! I'd come home and gone straight out into the garden, when I knew Mother did her nut if she saw me messing about in my school uniform.

'Come here please,' Mother hollered.

I was going to shout 'why' but I thought better of it. For the last couple of weeks, Mother had got worse and now I just did as I was told and kept my head down as far as she was concerned. And for the most part it worked. Jumping off the swing, I ran to the house.

'Go to your room and put on your navy-blue dress and your blue shoes.'

'Which blue dress?' I frowned.

'Your Jackson Spacey one,' Mother told me as if it was obvious.

My eyebrows went up at that. That dress had cost over one thousand pounds and Mother told me I was not to wear it without her express permission. The last time I'd worn it was when I'd snuck out of the house to Callum's after Lynette had died. I and my dress had gone down like a lead balloon then. It kind of made me loath to put the thing on again.

It wasn't a special Saturday and it wasn't anyone's birthday. Or had I forgotten someone? No . . . Today was 24th July and the next birthday was my sister's and that wasn't until the middle of August.

'Why do I have to get dressed up?'

'Because I said so,' Mother snapped. 'Do as you're told. And tell your sister to hurry up as well.'

'Where're we going?'

'No more questions,' Mother said, edgily. 'Go!'

I headed for the kitchen door, turning in the doorway to ask Mum what was going on. She was pouring out a glass of Chardonnay, which she downed in a one-er. She poured out another one. I left the room and headed upstairs.

Minnie didn't know what was going on either – not that she would've volunteered to tell me if she had. Apart from the one time we'd confided in each other in Minnie's bedroom, my sister and I have never had much to say to each other. But I knew it was something very serious indeed when Mother opened our front door and Dad's official government Mercedes was parked on the driveway. And Dad was in the back. My face lit up like a Crossmas tree at the sight of him.

'Dad!' I ran over to the car and threw open the door before Karl had the chance to do it for me. I hadn't seen him in over a week.

'Sephy, get in this car and try to show that you've been brought up, not dragged up,' Dad ordered, his face as stiff a door.

It couldn't've hurt more if he'd slapped me across the face. One week apart – and that was all he had to say to me. Mother and my sister Minerva had reached us by this time. Karl held the door open for them. I hung back, waiting for them to get in first before I did. No way was I going to sit next to Dad. No way was I even going to say a word to him until he apologized. Mother sat next to him, very careful not to actually touch him. Next Minnie, then me. Less than a minute later, we were off – and I still had no idea where. I glanced down at my watch. Four-thirty. I looked at Mother and Dad and Minnie, hoping that someone would let me know what was going on without my having to ask. Nothing doing. I turned and looked out of the window. If everyone else wanted to be mysterious, then let them get on with it. I wasn't going to join in.

Our car drew up outside Hewmett Prison. Ten to six. There were cars ahead of us and cars behind and people walking in on foot. All the noughts walking through the pedestrian entrance were dressed in black and not one of them spoke. Every expression was a reflection of the one before it and the one after. When we reached the entrance of the prison, Dad flashed his ID card at the two security guards by the gates. We were waved straight through. What on earth were we doing in Hewmett Prison? Why did I have to put on my Jackson Spacey dress no less to go to a *prison*?

We were taken out into the prison courtyard. The early

evening air was humid and uncomfortable. Our car was air-conditioned so I hadn't realized how unpleasant it had become outside. Already my dress was beginning to stick to me. Half of the prison courtyard was taken up by seats placed in tiers, whilst most of the rest of the space was bare. At the far end of the courtyard was a scaffold. And still I didn't click. We were shown to our places right at the front of the seated area.

I looked around, puzzled. All the noughts were standing. Some were looking at the scaffold, a few were crying, some were looking at us Crosses on the seats, burning hatred on their faces. Without warning, my eyes caught and locked with Callum's. Shock, like a bucket of ice-water, flowed over me. What was going on? He stared at me. I hadn't seen him for so long that the jolt was all the greater for seeing him here.

'Ladies and gentlemen and noughts, we are here today to witness the execution of Ryan Callum McGregor of 15 Hugo Yard, Meadowview, having been found guilty of seven counts of murder and the charge of political terrorism. His appeal having been denied, the sentence of hanging by the neck until he is dead will now be carried out. Bring out the prisoner.'

And only then, when it'd been spelt out for me, did I finally realize what I was doing there. They were going to hang Callum's dad. I turned to the scaffold, appalled. A door opened to the left of the scaffold and Callum's dad was led out.

I turned to Mother and Dad. They were looking straight at the scaffold, their expressions grim, sombre. I tried Minnie. Her head was slightly bowed but she kept stealing glances at the scaffold. And still no-one spoke. We might've been in a graveyard.

We *were* in a graveyard.

I turned to Callum. He was watching me with a look on his face I'd never seen before. A look that cut right through me like the sharpest, keenest scalpel. I shook my head slowly.

I didn't know, I mouthed. I looked from the scaffold back to Callum, from Callum's dad to Callum, from my parents to Callum, from the crowds all around and back to Callum.

I swear I didn't know.

How to make my desperate thoughts reach him? I wouldn't have come if I'd known where we were going. Wild horses couldn't have dragged me through those gates. That's the truth. Callum, you must believe that.

' Mother, I want to leave,' I whispered furiously.

'Not now, Sephy.' Mother looked straight ahead.

'I want to leave – NOW!' I jumped to my feet, raising my voice.

Heads were turning in our direction but I didn't care.

'Sit down Persephone and stop making an exhibition of yourself,' Mother snapped.

'Nothing is going to make me sit here and watch this. I'm leaving,' I turned on my heels, trying to push past the other dignitaries in my row.

Mother stood up, spun me around and slapped my face. 'Now sit down and don't say another word.'

Cheek smarting, eyes stinging, I sat down. Some eyes were watching me. I didn't care about that. More eyes were watching the scaffold. Well, maybe I couldn't leave but they couldn't force me to watch. They couldn't force me to raise my head. And if they did, they couldn't force me to open my eyes. And if they did, they couldn't force me to *see*. But I couldn't keep my gaze lowered . . . Slowly, I raised my head, my eyes drawn to the sight, my heart disgusted by it. Angry with myself, I turned away, only to find myself looking straight at Callum. He wasn't watching his dad either. He was looking at me – and wishing me and every other Cross as dead as dead could be. I'd seen that look on other's faces – noughts looking at Crosses, Crosses looking at noughts. But I'd never seen it on Callum's face before.

And I knew in that moment that now I'd never ever stop seeing it. Flinching, I turned. Back to the scaffold. A choice of views. Hatred or hatred. They were putting a black hood over Callum's dad's head now. The prison clock began to strike the hour. When it struck six, it'd all be over.

One . . . All eyes on the scaffold.

Two . . . The noose around Callum's dad's neck.

Three . . . Someone begins to weep. Loud, heart-wrenching sobs.

Four . . . A man at the scaffold nods to someone behind him.

'Long live the Liberation Militia . . .' Callum's dad shouts at the top of his voice.

Five . . .

seventy-six. Callum

The clock struck five. One more . . .

'WAIT! WAIT!' A voice called out from beneath the scaffold.

'The governor . . .'

'That's the prison governor . . .'

I strained to see him, but part of the wooden scaffold structure was in the way. I wanted someone in the crowd around us to say what was happening, but now there was just silence. No-one spoke. No-one moved.

Six . . . The clock struck six times. I hardly dared to breathe, afraid the slightest motion would spring the trap beneath Dad's feet.

'Mum . . .' The merest whisper.

'Shush!'

'THE EXECUTION IS STAYED,' the same voice shouted out. I saw a Cross move from behind the lattice of wood-work and beckon to the guard up on the scaffold with my dad.

The peculiar thing was, there were no cheers, no shouts, no sounds at all. Maybe everyone was like me, unable to believe or understand what was going on. What did it mean? Were they going to let Dad go? Did they have new evidence to prove he was innocent? Maybe

Dad's lawyer had done it! From the moment Dad was found guilty, Kelani Adams had parcelled out all her other cases to her colleagues to concentrate solely on Dad's appeal. She'd told Mum and me that she wouldn't rest until Dad was a free man. I know that even as they were waiting to lead Dad out of the prison and up to the scaffold, Kelani had been busy making desperate phone call after desperate phone call. Obviously the phrase 'a lost cause' wasn't part of her vocabulary. Funny . . . it seemed to be a major part of mine.

The man who'd stopped the execution walked up the steps to the scaffold. He nodded to the guard who immediately took the hood off my dad's head. Dad blinked crazily for a few moments, his eyes wide like he was in the middle of a nightmare and even with his eyes open, he couldn't wake up. The governor walked up to Dad and said something to him. It looked like he had to repeat it, asking Dad if he understood. Dad shook his head. The governor put one hand on Dad's shoulder. Dad nodded. Murmurs sprang up through the audience. This not knowing was killing me. *What was going on?* The governor raised his hands for silence.

'Ladies and gentlemen and noughts, I am Governor Giustini. I have just this moment been informed that Ryan Callum McGregor has received a reprieve. His sentence has been commuted to life imprisonment. There will be no hanging today.'

'LONG LIVE TH . . .' Dad's knees buckled as if the ground had suddenly disappeared beneath him. The prison officer standing beside him only just managed to grab him in time to stop Dad from keeling over completely.

And then the whole place erupted. It was only because there were tall metal barriers between us and the scaffold that it remained in one piece. Our fury was so deep, we were all drowning in it. We wanted to get to Dad, to sweep him away, to get him out of there. But we couldn't get to him. Mum tried to pull me back but I was one of the first to push and shove my way forward.

'Dad! DAD!' I yelled until my throat hurt, but the tide of voices around me carried my words away.

Dad was hurried down the scaffold steps and back into the prison, along with the governor, but that didn't stop us. We could've torn down Hewmett Prison brick by brick. *We would've* – but we couldn't get past the barriers. I turned my head whilst being pushed forward. Turned to where *they* were sitting. I couldn't see her. Where was she? Watching all this and enjoying the free entertainment? The Crosses were all leaving in a hurry. We were penned in and had to stand up like cattle; they had seats. We were herded in through a side gate and ushered to our part of the courtyard. The Crosses got to drive in and sit down, like they were having a night out at the ballet or going to the cinema or something. Each one of us was scanned and searched. I bet not one single Cross was even stopped.

And then they wondered why we hated them so much.

People were beginning to get hurt. I saw a man in front of me fall, and whilst those around him tried to help him up, the ones behind still pushed forward. There were screams and shouts and shrieks and chaos. And I loved it. 'Cause it was just what I needed. A place to shout and kick out, where no-one could stop me because I was just one of many. At that precise moment I felt like I could rip the metal barriers out of the concrete beneath my feet with my bare hands. I was invincible because I was so filled with rage. It was a giddy feeling and I revelled in it. Someone grabbed my arm. I turned, ready to lash out. It was Mum.

'Callum!' she shouted. 'Let's get out of here. I want to see your dad.'

'Mum . . ?'

And just like that all my anger that was just about to break out subsided. I stood watching Mum, waiting for the pain inside to dampen down, waiting for the world around me to turn multi-coloured again instead of blood red.

'Come on.' Mum pulled me after her, in the opposite direction to the crowd. And with an overwhelming sense of regret and frustration, I let her.

seventy-seven. Sephy

'DON'T YOU EVER DO THAT TO ME AGAIN!'

'Don't talk to me like that,' Mother frowned.

But I was too far gone by now. Dad had gone straight back to his office in one of his colleague's cars, leaving me, Mother and Minerva to go home alone. And with each passing second, the fury in me had dug deeper and deeper. Mother had come home and gone straight to the kitchen. Minnie ran up to her room. I followed Mother.

'How dare you take me to that . . .that . . . thing? How *dare* you?'

'We had to go. It was our duty.' Mother took a half-empty bottle of Chardonnay out of the fridge.

'Our duty? To see a man get hanged?'

'Yes.' Mum poured out some wine into a tumbler. 'Because like it or not we have to support your dad, whether or not we agree with what he's doing.'

'But that was . . . barbaric. Taking us to watch a man die. Dad's sick. So are you.'

'I didn't like it any more than you did.' Mother downed her half pint of wine without even gasping.

'Liar. You couldn't take your eyes off it. I saw you.'

'I wasn't watching,' Mother said quietly, pouring herself another drink.

I'd had enough by then. I snatched the bottle out of her hand and threw it across the kitchen. It hit one of the cupboards and bounced off to spin around on the floor. But it didn't break. What little wine there was left, trickled out in a silent puddle.

'Go to your room,' Mother stormed at me.

Finally, a reaction. And it left me cold. 'You really don't care, do you?' I said, making no attempt to hide my disgust. 'You would've cared more if they were hanging a wine bottle instead of a person.'

Mother slapped me hard – but I was ready for it this time. I turned back to face her almost immediately.

'There's wine spilling out over there. Go and lick it up then. You wouldn't want to waste any, would you?'

Mother gasped, a sound she tried to smother at once, but she was too late. I heard it.

'Waiting for me to leave before you get on your hands and knees?' I sneered. 'OK then. I'll leave you to it.'

Mother grabbed my arm and swung me around to face her. 'You don't know every damn thing, Persephone,' she hissed at me. 'You think you're the only one hurting here? Ryan McGregor was my friend. So was Meggie McGregor. D'you think I wanted to see him hang?'

'Why did you go then?' I shouted at her.

'One day you'll realize that you can't always do what you want to do in this life. And when you realize that, maybe you'll think of me,' Mother told me.

'I want to think of you as little as possible,' I said bluntly. 'You say they were your friends? Nothing would make me go to the hanging of one of my friends. Nothing. Not even Dad.'

'I tried to help . . .' Mother whispered.

'How? By getting blind drunk before and afterwards?'

'You stupid girl. Who d'you think paid for their lawyer and all their legal fees?' Mother took hold of my shoulders and shook me. 'I prayed and paid and did everything I could to make sure that Ryan wouldn't hang. What more could I've done? You tell me?'

'*You* paid for their lawyer?'

Mother turned away from me. 'Yes, and that's not to leave this room. And not for the reason you think either.'

'That was just your guilty conscience,' I told Mother. 'You've never done anything for anyone other than yourself in your life. So go back to your bottle. You've earned it.'

And I ran out of the room, knowing that Mother was

watching. I bolted up the stairs like the devil himself was chasing me.

Strange how much you can cry, don't you think? Strange how many tears you can hold inside. I lay on my bed and cried until my whole body shook and my head pounded like a pneumatic drill, and even then I couldn't stop. And I knew no-one would hear me cry either. Minnie's room was next to mine but our rooms were practically soundproofed. So I didn't need to bury my head under my pillow, or choke back my sobs. I just cried. For Callum, for his dad, for the day – and for myself, I admit it.

seventy-eight. Callum

Two hours and a lot of arguing from our solicitor later, we were finally allowed in to see Dad. Mr Stanhope, our solicitor, said he'd wait for us outside as we were shown into the visitors' hall. Mum and I sat in silence, our eyes trained on the door. At last the door opened – and I almost wished it hadn't. Another anonymous prison officer entered, followed by Dad. And he looked terrible, half-deflated and pale as a ghost. On the scaffold, he'd been tall and straight and in a funny way I'd felt so proud of him. But now he looked . . . old. Stooped and shrunken into himself. Mum stood up. I did the same.

Dad saw us, but he didn't smile. Mum opened her arms. Dad walked into them and they hugged silently for a long, long time.

'I hear I'm being blamed for the riot outside,' said Dad, his voice almost a monotone.

He pulled away and sat down. All of us, except the prison officer, did the same. I glared at him. Was he going to just stand there, listening to our private conversation? Obviously he was.

'How are you, Ryan?' Mum couldn't care less what was happening outside.

'How d'you think?' Dad said bitterness modulating his voice slightly.

'At least you're still alive. I'm grateful for that . . .'

'I'm not. I was ready to die,' said Dad sombrely.

'Ryan . . .'

'I mean it, Meggie. D'you really think I want to stay here, rotting away in a prison cell. They should've hanged me. It would've been kinder.'

'Don't say that!' Mum cried.

'Why not? It's the truth, isn't it?'

Mum glanced down, struggling for something to say. The click of the door had us turning around. Kelani Adams swept in, her arms out, her expression triumphant. We all stood up. Kelani hugged each of us in turn, even hugging me for good measure.

'Well, we've won the first battle. On to the next one,' Kelani nodded. 'I've already launched an appeal and . . .'

'With all due respect, Miss Adams, this is as far as you'll get,' Dad interrupted.

'Oh no it's not,' Kelani denied. 'I'm calling in every

favour I'm owed – and then some. You're innocent of these charges and I'm going to prove it.'

Mum grasped Kelani by the hand, her smile sincere. 'I want to thank you for your help in all this, Miss Adams. If it wasn't for you . . .'

'Your thanks are a tad premature.' Kelani returned Mum's smile. 'But that's OK.' She turned to Dad. 'What we need to do now is . . .'

'Kelani, it's over,' said Dad. 'They didn't kill me quickly. They just decided to draw it out instead. I'll never see the outside of this prison and we both know it.'

The conviction in Dad's voice silenced us all – but only momentarily.

'You may know it, but I certainly don't,' said Kelani firmly.

But I don't think Dad heard her.

'Ryan, please don't give up,' Mum begged. 'There's still hope. We can appeal. There are lots of things we can do . . .'

'I don't want you to do anything. There has to be a way out of here and *I'll* find it . . .' said Dad.

'Ryan . . .' Mum was worried.

'It's OK, love. I've got it all figured out,' said Dad.

I shook my head slowly as I watched Dad, before stopping abruptly when I realized what I was doing. I glanced up at the officer. He was still looking straight ahead but now his expression was troubled rather than neutral. He glanced down at Dad, then turned to Mum and shook his head.

'I don't wish to interfere,' he began softly. 'But please tell your husband there is no way to escape from this prison. He's been talking about nothing else since his reprieve. Tell him the security gates are guarded at all times and the fence is electrified twenty-four hours a day, seven days a week.'

Mum looked from the guard to Dad. 'Ryan, you're not going to do anything stupid, are you? Promise me . . .'

Dad smiled, a slow, frightening smile, and opened his mouth to answer but at that moment a buzzer sounded.

'Ryan, please, *please* trust me to do my job,' Kelani said to Dad. 'I *will* get you out of here. You have to believe it.'

'I'm afraid visiting time is over,' the officer said.

Dad headed for the door.

'Ryan . . ?' Mum called after him.

'Meggie, don't worry about me. I'm getting out of here,' said Dad. 'You just see if I don't.'

And he carried on walking away from us, towards the exit. The prison officer nodded politely to my mother and Kelani. Kelani nodded back. But Mum didn't even see him. She was watching my father leave. The prison officer followed Dad out of the room. Mum muttered something to herself, utterly desolate.

'What did you say?' I asked her as gently as I could.

Mum turned to me, tears in her eyes. 'He didn't even say goodbye.'

seventy-nine. Sephy

It took a while before I heard the strange tip-tapping at my window. And once I was conscious of it, I instinctively knew that it'd been going on for a while. Not bothering to wipe my face, I headed for my window and opened it. Tiny stones lay at my feet.

Callum . . .

Callum in our back garden. I leaned over my balcony and saw him at once.

'What . . ?' I lowered my voice. 'What're you doing here?'

'I need to see you.'

'I'll come down.'

'No. I'll come up.'

I looked around anxiously. 'OK. But be quick.'

'How do I get up there?'

'Just a sec. Er . . . can you climb up the drainpipe and use the ivy for footholds?'

'I'll break my neck.'

'Hang on, I'll tie some sheets together then.'

'No, don't bother.'

Without another word, Callum clambered up the drainpipes and the ivy, reaching my balcony in about ten seconds flat. My heart leapt up into my throat as I watched him. If he fell now . . . The moment he reached my balcony, I hauled him over, terrified he'd plummet to his death.

'Did you phone me? I didn't hear your signal,' I told Callum, confused.

'I didn't phone. I came straight here,' Callum replied. 'I hid in the rose garden until the coast was clear.'

We stood in the middle of my room. He looked at me and I looked at him and all the events of our lifetimes finally caught up with us. I wanted to say sorry for everything that'd happened to his dad, sorry for everything that was still happening, but even in my head the words sounded trite and totally inadequate. Better to say nothing. Safer. And I couldn't forget the way he'd looked at me as the prison clock struck. I was the first to look away. I'd known Callum all my life and yet I felt as if we'd only just met.

'Is there anything I can do?'

Or maybe I'd done enough. Me and my kind . . . I risked a glance at Callum. He didn't answer. He just watched me.

'How's your mum . . ?' Stupid question. 'Is she still staying with relatives or friends? Is she . . ?'

'She's at my aunt's house,' Callum replied.

I looked around my room. Should I sit or stand? What should I say? What should I do? Inside, I was beginning to panic.

I ran to lock the door. The last thing either of us needed was to have my mother or sister enter the room. Sighing with relief at the click of the key in the lock, I turned, only to bump straight into Callum. Dazed, I looked up at him.

'I . . . I thought you were going to get help,' Callum told me.

I shook my head, shocked. Why would he think such a thing? 'Listen, if I wanted to get help, you wouldn't have made it to my bedroom window,' I told him.

But he was hardly listening. He just kept staring at me, his expression freezing by degrees.

'Callum . . ?'

'Your father must be so proud of himself,' Callum's eyes narrowed. 'An innocent man is going to rot in prison and just like that his political reputation is restored.'

'No . . .' I whispered. 'It wasn't like that . . .'

But it was — and we both knew it.

'Is this the way it's going to be from now on? Whenever a politician is in trouble in the polls, if they can't start a war, they'll just search out the nearest nought to imprison or hang — or both?'

I didn't take my eyes off Callum's face. Out of the corner of my eye I saw him slowly clenching and unclenching his fists. I didn't move. I didn't blink. I hardly dared to breathe. Callum was hurting so much, it was tearing him up inside. And he wanted to hurt someone.

'And what about you, Sephy?' he asked.

'W-what about me?' I whispered.

'No more you and me, I take it,' Callum said with contempt. 'After all you wouldn't want to ruin your future career prospects by being spotted with the son of the Dundale bomber.'

'I know your dad didn't do it.'

'Oh yes? Well, so did the jury — for all the difference it

made. D'you know how long they deliberated? One hour. One lousy, stinking hour.' His head slumped in despair.

'Callum, I'm so sorry . . .' I touched his cheek.

His head shot up. He glared at me with white-hot, burning hatred. My hand fell quickly to my side.

'I don't want your ruddy pity,' he shouted.

'Shush . . .' I pleaded, glancing at my bedroom door.

'Why should I?' Callum challenged. 'Don't you want anyone to know you've got a blanker in your room?'

'Callum, don't . . .' I didn't even realize I was crying until a salt tear ran into the corner of my mouth.

'I want to smash you and every other dagger who crosses my path. I hate you so much it scares me,' he told me.

'I . . . I know you do.' I whispered. 'You've hated me ever since you joined Heathcroft and I called you a blanker.' I realized it as I said it. And in that moment I realized a lot of things, including why I'd started knocking back wine.

'And you've hated me for turning my back on you at school and not being there when you needed me,' said Callum.

I didn't deny it.

'So why're we still together?' Callum spoke softly to himself, almost forgetting that I was right in front of him. 'Why do I still think of you as . . ?'

'As your best friend?' I supplied. 'Because you know that's how I think of you. Because . . . because I love you. And you love me, I think . . .'

My words snapped Callum out of his reverie with a

vengeance. A hard, mocking look flashed over his face. I waited for him to do something; laugh, lash out, deny it, leave – anything. But he didn't.

'Did you hear what I said?' I tried again. 'I love you.'

'Love doesn't exist. Friendship doesn't exist – not between a nought and a Cross. There's no such thing,' Callum replied.

And he meant every word.

'Then what're you doing in my room?' I asked, choking inside. 'Why did you come?'

Callum shrugged. 'I'm damned if I know.'

With a sigh I moved over to the bed and sat down. After a moment's hesitation, Callum came and sat down beside me. I can't remember either of us ever feeling more awkward. I struggled desperately to find something to say. Risking a glance in Callum's direction, I saw at once from the look on his face that he was having exactly the same problem.

I had so many things I wanted to tell him. The words tumbled and jumbled around in my head, making me dizzy. But nothing would come out. I turned to Callum and slowly held my arms out towards him. He looked puzzled, then his expression cleared. He watched me intently. My gaze dropped. Another of my stupid ideas. I started to lower my arms. Taking hold of my hands, he shuffled along the bed towards me.

Wrapping his arms around me, he lay down on the duvet cover, taking me with him. We faced each other, our eyes locked. I licked my lips nervously. Now what? Callum kissed me. And I kissed him back. We were comfort kissing, that's all. We wrapped our arms around each other for solace. Bear hugging. Squeezing the life out of each other as if we were trying to merge together. When at last we loosened our grip, in a strange way we were both more . . . calm. Physically, at least. Not mentally.

'Turn around,' Callum whispered.

I was about to argue but then I thought better of it. I did as I was asked. He wrapped his arms around me. We were cuddled up like a couple of spoons in a cutlery drawer. I toyed with the idea of suggesting that we get under the covers but I decided not to push it. I didn't want to give Callum a reason to panic and leave. Maybe there was some way to suggest it . . . gently? I raised an eyebrow. Gently? Yeah, right! But it would've been wonderful. Just Callum and me locked together, locking out the whole world. Bliss. But one step at a time. And besides, what we were doing now wasn't too shabby! Better to settle for this than his hatred. Better this than nothing at all.

Callum sighed. I shuffled back to get closer to him. I felt him relax, his body warm against mine. My sigh echoed his.

'Are you OK?' His breath was warm and soft in my ear.

'Uh-hm!' I mumbled.

'I'm not squashing you'

'Uh-uh!'

'You're sure?'

'Callum, shut up.'

I felt rather than saw him smile. His first smile in a long while, I think.

'Don't leave without giving me your new address and phone number,' I murmured. 'I don't want to lose you again.'

I don't even know if he heard me and I was too comfy to find out. Then I thought of something else. Something which struggled through my lethargic haze. Something that'd been troubling me for a while now.

'Callum,' I whispered. 'I'm sorry I sat at your table.'

'What're you talking about?'

'Your table. At school,' I said, sleepily. 'And I'm sorry for what happened at Lynette's funeral.'

And sorry for all the million and one other well-meant but badly thought out things I'd done in my life. Acts to make me feel better. Actions that had hurt Callum rather than helped him. Sorry, Callum. Sorry. Sorry.

'Forget it. I have,' Callum's warm breath whispered across my cheek, before he kissed it.

I closed my eyes and allowed my mind to drift away. I was cuddled up with Callum and for once this time was ours and no-one else's. With that thought in my mind, I drifted off to sleep, with Callum still holding me.

eighty. Callum

Sephy was out like a light. Lucky her. I lay on her bed with my arms wrapped around her, wondering how on earth we'd managed to end up like this. I'm not sure what'd been on my mind when I came to see her, but this wasn't it! Strange the way things turn out. When I'd come into her room, I'd been burning up with the desire to smash her and everything else around her. Sephy was a Cross I could actually hurt. And yet here she was, asleep and still holding on to my arms like I was a life-raft or something. There's not a single millimetre of space between her body and mine. I could move my hands and . . . And. Anything I liked. Caress or strangle. Kill or cure. Her or me. Me or her.

I lifted my head, to make sure she was really asleep. Eyes closed, regularly breathing, in-out, in-out. Dead to the world. Lucky her.

She turned in her sleep to face me, her arms instinctively reaching out to hug and hold me close to her. I lowered my head back down to the pillow. Each time Sephy exhaled, her breath tickled my cheek. I moved my head down slightly so that our noses were almost touching. So that when she breathed, she'd have to breathe my breath and I'd have to breathe hers. And then I kissed her. Her eyes opened almost immediately, sleepy but smiling. Her hands crept up to frame my face and, closing her eyes again, she returned my kiss, her mouth open, her tongue dancing against mine. Fireworks were shooting through my body. I was finding it hard to breathe. So was she. I pulled away abruptly.

'Why are you kissing me?' I asked, frustrated anger creeping into my voice. 'Passion or guilt?'

Sephy looked so sad, so hurt, that I instantly regretted my words. She went to roll away from me, but I held her arm and wouldn't let her.

'Sorry,' I murmured.

'Maybe you should go . . .' Sephy whispered, still not looking at me.

'Not yet. Please. I'm sorry.' I placed my hand under Sephy's chin and raised her head so that she could look at me and know I meant it. She tried to smile. I tried to smile back.

I opened my arms for her. 'Let's just get some sleep – OK?'

Sephy nodded. I lay on my back and Sephy settled down to lie with her head on my shoulder. She was asleep again in less than a minute. Lucky, lucky, lucky. Ten minutes must've passed. Then fifteen. I couldn't stand it any longer.

'Sephy, d'you want to know a secret,' I mouthed against her ear.

She moved her ear slightly away from my mouth. My breath must've tickled her. But she was still fast asleep.

'Here is my confession,' I whispered. And I told her what I'd never told anyone else. What I hadn't even admitted to myself. The biggest secret of all.

God, if you are up there – somewhere – you've got a very peculiar sense of humour.

eighty-one. Sephy

'Miss Sephy? Are you all right in there?'

'Persephone, open this door. At once.'

The dream I was having was so warm and comfortable,

apart from that incessant calling somewhere in the background. I opened my eyes slowly, only to have them fly right open when I saw whose shoulder I was perched upon. Callum's. His arm was around my shoulders and he was fast asleep.

'Persephone, open this door right this second or I'll get someone to break it down,' Mother yelled.

'Miss Sephy, are you OK. Please.' Sarah pulled at the door handle.

I sat bolt upright. 'Just . . . just a minute,' I yelled, shaking Callum awake.

'What . . . what's the . . ?' Callum began sleepily.

Putting one hand over his mouth, I pointed to the bedroom door. He got it at once. I pointed to my bathroom door. Callum jumped off the bed and ran towards it.

'Look, why don't I just let them in,' I whispered. 'I want Mother to know about us. Besides, we haven't done anything wrong.' The look Callum gave me instantly changed my mind. 'Bad idea?'

'Duh!!' Callum replied.

I looked down at my clothes. I still had my Jackson Spacey dress on – although by now it had so many creases in it that it looked like the skin on a day-old macaroni cheese. If Mother saw it, she'd kill me.

'Just a minute, Sarah. I'm just putting on my dressing-gown,' I called out.

After pulling the belt tight and making sure none of my dress could be seen, I ran to the door, waiting until Callum had scooted into my bathroom before I turned the key in the lock.

'What's the matter? Is the house on fire?' I asked as

Sarah and Mother bustled past me.

'D'you know what time it is?' Mother asked.

'So I overslept a few minutes. Big deal,' I said, annoyed.

'Ten minutes? It's almost noon and your door is locked. You never lock your door,' Sarah said suspiciously.

'Maybe I decided to bring a little excitement into your lives,' I yawned.

And then I saw them. Callum's trainers, right by my bed in plain, full, multi-colour view. My heart dropped to my ankles then bounced right up to my mouth.

'I'll be down as soon as I've had my shower,' I smiled brightly. 'I promise.'

'There's nothing wrong?'

''Course not. What could be wrong?' I said, a little too emphatically judging by the deepening look of suspicion on Sarah's face. She looked around slowly, stopping abruptly when she caught sight of the men's trainers on the floor. She gave me a profoundly shocked look and I knew at once what was going on in her head. Pursing my lips, I fought hard to stop myself from looking guilty. I hadn't done anything wrong. And if Callum and I had been at it all night like bunny rabbits instead of fast asleep, it still wouldn't have been any of her business.

'There's something strange going on around here,' Mother said slowly.

'Just 'cause I overslept?' I asked, more to focus her attention on me than for any other reason.

Sarah walked towards Callum's shoes as Mother scrutinized my face. Although my eyes were on Mother, I was aware of Sarah's every movement. She was going to hold up Callum's trainers with a flourish for Mother to feast on.

'Sarah, what . . ?'

As Mother turned around, Sarah kicked the trainers under my bed. All Mother saw was Sarah tidying up my bedclothes as if she was making my bed.

'Don't do that, Sarah,' Mother admonished. 'My daughter is quite capable of making up her own bed. That's not your job.'

Sarah dropped my duvet with a prim 'Yes, Mrs Hadley.'

Mother marched out in high dudgeon, followed by Sarah trotting behind her.

'Get Callum dressed and out of here!' Sarah whispered urgently as she passed me.

'How did you . . ?' My mouth snapped shut. I shut the door behind them, carefully locking it so neither of them would be alerted by the noise.

'OK, Callum. You can come out now.'

Callum popped his head around my bathroom door and had a look around before he came back into my bedroom. We looked at each other and burst out laughing. And it felt so good.

'How am I going to get out of here?' Callum asked.

I had a long, hard think. 'We'll have to sneak out of the house and across the grounds to the beach. If we see anyone, I'll distract them whilst you sneak past.'

'Just your ordinary average Sunday-morning activity!' Callum said dryly.

'Never a dull moment,' I agreed.

'Fancy another cuddle in the bed first?' asked Callum.

I smiled. 'You betcha!'

eighty-two. Callum

'Ryan Callum McGregor, the convicted bomber of the Dundale Shopping Centre, was killed this morning whilst trying to escape from Hewmett Prison. He was electrocuted whilst trying to scale the electrified fence surrounding the prison. Ryan McGregor, who was due to hang four days ago, received a dramatic last-minute reprieve from the Home Office. His family are said to be devastated at the news and were unavailable for comment. Officials have launched an immediate enquiry.'

eighty-three. Sephy

Dear God,
  Please leave Callum's family alone. But it's not you, is it? My mistake. This has nothing to do with you. This is more like the devil's work. Another mistake? Maybe hatred has nothing to do with the devil either. Maybe it's something we've invented. And then we just blame it on you, God, or on the devil, because it's easier than blaming ourselves. I'm not thinking straight. I can't think. Dear God, look after Callum and his family. Help them. Help us all.

eighty-four. Callum

I entered the burger bar and waited my turn in the long queue. This Friday was just like the Friday before and would probably be exactly like the Friday to follow. My days stretched out before me like some kind of galactic desert. Funny how the days could go so slowly and time could pass so fast. They'd killed . . . they'd murdered my dad in July and when he died, I think something inside me had died as well. And although since then the weeks had come and gone, it still cut like a knife every time I thought of my dad – which was all the time. Officially, the authorities might call it suicide, but I and every other nought knew differently.

And I hadn't seen Sephy since the Saturday night-Sunday morning I'd spent with her. Sarah hadn't given us away but she'd made sure it was practically impossible for me to slip back into the house again. A guard was now on permanent patrol.

I'd visited the beach a few times but to be honest I never stayed very long. Going to the beach felt like trying to recapture the past – an impossible task. Too much had happened over the last year. I never saw Sephy anyway, which was probably just as well. At least the memory of that night in her bed was beginning to fade a little. Not much. But a very little. If I tried very hard to think about something else – and rubbed my stomach and patted my head at the same time! I forced myself to think of Dad. What were the thoughts running through his head as he stood before the fence? What was the last thing he thought of before he died? I'd never know. Something else to hate the Crosses for.

I gave my order to the cashier, ignoring the plastic smile on her face as she served me, and waited for my food. When I'd received my burger, french fries and milk, I sought out the darkest corner of the burger bar. I finally sat down with my back to the throng and slowly chewed on a chip. I wasn't even hungry. It was just something to do to pass the time until the afternoon had passed. Now that I wasn't at school, I never knew what to do with myself. Totally aimless, I had nothing to do and nowhere to go. Since Dad's death, Mum was lost somewhere deep inside herself where I couldn't reach her. No-one could. I had tried, but it was hopeless. Maybe if I'd been Lynette, her favourite child, or Jude, her first-born son, but . . . I chewed on another chip. I was sixteen and a half, and already it felt as if my life was over. The good times, the *best* times, were over.

'Hi, little brother.'

I looked up and my eyes began to hurt I was staring so hard. Jude . . . *Jude!* I leapt up and, leaning across the table, I hugged him – hard!

'I've missed you,' I told him.

'Get off. Are you mad, or what?' Jude glanced around

before sitting opposite me. I sat back down, beaming at him.

'Stop grinning like an idiot!' Jude told me sourly.

'It's great to see you too!' I replied. 'Where've you been? I really have missed you.'

Jude took another look around. 'I've been keeping my head down for a while.'

My smile disappeared. 'You ... you know what happened to Dad?'

'Oh yes, I know,' Jude said grimly. 'I know all about it. And it's payback time.'

'What d'you mean?'

Jude sat back in his chair. His eyes darted here, there and everywhere and although he sat perfectly still, he reminded me of a nervous cat, ready to leap off at a nanosecond's notice.

'I hear they booted you out of Heathcroft,' Jude said at last.

'I wasn't booted. I walked,' I told him huffily.

'Good for you. That wasn't the place for you, little brother.'

'I know that now.'

'It's a shame you didn't listen to me when I told you months ago. It would've saved you a lot of grief.'

I shrugged. What else was there to say?

'So what're you up to now?' Jude asked.

'I eat chips.' I pointed at my polystyrene tray.

'Would you like to do something more worthwhile?'

'Like what?'

Jude stood up. 'I have to go now. Someone will be in touch.'

'Jude, don't do your "Man of Mystery" routine on me.'
I frowned. 'What am I meant to tell Mum?'

'Don't tell her anything,' Jude said vehemently. 'Where we're going, she can't follow.'

'And where are we going?'

'I think you know, little brother.'

'Stop calling me that,' I protested. 'What're you up to, Jude?'

'Just tell me one thing,' Jude said. 'Are you in or out?'

He was deliberately being enigmatic, answering each of my questions with a question of his own. And it was really cheesing me off. But I knew what he was asking. This was my chance to link up with the Liberation Militia. And I knew in my gut that if I turned Jude down now, I'd never be asked again.

'Well?' Jude prompted.

I licked my lips, trying to delay the moment of decision.

'This is your chance to make a difference,' Jude told me.

And just like that, I felt a calmness, a *purpose* I hadn't felt in a long, long time. I looked at Jude and said, 'I'm in.'

Jude nodded, satisfied. 'Then go home, pack your bags and make your peace with Mum. You'll be contacted tomorrow some time. After that you won't be seeing Mum or anyone else we know for that matter for a while. Are you still in?'

I nodded.

'Welcome to the lifeboat party, little brother,' Jude said adding, 'I hope I can trust you.'

And a moment later, he was gone.

eighty-five. Sephy

Dear Callum,

I was going to phone you but I knew I'd bottle out and never say what I wanted to say. So I've decided to write it all down. I've thought and thought about it and I think I've found a way for both of us to get away from all this madness. You're sixteen, nearly seventeen and I'm almost fifteen so don't say I'm too young or anything stupid like that. Just read this letter with an open mind, that's all I ask.

I think you and I should go away together. Somewhere. Anywhere. Just the two of us. For good. Before you throw this letter in the bin, my brain hasn't dropped out of my ear. I know what I'm saying is right. I want to be with you and I think you want to be with me. I'm not going to swear undying love or any of that other stuff you despise so much, but if we don't leave now and together, then something tells me we never will. I'm not talking about the two of us becoming lovers or anything like that. I don't think either of us is ready for that. Besides, I know that's the last thing you'd want. But the two of us could set off together. Set up together. Stay together. Save each other — if that doesn't sound too melodramatic. I think it probably does. But I mean it. And if you think about it, you'll realize deep down that I'm right.

So let's just do it before we get too old and scared. Let's do this before we turn into <u>them</u>. I've got plenty of money saved in my own personal bank account, plus there's my regular monthly allowance from both Dad and my grandmother's trust fund. And we can both work. Just as long as we're together. All you have to do is say yes. I thought we could move right away from here. Maybe rent a place up north somewhere. Maybe in the country.

If you say yes.

Mother has finally agreed to my going to Chivers Boarding School and I'm leaving at two o'clock on Sunday afternoon. If I don't hear from you by then I'll know what your answer is. I'll wait for you right up until the moment I have to leave. But either way I'm going to get out of here.

Take me away from all this, Callum. Don't let me leave for Chivers. I want to be with you. Please don't let me down.

~~All my love~~

Yours for ever,

Sephy

I stuffed the letter back into its envelope as I heard footsteps approach the kitchen. I was in luck. It was Sarah.

'Sarah, I . . . could you do me a favour? A really big one.' I chewed on my lip nervously, trying to read her expression.

'Oh yes? What's that then?'

'Could you deliver this letter to Callum McGregor? He's staying with his aunt. I've written the address on the front.'

'I don't think so!' Sarah scoffed. 'I need this job.'

'Please, Sarah. I'm begging you. It's really important.'

'What is it?' Sarah asked.

'A letter.'

'I can see that. What does it say?'

I chewed on my lip some more. A horrified look appeared on Sarah's face.

'You . . . you're not pregnant, are you?'

I stared at her, then burst out laughing.

'I guess not,' Sarah said dryly.

'Please,' I pleaded, my smile fading. 'I wouldn't ask you if it wasn't really, *really* important.'

Sarah regarded me thoughtfully. 'OK,' she said at last. 'I'll deliver it on my way home tonight. But only on one condition.'

'What's that?'

'That you don't do anything . . . hasty.'

'It's a deal!' I wrapped my arms around her and hugged her tight. 'Thank you. Oh, thank you.'

'Hhmm!' Sarah didn't sound convinced that she was doing the right thing at all.

I licked the envelope and sealed it before pressing it into her hand before she could change her mind.

'Thanks, Sarah. I owe you one.' I grinned at her as I skipped off.

'You owe me several, Miss Sephy,' Sarah called after me.

'I know.' I twirled around before heading up the stairs.

Hasty! This wasn't hasty at all. I'd thought and considered and planned this for days, weeks, months, all my life. Everything Callum and I had ever done had been leading up to this moment.

Callum would read my letter and come for me and together we were going to *escape*.

Wasn't life glorious?!!

eighty-six. Callum

'Callum, there's someone downstairs to see you ...
What're you doing?'

I closed my eyes briefly, my back towards Mum. I'd
hoped to escape any kind of explanation.

'I'm going away, Mum.'

'Where?'

'Away,' I replied. 'Somewhere where I can make a
difference.'

Silence. When I could bear it no longer, I turned to see
what Mum was doing. She stood in the doorway, watching me.

'I see,' she said at last.

And she did see. That was the trouble.

'When will you be back?'

'I don't know,' I answered truthfully.

Pause. 'Will you see your brother?'

'I don't know. Probably.'

'Tell him ... Give him my love,' Mum said at last,
adding, 'Do one thing for me, will you?'

'What's that?'

'Keep your head down. And tell your brother to do the
same.' Mum turned to walk out of the door, her whole
body slumped and drawn in on itself. She turned her head.

'What about Sarah downstairs?'

'Sarah?'

'Sarah Pike who works for Mrs Hadley. She's downstairs.'

'Tell her I'm busy at the moment. I don't want to see her.' I shook my head. The last thing I needed right now was a stale morality lecture from Mrs Hadley's dogsbody. 'I can't take all my stuff,' I decided. 'I'll be back tomorrow afternoon for the rest.'

Mum carried on downstairs. I flung a clean T-shirt into my rucksack and closed it, waiting for the sound of the front door to close downstairs. My leaving would please Aunt Charlotte at any rate. I'd already received my orders. Go to the bus garage just outside town, sit on the bench outside the bus garage and wait. All very hush-hush, cloak-and-dagger. It was a big waste of time and effort if anyone were to ask me, which no-one did. But if it kept my brother happy then fair enough.

I felt quite upbeat about what was going to happen actually. I was going to join the Liberation Militia. It wasn't what I'd planned for myself a couple of years ago, but at least I'd stopped drifting. At last, I belonged.

The moment I heard the front door shut, I headed downstairs.

'Sarah left this for you,' Mum pointed to a letter on the hall-table.

'I'll pick it up tomorrow with the rest of my stuff,' I said, impatiently, without even looking at it. What Sarah couldn't say to my face she'd written down, eh? Well, it could wait. I was off to spend my Saturday evening outside a bus garage.

'I'm off now, Mum.'

Mum nodded. 'Take care of yourself.'

'You too.'

We stood in the hall like two lemons on display.

'See you, Mum.'

'Bye, son.'

I skirted round Mum trying to make sure I didn't knock her with my rucksack. And then I was out of the door. Mum closed it quietly behind me as I walked off towards the other end of town.

eighty-seven. Sephy

He's coming. He's not going to come. He's coming. He's not going to come. He's . . .

'Persephone, move it!' Mother snapped. 'D'you want to go to Chivers or not?'

'I'm coming,' I called out. I took one more look around, searching the grounds, the path, towards the gate.

Nothing.

He wasn't going to come. The desire to cry came and died. Dry-eyed I moved towards the car. Karl, the chauffeur, stood by the passenger door, holding it open for me.

'Sephy!'

I turned as Minnie came hurtling out of the door. She

stopped right in front of me.

'Enjoy yourself at Chivers,' she said at last.

'I wish you could come with me,' I told her.

'Do you?'

I nodded.

'Well, Mother can't do without both of us and as I'm the oldest and my exams are only just around the corner, and going to a new school would be too disruptive, so I might as well stay here . . .'

Mother's arguments, not Minnie's.

'I'm sorry, Minerva.'

Minnie shrugged. 'Yeah, so am I.'

'Couldn't you have another word with Mother? Maybe she'll . . ?'

'It wouldn't do any good,' Minnie interrupted. 'She's determined that I should stay.'

'You worry too much about pleasing everyone,' I told her.

'Unlike you. You couldn't give two hoots for anyone else's opinion,' Minnie smiled.

If only that was true. I sometimes acted first and thought about it afterwards but I did care what other people thought. That was the trouble.

'Don't . . . don't get too . . . like Mother – OK?' I said.

'I'll do my best.' Minnie winked conspiratorially. 'And you lay off the booze. Agreed?'

'I'll try,' I told her.

'I thought you stopped for a while?'

'I did.'

'What made you stop?'

I shrugged. How to answer that? Feeling wanted. Being

cuddled. Not feeling sorry for myself any more. Any number of answers. Lots of reasons.

'Well, what made you start again?'

I shrugged again. Being lonely. *Missing him*. The absence of hope until I'd written my letter.

'Sephy, you're not Mother. Stop trying to be,' Minnie said.

I started at Minnie's words, staring at her. Is that what I was doing?

'Sephy, please come on,' Mother called out from behind us.

'Bye then.' Minnie bent forward awkwardly and kissed me on the cheek. I couldn't remember the last time she'd done that. I couldn't remember the first time come to that! I headed for the car, still looking around.

He wasn't coming.

Wave goodbye to Dreamland, Sephy. I sat down next to Mother.

'At last!' she said, annoyed.

Oh Callum ... Why didn't you come? Didn't you believe me? Or maybe you didn't believe in me? Or maybe you were the one who had to have sense enough for both of us. Or maybe you were just scared enough for both of us.

Karl walked around the car to the driver's seat – and we were off.

Callum, why didn't you come?

eighty-eight. Callum

Faster. Move. I have to do it. I just have to. Wait. Please wait.

I race like the wind towards Sephy's house. Faster than I've ever run before. As fast as if my life depends on it.

Please God, if you're really up there . . .

I clamber up the rise to the rose garden, just in time to see a car turn out of the security gates. Sephy is in the back, next to her mum. But she's looking down, not at me, not anywhere near me.

Please God . . .

'WAIT! SEPHY, IT'S ME. WAIT!'

Run. Move. I sprint after the car. I stop breathing so drawing breath won't slow me down. Run. Race. Sprint.

'SEPHY . . .'

The car is several metres ahead of me now. The driver's eyes meet mine in the driver's mirror. Sephy's Mercedes accelerates smoothly but noticeably away from me.

'SEPHY . . .' I speed after the car. My lungs are about to implode and every muscle, every bone in my body is on fire. But I'll follow that car to hell and back, if I have to. If I can.

Please, please God . . .

I trip over my feet and hit the ground face first. Dazed,

I look up, but the car is almost out of sight. I grip Sephy's letter in my hand, lying on the ground, listening to the sound of all my hopes and dreams moving further and further away. Like listening to the sound of a door being slammed in my face.

THE HOSTAGE . . .

eighty-nine. Sephy

Funny the way things work out. When I first arrived at Chivers, I thought I'd made the biggest mistake of my life. I'd cry myself to sleep over what had been and what might've been, over Callum not wanting to leave with me, live with me. He didn't even bother to say goodbye. It took a long time to stop crying.

And shaking.

I didn't really believe I was drinking that much and I certainly wasn't an alcoholic, but after the second day of feeling wretched and wrung out, I finally realized I was suffering from alcohol withdrawal pains. The school nurse reckoned I had the flu and was very sympathetic, but I knew differently. It took three weeks before I could call my body my own again – and even then, I had to fight hard against the sudden cravings I got for a glass or two or three of wine or cider. So I buried myself in schoolwork and activities, the more physical the better. And it had slowly but surely begun to pay off.

Chivers is definitely the best move I could've made – under the circumstances. It gave me a chance to remake myself, start from scratch. I stopped hanging on to my childhood and started moving forward. I made new friends like Jacquelina and Robyn, who saved my sanity because they liked me for who I was, not for what my father did, or the money my mother had.

The schoolwork was harder than it'd been at Heathcroft, because at Chivers no-one pushed me, so I had to push myself. And I was terribly homesick for the first few months. I still get homesick if I allow myself to think about home for too long, but I don't allow that to happen any more – much. I spent the whole Crossmas holiday with Jacquelina and the Easter holiday skiing with Robyn. It was great. I talk to Mother on the phone of course, and she'd been up to see me a few times, but so far, I'd managed to stay away from home.

And I joined a dissident group. We were Crosses fighting for change in the system. But we had to be careful. We each made a pledge to do what we could – now and in the future – to further the cause of true integration between noughts and Crosses. I think we all felt that the only way we'd achieve real progress was to wait for all the old dogs to die so that us new dogs could replace them and their thinking. Old dogs like my father who couldn't see beyond the fact that noughts used to be our slaves. As far as he was concerned, they'd never be much good for anything else. The dissident group was the one thing that kept me focused when I was at Chivers. It was my reason for doing well, for succeeding. Our group kept me sane. It was a shame my sister didn't have something similar to believe in.

I used to comfort myself with the belief that it was only certain individuals and their peculiar notions that spoilt things for the rest of us. But how many individuals does it take before it's not the individuals who are prejudiced but society itself? And it wasn't even that most Crosses were prejudiced against noughts. I still didn't believe that. But everyone seemed to be too afraid to stand up in public and say 'this is wrong'. And, by everyone, I meant me included. No-one wanted to raise their head above the parapet. At least our group knew that the way things were was wrong. At least we were trying to do something about it – albeit from behind the scenes. We moved quietly but irrevocably, like a relentless army of tiny termites eating away at the rotten fabric of a house. And we would succeed. Each of us believed that, for the simple reason that we had to.

A few months after joining our group, I thought long and hard about asking Minnie to join us, but in the end I decided against it. Minnie's only got one more year at school and judging from the twice I've spoken to her, she's finding being at home difficult to say the least. She's determined to go to a university as far away from our home as she can get, but Mother cries or throws a tantrum or both if she even so much as mentions it. I'm glad I got out before her. Selfish but true.

According to Minnie, Mother's still drinking. I'm not. Even when some of the girls sneak the odd bottle or two into the dorm at night, I don't touch the stuff. I don't trust myself. It's very easy to hide away in a wine bottle, but very hard to come out again. Besides, that's part of my past too. I'm designing my future.

A future without Callum.

I've decided to be a lawyer. But I'm only going to work on those cases that I believe in. I'm going to be another

Kelani Adams. I'm going to stand up and speak out and I'll be so famous and popular that no one will be able to touch me. Not the government, not the P.E.C., no-one. It's great to finally have some direction to my life.

I admit that I think about Callum. Often. But I've stopped brooding and I've stopped yearning for the impossible. Maybe in another lifetime or in a parallel universe somewhere Callum and I could be together the way we should be. But not here. Not now.

And that's OK too. He's moved on with his life, and now so have I.

I wonder if he ever thinks of me? I doubt it, but just occasionally, when I'm doing my homework or washing my hair or cutting my toenails, I pause for a second or two and wonder.

But only for a second.

Or two.

ninety. Callum

My dad said something once about the Liberation Militia. He said that once they had you, they never let you go. I learnt exactly what he meant over the next couple of years. I started off as little more than the tea boy, but I was eager and keen. I soon worked my way up the ranks. I moved on from tea boy to grunt, following the orders of anyone and everyone in my cell of six men and three women. From grunt I moved on to private and on up the ranks until I earned the rank of sergeant and joined a new cell. Sergeant at nineteen — I was proud of that.

And whilst I was working my way up the L.M. ranks, I took the time to take care of some personal business. Namely, Dionne Fernandez, Lola Jordan and Joanne Longshadow — the ones at Heathcroft who'd beaten up Sephy for sitting with me, for being with me, for not knowing her place — which was kilometres above mine. With the contacts and resources now at my disposal it wasn't difficult to find out where they lived. I made it my business to find out all about them: their home lives, their family circumstances, their likes and dislikes — everything. If there's one thing that being in the L.M. taught me, it was that everyone had a weakness. You just had to know where and how to look for it.

I dealt with each of them in turn. Lola first, then Joanne. Dionne last, but by no means least. I took particular trouble to make sure that Dionne suffered — just as she'd made Sephy suffer. They say that revenge is a dish best served cold — and they're right. I served it icy-cold. And I lost more of myself as I did so. But that was OK. Because the Callum Ryan McGregor who loved to sit on the beach and watch the sun go down didn't exist any more. He'd been taken and I'd been left in his place. A poor trade, but an inevitable one.

In the new cell, there were four of us altogether. Pete, Morgan, Leila and me. Pete was in charge. We called him the quiet one. He didn't say much, but he smiled a lot. I was careful to watch my back around him. He was deadly with a knife and had at least four that I knew about always stashed on him somewhere. Morgan was twenty and the joker of the pack. He was our computer expert and the best driver in any L.M. cell for kilometres around. Leila was my age and knew everything there was to know about breaking into buildings and blowing stuff up. She'd been my call.

One evening, just a couple of months after my eighteenth birthday, I'd been sitting sipping a coffee outside a café in the city and surreptitiously timing the guards' movements in the glass-fronted office block opposite when I first spotted her.

It was one of those cafés which likes to pretend it's *très chic* by serving croissants at night and coffee that's all foam and no flavour – or liquid for that matter. The evening was quite chilly so apart from me, there were only three other men huddled at another table about two metres away from me.

Leila came over to me first.

'Spare some change for a coffee?'

I looked at her and shook my head. She moved on to the only other occupied table outside the café.

'Spare some change please?'

'Here's five quid.' One of the morons at the table waved it under her nose. 'What will you do for it?'

I turned to watch, interested to see what she'd do next.

'Well?' The man winked at his friends and continued to wave the money under Leila's nose.

I could tell from her tense stance that she was furiously angry, but the guy who was showing off to his mates was too thick-skinned to realize it. Or maybe he just didn't care? Leila lurched forward to try and snatch the money from the moron's hand, but he snatched it back.

'Come on, you tart! You can do better than that.'

'What did you call me?' Leila asked softly.

I moved my coffee to the other side of my table.

'If the shoe fits . . .' The moron laughed and his friends joined in.

'Stand up and I'll show you what I'll do for that fiver,' Leila said silkily.

And like a jackass the man stood up. Seconds later he was doubled over after Leila's foot made painful contact with his goodies.

'You were right. The shoe does fit!' Leila hissed at him, snatching the five pounds out of his unresisting fingers.

Moron number one collapsed to the floor, coughing his guts out. Morons two and three should've remained seated but they decided to go for it. Big mistake! It took less than fifteen seconds for Leila to sort out those two. By the time she'd finished, they were all rolling on the ground like human skittles.

I waved to one of the waiters inside the café who was watching the proceedings with horror.

He edged out, giving Leila a wide berth.

'My bill, please,' I told him. I turned to Leila. 'Would you like to have dinner with me?'

Leila spun around, belligerence all over her face. 'Are you talking to me?'

'Yes. Would you like a dinner – somewhere away from here though. The police will be here in about five minutes.'

She looked me up and down – and more than once

before she answered. 'Yeah, OK then.'

I glanced into the café but my waiter was taking his time. So guessing at the price then doubling it, I put my money down on the table. We strolled off down the road towards a good meat restaurant I knew. I'd been poor for too long to be a vegetarian. And as we walked along, Leila never said a word. When we got to the restaurant, she sat down on her chair poised to leap straight on to her feet if the situation demanded it.

'Two menus please,' I said to the waitress. 'I'm Callum,' I told my new companion, holding out my hand.

'Leila,' she replied, digging her hands deeper into her pockets.

And that was the beginning of our friendship. It'd taken me a while to get to know her but it was well worth the effort. She and I had a similar sense of humour – which always helps. I was the one who recommended that she be taken under our wing. She'd been on her own for a long time before she joined our cell, so she was ridiculously grateful at belonging to the L.M. So grateful that she suggested becoming my lover. It was a couple of months later when we were held up in one of our safe houses, waiting for Pete and Morgan to return from a reconnaissance trip.

'Thanks for the offer,' I told her. 'And I'm very, very flattered but I've only got room for one thing in my life now – and that's my work.'

'You're sure?' she asked.

I nodded. To my surprise, Leila put her hands on my shoulders and kissed me. It was nice too, but that's all it was.

'You're sure you won't change your mind?'

'I'm sure,' I smiled.

'Well, the offer is always open,' she shrugged.

'I'll remember that.'

And we'd both carried on cleaning our field guns. I didn't want to get involved. In fact, I didn't want any distractions, no matter how lovely they were – and Leila was lovely. She was as tall as me and super-fit with dark brown, short-cropped hair, cat-green eyes and a ready smile in spite of all the crap that'd happened to her. Of course, Morgan and Pete couldn't believe the fact that I'd turned her down. I heard the two of them discussing whether or not I batted for the other side. That made me laugh wryly, but I left them to wonder. Sometimes I felt lonely enough to take Leila up on her offer, but I never did. The last thing any of us needed were lovers' quarrels taking our minds off what we were meant to be doing.

So in a short space of time, I made quite a name for myself. I was known as the crazy one – the first one into danger and the last one out. Everyone in my cell was convinced I had nerves of steel. So much so that Pete had to take me to one side and tell me to take it a bit easier or I'd wind up dead. No-one realized that that was the whole point.

By the time I was nineteen, I'd gained my stripes – and lost my soul. But a soul was unnecessary in my line of work. To make it as a grunt I had to beat up a dagger. I ambushed one on his way home from work and knocked seven bells out of him. To prove myself as a private I had to take on three of them, but for that I was allowed to be armed. I had a knife and I'd been taught how to use it. I won that fight as well. And one of the daggers died later from his wounds. I waited for days to feel something, anything, but I never did. Confirmation, if I needed any, that I was dead inside.

And to become a sergeant . . . Well, it doesn't make any sense to dwell on it. I did what I had to do. I did the only thing I could do. I became one of the youngest sergeants in the whole of the Liberation Militia. Second-in-command of our well respected cell. One of the most respected. And one of the most wanted.

I missed my mum. I sent money to her whenever I could, but I never made any attempt to see her. It would've been too dangerous, for both of us. And I never posted the money from the same place twice either. In my line of work, there was no such thing as being too careful. Poor Mum! One way or another, she'd lost us all – through no fault of her own.

I never once saw my brother. I heard he was in charge of a cell further north. We never had any contact with each other. I was told not to expect any favours because I was Jude McGregor's brother and Ryan McGregor's son – and I didn't. I didn't expect anything. I didn't want anything. I didn't ask for anything – except complete loyalty from those in my cell. And absolute obedience the couple of times I had to take charge. And I got it too.

The police didn't know my identity, my real name. They didn't even know what I looked like, I was careful that way. They just had the codename of our cell – *Stiletto* – like the very sharp, very deadly dagger. Isn't that ironic?

My cell was never given anything too onerous to do, or too dangerous for that matter. We were more of an acquisitions cell than otherwise. Money, explosives, guns – you name it, we did what we had to do to get it. I was on my way up and nothing was going to get in my way. Nothing.

Our cause was just.

Our aim was true.

A couple of months after my nineteenth birthday, Pete received a direct order from L.M. command. They were sending a lieutenant to assess his cell's 'efficiency'.

'Efficiency, my left buttock!' Pete fumed. 'There's nothing wrong with my cell's efficiency.'

The rest of us could see the strop the message had put Pete in, from over five kilometres away and wisely kept our distance for the rest of the day. There was no word as to when we could expect this lieutenant and Pete was determined he or she wouldn't be able to fault any of our work or procedures. He made Leila go through our inventory with a fine-tooth comb to make sure that everything was accounted for. Pete went through our accounts himself, whilst Morgan and I grumbled like hell about having to clean our main headquarters in the tunnel complex beneath Celebration Park from top to bottom. We were holed up in the old access tunnels which were no longer used by anyone but the rats. We received reasonably fresh air from the ventilation grills still scattered throughout the park, but nothing we did got rid of the permanent sewer stench. To be honest, after a couple of weeks in the tunnels, I didn't even notice the smell any more. We weren't going to be in the tunnels for longer than a month or two, so there was no point in belly-aching about it. We all just got on with it. Morgan and I made sure each tunnel was secure and our warning devices on the grills were in place and working.

At last, when Pete was reasonably satisfied, we all sat down for our dinner – a take-away meal of burger and chips.

'Why isn't there anyone outside guarding the main entrance?'

I recognized that voice at once. I leapt up, shocked. 'What the hell are you doing here?'

'Unless you're in charge here, I'd sit down and shut up if I were you,' came the reply.

'I'm in charge,' Pete stood up slowly.

'You should've been expecting me. I'm your new lieutenant,' said my brother, Jude. 'And I asked you a question. Why is no-one outside guarding the main entrance?'

I sat down slowly, never taking my eyes off my brother. He turned and looked at me, his eyes burning into mine and I knew right then and there that he still didn't quite trust me. And that everyone in our cell was in danger because of it.

ninety-one. Sephy

It was time to go back home. I'd finished my end-of-year exams and the summer holidays had already started. And I didn't have to wait for the results to know that I'd passed all my subjects. So, as Mother had tersely pointed out, there was no reason for me not to go home. Except that I really didn't want to go back. Over two and a half years away from home and to be honest, I had no desire whatsoever to return. I'd dragged my feet for two weeks but August had started and Mother wasn't taking no for an answer. I'd run out of excuses. Mother and Minnie had been up to see me a few times – sometimes together, a few times apart, but somehow I'd always managed to avoid reciprocating. There was always something stopping me – a holiday with this friend, a long visit to that friend, the excuses had been trotted out one after another. Backpacking, camping, overseas expeditions, you name it, I went on them. Anything to keep me away from home. And I'd got away with it.

But not this time. Mother was putting her foot down and insisting. So I had no choice. If I'd had my way, I'd've been seventy not seventeen-going-on-eighteen when I returned home. I hated that place. So many bad memories. Too many.

Karl was sent to pick me up at Chivers. On the long drive home, we barely exchanged a word once the platitudes were over. He was fine, everyone in his family was fine, I was fine, school was fine – end of conversation! It was a long drive home!

Getting home was a bit of an anti-climax too. Minnie was spending the week with one of her friends and Mother was out on one of her rare visits to her Aunt Paulina and had left a message on our answering-machine saying that her car had broken down on the motorway so she'd be late getting home. To be honest, not meeting up with Mother immediately was a bit of relief. I still hadn't worked out how I was going to handle her. Should I be all sunshine and flowers and smile and take nothing seriously? Or should I be morose and sombre and take everything she said too seriously? Either way, there was no way I was going to stay put for more than a few days. I'd lined up a summer job with a law practice near to Chivers school and I had one week before I was due to start. One week. The new term didn't start until October and Mother was expecting me to stay for the rest of the summer break. Some hope.

'Welcome home, Miss Sephy,' Sarah hugged me as she emerged from the study. I hugged her back.

'It's good to see you, Sarah,' I smiled.

Sarah looked around quickly. 'A certain someone found out that you were due home today and he left a message for you.'

She whipped out a folded brown envelope from her pocket and stuffed it into my hand. Without another word, Sarah disappeared back into the study. No need to ask who it was from. I recognized the handwriting on the envelope at once. My heart bounced about at the mere sight of it. What did he want, after all this time? I should just put the letter in the bin. Yeah, right! In another lifetime maybe. I tore open the carefully sealed letter and began to read.

Dear Sephy,

I know it's been a long time since we last met and you probably don't even remember me any more. But if you do, please could we meet tonight around nine o'clock at our special place. It's very important. But I'll understand if you can't make it. Two, almost three years is a long time. A lifetime.

   C.

Why did he want to see me? Why was it important? All the feelings I thought I'd bundled up and thrown away years ago suddenly came rushing through me again. Did I really want to see him again? It didn't take much intuition to realize that Callum was the one person who could upset my carefully constructed plans for what I wanted to do with the rest of my life. Look at this! One letter and I was already confused and uncertain about what I should do next.

No! I wouldn't do it. Callum had his life now and I had mine and they were worlds apart. But I hadn't seen him in such a long time. And what harm could a short ten-minute meeting do? I was a big girl now! Not a child any more. I'd go and say hello and we'd pass the time by catching up with each other's lives and then we'd part on better terms than happened years ago. Where was the harm in that?

Don't go, Sephy . . .

Where's the harm in that?

Don't go . . .

Where's the harm?

Don't . . .

ninety-two. Callum

'Is everyone clear about what they're supposed to do?' Jude asked.

Nods and grunts and a low-pitched, grumbled 'Yeah! How many more times?'

'She might not even come,' I warned.

'If she got your message, she'll come,' Jude announced. He gave me an assessing look. 'What about you, little brother? You up for this?'

'Why wouldn't I be?' I asked, pulling on my black leather jacket.

'We need to know we can count on you, on your loyalty,' said Jude.

Everyone stopped what they were doing. The room grew very still. I regarded my brother, not attempting to disguise my hostility.

'Meaning?'

Jude looked at me, but he didn't say anything.

I looked around. 'Which one of you doubts my loyalty then?'

Silence.

'I'm glad to hear it,' I said.

'You let us down, and I'm going to forget you're my brother. Understand?' said Jude.

I didn't deign to answer. My brother could go rivet himself.

'This is going to make us famous,' said Morgan as he and Pete slapped hands in gleeful anticipation.

'And rich!' Jude grinned. 'Just think about all that lovely money we're going to be able to add to the Liberation Militia's coffers.'

'Come to Papa!' Morgan laughed, rubbing his hands together.

'And if this comes off,' Jude said to Pete, 'you'll be able to write your own ticket. You'll be able to set up your own L.M. division anywhere in the country.'

'Sounds good to me,' Pete smiled.

It was the first smile he'd directed at my brother. The promise of a bigger and better army to lead had sweetened him up no end and all his resentment about being usurped by Jude seemed to have melted away.

'Let's not count our chickens,' I said brusquely.

'Ever the voice of doom, eh?' Jude smiled. 'If you do your part, nothing will go wrong. Nothing.'

ninety-three. Sephy

I took off my sandals and headed for the moonlit water. I couldn't remember when I'd felt more at peace with myself. I'd finally got a lot of things straight in my head.

Like Dad. For him, his political career came first, last and every number in between. Dad was never going to have any time for me and my sister and my mother. The only reason we'd been around at all was because a 'stable' family was a necessary, compulsory adjunct for a politician. And that was OK. That was the life Dad had chosen for himself and my days of pining about it were over.

I shifted my heels, then toes, to stop my feet from sinking into the wet sand. I kicked up the water lapping over my feet and ankles, watching it fly up and out in an arc of silvery droplets. Laughing, I did it again and again, alternating kicking feet, delighting in my childish game. And then I thought of my mother, and the game stopped.

Mother. I'd always be a disappointment to her. That was never going to change. I was simply not enough. Not ladylike enough, not smart enough, not pretty enough. Not enough. And that was OK too. Her life was her major disappointment, her mistakes carved into every premature line in her face, but I wasn't going to let her use my life as her second chance. I had plans. In September I'd be eighteen years old and I had my whole life and the whole world in front of me. A world full of choices and decisions and opportunities – and they were all mine for the taking.

And as for Callum and me? Well, I didn't want the moon. I was prepared to settle for friendship between us. It would never be the way it was years ago and it'd never be the way I wanted it to be, but maybe we could find something new to take the place of what we had before. Maybe.

I glanced at my watch, wondering where Callum had

got to. I turned, almost as if thinking about Callum would conjure him up. I gasped. Callum was standing right behind me, his appearance so sudden that he might've been a ghost, able to appear and disappear at will. And he looked so different. He'd shot up like a beanstalk. He was lean now, rather than skinny. He'd definitely sprouted muscles! And his dark cords and leather jacket made him look . . . mysterious somehow. His hair was longer too, almost shoulder-length. It suited him. Everything about him seemed different. Callum the boy had disappeared and in his place . . . I smiled, chiding myself. It was as if I'd expected time to stand still for him. I'm glad it hadn't though! Had I changed as much? I guess I must've.

'Good sneaking!' I congratulated him with a wry smile.

Slipping on my sandals, I stepped forward, my arms outstretched for a hug. I expected a similar jovial reply in greeting, but he didn't even smile. And even in this light, I could tell something was wrong. My arms dropped to my sides.

'Callum?'

Callum stepped forward and kissed me. A brief, icy-cold kiss on the lips. He stepped away from me, his eyes filled with regret. And then I saw them behind him. Four of them. Four noughts. Walking towards us. Towards me. A quick glance at Callum. Shock on my face. Confirmation, resignation on his. And I didn't wait to see any more. I turned and ran. Ran along the shore. Away from them. Away from Callum. Ran for my life. I could hear them yelling behind me. Not the words. I didn't try to decipher the words.

Run, Sephy. Don't stop . . .

No sounds of footsteps on the sand. Just shouts and curses and laboured breathing. No lights to guide my way. Even the moonlight was fading as a cloud hid the moon's face from me. Salty, damp air caught in the back of my throat. Run. *Run*. RUN.

Don't look back . . . They'll catch you if you do . . . Don't look . . .

And most of all, don't think. Don't think about *him*. Don't think about anything. JUST RUN.

And then I realized my mistake. I was kilometres from anywhere. And I was running away from the cliff steps, not towards them. And I had four noughts after me . . . Five.

Head for the sea . . .

I turned on my heels and sprinted towards the darkness. Before my third step, I was grabbed by the waist and swung around. I kicked back with my heels and swung my head back at the same time.

'Oof!'

He dropped me and I hit the ground running.

'Bloody dagger bitch!'

I ran straight into a crucifying punch to my stomach that had me instantly doubled over and retching onto the sand.

'That's for my sister,' a voice above me said. At least I think it did. My stomach was on fire and all I wanted to do was curl up in a ball. Arms clamped around my waist from behind and lifted me up, tightening until I could hardly breathe. The man who held me shook me hard then banged me down onto my feet. Without giving me a chance to catch my scattered breath, he immediately began to drag me backwards, his hands under my arms.

My bare heels dragged over sharp rocks and stones. I raised my arms to try and slide out of the man's grasp. But he was ready for that one. My arms slid down his but he grabbed my hands before I could free myself and now I was being pulled backwards by my hands. My legs and my back were being punctured by the rocks and stones. The man holding me jumped up onto a boulder, almost pulling my arms out of their sockets as he dragged me after him. My whole body was pain now. Closing my eyes, I whimpered.

Don't pass out! Open your eyes . . .

I opened my eyes to see the moon almost directly above me and just for one split second my body no longer hurt. Then a dark bag was shoved over my head and the world turned to blackest ink.

ninety-four. Callum

'We did it!' Jude was jubilant. 'We ruddy DID it!'

Pete and Morgan danced an impromptu jig around each other. Yes, we had done it. We had Persephone Hadley, Kamal Hadley's daughter. And she wouldn't see the light of day again if Kamal didn't agree to our demands. As simple as that. We'd bundled the unconscious Sephy into the boot of our car and now we had her stashed away where no-one would ever find her – or us. We were in the middle of nowhere — the perfect location. Weren't we clever?

'I'm proud of you, little brother.' Jude slapped me on the back.

I spun, grabbed his jacket and shoved him against the wall, all in one movement.

'Don't you ever doubt my loyalty again. D'you understand me?' I hissed, my face only centimetres away from Jude's.

Out of the corner of my eye I saw Morgan step forward, only to be pulled back by Pete. I didn't care. I'd take on all of them to get to Jude if I had to. My brother and I watched each other for silent moments.

'D'you understand?' I repeated, slamming him against the wall again.

'I understand,' Jude said.

I released him at once. We regarded each other.

'So the mouse can roar, can he?' Jude smiled.

I took a step forward, my fists clenched.

'Peace, brother. Peace.' Jude held up his hands, laughing at the expression on my face.

I clenched my fists even harder at that. Never before had I wanted to hurt him as much as I did now. I wanted to *destroy* him. Hatred churned inside me, feeding on itself and growing bigger.

'You did a good job,' Jude told me softly.

I turned away from the approbation on his face. Morgan, Pete and even Leila had the same look of praise and admiration all over their stupid faces too.

'What's our next move?' Pete asked Jude, all past resentments forgotten.

'We deliver the ransom note with proof we have her to the girl's father,' Jude replied.

'What kind of proof?' I asked more sharply than I intended.

'What would you suggest, little brother?'

Another test. 'I'll sort that out. I'll cut off some of her hair and film her holding today's paper.'

'Maybe we need something more convincing than just her hair?' Jude suggested.

Another test.

'What did you have in mind?'

'You tell me, little brother.'

I made my mind go blank. It wasn't Sephy in there. It was just some Cross female who we needed to get what we wanted. It wasn't Sephy . . .

'Something of hers that's bloodstained might be more effective,' I suggested.

'Good idea.' Jude nodded. 'What would you suggest?'

'Leave it to me. I'll sort that out too.' I took the camcorder down from the shelf and put a fresh disc inside it. A strange silence filled the room. I looked up to find all eyes upon me.

'Yes?' I said through gritted teeth.

Everyone made a big display of going about their business at that. I took some scissors and a sharp knife out of the drawer and, tucking today's paper under my arm, I headed for Sephy's prison cell. I walked along the short corridor of our three-room brick cabin. It wasn't much. The kitchen was disgusting, with years of neglected grease and grime over practically every surface. Jude had suggested that someone clean it, looking pointedly at Leila as he said so. In response, she'd let her fingers do the talking. Apart from the kitchen there was the living room, full of rolled-up sleeping bags, a small oak table and all the equipment we might need in a hurry: tins of food, weapons, a few explosives, a small TV, a radio, that sort of thing. The third room had been turned into a cell. Not by us. That was just what this place was used for, a place to hold a prisoner or two and their wardens.

Ever since the information had filtered down over two weeks ago now that Sephy could be on her way home, Jude and Pete had been plotting and planning for this moment. They'd got permission from the General himself to go ahead. And the General's second-in-command was due to come and see us the day after it happened. So much scheming and calculating to bring us to this moment. We were pretty safe in this cabin; it was known to a select few on a need to know basis only. But we weren't going to take any chances. Two of us would be on guard at all times, one out front and one out back. And as the cabin was in a clearing in some woods, anyone coming towards us would find themselves without cover of any kind before they reached us.

Everything was taken care of.

And we'd succeeded. We had Sephy. NO! Not Sephy . . . Just a Cross girl – who deserved everything she got, who'd get us everything we needed. I paused outside the cell door. I could do this. I had to do this.

Be what you have to be, Callum, not what you are . . .

I repeated that phrase over and over in my head, the way I used to do when I first joined the L.M. The way I had to whenever there was something . . . distasteful that needed to be done.

Be what you have to be, Callum, not what you are.

I unlocked the cell door and went inside.

ninety-five. Sephy

At the sound of the door being unlocked, I struggled to sit up. My bed was just a wire spring base with a mattress as thin as a carrier bag. I groaned and winced, wrapping my arms around my painful stomach. It ached like nothing I'd ever felt before. My whole body hurt, from my heels to my nape. Had they tried to strangle me? My throat certainly hurt as if someone had done exactly that. The door opened. I moved my hands away from my abdomen. I wasn't going to show any of my captors how badly hurt I was.

Callum . . .

The sight of him standing in the doorway was like an arrow whizzing straight through my body. He wasn't the Callum I'd grown up with and I'd been an idiot to think he would be. It had all been a trick. A trap. And like the biggest fool in the universe, I'd fallen for it. He took a step towards me. Afraid, I drew back. For a briefest of seconds, I thought he flinched. But I was just imagining things. He couldn't care less how I thought of him.

He came over to me. I drew back even further. What

was he going to do? It was only when he was leaning over me that I noticed the scissors in his hands. I trembled, terrified, then clamped my teeth together hard in an effort to stop myself from shaking.

Whatever happens, don't cry. Don't beg.

As Callum's hands touched my hair, I froze. I looked up at him without even blinking. I couldn't even wonder what he was doing. My mind was shutting down. Then I heard the clip of the scissors and Callum moved away. Only then did I look away, my body slumping with such relief that I felt sick with it. My hand flew to my head. He'd cut off some of my hair. That was all. Just some of my hair.

'I want you to hold this newspaper,' Callum told me.

His voice was different. Deeper. Gruffer. And I'd missed it. I'd missed a lot of things.

'Why?' I asked.

'I need to film you holding today's paper.'

That wasn't what I was asking.

'I'm not going to help you.' I folded my arms across my chest. No way was I going to hold that paper or do anything else he told me to do.

Two other noughts appeared behind Callum in the doorway. With a start, I saw that one of them was a woman, not the man I'd thought her on the beach.

'Hold that paper or we'll break your arms and arrange them in such a way that you'll have no choice,' the man behind Callum hissed at me.

Callum turned to look at him. I'd seen him somewhere before, if I could just figure out . . .

'I don't need you standing over me, supervising,' Callum fumed.

'Not supervising. Just observing, little brother.'

And only then did I recognize him. Jude, Callum's brother.

'Nothing like keeping kidnapping in the family, is there?' I told them.

'Hold the newspaper, Sephy,' Callum held it out for me.

Reluctantly I took it. Callum lifted up his camcorder, only to lower it again immediately.

'Look, I don't need an audience,' Callum told the spectators.

'I've come to see the daughter of the famous Kamal Hadley,' the woman replied. 'Let's see the silver spoon then.'

I regarded her, trying not to cringe at the venom in her voice. Without knowing a single thing about me, she hated my guts. I was a Cross and that was all she wanted or needed to know.

'I bet you've never had more to worry about in your life than chipping the odd fingernail,' the woman hissed at me.

'Leila, go and do your job. Guard the front,' Jude told her.

Casting one last poisonous look at me, Leila did as directed. I'd have to be careful of that one. She wouldn't spit on me if I was on fire. None of them would.

'I want you to read out that message for your father,' Callum told me, handing me a piece of paper with my lines on it. He held up the camcorder to watch the preview screen. I glanced down at the sheet. If he thought I was going to say any of this then he was crazy. I scrunched it up and threw it across the room.

'Dad, don't give them a penny,' I shouted.

Callum lowered the camcorder but before he could say a word, Jude flew across the room, grabbed hold of both my jacket lapels with just one hand and slapped my face, before shaking me viciously.

'You're not in control here. We are. And you will do as you're told or you won't leave this place alive. D'you understand?'

I rubbed my cheek, fighting to hold back the tears.

'You will do *exactly* as you are told or I will make this place your hell on earth. None of us are going to take any of your crap,' Jude said softly.

He let go of me so suddenly I fell backwards onto the bed, hitting my head against the brick wall behind me. Jude straightened up and headed out of the room, pausing briefly as he reached Callum.

'Make sure she does as she's told,' he said, making sure I could hear.

Moments later he was gone.

I wondered about making a break for it but Callum was between me and the door, plus from the sound of it the front door was guarded by that girl, Leila. And Jude wouldn't hesitate to take me down if he reckoned it was required. I had to bide my time. If only my head would stop ringing so that I could think straight. If only my stomach would stop hurting so I could at least sit up without pain. If only . . . if only . . .

I had to get him talking. I had to get him to remember me, remember us as we used to be. I had to get him to think of me again as a fellow human being with a name and thoughts and feelings, instead of the nothing I obviously was to him now.

'Callum, I understand why you feel you have to do this,' I began. 'I really do. But this isn't the way.'

Nothing.

But I wasn't going to give up. 'Callum, listen to me. At Chivers I became involved in protests and debates and sit-ins. If you try to change the world using violence, you'll just swap one form of injustice for another. This isn't right. There are other ways . . .'

'Like what? Like being educated to fight the system from within?' Callum challenged. 'I tried that – remember?'

'I know, but if you'd just give it another try . . . I could help you . . .'

'I don't want to hear it. And I don't want your ruddy help. I'm sick of your charity and your handouts,' he interrupted. 'You're just like all the others. You think we noughts can't do a damned thing unless you Crosses are there to help or supervise.' And his body shook with such rage that I had to force myself to continue.

'Don't hate me for wanting to change the way things are. I believe in you, Callum. You can change the world, I know you can. But not like this,' I said. 'I'm not trying to be magnanimous or patronizing. I genuinely want to help but . . .'

'Enough! Hold up the newspaper and read the words on this,' Callum ordered, handing me the now smoothed-out sheet of paper again. I looked up at Callum.

'Read it,' he said, his attention on the camcorder and nothing else.

'Callum, please . . .'

'READ IT.'

After a moment's pause, I began to read.

ninety-six. Callum

'Dad,

I've been ordered to read what's on this sheet. I've been kid-napped and the kidnappers say you'll never see me again unless you do exactly as instructed. Your instructions will be in the envelope along with this video disc. You have twenty-four hours to follow their instructions to the letter. If you don't, I'll . . . I'll be k-killed. If you go to the police or tell anyone, I'll be killed. The kidnappers will know every move you make and every person you talk to. If you ever want to see me alive again, please do as they say.'

Sephy looked up from her sheet of paper, tears trickling down her cheeks. I moved my hand up to indicate that she should lift up the newspaper. She did so at once. I zoomed into the paper so there could be no doubt about the date, then I moved to zoom into Sephy's face. She quickly wiped her eyes with the back of her hand. She wasn't looking at the camcorder. She was looking at me. I switched off the camcorder.

'That ought to do it.' I took the newspaper from

Sephy's unresisting hand. I looked her up and down critically. 'What're you wearing?'

'Pardon?'

'You heard me.'

Puzzled, Sephy said, 'Trousers, a jacket, a jumper.'

'Tell me everything you're wearing,' I ordered.

Silence.

'I can always find out for myself,' I threatened.

'Sandals, jeans, knickers, watch, bra, T-shirt, jumper, necklace, jacket, earrings. Satisfied?'

'Take off your T-shirt.'

'No way.'

'Take off your T-shirt or I'll do it for you.'

Sephy gave me a long, hard, fearful look. She obviously decided I was serious, which I was, because she started to take off her jacket.

'Are you going to kill me, Callum?'

'Don't be ridiculous!' I closed my eyes and turned away so Sephy couldn't see my face. Why couldn't she just shut up? Why did it have to be her? I thought I could do this . . .

'I never realized just how much you and your family hate us,' Sephy whispered. 'Jude looked at me like he wanted to kill me just now. Why does he hate me so much? Is it me personally or just what I am?'

I didn't answer. I squatted down to pack the camcorder back into its holdall as she carried on undressing.

'I'm not stupid, you know,' Sephy said wearily, taking off her jumper. 'None of you are wearing masks or disguising your voices. I could identify each and every one of you, but you don't care. Which means only one thing.

You have no intention of letting me go, even if my father gives in to all your demands.'

My head shot up at that.

We regarded each other as Sephy continued. 'One of you is going to kill me. It's just a question of when . . . and who.' She pulled her T-shirt over her head and threw it down on the floor. 'W-what now?' she asked.

'You can put the rest of your clothes back on,' I told her, picking up the T-shirt.

As she pulled on her jumper, I tried not to stare, I really did. But her body had changed so much in the years we'd been apart. She had breasts now! Her purple lace bra just emphasised them rather than hid them. And her waist went in, instead of straight down, and her stomach was flatter and her legs were longer and her face had lost its baby fat – and she was so very, very beautiful. I turned away as Sephy pushed her head through the neck of her jumper. I didn't want her to catch me staring.

'If your father does as he's told, you'll be OK . . .'

'OK? Like I'm OK now?' Sephy scoffed. 'Come on, Callum, this is your chance to really take your revenge. Don't you want to get your own back for all those times you had to put up with me on the beach? And all those years pretending to be my friend, just praying for this moment.'

Shut up! Shut up . . . Ignore her, Callum. Just ignore her. Put a strait-jacket on your feelings. Don't let her see how much she's getting to you . . .

'What about the night we spent together in my room?' she asked. 'Didn't that mean anything to you?'

'You mean, the couple of days before you murdered my father?' I asked, harshly.

'Your father died trying to escape . . .'

'My father chose to die because he didn't want to spend the rest of his life in prison for something he didn't do.'

Sephy's gaze lowered briefly. She looked up again and said, 'I didn't murder your father, Callum. I didn't want him to die.'

'You and your kind killed him,' I told her, zipping up the camcorder case.

'So you *are* going to kill me. But not you personally, I bet,' Sephy's voice trembled. 'That's not your style, is it? You set me up so your friends could capture me. You're real good at letting others do your dirty work for you.'

I spun around at that. 'You wouldn't be the first dagger I've killed. Not by a long shot.'

'And I'd be easy to kill, wouldn't I?' Sephy said quietly. ''Cause I don't count. I'm nothing. Just a black dagger bitch. Just like you're a white blanker bastard.'

And now I was furiously angry. Just like I'd wanted to be before I could do what I had to do next. I grabbed her left hand and before she could pull away, I drew my knife across her index finger. Sephy gasped, tears instantly springing to her eyes. And my anger died with such a suddenness that I knew it hadn't been real to begin with. Manufactured to get me through the moment. The day. My life.

'Sorry . . .' I mumbled, wrapping her T-shirt around her finger. I concentrated on getting her blood on to the T-shirt. I didn't look at her. I couldn't. The white cotton of her shirt soaked up the blood like blotting paper. I unwrapped the shirt and dragged her still bleeding finger up and down it. The final proof for her father that we were deadly serious. The final proof that we were deadly. Sephy kept trying to pull her hand back but I wouldn't let her.

'I bet you enjoyed that,' Sephy hissed at me.

'No, I didn't,' I snapped back, letting go of her wrist at last.

Sephy put her finger into her mouth, wincing as the wound stung anew. She took her finger out of her mouth to look at it. It was still bleeding. The cut was deep – for both of us. Deeper than I'd intended. A scratch would've been deeper than I intended. She went to put her finger back in her mouth but I grabbed her hand again. She struggled, trying to pull her hand away. Maybe she thought I was going to cut her again. I put her finger in my mouth. And she was instantly still. I don't know how long we sat there, watching each other. A second? An hour? Sephy moved first. She slowly pulled back her finger.

'When you all decide you don't need me any more,' Sephy whispered, 'I want *you* to . . . do it. One favour though. It's the last thing I'll ever ask you. J–just make it quick. OK?' And she turned around and lay down on her side of the bed, her back towards me.

I stared at her back, my fists clenched, reining myself in so tightly, I thought my back would snap. Only when I could trust myself to stand without falling to the floor did I get up. I left the room, carefully locking the door behind me. I leaned against the door, my eyes closed. I had to do this, make it through this. And I would. I turned to walk back to the living room, only to find my brother further down the corridor, watching my every move.

'Yes?' I asked, annoyed.

Everywhere I turned at the moment, Jude seemed to be watching me.

'Give me the disc.'

I handed over the T-shirt and Sephy's hair before taking out the camcorder. I opened it up, took out the video disc and put it in its case before handing it over.

Jude held it up carefully, before slipping it into his pocket. He looked long and hard at the T-shirt. When at last he looked at me, his grin was full of admiration and relief. 'Now I know for sure whose side you're on. Well done, little brother. Pete and I are going to deliver all this as well as our demands. Leila and Morgan will guard the house. Sephy Hadley is your responsibility. Understand?'

I didn't answer. It was unheard of for the first- and second-in-command to go off on a joint mission together like this. Why wasn't Jude going with Morgan? Or Pete going with me? Why did Jude want to be with Pete? There was something going on here . . .

'We should be back by morning,' Jude continued. 'If the General's second-in-command arrives before we get back, make him welcome – after he's given you the password.'

'Which is?'

'Golden Man.'

Jude went to move past me. I stood back against the wall to let him go. Jude was my brother but I trusted him less far than an elephant could jump. More than ever I sensed the need to watch my back, my front, my sides and every other part of me – if I wanted to keep them in one piece, that is.

ninety-seven. Sephy

The door opened again. I didn't even bother turning around this time. I lay on my side facing the wall. Rubbing my sore hand over my aching stomach, I fervently wished the pain away.

'Dinner,' came Callum's rough voice.

I ignored him and carried on rubbing my stomach, waiting for the sound of the door closing. It didn't come. Callum's footsteps echoed across the hard cement floor. I stopped rubbing my stomach at once, but I still didn't turn around. Callum put his hand on my shoulder and pulled me round to face him.

'Dinner.'

He thrust the plastic plate into my hands. I sat up and after firing a lasering look in his direction, I threw the plate across the room. It hit the wall with a thud and the plate fell first, followed by a brown sticky mess trickling its way down the wall towards the floor.

'You shouldn't've done that.'

I deliberately turned away from him and lay down again. Silence. But I wasn't going to turn around to see what he was doing. After a short while, I heard him cross the room and leave, locking the door behind him.

He never forgot to lock the door.

ninety-eight. Callum

If I could just stop thinking for five seconds then I could get some shut-eye. But it wasn't happening. And the sleeping bag seemed to twist in the opposite direction to whichever way I turned. I couldn't get Sephy's words out of my head.

One of you is going to kill me . . .

But we didn't have to do that. OK so she'd seen us, but once her dad met our demands we could be long gone. But even as I thought it, I knew I was just deluding myself.

One of you is going to kill me . . .

'You look like you could use some company.' Leila's voice above me was the last straw. I opened my eyes, giving up all pretence of trying to sleep.

'Who's guarding the front?'

'I came in for a loo break – if that's all right with you.'

I unzipped my bag and sat up. 'No, it's not OK with me. You want to take a leak, do it in the woods, but don't leave the front of the cabin unmonitored.'

'I'm not a man,' Leila protested. 'I can't wee standing up.'

'That's no excuse.'

'Callum, you're mad as hell at something, but don't take it out on mc.'

I pulled on my T-shirt. 'I don't know what you're talking about.'

'You don't have to get dressed on my account,' Leila said silkily, running her hands lightly over my chest.

'Go and guard the front like you're supposed to,' I told her.

Leila stood up. 'Suit yourself. D'you know, I think that's why I like you.' At my puzzled look she explained. 'You're the only man I know who hasn't tried to get on my good side in five seconds flat!'

I smiled. 'Nothing personal, Leila.'

'Thanks!' She raised an eyebrow. 'That makes it worse!'

I got to my feet as she left the room. Pulling on my boots, I decided to hunt down a beer and join Morgan out back. Without warning, there was a sudden commotion out front. I ran towards the front door when it burst open. For one split second, I thought we'd been rumbled, that the police had somehow tracked us down. But it wasn't the police. It was Leila and a stranger. He was as tall as me, with blond hair tied back in a pony-tail. He wore a dark polo shirt and expensive brown trousers tucked into fancy boots. His long, dark trenchcoat had the collar turned up and flapped open like a cloak or a cape. The peculiar thing was, the stranger had Leila in an armlock, not the other way round. Morgan came running up behind me.

'Who's in charge here?' the stranger asked.

Morgan looked at me. I didn't take my eyes off the intruder. The stranger turned to me. 'I see that you are. I believe you've been expecting me.'

'Let me go!' Leila hissed, trying to twist away from the man who held her.

The man pushed her forward – hard. She only just kept her balance. She spun around, arms raised, ready to take him out. The man raised one hand.

'I wouldn't if I were you,' was all he said. But it was enough.

A second or two later, Leila dropped her hands.

'So this is the famous *Stiletto* unit, is it?' The man looked at each of us in turn. 'So far, I'm not very impressed.'

'We've been expecting you, have we?' Morgan said.

'That's right.'

'What's the password then?' I asked.

'You first,' the man ordered.

I regarded him. 'I don't think so. You're the guest here, not us.'

I signalled to Morgan behind my back to get ready. We'd been caught on the hop but there were three of us and only one of him.

'How about Gold Man?' said the stranger.

'Not even close.' Morgan and I started forward.

'Then how about Golden Man,' the stranger laughed.

I regarded the man with undisguised venom. I didn't like to be made a fool of and that was precisely what he was doing.

'Hi. I'm Andrew Dorn.' He held out his hand.

After a moment's pause I took it, still on my guard.

'You're the General's second–in–command?' Morgan said sceptically.

'Yeah. D'you want to make something of it?' asked Andrew.

'Only asking,' Morgan shrugged. 'Excuse me. I'm on guard duty.'

With a brief nod of his head, Morgan turned and headed for the back door. Leila followed his cue by heading out the front, still rubbing her upper arm where Andrew had twisted it behind her back.

'Congratulations on the success of the first part of your mission,' Andrew told me when the others had gone. 'Let's hope the rest runs as smoothly.'

'No reason why it shouldn't.'

'No reason at all,' Andrew agreed.

'Want some coffee?'

'Wouldn't say no. Can I see the prisoner first?'

I opened my mouth to say that she was probably asleep, but I managed to snap it shut in time. We moved along the hall to the door. I dug into my trouser pocket for the key and unlocked it. Sephy was sitting up on her bed, facing the door. She regarded both Andrew and me without saying a word.

'I hope for your sake that your father loves you very, very much,' Andrew told her.

Sephy stared at him, frowning. I saw her glance down at Andrew's boots, then start. I glanced down at Andrew's boots myself. They were brown with silver chains just above the heel of each one. A bit too ostentatious for my taste but nothing special. So what was it about them that had caused such a reaction?

'Be a good girl and you'll soon be out of here,' Andrew told her.

And still Sephy didn't speak. If anything, her frown deepened. Andrew left without another word. I followed him out, locking the door behind me.

'Make sure she doesn't leave that room alive,' Andrew said quietly. 'Orders from the General himself. Understood?'

The ground started rocking beneath my feet. 'Understood, sir. I'll take care of it myself.'

'Good man. Make sure you do.' Andrew headed towards the kitchen.

I stood totally still, waiting for the earth to stop moving.

ninety-nine. Sephy

The moment Callum locked me in again, I carried on exploring my room. A forty-watt bulb gave the only light in the room. There were no windows and the locked door could've been reinforced steel for all the good it did me. The floor was cement and the walls were bricks and plaster. I thought again about shouting for help but logic told me that we had to be kilometres away from anyone who could help me, otherwise they would've tied me up and put a gag in my mouth. I tapped my way around the walls, not really sure what I was listening for, but listening for some change of note, a hollow sound that could rekindle some hope within me.

But there was nothing.

That man who'd come in with Callum . . . I'd seen him

somewhere before. I knew I had and yet I couldn't quite place him. It was frustrating the hell out of me. I pulled the bed away from the wall. It dragged across the floor with enough noise to wake the dead. I stopped at once and listened. I couldn't hear anyone coming. I moved the bed more slowly. Was there anything behind it that could help me?

What was that scratched into the plaster behind the bed?

To my fellow Crosses, keep the faith.

The writing was jagged and uneven. From the look of it, it could've been written with a fingernail. *Keep the faith* . . . God knows there was little else to do in this hell-hole.

There was nothing in the room, apart from the bed with its one blanket and a bucket in the opposite corner. And short of standing behind the door and using the bucket to brain the first person who came in, there was nothing in the room I could use as a weapon of any kind.

Keep the faith . . .

I pushed the bed back and lay down again. I wondered what my family were doing at that moment – Minnie and Mother and Dad. Did Dad know that I'd been kidnapped yet? I hadn't seen him in almost six months. How would he take the news? How much money did the kidnappers want anyway? How much was I worth to them? Maybe they didn't want money. Maybe they were after something else, like the release of L.M. prisoners or something like that. I didn't even know. How long ago was it that I hadn't wanted to go home? A day? Two? It was hard to tell how long I'd been in this place.

A strange joke. I hadn't wanted to be at home and now

I'd got my wish. I would've given my right arm to see my family one more time. Just once more. And with that thought I knew that I'd given up on any chance of seeing any of them, ever again.

one hundred. Callum

'We interrupt this programme to bring you a newsflash.'

We sat forward, all eyes on the telly. The atmosphere in the room was edgy as we waited to hear. I glanced at my watch. Kamal Hadley appeared at seven o'clock precisely, just as he'd been instructed.

'I am here to announce that I shall be temporarily withdrawing from public office for personal family reasons,' Kamal announced. 'I don't wish to say anything further at this time. Thank you.'

And then he was out of the press office like a rat up a drainpipe. Jude punched the air.

'Yes! He's agreed to our demands.'

'I don't trust him,' I said, still watching the telly as the newsreader discussed Kamal Hadley's surprise announcement with the channel's political correspondent.

'I don't trust any of them,' Jude replied. 'But we've got him over a barrel – and he knows it.'

It was a crisp early autumn evening: the perfect evening to pick up our ransom money and let Kamal Hadley know we had further demands before he could see his daughter. At least, that's how Jude had described it. The money would fund future L.M. activities but Sephy wouldn't see her dad again until five L.M. members had been released from prison. The authorities didn't realize that three of the five we wanted released were key members, not just the underlings they thought they were.

'You're all ready for the telephone relay?' Andrew asked.

'Of course,' Jude frowned. 'We've been through it a dozen times. Leila will stay here with the girl. Pete, Morgan and I make our relay phone calls from three different locations around town to stop them tracing the calls. Callum will drop off the second set of instructions, pick up our money and head straight back here. It's all arranged.'

'And you'll each be in your proper places at the right times?' asked Andrew.

'Of course.' Jude was getting annoyed now and not doing a very good job of hiding it. 'This isn't amateur hour, you know. We know what we're doing.'

'Good! Good! But I think it'd be better if Leila makes the pick-up,' said Andrew. 'That's always the most dangerous part of a kidnapping and as a girl she's more likely to go unnoticed.'

'Then I'll go in Pete's place and make one of the phone calls,' I volunteered.

'No. Of all of us, you're the one Hadley knows the best. We can't take any chances of him recognizing your voice,' Andrew said at once.

'I'm not staying here,' I said furiously. 'I'm not a ruddy babysitter.'

'You're needed here,' Jude told me.

'Why can't Andrew stay behind and look after her?' I asked.

'Because I'm off to another part of the country,' Andrew replied. 'And I'm here as an observer, not to do your dirty work for you.'

'You'll have to forgive my brother,' Jude smiled uneasily. 'He's still very young.'

'I'm not staying here,' I protested.

'You'll do as you're told,' Jude rounded on me.

I was embarrassing Jude in front of the General's second-in-command. I'd get it in the neck for that when they all got back.

'You're staying here and that's final.'

Reluctantly I kept quiet, but my outraged scowl told them all what I thought of that idea.

'Let's go, people. And remember to keep your eyes and ears open at all times,' said Andrew. 'Never underestimate the daggers. A lot of our members made that mistake and they're either languishing in prison or swinging at the end of a rope because of it. I'll be keeping a close eye on your situation. A very close eye.'

They all headed out of the door with me trailing miserably behind them.

Andrew turned to me. 'If the police or anyone suspicious arrives, you shoot the girl first and ask questions afterwards. Get it?'

'Got it.'

'Good.'

Jude was the first one to the front door but the last one out of it. 'Don't let us down, brother – OK?' he whispered to me.

'I won't,' I replied.

'I know you won't.' He slapped me on the back and then they went off. I shut the door behind them, and stood in the hallway. I didn't want to be here. I didn't want to be anywhere near here where I could hear Sephy's voice, or see her face.

Let me leave, before I forget why I'm here.

Get me out of here, before I break down or lose my mind at all the things I've done since we've been apart.

I didn't even have to close my eyes to remember the sight of Sephy's car driving away from me that day. My life might've been very different if I'd read her letter in time, if I'd managed to reach her car before it sped away from me.

I might've been very much alive, instead of ice-cold inside.

At least I thought I was – until I saw her again.

Get me out of here, before I do something I'll regret.

one hundred and one.
Sephy

Lying on my back, I concentrated on breathing regularly. In. Out. In. Out. The pain in my lower abdomen was less than it had been but it was still sharp. My eyes closed and, still forcing myself to breathe in a slow, regular pattern, I moved my hand in a circular motion over my abdomen below my navel.

'What's the matter?'

My hand slowed for a moment but did not stop. I turned to lie on my side, my face averted, my eyes now open and wary.

'Sephy, what's the matter?' Callum moved further into the room to stand beside my bed.

'It's nothing. Go away.'

I kept my back towards him. Even if I'd been ordered and chastised, I couldn't have looked at Callum. To look at him would be to weep and scream and beg. And I wasn't going to do any of those things. Ever. I'd never give him the satisfaction. He was one of them now. My Callum was dead. The mattress sank where Callum sat down. Neither of us spoke. I continued to rub my abdomen. Slow, circular strokes. If only this pain in my stomach would ease – just for a second. Callum's brother must've really enjoyed that thump he gave me. From the continuing feel of it, he'd put his whole heart and soul into it. And my finger was as sore as blazes. Every time I stretched it out, the wound opened up again. Between them, the McGregor boys had really sorted me out.

Without warning, my hand was moved away from my body and moments later, Callum's hand replaced it. I turned to Callum, eyes wide with shock. I tried to push his hand away. Gently but firmly, Callum placed my hand at my side and continued rubbing my abdomen. I couldn't breathe. My heart slammed against my ribs as I stared at my captor.

'What're you doing?' I whispered.

'You're hurting.'

'Like you care.'

At first I thought that Callum wasn't going to reply.

'I care,' he said at last.

'Then let me go. *Please.*'

'I can't.'

Ashamed of myself for having asked, I tried to turn my head away, but Callum's restraining hand on my cheek stopped me. He carried on rubbing my stomach. We watched each other in a silence that surrounded us like a bubble of barbed wire. There was no outside, no sight, no sound. The world was reduced to the room we were in. Time was condensed to the moments that passed between us.

'I love you,' Callum said softly.

'Then let me go. Please . . .'

Callum's finger on my lips stilled the words. 'I love you,' he repeated. 'I told you once before – when you were asleep and couldn't hear me. I was afraid for you to hear me. But I'm not any more.'

Callum *loved* me . . .

My heart began to rocket against my ribs again. Yesterday those words would've enabled me to fly. But that was yesterday.

'You don't. You can't love me. It doesn't exist. You told me so.'

'If it didn't exist, I wouldn't've cared when I saw you drive off for Chivers. I came after you, you know. But I was too late.'

'Y-you . . . came after me?'

Callum smiled sadly. 'I didn't read your letter until

about twenty minutes before you were due to leave. I ran and ran all the way, but I was too late . . .'

I closed my eyes to stop my tears from escaping, but they did anyway. They trickled slowly down my face like solitary raindrops on a window pane. What might've been . . .

'Ignore me,' I said, wiping my eyes. 'Just go away, please.'

'Do you hate me?' asked Callum.

I was finding it hard to think straight. *Callum had come after me* . . . He had wanted us to be together. His hand was still stroking my abdomen but it was no longer soothing. Instead it seemed to burn through my clothes and straight down into my insides.

'Do you?' Callum prompted.

I shook my head. 'Another place . . . another time . . . you and I . . .'

'I don't know anything about another place and another time,' Callum interrupted. 'All I know is here and now.'

And he bent his head to kiss me. He moved so quickly, I had no time to even be surprised. Before I could make a sound, his lips were on mine and I could see nothing but his face, his eyes. His lips were so soft. Even softer than I'd remembered. I'd daydreamed so many times of doing this, until I'd realized that I was dreaming about something that was never, ever going to happen. And then the dream had been, not exactly abandoned, but buried deep where not even I could reach it easily. But now the world had turned upside down and Callum was kissing me. His lips coaxed open my mouth, but there was very little coaxing to be done. I closed my eyes.

This wasn't real.

None of it was real.

It couldn't be.

It was forbidden.

Against the law.

Against nature.

So I was dreaming again. Lost in my own world where there were no noughts and Crosses. Just me and Callum, as Callum and I should be, whilst the rest of the world smiled kindly at us or turned their backs on us – but either way, we were left alone. Callum's hand moved from my abdomen to my waist and higher. I pushed at his hand but it didn't move. His kiss became gentler.

'Callum . . .'

'Shush! I won't hurt you. I'd never hurt you. I love you,' Callum whispered against my mouth. His breath was hot and made my insides melt. Uncertain, confused, I tried to pull away, but his kiss grew more urgent and all at once I didn't want to move away any more. I pulled him closer to me, wrapping my arms around him, kissing him just as desperately as he was kissing me. Like if we could just love long enough and hard enough and deep enough, then the world outside would never, could never hurt us again. And then, it was as if we'd both caught fire. Sort of like spontaneous combustion and we were burning up together.

'I love you,' Callum whispered again.

But I could hardly hear him over the sound of my blood roaring in my ears. His hands were everywhere, moving over my arms, my breasts, my waist, my thighs.

And every caress, every stroke robbed me of my breath and burnt through my skin. I pulled him closer and closer, my hands moving over his back and his bum and his legs. He sat up, pulling me with him. He raised my hands to pull off my jumper. I unbuttoned his shirt. He unfastened my bra. I unzipped his trousers. We stripped each other until we were both naked. And I was shaking. But not from the cold. I was melting inside. Never had I felt so scared and exhilarated and *alive* all at once. We both knelt on the bed, facing each other. Callum's gaze moved down over my body. I'd never realized before just how physical a mere look could be. Callum reached out with both hands and touched my cheeks. He ran his hands over my lips and my nose and my forehead. I closed my eyes, just before his fingers softly touched my eyelids. And then moments later, his lips were exploring my face the way his hands had done. He lay me down gently, his hands and lips still exploring my body. I wanted to do the same to him. I was going to do the same to him. We were going to make this time last for ever. Callum was right. We had here and now. And that was all that mattered. I let myself drift away, following wherever Callum led. Beside him all the way as he led me into a real, unreal world. Not quite heaven. Not quite hell.

I sat up, scrambling for my jeans and my jumper. I couldn't stop sobbing. My head was pounding and my nose was running and my throat was hurting, but I couldn't stop.

'Sephy . . .' Callum began.

Did I look like him? So miserably unhappy after what had just happened to us? If I did, then I wouldn't look at him again. His expression was my reflection. I pulled on my jeans and my jumper and hunted frantically for my sandals. I was aware of Callum getting dressed even though I couldn't bring myself to look at him.

Stop weeping . . . Just stop . . .

But I couldn't. More tears for the impossible. My sandals were on the wrong feet. I didn't know what I was doing. I kicked them off and tried again, still weeping.

'*Sephy, please . . .*'

Callum tried to put his arms around me. I pushed him away. He pulled me toward him again, which just made me cry harder and push against him more frantically.

The door of my prison cell was flung open and in ran Jude and Morgan, only to stop abruptly when they saw Callum and me together on the bed. Callum leapt up, but it was too late.

Stop crying . . . If only I could stop crying . . .

one hundred and two.
Callum

It's not what you're thinking . . . It's exactly what you're thinking . . . Someone say something. Anything.

Nothing.

'What's happened?' I asked at last.

'You tell us,' Jude said with quiet menace.

He kept looking from me to Sephy and back again.

'Where's Leila?'

'Arrested,' Morgan replied.

'Where's Pete?'

'Dead,' said Jude. 'They had undercover police everywhere. They must've been monitoring every phone box in town. Either that or they knew exactly where we'd be. Morgan and I changed our locations at the last moment otherwise they might've captured us too. We were lucky to escape in one piece.' Jude looked at Sephy, his face sombre. 'I thought we could take the girl and move out of this town to somewhere safer, but now . . .'

He turned to me, the rest of his sentence clearly spoken but unsaid.

What have I done? Sephy, forgive me. I've killed us both.

'I'll pack up all our equipment . . .' I said.

'I don't think so,' Jude replied. 'Morgan, go and pack up everything essential. Leave the rest. We've got to get out of here.'

Morgan left without a word.

'Why is she crying?' Jude indicated Sephy.

My face began to burn. I kept my mouth shut.

'And her jumper is inside out.'

Jude and I glared at each other. What was I meant to say to that? Nothing. Jude had already made up his mind what had happened in his absence.

'You stupid, stupid berk. You've put a noose around all our necks.' Jude grabbed me by my T-shirt. 'We could've got what we wanted and let her go, in spite of what Andrew Dorn said. They'd never have found us.' He punctuated each half-sentence by backhanding me around the face. 'But not now. You raped her and now it's her or us. You stupid, stupid . . .'

I clenched my fists and the next thing I knew Jude was flat on his back with blood trickling down from his nose.

'Don't you ever hit me again as long as you live,' I hissed at him.

He sprang up and swung at me. I blocked his arm easily and hit him again. And then we were at it. A vicious, scrappy brawl, with each of us determined to hurt the other more than we were hurting. Something rushed by me but I barely noticed.

'Stop her! Stop!' Jude pushed me away. 'She's escaping. Get her.'

We both sprung to our feet. I looked around, confused. Where was Sephy? I looked towards the open door and realized. Jude and I both took off after her. We raced out of the front door.

'Morgan! Round here!' Jude yelled. 'She's escaped.'

I looked around but I couldn't see her. It was night-time now, almost midnight, but we had a full moon on our side and there were no clouds, so that was something.

'There she is!' Morgan pointed over to the left towards the trees.

I turned, just in time to see Sephy disappear into the darkness of the wood. All three of us chased after her. I had to find her before the others. I needed to find her.

God help me if I didn't.

one hundred and three.
Sephy

Run, Sephy. Just keep running.

The shadows were long and ominously silent all around me. I ran round tree-trunk after tree-trunk, the moonlight dappling through the branches and leaves above me.

And still I ran. Whatever happened I couldn't let them catch me. Something sharp dug into my right foot. I cried out, biting my lip a moment later – but too late.

'Over there!' A voice cried out from behind me. Too close behind me.

I darted to the right. Where was I? I couldn't tell. I couldn't see where I was going. It was just – away.

I could hear leaves and bracken crunching behind me. Getting closer.

Hide, Sephy!

I made out the outline of some undergrowth between a clump of trees. For a second, I considered hiding in it but I didn't want to have to lie down. If I did that and I was discovered, I'd never get away in time. Footsteps approaching. I made for the nearest, darkest tree and hid behind its trunk. I leaned back against it, trying to merge with it, desperate to disappear.

Please, God . . .

The footsteps slowed then stopped. And they were so close. I stopped breathing. I couldn't breathe. I didn't dare. *Please, God . . .*

'Persephone, I know you can hear me . . .' Jude's voice. 'We're kilometres from anywhere here. You'll wander around this forest for days without seeing another soul. With no food. No water. Come out now and we won't harm you – I promise.'

Silence. Moments later, a muffled curse fractured the silence. I drew a hasty breath before my lungs could burst and held it. The night wind rustled through the leaves all around, making them sound like they were whispering, commenting on what was happening on the ground below them. I opened my mouth and exhaled softly, feeling the warm air dance across my lips, terrified that what I could feel the others would hear. I closed my eyes.

Please, please God . . .

'Sephy, come out now and nothing will happen to you.' Jude's voice seemed further away.

Or was that just wishful thinking.

'But if you don't show yourself and we find you . . .' The threat hung in the air like the very darkness around me.

Footsteps sounded, getting further away. I opened my eyes, my feet already moving to head in the opposite direction only to stop abruptly. I gasped. Callum stood right in front of me, less than a metre away. And the fear I felt then was like a moment spent dying.

'Callum . . .' I breathed.

'What was that?' A voice I hadn't heard before asked.

Callum put his finger to his lips.

'It's only me,' he called out. 'I tripped.'

'We've got to find her.' The other man's voice was getting closer.

'I SEE HER!' Callum yelled suddenly.

I shook my head, my eyes pleading with him, my heart about to crack.

'She's trying to double back on us. She must be heading back for the cabin,' Callum shouted out.

'Blast!'

The immediate sound of running. Away from me. Away from us. Callum stepped towards me. He took my unresisting hands in his. He looked up.

'D'you see Orion's Belt?' he said softly.

I looked up and nodded.

'Always keep it immediately behind you. When you reach the road, turn left on to it and keep going.'

'Callum . . .'

'Just go, Sephy.' He let go of my hands and turned away.

'Callum, we have to talk . . .'

'No. Just go.' He turned away again.

'Callum . . .' And then I remembered what had been bothering me about the stranger since I'd first seen him. I grabbed Callum's hand. 'Wait. That man with the blond pony-tail, the one who came in with you to see me?'

'What about him?'

'He works for my father. I saw him a couple of years ago at our house.'

'You're sure?' Callum frowned.

'Yes. I'm positive. It was him. He works for Dad. He wore the same boots with the silver chains. I recognized them. It's definitely him.'

'Thanks.' He pulled away from me and a moment later he'd melted into the shadows. I tried to train my eyes to see him but he'd gone. I turned and ran.

THE CONFESSION . . .

one hundred and four.
Callum

Reporters surrounded Kamal Hadley. And there were so many cameras flashing around him that it looked like a firework display. Kamal Hadley raised his hands and immediately the clamour around him died down. The firework display didn't.

'I . . . I will make a short statement and t–that's it.' Kamal Hadley wiped the back of his hand across his cheeks before continuing. 'My daughter is still unconscious after being found this morning. Her doctors describe her condition as critical but stable. The police are present and will interview her the moment she regains consciousness. Acting on information received, we captured one of the kidnappers and another opened fire on the police and was killed as a result. No ransom was paid. That's all I'd like to say at this moment.'

'How many kidnappers were there?'

'Where was your daughter held during her ordeal?'

'What are the extent of her injuries?'

Kamal Hadley turned without another word and headed back inside the hospital. Jude pressed the mute button on the TV remote control just as the newsreader's face appeared on screen. I slumped back in my chair, dog-tired. We were hundreds of kilometres away from the cabin in the woods, having got out of there in a hurry once it became clear that we'd lost Sephy. We were holed up in one room in a seedy bed-and-breakfast hotel, with twin beds for Jude and Morgan and a sleeping bag for me. The walls looked like they hadn't seen a lick of paint in at least three generations and the windows and fittings were caked with grease and grime. There was a carpet on the floor which I think had a pattern once, a long time ago, but it was so worn it was impossible to tell what the pattern might've been or even its original colour. Not that I had much time to dwell on our surroundings. Morgan and Jude were all too ready to beat the crap out of me – at the very least – until I told them what I'd learnt about Andrew Dorn.

'Where did you get this information from?' Jude asked.

'Sephy,' I replied.

'And it never occurred to you that she could be lying.'

'She wasn't.'

'How can you be so sure?'

'Because I know her. If she says she saw Andrew Dorn with her dad then she did. Besides, she volunteered the information.'

'Because she wanted us to be paranoid about each other,' Morgan said scornfully. 'Andrew Dorn isn't a traitor. He's the General's second-in-command for God's sake!'

'Then tell me this. How did the police know where each of you was going to be when you went to set up the telephone relay and pick up the ransom? We set up different locations for everyone precisely so that wouldn't happen. Only five people knew our plans apart from Andrew. One is dead. One is captured and us three are here up to our armpits in alligators. So you explain that then?'

Jude and Morgan exchanged a long look. At least I had them thinking.

'You said you changed your positions at the last minute?' I carried on. 'So you didn't have a chance to tell Andrew what you were doing and I bet that's the only reason you're both still here to talk about it now. He betrayed us. Sephy was right.'

'But she can't be . . .' Morgan couldn't believe it.

I remembered something else. 'He kept whispering to me that Sephy wasn't to leave the cabin alive. I think that's because he knew she'd recognized him. He ordered me to kill her first and ask questions later if anyone came to the cabin. But if I'd done that, I wouldn't've stood a chance of getting out alive.'

Jude and Morgan were silent as they considered what I said.

It took a while to convince them but, in a way, Leila being captured and Pete being killed finally did it for me. The police must've known our plans to be able to round up two of us. And Andrew must've told them. No-one else could've.

'I'll find him if it takes the rest of my life.' Morgan was spitting mad by now. 'And when I do, my hands and his throat are going to make long and painful contact.'

We discussed various ways of stopping Andrew from betraying us or anyone else in the future but the problem was, we had no proof. And you didn't go round accusing the General's second-in-command of being a traitor without proof, not if you wanted to live to a reasonable age.

'Besides,' said Jude, looking directly at me, 'we have a more pressing problem.'

'We'll never be able to settle in one place long enough to figure out what we're going to do next.' Morgan said grimly. 'They are never going to stop looking for us.'

'I didn't rape her,' I said through gritted teeth.

'So you say,' Morgan sneered. 'But here's some free advice. If you can't keep your trousers on, don't leave any witnesses next time.'

'I didn't rape her.' I turned to Jude. From his expression, he obviously didn't believe me either.

'You shouldn't've done it,' he said at last.

I closed my eyes briefly and looked away. Talking to those two was like banging my head off a brick wall.

And the worst thing of all was, Jude was right. I shouldn't have done it.

'Morgan, I think it'd be better if we all went our separate ways for a while,' Jude said carefully. 'Together we'll be much easier to track down. We should each fend for ourselves for say, six months and then meet at a pre-arranged time and place.'

'That's a good idea,' Morgan agreed.

'We'll meet up on Callum's birthday. And no-one is to go blabbing about Andrew Dorn in the meantime,' Jude warned. 'If he suspects we're on to him, he could have other cells pick us off one by one before we could do anything about him.'

'But we can't just let him carry on betraying the L.M.

to the Crosses,' Morgan protested.

'None of us has the ear of the General. We don't even know who the General is. And if we tried to get a message to him, it's bound to go through Andrew first. So we're going to have to bide our time.'

'So in the meantime more of our people will go to jail or swing from the scaffold at Hewmett Prison?' said Morgan.

'If that's the way it's got to be until we can expose him – yes.' Jude replied fiercely. 'We have to lose this battle to win the war.'

'That sucks!'

'Tough,' Jude snapped. 'I don't like it any more than you do, but we have no choice. Morgan, could you go out and get us a meal?'

'What kind of meal?'

'I don't know.' Jude frowned impatiently. 'Get a curry or a chicken wrap or some burgers or something.'

Grumbling, Morgan left the room.

'You do know we'll be lucky if we survive a month without being wiped out by either our own side or the police, don't you?' Jude said quietly. 'Andrew has probably already got the word out that we're to be . . . eliminated.'

I'd figured that out for myself.

Jude sat back on his single bed and rubbed his eyes wearily. 'D'you want to hear something bust-a-gut funny, little brother?'

The last thing in the world I felt like doing was laughing.

'D'you remember when Mum had to go to hospital

because she broke a finger slapping Dad's face?'

I nodded.

'Remember when she asked you to disappear because she had something to tell me?'

'Yeah, I do.' I frowned.

'You see her?' Jude pointed to the photo of a smiling Sephy now being shown on the TV screen.

I looked away, unable to look at her for longer than a microsecond. Just that quick sight of her had my heart drumming.

'She and her whole family have ruined our lives. It's as if they've made it their business to mix up their lives with ours,' said Jude. 'They've always believed they were better than us and they weren't.'

I frowned at him. 'What're you talking about?'

'Mum's grandfather, our great-grandfather was a Cross. That's what Mum told me that day. We've got Cross blood in our veins.'

'I . . . I don't believe it,' I whispered.

'It's true. Mum only told me because I joined the L.M. She said I was part Cross, so killing them would be like killing my own. Poor Mum! That backfired on her.'

'What d'you mean?'

'None of them ever wanted us. What has any Cross ever done for me except look down at me? I hated all of them even more after Mum told me the truth. Poor Mum.'

I was drowning in Jude's words, trying to find something of sense to hold on to.

'I had no idea . . .'

'There's no reason why you should.' Jude shrugged.

'We're going to split up soon and I don't even know if I'll see you again. But I've got some free advice for you, Callum. Stay away from Persephone Hadley.'

'I . . . of course I . . .'

'Stay away from her, Callum,' Jude interrupted. 'Or she's going to be the death of you.'

one hundred and five.
Sephy

Not again! I only just made it to the bathroom, collapsing with my head over the toilet bowl before I brought up what felt like most of the acid in my stomach. It was seven o'clock in the morning and I'd only just woken up, so my stomach was totally empty. And retching on an empty stomach was far worse than vomiting with a full one. My stomach acid stung my nose and made my mouth taste bitter and nasty. And this was about the fifth morning in a row that I'd woken up feeling like last Crossmas's left-over turkey.

Only when I was reasonably sure that I could get to my feet without keeling over did I stand up. I cleaned my teeth and gargled for at least a minute with mouthwash. But I still felt wretched. I made my way out of my bed-room and headed downstairs, feeling very sorry for myself. As if everything that'd happened to me in the last five weeks wasn't enough, now I'd caught a tummy bug.

The last five weeks . . .

After I'd regained consciousness, it seemed like every doctor in the northern hemisphere had prodded and poked me and given me test after humiliating test until I felt more like a specimen in a lab than a human being. And the police had asked me question after embarrassing question.

Especially about what my kidnappers had done to me.

'Whatever happened, you mustn't feel it was your fault. You were powerless. You can tell us *everything* that happened, we'll understand . . .' The policewoman had smiled and hugged and tried to get me to confide in her until all I wanted to do was slap her senseless. She interviewed me in a room with a huge mirror on one wall and kept stealing quick glances at it when I wouldn't answer her questions. I mean, did she really think I was that stupid? Jeez! I knew a one-way mirror when I saw one.

I had nothing to say to them. I had nothing to say to anyone about my ordeal in the cabin in the woods. I didn't even want to think about it. It hurt my head and stung my eyes and broke my heart to think about it. Not the kidnapping so much, although that'd been bad enough. But Callum . . . I couldn't bear to think about Callum. And yet every thought seemed to find its own way back to him. He was never out of my mind. And it was driving me crazy.

I entered the kitchen and made myself some dry toast and a cup of weak blackcurrant tea. It helped. A bit. A very little bit.

'Oh, there you are,' Minnie entered the kitchen to sit

opposite me at the breakfast bar. 'You OK?'

'Yes. Apart from this tummy bug?'

'You've been sick for the last couple of mornings, haven't you?' Minnie frowned.

'How d'you know?'

'I've heard you calling on the porcelain telephone!'

I raised an eyebrow and carried on eating my toast. I wasn't in the mood for any of my sister's so-called jokes.

'When're you going to talk about what happened to you when you were kidnapped?' Minnie asked.

'Never.'

'You shouldn't bottle it up inside . . .'

'Back off, Minnie. OK?' I snapped. 'My being kidnapped won't reflect badly on you in any manner, shape or form so you can leave me alone now.'

'What're you talking about? I'm concerned about you.'

'Yeah, right!' I took another bite of toast.

'What happened to you out there?' Minnie asked softly.

'I was kidnapped. I escaped. Now you know as much as I do.' I chewed my last piece of toast and swallowed it down with a sip of rapidly cooling fruit tea.

'Sephy, are . . . are you pregnant?'

'What're you talking about? Of course I'm . . . not . . .' The words trailed away to nothing. I stared at my sister, in a daze.

'So you could be?' Minnie said grimly. 'Who was it? One of the kidnappers?'

'I can't be . . . I can't be pregnant . . .' I whispered, aghast.

'Who was it, Sephy? You can tell me. I won't tell anyone, I promise.'

I sprang up and raced from the room, like if I could only run fast enough I could leave my sister's words far behind me.

Come on, Sephy! Just do it. The pregnancy test doesn't work unless you actually use it! Just do it. And one minute later, you'll know. If it stays white you're not pregnant. You'll have ducked a bullet and no one need ever know. And if it turns blue . . .

For heaven's sake, do it. Anything's better than this not knowing.

I picked up the leaflet and read the instructions again. It seemed straightforward enough. One indicator stick included. Just add urine. Nothing to it. So get on with it. I took a deep breath and followed the instructions. Which was silly of me, because I knew I wasn't pregnant.

I couldn't be. Not now. Not like this.

I placed the now-wet indicator stick on top of the toilet cistern whilst I washed my hands.

All I had to do now was wait. Just one minute to go.

The longest minute of my life. I sat down on the closed toilet lid, my back to the indicator stick as I counted up to sixty. I stopped at fifty-nine, unable to even think the next number, never mind say it.

I'm *not* pregnant. Just because I've been a bit sick in the mornings . . . That doesn't mean anything. It's just a delayed reaction to everything that's happened to me over the last few weeks. That's all. Steeling myself, I turned around, my eyes closed. I opened my eyes slowly. I didn't even have to pick it up. I could see its colour very clearly.

What am I going to do? God help me, what am I going to do?

one hundred and six.
Callum

Now I don't have anything. Not even the Liberation Militia. And there's still three months to go before I meet up with Morgan and my brother again. I miss them. When you work with people for so long, your life in their hands and their lives in yours, they almost become family. Sometimes even closer than real family. I thought about going to see Mum. I even got so far as to stand outside my aunt's house. I had so many questions I wanted to ask her. But then I changed my mind. Some things are best left unsaid. And seeing me would hurt Mum even more than not seeing me, especially as there was no way I could stay.

Sometimes when it's late at night and I'm all alone in a room or sleeping rough on the streets, I look up at the moon or one of the stars and imagine that at that precise moment, *she* is looking at the very same thing.

Why did she cry?

I guess I'll never know. I doubt if I'll ever see her again.

I've finally figured it out. I'm dead. I died a long time ago, woke up in hell and didn't even realize. Thinking about it, I must've died just before I started at Heathcroft school. That's what happened.

I know I'm right.

one hundred and seven.
Sephy

There came the lightest of taps at the door. I quickly wiped my eyes and jumped off the bed to sit at my dressing-table. I picked up the first thing to hand, a comb, and began to comb my hair.

'Come in.'

Minnie entered my room, closing the door quietly behind her. I watched her via my dressing-table mirror. She'd been watching me very strangely for the last few days. Or was it the last few weeks?

'Sephy, are you OK?'

'Is that what you came in here to ask me?' I frowned. Minnie nodded.

'Yes, I'm fine. Now stop asking me that,' I snapped.

'I'm concerned about you.'

'Well, you're wasting your time. I've already told you, I'm brilliant, wonderful, marvellous. I've never felt better in my life. So back off.'

Minnie gave me a deeply sceptical look. 'Then why haven't you gone back to school?'

' 'Cause I don't want everyone pointing their fingers at me and whispering behind my back and feeling sorry for me.'

'And why do you always look like you've just stopped crying or you're just about to start?'

'You need to get your eyes tested.'

'And why have you taken to wearing leggings and baggy T-shirts and jumpers?'

I was really beginning to lose it now. 'Minerva, what's the matter with you? Since when have you been the least bit interested in what I wear?'

'You *are* pregnant, aren't you? The T-shirts and jumpers are just to hide the fact that your pregnancy is beginning to show.'

'No, they're not. I'm only wearing them because . . . because . . .' And like a moron, I burst into tears, burying my head in my hands.

Minnie was immediately at my side, her arm around my shoulders.

'Oh, Sephy, you idiot! Why didn't you just come right out and say so? I could've helped you. We all could've helped you. Why d'you always insist on doing everything the hard way?'

'Minnie, I don't know what to do,' I sniffed. 'I've thought and thought and there's no way out.'

'Ignoring your growing stomach isn't going to alter the fact that you're pregnant,' Minnie said, exasperated. 'What were you thinking?'

'It's all right for you. You're not the one who's pregnant. I am,' I said angrily.

'You're going to have to tell Mother . . .'

I pulled away from Minnie and stared at her. 'Have you lost your mind?'

'Sephy, sooner or later she's going to find out for

herself. Even if you manage to hide your entire pregnancy, how d'you expect to hide a baby?'

'I don't know. I haven't thought that far ahead.'

'Well, you'd better start.'

'Minnie, promise me you won't say a word to anyone,' I begged.

'But Sephy . . .'

'Please. Promise me. I'll tell Mother but it has to be in my own time and in my own way. OK?'

'OK, I promise. But don't leave it much longer or I may change my mind.'

I nodded gratefully. I'd bought myself a few more days, possibly a few more weeks.

'D'you want to talk about what happened with the kidnappers?'

I shook my head.

'I take it the father is one of your kidnappers?'

I didn't answer.

Minnie stood up. 'Well, just remember, if you do want to talk, my bedroom is right next door to yours. OK?'

'OK.'

The moment Minnie left my room, I flung myself down on my bed, weeping like I'd only just discovered how to do it. All my plans had turned to ashes and dust. All my dreams and schemes for the future had turned into . . . a baby.

one hundred and eight.
Callum

'What about you, Callum? What would you do with all the money in the world?'

Gordy must've seen from my face what I thought of the question.

'Oh, come on. It's just a bit a fun,' Gordy teased.

Four months had passed since . . . since the kidnapping. I was working as a car mechanic three hundred kilometres away from home in a place called Sturham. The December afternoon was already getting dark. The heating in the garage was supposedly turned right up, but it was still chilly, and the work was mind-numbingly boring but I was glad of it. It stopped me from brooding all day, every day. And the guys I worked with weren't bad. Gordy was a nought who'd worked as a car mechanic since he was thirteen. He was now fifty-seven and he was still a car mechanic. Nothing had changed for him. Tomorrow was going to be the same as yesterday as far as he was concerned. He was just punching time until he died. I looked at him and saw my uncles and Old Man Tony and even my dad – until Lynette had died. I looked at him and was so afraid I was seeing myself in ten, twenty, thirty years time.

Rob was a couple of years older than me. He was a talker. He was going to change the world by using the only means at his disposal, by grumbling about it. I'd only been working here for three weeks and already I'd had to hide my fists behind my back and go and sit in the toilets for a good ten minutes to stop myself from swinging for him. He drove me nuts.

'Well? Don't you have any dreams – or are you too good to share them with the likes of us?' Gordy teased.

I forced myself to smile. 'I don't like to dwell on what I'll never have,' I shrugged.

'You never know,' Rob said, inanely.

'So what *would* you do?' Gordy urged.

'Build a rocket and leave this planet. Live on the moon or some place else. Any place else,' I answered.

'If you had all the money in the world, you wouldn't have to live on the moon. You could do whatever you liked right here,' said Rob.

'D'you know what they call a nought with all the money in the world?' I asked.

Rob and Gordy shook their heads.

'A blanker,' I told them.

They didn't laugh. They weren't supposed to.

'Things would change if we had a ton of money,' Rob tried to tell me.

I tried – and failed – to keep the pitying look off my face. 'It takes more than money, Rob. It takes determination and sacrifice and . . . and . . .'

Rob and Gordy were both looking at me like I'd lost my mind. I shut up.

'Just ignore me,' I told them ruefully.

'We'll have to call you the deep one,' Gordy said. 'Or better yet, the *profound* one.'

'Don't you dare,' I warned him.

'We will come to you for spiritual guidance!' Gordy bowed low, his hands together as if in prayer. 'Oh, profound one, share your mystical insights with us. Enlighten us . . .'

'If you three can't be bothered to get on with your work, there are hundreds of others out there who'd be only too happy to take your jobs,' Snakeskin emerged from his office to holler at us.

Without a word we got back to work, waiting until Snakeskin had slammed his way back into his office before adopting our previous positions.

'What a horse's ass!' Rob sniffed.

'There's a lot of it about,' I said.

'Amen to that,' Gordy agreed.

'What I want to know is, how does . . ?' Rob began.

'Shush! *Shush!*' I hissed at him. I moved over to the workbench to turn up the volume on the radio. Something on the news had caught my attention.

'. . . *has refused to confirm or deny that Persephone Mira Hadley, his daughter, is pregnant, and that this is the result of her ordeal a few months ago at the hands of her kidnappers. We can only speculate as to what this poor girl has been subjected to at the hands of the nought men who abducted her. Persephone herself has so far refused to speak of her two terrifying days in captivity, the memories being obviously too painful, too shocking . . .*'

'Hey!' Gordy was staring at me and I had no idea why, until I saw the radio lying on the floor, smashed to smithereens where I'd thrown it against the wall.

'I've got to get out of here.' I headed for the exit.

'Er . . . Callum, where d'you think you're going?' Snakeskin called after me.

'I've got to leave.'

'Oh no you don't.'

'Watch me!'

'If you go out that door, don't bother to come back.'

I carried on walking.

one hundred and nine.
Sephy

Mother sat down beside me in the family room. Dad paced up and down in front of me. I turned to glare at Minnie.

'So much for your promises,' I said bitterly.

At least she had the grace to be embarrassed and look away, unable to meet my stare. I should've known she wouldn't be able to keep her mouth shut. Some secrets are obviously too juicy to keep. And no doubt this was her chance to get back at me for all those years of 'Minnie' instead of 'Minerva'. As well as telling Mother and Dad, she'd probably told one person, who'd told someone else, who'd told someone else and before you knew it, it was the world's best-kept shared secret. It was inevitably only a matter of time before the press found out. Maybe that's what Minnie wanted all along. Whatever else happened, I'd never forgive her for this, never if I lived to be five hundred.

'What we have to do,' Dad began, 'is deal with this situation as quickly and discreetly as possible.'

'It's for the best, darling,' Mother took one of my hands in hers and patted it gently.

'We've already booked you into a clinic for tomorrow morning,' said Dad. 'By tomorrow evening it will all be over. You won't be pregnant any more and we can all put this whole thing behind us.'

'I know it's hard, love, but it's definitely for the best,' Mother agreed.

'You want me to have an abortion?' I asked.

'Well, you don't want to keep it, do you?' Mother said, puzzlement in her voice. 'A child of your kidnapper? The bastard child of a raping blanker?'

'Of course she doesn't,' Dad said brusquely. He turned to me. 'You should've told us, princess. You should've told us what they did to you. We could've sorted all this out so much sooner and avoided all this press speculation.'

'I'll take you to the clinic myself,' said Mother, trying to dredge up a smile from nowhere.

'We'll both go,' said Dad. 'This time tomorrow, it will all be over.'

'Leave everything to us,' said Mum.

'You can hardly be expected to make decisions for yourself or even think straight at a time like this,' Dad said.

Mother and Dad – together at last. Reunited. Acting, moving, thinking as one. And I'd done that. I couldn't help but wonder. The thoughts going through my head, were they the result of straight thinking or crooked thinking? How could I tell which was which?

'We're all behind you on this, love,' said Dad. 'And once it's over we'll all go away somewhere on a holiday. You can put it behind you and get on with the rest of your life. We all can.'

Put it behind me . . . Is that what he thought? A quick operation and just like that, my baby would be gone and forgotten? Looking at Dad was like looking at a stranger. He didn't know me at all. And I couldn't even feel sad about it.

'I'm not going to the clinic tomorrow,' I said softly.

'You won't be alone. We'll be with you . . .'

'You'll be on your own then, because I'm not going.'

'Pardon?' Dad stared at me.

I stood up to face him directly.

'I'm going to keep my baby.'

'Don't be ridiculous,' Dad wasn't shouting. He was merely incredulous. He didn't believe I meant it.

'I'm going to keep my baby,' I repeated.

'No, you are not.'

'It's my body and my baby, and I'm keeping it.'

'Persephone, be reasonable. You're not being sensible. You're only just eighteen. How can you keep the baby? Everyone will know how it was conceived. You'll be pointed at and scorned and pitied. Is that what you want?'

He really didn't know me at all.

'I'm keeping it.'

'You'll change your mind tomorrow,' Dad decided.

'No, I won't,' I told him. 'I'm keeping it.'

one hundred and ten.
Callum

All the way down to the coast, I phoned Sephy's house using our signal from years ago. I had no idea if she was at the house by the coast or even if she heard my signals but I wasn't going to let that stop me. I had to see her. I had to *know*.

It took me a whole day to get back to our home town and then I had to wait until nightfall to sneak up from the coastal cave to the rose garden outside her bedroom window. It was the longest, hardest wait I've ever had to endure. I was so close to her, just a couple of kilometres but she might not be there or she might not want to talk to me. A world of doubts and fears stretched between us. And planning to go to her house had to be one of the stupidest things I'd ever attempted. And yet I wasn't even close to reconsidering my actions.

I had to see her.

I was going to see her.

one hundred and eleven.
Sephy

He's out there. I don't have to see him to know he's out there. He's down there in the rose garden, just below my window. I can sense it. I can sense *him*. My whole body is tingling and my mouth is dry and my stomach keeps flipping over like a pancake. What should I do? What will I do if he says the same as Mother and Dad?

Go and see him, Sephy. You owe yourself that much. You owe him that much.

Go and see him.

one hundred and twelve.
Callum

The entire rose garden was now under glass in what had to be the biggest greenhouse I'd ever seen. I'd snuck into it past the guard, only to be knocked back by the overpowering scent of the roses. They'd grown since the last time I was here – a lifetime ago. The arches and trestle woodwork were now completely covered with rose stems and thorns and flowers. It was hard to make out all the colours in the dark. Each flower melted into the next and the next.

Was she up at the house now?

Would she come?

'Callum?' The merest whisper behind me but it was enough. I spun around, my heart racing, my palms sweating. She stood less than a metre away. How had she managed to get so close without me hearing her? My mind had been pre-occupied, remembering . . . But seeing her again was like . . . was like a lightning bolt hitting my heart. She was wearing a dark-coloured dress, burgundy or maybe blue. It was hard to tell. And her hair was shorter. But her eyes were the same as they always were.

I opened my mouth to speak but the words wouldn't come. Instead I gaped pathetically like a drowning fish.

'You shouldn't've come here,' Sephy whispered, her gaze never moving from my face. 'It isn't safe.'

'I had to,' Was that really my voice, so hoarse and strange? 'I had to.' I tried again. 'Is it true?'

'Yes.'

We watched each other. And then she stepped forward and put her arms around my waist and rested her head on my shoulder. I immediately pulled her closer. She was having a baby. *Our baby*. I could hardly breathe for the wonder of it. I placed a finger under her chin to raise her head, and I kissed her. She hugged me tighter, returning my kiss, our tongues dancing together. And in that moment, the ice inside me shattered into a trillion pieces.

We shared a world of hope and regret and pleasure and pain in that one kiss, until we were both breathless and dizzy. I moved away slightly to rest my hands on her abdomen. Her hands covered mine. Her stomach was only sightly rounded but the moment I touched her, a frisson of electricity passed right through me. Like my child inside her was trying to connect with me somehow. She was carrying our child. I looked into Sephy's face but I could hardly see her for the tears in my eyes.

'If it's a boy, I'm going to call him Ryan after your dad.'

'If it's a girl, call her . . . call her Rose,' I said, looking around.

'Callie Rose.'

'Hell, no!'

'Hell, yes!'

We both started to laugh. It felt so strange. Unusual. Peculiar. One look at her face and I knew Sephy wasn't going to give in on this. 'OK. Callie Rose, it is.'

Sephy moved to hold me once more. 'I thought I'd never see you again.'

'Sephy . . .' I had to ask. 'A-about that night . . .'

'Yes?'

'Why did you cry?'

Sephy stepped away from me, her gaze dropping. 'Don't ask me that.'

'Did I hurt you? If I did, I'm sorry. I . . .'

'Of course you didn't. You know you didn't.'

'Then why?'

At first I thought she wasn't going to answer, but then she looked straight at me and I held my breath as she began to speak. 'When we made love, I knew I loved you. That I always have and that I always will. But I also realized what you'd been trying to tell me all these years. You're a Nought and I'm a Cross and there's nowhere for us to be, nowhere for us to go where we'd be left in peace. Even if we had gone away together when I wanted us to, we would've been together for a year, maybe two. But sooner or later, other people would've found a way to wedge us apart. That's why I started crying. That's why I couldn't stop. For all the things we might've had and all the things we're never going to have.'

'I understand.' And I did. I'd been hurting inside over the same thing for most of my life.

'When you said . . .' Sephy paused, looking embarrassed. 'When you said you loved me . . . Did you mean it? I don't mind if you didn't . . .' She rushed on. 'Well, I do but . . . I mean . . .'

I held out my hands and she put hers in mine, looking at me ruefully. Love was like an avalanche, with Sephy and I hand-in-hand racing like hell to get out of its way – only, instead of running away from it, we kept running straight towards it.

'Let's get out of here,' I smiled. 'Let's go away. We can be together, even if it's just for a little while, we could tr . . .'

Light after light after light clicked on around us, dazzling and blinding.

'Callum, run. RUN!'

I put one hand up to my eyes but I couldn't see. And then something hit my head and I was knocked to the ground and all the lights in the world went out.

one hundred and thirteen.
Sephy

'I thought one of the kidnappers might try again, or maybe try to get to you so that you wouldn't be able to identify them, so I had extra security installed throughout the premises when you were in hospital.'

'You've got the wrong man,' I screamed at him again. 'Why won't you listen to me. Callum hasn't done anything wrong.'

No-one was listening to me. I'd screamed at the police to let him go as they carried Callum away, but they'd ignored me. I'd tried to hold on to Callum, to pull him back but Dad had dragged me inside the house with an angry demand that I stop making such a spectacle of myself.

'Callum hasn't done anything. We were just talking,' I lowered my voice. Maybe if I stopped shouting, he'd listen to me . . .

'You're lying,' Dad replied at once. 'I know for a fact that Callum McGregor was one of your kidnappers.'

'Then you should also know for a fact that he saved my life. When I escaped from my prison cell into the woods, Callum found me. He could've told the others where I was but he didn't . . .'

'No, he just raped you and made you pregnant instead,' Dad said bitterly.

'Kamal, please . . .' Mother began.

'Callum didn't rape me. He didn't.'

'But you're pregnant so he must've done,' Mother frowned.

'I'm pregnant because we made love to each other,' I shouted angrily. 'And it was the most magical, wonderful night of my life. My only regret is Callum and I can't do it again . . .'

Dad slapped me so hard he knocked me off my feet. Mother tried to rush to my side but Dad pulled her back. He drew himself up to his full height, looking down on me with an expression on his face I'd never seen before.

'You are no longer my daughter. You are a blanker's slut,' Dad said with quiet venom. 'But I'll tell you this, you *will* go to the clinic and you *will* have an abortion. I will not allow you to embarrass me any further. D'you hear me? D'YOU HEAR ME?'

'I hear you . . .' I rubbed my cheek, ignoring the tears streaming down my face. Dad turned and marched out of the room.

Mother looked down at me, anguish filling every curve and line of her face. 'Oh, Sephy . . . Sephy . . .' she whispered. And then she turned around and left me. Alone.

That's what I was now. That's all I was now, according to my dad. A blanker's slut. I buried my face in my hands and cried.

DECISIONS . . .

one hundred and fourteen.
Callum

I lay on the bunk bed in my prison cell, reading the news-paper. I was still in the newspapers but now that my trial was over I was no longer front-page news. I'd been rele-gated to the third or fourth pages. And they were no more accurate than the front page. I was only reading it to pass the time. After all, I had nothing better to do. One article did catch my attention though.

SUSPECTED 'MOLE' WITHIN THE LIBERATION MILITIA
Sources from within the Liberation Militia stated that the whole movement is in turmoil over a suspected mole who, it is believed, is actually working for the government. The mole is rumoured to be someone high up in the party echelons. Our sources have revealed that all LM activity has been suspended until the mole is found.
The editor says . . . See page 7

'Well done, Jude,' I thought. That's if it was Jude. If he wasn't dead yet.

There was no way to get to the General so a few

rumours in the right places, a couple of discreet interviews, and the General would become aware of our suspicions. I could only hope that the General would catch Andrew Dorn before he had a chance to cover his tracks or disappear. I scrunched up the newspaper and dropped it in the bin beside my narrow bed. What was the point of reading the news? No point at all. My thoughts turned to my sister, Lynette. Funny, but I thought of her more and more often these days. She'd always been there for me. She made our home bearable. Each time I thought I couldn't take it any more, she'd smile or put her hand over mine and I'd calm down inside. When she'd died, part of me had despised her for being a coward. Part of me had hated her for leaving me. It'd all been about me. Now I thought about all the things Lynny had been through. I'd allowed all the things that'd happened to me to rob me of my humanity. Do unto others before they did unto you, that'd been my philosophy. That's how I'd coped with the world. Lynny's solution was better. Just fade out, until you were ready to fade back in. Only she hadn't been ready. Maybe that's why she'd died. She'd been pulled out of her unreal world too soon.

'Cal, you have a visitor,' Jack told me.

'A visitor?'

Jack nodded, his expression sombre. Jack was a Cross prison guard but in the short length of time I'd been at Hewmett Prison, we'd become friends. I'd even say good friends. Something I'm sure was against the rules. But if Jack didn't mind, why should I? I looked at him now. Judging from his expression, this visitor was obviously someone I wouldn't particularly welcome. I had no idea who it could be. I hadn't been allowed any visitors at all since I'd been brought to Hewmett Prison, so I was curious – to say the least.

'Man or woman?' I asked.

'Man.'

'And I take it I have to see him?'

Jack nodded again.

'OK,' I said, picking up my T-shirt. 'I'll just put on . . .'

'Don't bother. You're not going to the visitors' hall. He's coming to see you.'

'Here?'

'Yep!'

I put my T-shirt back on anyway. The prison cells were like ovens during the day and although we were meant to keep our clothes on, most of the guards turned a blind eye if we took off our shirts. I'd taken mine off when it'd started to stick to my sweaty body like clingfilm. Heels clicked along the corridor. A man's heavy, determined footfall. And angry too by the sound of it. I stood up and waited. Then the man appeared before my cell bars. My mouth fell open. Kamal Hadley. He was the very last person I'd been expecting.

He entered my cell. Jack stood outside. Kamal wore a dark charcoal-grey suit and a royal-blue shirt with matching tie. His black shoes were so highly polished I could see the light strip above reflected in them.

'You can leave us now,' Kamal ordered, his eyes never leaving my face.

'But . . .' Jack began.

Kamal turned to him with a look that brooked no disagreement. Jack set off down the corridor. I considered knocking out Kamal and taking off down the corridor. But how far would I get? I considered knocking out Kamal just for the hell of it. It was definitely tempting.

'I'm sure you can guess why I'm here,' said Kamal.

I couldn't actually, so I kept my mouth shut.

'I'm here to offer you a deal,' Kamal went on.

'What kind of deal?'

'If you do as I say, I'll make sure you don't hang. You'll be sentenced to life imprisonment and I'll make sure you serve no more than eight to ten years. You'll come out of prison still a young man with your whole life ahead of you.'

I studied Kamal as he spoke. He hated being here, he despised having to ask me for anything and he was having trouble hiding just how much he loathed it. It made me smile inside. I had something he wanted very, *very* badly. But I had no idea what.

'And what exactly do I have to do for this . . . largesse?'

'I want you to state publicly that you kidnapped and . . . raped my daughter. I want you to freely admit to the crimes you're charged with. No more denials.'

'Why?'

At first I thought Kamal wasn't going to answer. I waited. I had all the time in the world. I wasn't going anywhere.

'My daughter won't be able to put this whole business behind her and get on with her life if you don't,' he said at last. 'She feels she owes you something because you saved her life in the woods. If she knew you weren't going to die, then she'd be only too willing to get rid of your child. A child she never wanted. A child she still doesn't.'

Every word he spoke was well rehearsed and deliberately wielded to cause the maximum amount of pain. And it worked too. I half-sat, half-collapsed down onto my bed, looking up at him. My guts were being shredded and he knew it.

'And she told you this, did she?'

'Of course.'

I didn't believe him. I almost didn't believe him. He was lying. But suppose he wasn't?

My life or my child's?

Was that really the only reason Sephy was still carrying it? Because of misplaced guilt over me? I didn't want to believe it. I didn't know what to believe.

My life. Or my child's?

'Is it just the thought of Sephy and I having a child together that you can't stand, or is it all mixed-race children in general?' I asked.

'We're not here to discuss my feelings.' Kamal waved aside my words like he was swotting flies. 'What's your answer?'

My life? Or my baby's?

Oh Sephy, what should I do? What would *you* do?

'I need to think about it.'

'I want your answer here and now,' Kamal demanded.

I stood up slowly.

'Well?' he prompted, impatiently.

Time to choose. A choice to live with or die with. I looked Kamal Hadley straight in the eye – and told him my decision. I knew it would damn me to hell, but I knew it was the right one.

one hundred and fifteen.
Sephy

Dad barged into my room without even knocking on the door first. It was very late, almost midnight, but I wasn't the least bit sleepy. I couldn't even remember the last time I'd had a good night's sleep. I sat at my table, writing in my diary when Dad came in. I shut the book and swivelled round in my chair. Dad stopped in the middle of the room. We regarded each other. We hadn't exchanged a word since he'd slapped me. Dad sat down on the corner of my bed, suddenly looking very weary.

'I'm not going to beat about the bush, Persephone,' he told me. 'Callum McGregor is going to hang for what he did to you.'

I swallowed hard but still didn't speak.

'And you're the only one who can stop it,' Dad continued.

Every cell in my body was put on full alert at Dad's words. I sat very still and watchful, waiting for him to carry on.

'It's within my power to ensure that he doesn't hang. I'll make sure he only goes to prison. He'll get a long sentence but at least he'll be alive.'

And where there's life . . . there's a price. I kept my

mouth shut, waiting for the other shoe to drop.

'And all you have to do is agree to have an abortion,' said Dad.

Like all I had to do was agree to eat my greens or go to bed early – that's what he made it sound like.

'Why?' I whispered.

'Why!' The incredulous word exploded from Dad's mouth. 'Because you're too young to have a child. Because it was a child forced on you . . .'

'I've already told you, Callum didn't . . .'

'You didn't set out to get pregnant either, did you?' Dad interrupted harshly.

'It's too late to get rid of it. I'm too far gone,' I pointed out.

'There are ways, drugs to take care of that.' Dad pointed to my stomach. 'Then they'd induce labour. It'd be relatively painless for you.'

And lethal for my child.

'If I say no, what will you do then?' I asked. 'Kidnap me like the noughts and force me to get rid of my baby?'

Dad stared at me. 'I know we're not close, Persephone, and I know that's my fault, but I would never, ever do a thing like that.' His voice held such incredible hurt that it got to me, in spite of myself.

'But what you're doing is no different,' I cried. 'You may not be using direct force but you're pressuring me into having an abortion. It's the same difference. Callum's life or my child's. You're trying to coerce me into making a decision. *Your* decision.'

'That boy's life is entirely in your hands.' Dad stood up. 'It's up to you. I know you'll make the right choice.'

And with that he left my room. I locked my diary and put it in its hiding place, moving around my bedroom on auto pilot. I wanted my brain to shut down so I wouldn't have to think, so I wouldn't have to decide. But it didn't work that way.

If I had an abortion I'd be saving Callum's life. He wouldn't spend the rest of his life in jail, either. I'd work every hour of every day for the rest of my life if I had to, to make sure that he was released from prison. And if he came out . . . *when* he came out, we could be together again. We could have more children. It was the chance of some kind of future together against no future at all. But if we were together would we be able to live with the fact that our first child died for us? Or would the ghost of our child eventually drive us apart?

Callum's life or our baby's? That was the choice.

Oh Callum, what should I do? What would *you* do?

And then just like that, there was no choice. I had my answer. I knew what I was going to tell my dad. God help me, I knew.

LOSING MY RELIGION

one hundred and sixteen.
Callum

'Jack, your mind isn't on this game, is it?'

Jack throws down his cards. 'I don't want to play any more.'

'I thought I was the one who was meant to be temperamental and moody, not you?' I say dryly.

'Sorry.'

I gather up the cards. Poor Jack! This is almost as bad for him. Almost! Bless him! He's the one who's kept me up to date with what was going on in the outside world. He's the one who told me that since my farce of a trial, Sephy has spoken out publicly against the guilty verdict and has openly declared that I didn't rape her. She's told anyone prepared to listen that the authorities refused to let her testify on my behalf. And apparently even some of the national papers are beginning to question the death penalty being given in my case. I'm hoping that Kamal Hadley doesn't emerge from this one smelling of roses, the way he always does.

A prominent psychiatrist stated in one of the so-called quality papers that Sephy was suffering from Kidnapper Empathy Syndrome. Some psycho-babble about the captive taking on the ideals and beliefs of the captor, to the extent that he or she begins to empathize with them. In Sephy's case that's just so much nonsense. If I could've spoken to Sephy, I would've told her not to say anything on my behalf. Once I'd been found guilty nothing on earth could've made the judges overturn the verdict. The reason is simple. I'm a Nought who'd dared to fall in love with a Cross. And worse still I actually made love with her. And even worse than that, she's pregnant with my child and doesn't care who knows it.

Poor Sephy! She never could tell when she was fighting a losing battle. I knew I was going to hang before the jurors were even sworn in.

And now I've come to my last day on this earth.

And I don't want to die.

'What time is it, Jack?'

'Ten to six.'

'Ten more minutes then.' I shuffle the cards. 'Time for a quick game of rummy?'

'Callum . . .'

I throw down the cards. 'It must be catching. I don't feel like playing myself now.'

Silent moments tick by. I don't want to spend my last ten minutes in silence.

'D'you ever wonder what it would be like if our positions were reversed?' I ask. At Jack's puzzled look, I continue. 'If we whites were in charge instead of you Crosses?'

'Can't say it's ever crossed my mind,' Jack shrugs.

'I used to think about it a lot,' I sigh. 'Dreams of living in a world with no more discrimination, no more prejudice, a fair police force, an equal justice system, equality of education, equality of life, a level playing field . . .'

'Good grief! Is that a thesis or a fairy tale?' Jack asks dryly.

'Like I said, I used to think about it a lot.'

'I'm not sure I share your faith in a society ruled by noughts,' Jack tells me, thoughtfully. 'People are people. We'll always find a way to mess up, doesn't matter who's in charge.'

'You think so?'

Jack shrugs.

'You don't believe that things get better? That they have to, one day, some day?'

'When?'

'It takes a long time.'

'But they do?' asks Jack.

'They do.'

But not for me. A long silence fills the gap between us. Until at last, I open my mouth to speak but Jack gets in first.

'Your girl, Persephone Hadley, tried to get in here to see you – and more than once as well,' Jack tells me softly. 'But orders came from way above the governor's head that you were to have no visitors whatsoever under any circumstances.'

I digest this piece of news with regret. Kamal Hadley's influence no doubt.

'Jack, can I ask you for a favour?'

'Just name it.'

'It might get you into trouble.'

'My dull life could do with a bit of sprucing up.' Jack grins.

I smile gratefully. 'Could you find a way to deliver this letter to Sephy?'

'Persephone Hadley?'

'That's right.'

'Sure thing.' Jack takes the envelope from me.

I hold his wrist. 'You have to personally put it into her hand. Promise?'

'I promise,' Jack replies.

I let him go and watch him put the letter into his pocket. Sighing, I sit back on my bed, my back against the cool wall. There're still so many things I want to do, so many things I want to find out. I would've loved to see my mum again, just once more. Just to say . . . sorry. But it hasn't been allowed. Heaven only knows what she's going through now. Her husband is dead. Suicide or murder – take your pick. Her daughter is dead. An 'accident'. Her youngest son is going to die because of his own self-inflicted stupidity. And her eldest son is . . . missing? Wanted – dead or alive. Poor mum. What has she ever done to deserve all this? My thoughts are flitting around now. I wonder about Jude? I miss him so much. I'd love to know if he's OK. Is he safe or in prison? Has he linked up with Morgan? Has he come up with a way to deal directly with that traitor Andrew Dorn? A newspaper article is all very well, but how can he be sure Dorn won't weasel his way out or just disappear? Dorn doesn't deserve to disappear after everything he's done. Will Jude catch up with him? I'll never know.

And Sephy, how does she feel about me now? Is she

still going to have our child? I'm sure her mum and dad are doing their best and then some to make her get rid of it. Maybe she has already. Our time together in the rose garden was so brief. All those things I'd wanted to say to her – and now they'll never be said. If I could just see her one more time then I could make sense of all this, I'm sure I could.

I hear the security door click at the end of the corridor. Jack jumps to his feet and heads out into the corridor to stand by my open cell door.

This is it then. I stand up and pull down my T-shirt. I can feel little prickles of heat break out all over my skin.

I don't want to die . . .

Governor Giustini stops in the corridor outside my cell. He looks at the cards scattered on the floor and the bed and then at me.

'Do you have a last request?' Governor Giustini asks sombrely.

'Just get it over with.' My voice trembles over the last couple of words. I'm going to break down.

Oh, please God – if you're up there, somewhere – don't let me break down . .

No more words. I can't risk it.

Don't show them how terrified you are, Callum. Don't show them how you want to clutch at them and beg them not to kill you. Don't show them . . .

'Put your hands behind your back, Callum,' Jack says quietly.

I look at him. Strange . . . His eyes are shimmering. I try to comfort him. No words, just the briefest of smiles in gratitude for his pity before I turn around, my hands behind my back as I wait to be handcuffed.

'D'you want a priest or some kind of spiritual counselling?' Giustini asks.

I shake my head. I never really believed in it when I was alive, so it would be hypocritical to call for it now.

When I was alive . . .

I'm not dead yet. Not yet. Every second counts. There's still time. I must have hope. Hope till the very end. Miracles have happened before. My cell door opens wider. Giustini leads the way, with two guards I've never seen before on either side of him. Jack walks next to me.

'You're doing fine, Cal,' Jack whispers. 'Be strong. Not long now.'

They lead me down the long corridor. I've never been this way before. Early evening sunlight streams in through the high windows and dances across the floor all around me. It's so bright I can see the dust motes swirling through the air. Who would've thought that dust could look so eerily beautiful. I try to walk as slowly as possible, to drink in every sight and sound. To make each moment last a lifetime.

'Good luck, Callum . . .'

'Spit in their eye, Cal . . .'

'Bye, Cal . . .'

Anonymous calls from the cells on one side of the corridor. I'm tempted to turn and study the faces behind the words but that would take too much time. And that's the one thing I don't have any more. I look straight ahead. The door opens at the end of the corridor. More blazing sunshine. Such a perfect day. We step out. I stop abruptly.

Faces. A sea of faces, even more than when my father was about to be hanged. Lots of Crosses, come to watch the show. But the sun is before me and dazzling my eyes. I can't see much. Besides, the scaffolding is in the way. And the noose up there, gently swaying in the evening breeze.

Don't look at it.

I want to cry.

Please God, don't let me cry . . .

Please God, don't let me die . . .

Giustini and his guards move to one side of the scaffold. Jack leads me to the stairs. I climb up them. He follows.

'Forgive me, Callum,' Jack whispers.

I turn my head. 'Don't be silly, Jack, you haven't done anything.'

'Neither have you,' says Jack.

I pause to smile at him. 'Thanks for that.'

We're at the top of the scaffold now. The noose is less than a metre away. And beneath it a closed trapdoor. I turn to look at the governor. He's standing beside another man, a nought with blond hair wearing a black suit. The nought stands behind a long lever. The lever for the trapdoor.

My life in your hands.

I don't want to die . . .

There's still time. There's still hope.

I look around, scanning the crowd, searching the audience for her. But I can't see her. If I could just see her one last time . . . Where is she? Is she even here? Sephy. And my child that I'll never see. Never hold. Never know.

Is she here?

Please, God . . .

'I've got to put your hood on now,' Jack says softly.

'I don't want it on.' How will I find her with a hood on?

'I'm afraid you have no choice. Those are the rules,' Jack apologizes.

He pulls the hood over my head. I try to pull back. I'm not trying to run away. I just want to see her . . . One last time . . . The hood is over my head and hangs down to my shoulders. The world is black as night. Jack pulls my arm to lead me to the rope.

Please God, I don't want to die . . .

Sephy . . .

Tears run down my face. Now I'm grateful for the hood.

'I LOVE YOU, CALLUM . . .'

Wait . . .

'I LOVE YOU, CALLUM. AND OUR CHILD WILL LOVE YOU TOO. I LOVE YOU, CALLUM, I'LL ALWAYS LOVE YOU . . .'

The noose is being pulled down over my head and around my neck. But I can hear her.

I can hear her. She's here.

'I LOVE YOU, CALLUM . . .'

Thank you, God. Thank you.

'I . . . I LOVE YOU TOO, SEPHY . . .' Can she hear me?

'I LOVE YOU, SEPHY. I LOVE YOU, SEPHY.'

Wait . . . Please wait . . . Just a moment longer . . .

'I LOVE YOU, CALLUM . . .'

'SEPHY, I LO . . .'

one hundred and seventeen.
Sephy

The trapdoor opens.

'I LOVE YOU, CALLUM,' I scream frantically.

He drops like a stone. My words die on my lips.

There's no sound except the rope creaking and groaning as Callum's body swings slowly to and fro.

Did he hear me? I don't know. He must have heard me. Did he say I love you '*too*'? Maybe I just imagined it. I can't be certain. I don't know.

Dear God, please let him have heard me. Please.

Please.

If you're up there.

Somewhere.

BIRTH ANNOUNCEMENTS

At midnight on 14th May
at Mercy Community Hospital,
to Persephone Hadley
and Callum McGregor (deceased),
a beautiful daughter, Callie Rose.

Persephone wishes it to be known that
her daughter Callie Rose will be taking
her father's name of McGregor.

AUTHOR'S NOTE

The African-American scientists, inventors and pioneers mentioned in chapter 30 are all real people and their achievements are very real. When I was at school, we didn't learn about any of them – except Robert Peary, the white European-American explorer. I wish we had done. But then, if we had, maybe I wouldn't have written this book...

Read on for **CALLUM**

introduction

I've had a vast number of letters and emails over the years regarding NOUGHTS & CROSSES, and how the lives of Callum and Sephy might have been very different, if only they'd made alternative choices. Some letters suggested that Sephy shouldn't have chosen her unborn child over Callum's life; others wondered if maybe the ending was a ruse perpetrated by Sephy's father, Kamal, and that Callum wasn't really dead. Some speculated as to what would have happened if Callum had read Sephy's letter in time.

Now, I love what if games! Constructing alternative realities and scenarios is something I've done since I was a child. When I was asked to write a World Book Day story, set at the time and in the world of NOUGHTS & CROSSES, it was my chance to play just such a what if game. As such, this story is not an amendment or true addendum to NOUGHTS & CROSSES, but a flight of fancy on my part. This story asks: What if Callum had run away with Sephy when he helped her to escape after she'd been kidnapped? I believe that sometimes alternative paths lead to different destinations, and sometimes they don't . . .

malorie blackman

CALLUM

malorie
blackman

CORGI

For Neil and Lizzy,
Mum and Wendy,
with love – as always.

What would have happened if . . . ?

CALLUM takes place within the timeline of NOUGHTS & CROSSES.

At this point in time, Sephy, a Cross, has been kidnapped by the Liberation Militia (LM) and is being held for ransom, thanks to the betrayal of her best friend and childhood playmate, Callum, who is a nought. This story takes place as the others in Callum's LM cell go to pick up the ransom money from Kamal, Sephy's father, leaving Sephy alone with Callum, as his prisoner.

one. Tears

Sephy must've dozed off. Her eyelashes are spiky from where she's only just stopped crying. The tracks of her tears have dried on her cheeks.

Tears caused by me.

Sephy told me once that I was the only one who could ever make her cry. I've never told this to her, or to anyone else for that matter, but it works the other way round as well.

How long have I been standing here now, looking down at her?

Too long.

The thoughts in my head are driving me crazy. Damn, but she's beautiful. Even more beautiful than I remember. And I remember a lot. I watch Sephy and memories of the two of us play in my head on an incessant loop. Some are bad, some are good. Some make me smile.

Some hurt.

Right now, the ones that hurt dominate. I'm standing right next to her and I don't think I've ever felt quite so far away, not even when she went away to Chivers Boarding School. To think that once, another lifetime ago, Sephy pleaded with me to run away with her. She poured out her heart to me in a letter, a letter I read too late.

She cared for me – once.

And now, as I stand watching her, I can't stop thinking about what might have been . . . I can't stop imagining the two of us together. My body burns at the thought of it. Sephy and I might've been together for ever.

We might've . . . flown.

Maybe in a parallel universe somewhere, Sephy and I are together and happy. Maybe in a parallel universe somewhere, there's no one but me and Sephy, like Adam and Eve. If Heaven exists, then that would be it.

But what's the point of thinking that way?

Better to deal with what is, rather than what might have been or some alternate reality somewhere else.

Sephy is our hostage, a prisoner of the Liberation Militia, and I've been left behind to watch her whilst the others pick up the ransom we've demanded from her father, Kamal Hadley. Will he pay it? It's not like we're asking for peanuts, but he can afford it – and more. There's no such thing as a broke politician. But Sephy's dad is such a shit. I wouldn't put it past him to have the police lying in wait, or to try and hand over a rucksack full of newspaper instead of money. I still don't understand how Sephy turned out the way she did when she's got such a bastard for a dad and such a stuck-up bitch like Jasmine Hadley for a mother. Her sister Minerva is no better. The few times I've come across Sephy's sister, she's always looked at me like I was something particularly revolting that had just been vomited all over her. How ironic, then, that Sephy should be the one in our clutches instead of any other member of her family. How ironic that Sephy, who has always supported the Liberation Militia's aim of equality for and between noughts and Crosses, should now be subject to our tender mercies.

The Liberation Militia have her now.

Thanks to me.

She would never have fallen into our hands if I hadn't set her up.

I betrayed her.

That thought, more than any other, rips strips off what's left of my soul like some kind of insatiable hell-hound.

I betrayed her.

Now every time she looks my way, her hatred for me inflicts third-degree burns up and down my body. And how can I blame her?

What's going to happen when the others get back? What's going to happen to Sephy if her dad pays the ransom?

Is it likely that he will?

My brother Jude seems to think so.

I'm praying, like I've never prayed before, that he won't. That might buy Sephy another day or two, but even that is doubtful. Whatever her dad decides to do, Sephy is as good as dead. It's a question of when, not if.

God, please, if you're out there . . .

But when did God – or anyone else for that matter – listen to any prayer of mine, let alone answer it?

The future stretches out before me like a long, hot desert road. I know only too well what Andrew and Jude and Leila and the others expect me to do. Once Kamal Hadley has paid up, it'll be my job to . . . to get rid of Sephy.

Get rid of . . .?

Tell it like it is, Callum.

It'll be my job to . . . to kill her and bury her in the surrounding forest where she'll never be found.

And I'll have to do it. What choice do I have?

It's her or me – or both of us.

Stop thinking about it, Callum. You're not fifteen any more. You're not the idealistic kid who thought that, deep down, somewhere, somehow, in some way, life had to be fair.

I know better now.

And yet, if I know so much better, why am I in this tiny, windowless box of a room, standing by Sephy's bed and staring down at her like some kind of low-life, no-class, predatory stalker?

Maybe because it's the only way I can look at her without her contemptuous glare burning holes straight through me. Maybe because I look at her as she sleeps and she reminds me of what I used to be, what I might have been.

And I hate her so much for reminding me.

And I love her so much for the exact same thing.

Jeez, this is doing my head in.

I've got to stop this. It does no good to brood on ifs and buts and maybes. 'If only' has to be one of the most pitiful phrases in the English language. I have to deal with what I've got now – which is my friends in the Liberation Militia, my brother Jude and the LM cause. At last, I have a reason to fight, to live.

So why do I feel so dead inside?

I need to think. I've got to sort out my head before the others get back.

But I don't want to leave Sephy alone in this room.

I'll sit here on the floor, just so I can keep an eye on her. Just to make sure she doesn't try anything desperate when she wakes. Just so she doesn't feel quite so alone. This concrete floor is cold and bloody hard but I need to stay put. And think.

two. Escape

Sephy opened her eyes and looked straight at me. And I didn't miss the way her body recoiled at the sight. I was still sitting on the hard, cold floor where I'd sat for the last hour, my back against the wall. Sephy sat up slowly, rubbing the sleep out of her wary eyes. She didn't take her gaze off me for a second. As I got to my feet, I waited for her to speak. She said nothing. She placed one hand over her stomach and began to rub it slowly, unaware that she was even doing it.

'What's the matter?' I asked, pointing to her stomach. Stupid question. Jude had hand-delivered a crippling punch with as much venom as he could muster. And even though I'd felt his blow like it had been directed at me, I hadn't stopped him. Even though my mind had screamed out 'NO!' I hadn't said a word. I answered my own question. 'You're hurting.'

Silence.

'Would you like some water? Or some aspirin?'

Sephy shook her head. She frowned, straining to hear beyond the silence between us. 'Are we alone?' she asked at last.

'Yes.'

'The others have gone to pick up the ransom?'

'Yes.'

'I see. Are you here to gloat?' Sephy asked.

Slowly I shook my head, not trusting myself to speak.

'Yeah, right. Go away, Callum.' Sephy lay down and turned away. I was effectively dismissed.

I was going to leave her alone, I really was, but somehow my feet had other ideas. Two strides later, I was at her side. I sat down at the edge of the bed, beyond weary. The unnatural stillness of her prone body indicated that she was very aware of me, but she still wouldn't look at me.

Sephy, don't treat me like I'm invisible. Please, don't do that. Not you, of all people. Not you too . . .

The words filled my head to overflowing but never left my mouth. I was being stupid. After what I'd done, was it likely that she was going to leap into my arms and smother me with kisses?

Maybe not, but I would've settled for a smile. One simple, genuine smile.

But that was asking too much.

What could I say to get her to look at me the way she used to? What could I do to help her, to make her stop hurting? To show her that I still . . . remembered the two of us in better times? No, not better, just more . . . innocent.

Tentatively, I replaced her hand with my own to rub her abdomen in gentle circles. Touching her was like touching lightning. A painful jolt of electricity stung my fingers and shot up my arm to cascade through my entire body. Sephy turned to look at me, her eyes wide.

'W-what're you doing?' she asked.

'You're hurting.'

'Like you care.'

We regarded each other.

'I care,' I replied at last.

Tears clouded Sephy's eyes. 'Then let me go. Please.'

I didn't reply. We both knew the answer to that one.

'Why're you in here?' Sephy asked with a sudden burst of anger. 'Are you afraid I'll somehow dematerialize if you don't keep your eyes on me twenty-four-seven and then you'll get the blame?'

'I want to make sure you're OK.'

'Oh, please. Spare me the platitudes,' Sephy scoffed.

'It's the truth.'

'Well, as you can see, I'm fine. Never been better.' Sephy removed my hand from her stomach. 'So feel free to leave the door open on your way out.'

Once again she turned away from me, muttering something under her breath.

'What did you say?' I asked sharply.

'Nothing. I didn't say anything,' Sephy denied. 'Go away.'

I knew what I'd heard. At least . . . at least, I thought I knew. It was something like, 'stupid to think you ever loved me . . .' I looked down at Sephy on the bed and the world stopped. Time stopped. At that moment, it was like I was looking down at myself and all the things I'd done and become since Sephy and I had been apart.

That's when I made my decision. And though every sense, every cell, every part of me roared, 'NO!' I knew I was going to ignore them all and be damned. Literally. I got to my feet and moved back a couple of paces.

'Sephy, stand up.'

Sephy turned to eye me warily. Moments ticked by, moments neither of us could afford to waste. But at last she did as I asked. I moved closer to her, trying to pretend I didn't see the way she flinched, trying to ignore the fear that darkened her honey-brown eyes. A stillness crept over her as she waited with trepidation to see what I'd do next. I took one of her resistant hands in mine.

'Come with me.' I started pulling her after me. She instantly tried to pull away.

'Sephy, we have to get out of here.'

'Callum, please . . .' Sephy's voice trembled. 'P-please don't kill me . . .'

I stilled. Is that what she thought . . . ? 'I'm not going to kill you.'

Sephy snatched her hand out of mine. 'What's that then?' she asked, pointing to the waistband of my trousers.

I glanced down, then saw the hand gun she was pointing to, its stock visible above my belt. The gun I'd forgotten that I was carrying, to be honest. It was a stupid place to carry a gun, really, but I had the safety on, so there was no danger of shooting off my bits. In our cell it was compulsory for every member to carry a gun at all times.

'Sephy, you have to trust me.'

'I've already made that mistake – remember?' Sephy said bitterly. 'There are plenty of new mistakes for me to make without repeating any. At least, I thought so until this moment.'

'This moment?' I frowned.

'I've run out of time, haven't I? You're going to kill me.'

I clamped my lips together. She really believed . . .

Callum, you betrayed her, so why are you surprised?

You asked her to meet you just so Jude and the others in your LM cell could kidnap her and hold her to ransom.

But the fact that she thought I could kill her without a moment's hesitation . . . Every time I thought I couldn't feel any lower, that I couldn't hurt any worse inside, Sephy always found a way to prove me wrong.

'Is this where you d-drag me outside and send a bullet through my brain?' Sephy whispered, her whole body trembling now.

A second or two passed before I could trust myself to speak. 'No, this is where I help you to escape.'

three. Going Once . . .

Sephy stared at me. 'W–what?'

'You heard me, but we have to hurry. You need to be long gone before the others get back.'

And still the shadow of suspicion clouded her eyes.

It hurt.

'Do you want to get back to your parents or not?' I held out my hand. 'This is a one time, never-to-be-repeated offer – going once, going twice . . .'

'OK! OK!' Sephy said quickly, putting her hand in mine.

Her head tilted to one side as she scrutinized me. And the clouds in her eyes hadn't dissipated. I forced myself not to look away.

'You have to trust me,' I said quietly. 'Now let's get out of here.'

Sephy nodded.

Callum, don't do this . . .

The dissenting voice inside my head had tried relentless shouting to no avail, so now it was an incessant, insistent whisper. A shout I could zone out, like so much static. This insidious, whispering voice inside my head was harder to ignore. This was madness. And even if I took Sephy back to her parents, how on earth was I going to explain her disappearance to Jude and the others? There was nothing I could say that they'd believe.

If I did this I'd be signing my own death warrant . . .

Sephy or me . . . ?

Me or Sephy . . . ?

We reached the front door. I let go of Sephy's hand, pulled my gun out of my waistband and flicked off the safety.

'Callum, what—?'

'Shush!' Turning to Sephy, I placed a finger against my lips, scowling at her. As she looked from my face to the gun and back again, her expression revealed that she was still more afraid of me than of anything or anyone that might be outside the cabin. Swallowing hard, I turned away. Slowly, I opened the door. Jude and the others shouldn't be back for at least another couple of hours, but I hadn't lived this long by assuming anything. I dropped my gun hand to my side so that I wouldn't alert anyone skulking as to what I was holding.

The coast looked clear. The two cars we had were gone; Jude and Morgan had taken one car, Pete and Leila had taken the other. I should've planned this better. I should've disabled one car and taken off in the other with Sephy whilst the others were in the back of the cabin. I shook my head. No, that would've been far more dangerous. We'd have stood more chance of getting caught if I'd tried to sneak Sephy out of the cabin whilst the others were there. Both of us would've ended up with bullets in our backs. Let's face it, there was no fool-proof way to do this.

I stepped outside, the night air cool and welcome on my fevered face. The newly minted moon was nearly full and low in the sky. All around us the leaves on the trees whispered in the night breeze. And I knew what they were whispering.

This was pure insanity.

I was going to get us both killed.

Better to turn round and lock Sephy back in her room. Better to wait for the others to arrive with the ransom and then follow my orders. But that was the trouble, because I knew – deep down in a place I could barely stand to acknowledge – that I wouldn't be able to do it. I just couldn't. So this was the only alternative.

A slim chance against no chance at all.

A swift look round was all I needed to show that we were still alone. I turned back to Sephy and beckoned her towards me. She hesitated. I put the safety back on my automatic and replaced it beneath my waistband. And still Sephy hesitated. I glared at her with impatience.

'This isn't going to work if you don't trust me,' I told her, my voice harsher than I'd intended. 'I'm trying to help you.'

Without a word, Sephy left the cabin doorway and walked towards me. I held out my hand.

'You need to stay close. If we get separated, we've both had it,' I told her.

She put her hand in mine. It was cool, almost cold.

I still scared her.

And no wonder, 'cause at this precise moment I was scaring myself.

This was beyond stupid, but there was no turning back.

four. Why?

We'd barely taken a couple of steps when Sephy asked, 'Callum, why are you doing this?'

I risked a swift glance back at her. 'Does it matter?'

'Yes, it does. To me it does,' Sephy replied.

'We don't have time for this,' I said impatiently.

Sephy's hand still in mine, I led the way through the trees. The rustling leaves all around us whispered their disapproval. 'We have to keep going,' I told her.

Sephy pulled away from me. 'Not until you answer my question. Why are you doing this?'

'You're really going to make me do this now?' I asked incredulously.

'Yes,' Sephy replied.

I recognized that look of old. Sephy was digging her heels in and they wouldn't shift until she got what she wanted. How on earth was I supposed to answer her? With a sigh of exasperation, I plumped for the inconvenient, angry truth.

'Oh, for God's sake! I'm doing this for us. For what we once were, for what we once had together. OK? Happy now?'

Silence. Except for my heart hammering in my chest there was absolutely no sound. Even the breeze whispering between the branches of the trees above us had stilled, as if waiting for Sephy to say something. Anything.

Sephy lowered her gaze. 'We'd better get going,' she said at last.

And it was ridiculous, I know, but – though I expected no less and deserved no more – I was still disappointed. I led the way through the forest. Sometimes the canopy of branches and leaves above us blocked out almost all the moonlight. Eerie sounds of nocturnal forest creatures broke the uneven silence. I was a city boy. Greenery made me nervous. Every cracking twig, every dry leaf bruised and protesting underfoot made me wince. If the others had arrived back at the cabin and were now chasing us then each of those sounds would've given away our position for sure.

Callum, calm down . . .

If any of my LM colleagues were following us, then I would know about it. My Liberation Militia training on that score had been second to none. But that knowledge didn't stop each and every sound from setting my teeth on edge.

Sephy's hand in mine was not quite as cold as it had been before, but I didn't try to kid myself that any other part of her was warming to me. So why was I doing this, burning my bridges behind me for someone who could hardly stand to look at me?

Stop pretending you don't know.

I might be fooling Sephy, but there was no way I could fool myself.

five. Painful Wounds

We'd been travelling through the forest for well over an hour, but it felt a damned sight longer. The floor of the forest was soft, almost sticky, but that made it hard going. The branches of the trees had been getting lower and thicker around us for the last thirty-odd minutes. I'd had to relinquish my grasp of Sephy's hand just to move them aside. I had no knife, no machete, no secateurs, just a gun. And I couldn't exactly shoot the bastard things out of my way. I'm super-fit but even my legs were beginning to ache.

This had to be the right direction, I was sure of it. Almost sure of it. When I was a kid, Dad used to bring the whole family to this forest for the odd day out. We'd have picnics and cycle round or play hide-and-seek. Trouble was, that had been a long time ago. And I'd never navigated my way through the forest in the dark before. All the recent times I'd made the journey to and from the cabin had been by car. But this was the right direction, it had to be. There was Orion's Belt. As long as I kept it directly in front of me that should lead us to the road – if I wasn't mistaken.

'Damn it! Ow!' Sephy's cry was choked off almost at once. I turned to see Sephy sitting in a collapsed heap on the ground, one fist cradled by her lap, her other hand rubbing at her ankle.

Less than a moment later, I was squatting down before her. Not just her forehead but her whole face was bathed in sweat. She looked like she was two seconds or less from passing out.

'What happened? What's the matter?'

'Nothing,' Sephy denied. 'Just give me a moment.'

'Sephy . . .'

'I was pushing one of the branches out of the way and it tore open the wound on my finger. That's all,' Sephy said.

'What's wrong with your ankle?'

'There was a hole, it must've been a rabbit hole or something. I twisted my ankle when I tried to jump out of the way of the branch as it swung back.'

'Can you stand?'

Sephy pushed against the ground with her still-clenched fist and struggled to get to her feet. I jumped up and tried to help her, one hand around her waist, the other beneath her tensed elbow. The moment she put some weight on her ankle, she cried out in agony.

'Shit!' The expletive burst from me. We still had quite some way to go and Sephy was having trouble even standing up. 'Let me see your finger.'

Sephy reluctantly held out her hand. I placed my palm under her fist, waiting for her fingers to unfurl. But already my palm was wet and a little sticky. Grasping her fist in both of my hands, I slowly straightened out her fingers. Blood ran from the knife wound I'd inflicted on her earlier.

I had done that . . . deliberately caused her pain.

I was the one who'd cut her finger so that we could send her blood-stained T-shirt to her father to show him we meant business. The deed had been bad enough, but it was the look of hurt and reproach clouding her eyes afterwards that I'd always carry with me.

Sephy winced.

'I'm sorry.' My voice was gruff. 'Can you walk if you lean on me?'

'I think so. Callum, c-can we rest first . . . just f-for a minute . . .?'

'Sephy, are you sure you're . . .?'

Sephy fell against me.

I wrapped my arms round her before she keeled over completely. She was drenched. And shaking. What was I thinking? I should've realized that she'd need to take a break before now.

'For God's sake, why didn't you tell me to stop?'

Sephy shrank away. I didn't mean for my words to bite and the harsh contempt lacing my tone wasn't directed at her, but she wasn't to know that.

'T-tell you!' Even though Sephy was still trembling, her voice held a trace of incredulity. 'I should've told you to stop?'

'OK, you could've asked me,' I replied, my tone equally dry.

'I just need to catch my breath.'

But that wasn't true. She needed to do more than catch her breath and we both knew it. I took a step backwards, still holding onto Sephy's hands which quivered in mine like trapped birds. Her breaths were short and raspy and she kept bowing her head as if its weight was too much for her neck. Even without the moonlight now bathing us, I would've been able to tell that Sephy was beyond exhausted.

'We'll rest for a couple of minutes,' I whispered. 'But we can't linger. The others have cars and if they catch us on the road . . .'

Sephy took a deep breath and raised her head to look directly at me.

'I'm OK. You can let go now.'

'Sephy . . .'

'I'm fine,' Sephy insisted though gritted teeth.

She took a step, then choked off an agonized cry as her weight descended on her ankle again. I moved forward to help her but she immediately pulled away. We stared at each other. At that moment, all I wanted to do was hold her and tell her everything was going to be all right, but that would just freak her out. And if I did say that, we'd both know that I was lying. Sephy should've been practically home by now. Instead we were still in this forest and with every second that passed, we ran the risk of being caught.

And God help both of us if that happened.

'I'll be all right, Callum. Just give me a moment.' Sephy took a deep breath, followed by another and then another.

'Unless the night air's laced with painkillers, deep breaths aren't going to help your ankle any.'

Sephy sighed with irritation. 'If you have a better suggestion, I'm all ears. I see your sarcasm hasn't deserted you.'

'My shadow and my sarcasm are the only things I have left,' I told her. 'And even my shadow has been known to desert me when the going gets tough.'

Sephy studied me. 'Sounds lonely.'

I shrugged. 'I survive.'

'Is that enough for you? Just surviving?'

'It's better than the alternative.'

Sephy nodded sadly. 'If you'll help me, I'm sure I can make it to the road.'

I had a decision to make. Even with my help, with Sephy's ankle the way it was, it'd probably take us until at least mid-morning to reach the road, by which time the others in my cell would be able to pick us up and pick us off with no trouble at all. Jude was an expert tracker, as were Leila and Morgan for that matter. Though I hadn't said anything, I was sure the others had to be back at the cabin by now. Once they discovered that we'd both disappeared, it wouldn't take them long to put two and two together and figure out what I'd done. Our progress had been much slower than I'd anticipated. I had hoped we'd have managed to hitch a ride and be miles away from here by now. If I'd planned this better, I would've left the cabin with water, blankets, a couple of knives and some food – at the very least. But helping Sephy escape had been a spur-of-the-moment decision. I couldn't shake the feeling that it was a decision that was going to cost both of us dear.

So what now?

'Sephy, I need you to stay here,' I decided after some thought.

'Why? You're not going to leave me here alone, are you?' The pitch of Sephy's voice rose by at least half an octave.

'I need to find us some shelter for the night. There used to be an old, abandoned shack around here someplace. If it's still standing, we'll head there. Then I can strap up your ankle and we can set off for the road at dawn.'

Sephy shook her head frantically. 'Callum, please don't leave me here alone. I couldn't bear it.'

'Sephy, I'll be back before you know it,' I tried to assure her.

'Don't leave me here.'

I took her hands in mine and looked her straight in the eye so she would know I was telling the truth. 'Sephy, I'm coming back. I promise. Trust me.'

Sephy scrutinized my face, her own expression sombre. 'Where are you going? Why d'you need to go?'

'We can't make it to the road any time soon, not with your ankle in that state. The shack is closer. It wouldn't surprise me if the roof is half-gone, but it'll do for the night, so you can rest. Then early tomorrow morning we'll set off and hope luck is on our side.'

'So why can't I come with you to look for it?'

'Sephy, talk sense. You can barely stand. I can travel faster alone, but I'll come back and get you. OK?'

Sephy's gaze fell away from my own, but not before I caught the fear creeping across her face, freezing her expression as it went.

'Which one is it?'

'Sorry?' Sephy raised her puzzled gaze to ask.

'Which one d'you think I'm going to do? Abandon you to your fate out here? Or d'you reckon this is your final resting place and I only brought you out here to save having to carry your body?' Frustration and more lent my voice an icy edge.

Silence. Then, unexpectedly, Sephy smiled, albeit faintly. 'I think you're going to find us some shelter for the night and then tomorrow you'll help me to get home,' she said softly.

'Are you sure that's what you really think?' I asked.

Sephy hobbled closer until she stood before me. 'Yes, Callum, that's what I really think.'

And then she placed a hand on either side of my face and leaned forward to kiss me. It was probably meant to be light and friendly and grateful, nothing more, but the moment her lips touched mine it turned into something else, something combustible. A second later, my arms were wrapped around her waist and her arms were wrapped around my neck, her fingers playing in my hair as we kissed. One kiss to share our mutual sadness and longing and hunger for something real, something more. And it wasn't like the last time either. This time, I could almost taste our shared desperation. She was so soft in my arms. Her kiss was burning my blood. I wanted her so much – not just her body, but her heart as well.

I was greedy. I wanted it all.

A malevolent voice sidled into my head, telling me that Sephy was only doing this because she needed my help, because she was desperate. I tried to smother the voice but it was too late. The thought entered my mind and took up residence. Abruptly, I pulled away from her.

Sephy stared at me, breathing heavily. She started to raise her hand to her lips. I got in first. I wiped the back of my hand across my mouth. The tips of two of Sephy's fingers lightly touched her slightly-parted lips, but her hand fell away from her face when she saw what I did. And the hurt in her eyes was just as bad as – if not worse than – the moment I had deliberately cut her finger.

Damn! I really thought she was going to wipe her mouth.

'Sephy, I . . .'

'I'll wait here by these trees.' Sephy turned away from me. That shimmer in her eyes – was it my imagination or a trick of the moonlight?

Sephy bent to gingerly pat the ground near the base of a tree with a broad trunk, before slowly sitting down, her legs curled to one side of her. She looked around nervously before studying her hands in her lap.

'Are you hungry?' I asked. 'I've got some mints.'

'No, thanks,' Sephy replied, her head still bent.

Say something, Callum. Explain.

But in the end, all I said was, 'I'll be as quick as I can.'

Sephy's voice, no more than a whisper, asked, 'Will you be able to find your way back to me?'

'I'll find you,' I told her.

She could be the proverbial needle and I'd turn into a magnet, just so I'd be able to find her and be with her.

'I'll see you really soon.'

'Callum . . . be careful,' Sephy whispered.

'Always,' I told her.

I tried to force a smile, but I was wasting my time. It was a smile she didn't see. Sephy still refused to look at me.

Not once since I'd wiped my mouth had she looked at me.

Not once.

seven. Let Me Help

'Sephy? Sephy, where are you?'

A twig or branch cracked from somewhere behind me. I whipped round, my hand on my gun.

It's not Jude or one of the others, I told myself.

If it was, I'd already have a bullet in me . . .

Unless they hadn't got Sephy yet and were waiting for her to reveal herself so they could get the both of us together . . .

Calm down, Callum.

It was a hard fight to bank down the panic flaring up within me. I'd been away for over an hour but I'd found the shack. It consisted of only two rooms, one room occupied by a chair which was no use for anything but firewood. After kicking in the locked door (I mean, why on earth would anyone bother to lock the door in the first place?), I'd spent at least two minutes making a thorough inspection of the place. The penlight attached to my key ring was barely up to the task but it was better than nothing. The shack was habitable – just. The roof was mostly intact, but there was no glass in the windows, just closed shutters. I'd spent a few minutes stacking what was left of the rotten furniture in one room so that we could use the other. And I'd used a couple of leafy branches to try and sweep the floor clean. I then took more time to try and make it comfortable for Sephy. It wasn't exactly five star, but it would have to do, at least until dawn.

With a lot of luck, the others in my LM cell would think that Sephy and I were long gone and wouldn't bother looking so close to home. In fact, with even more luck, they might pack up and leave believing that the police might be about to descend upon them at any moment.

I had to keep stopping to get my bearings, to make sure that I wasn't getting hopelessly lost – or worst still, wasn't inadvertently making my way back to the cabin. And time wasn't on my side.

By the time I got back to Sephy's location, I was heartily sick and tired of trees and leaves and nature. I longed for a greasy spoon café and a road filled with pot-holes and a pavement made up of broken slabs and roadwork signs. I would've paid good money to see some graffiti at that moment.

The only trouble was, Sephy wasn't where I'd left her.

She was nowhere in sight.

I was sure this was the right place. I'd left a trail for myself, a broken branch pointing down at the ground here, a gouged mark on a tree trunk there. Luckily the moon had remained bright, un-obscured so far by the clouds filling the night sky – but it had still taken a while to find the shack, and then find my way back.

'Sephy, answer me. Where are you?'

The darkness all round threw my words back at me. Until that moment, I'd never considered night to be a physical entity before, but it sure felt like that now. The night slunk its way around me, watching each misstep, like some malicious beast, just waiting for the right moment to pounce. The night air seemed to take on a living, breathing presence of its own. The leaves and the shrubs rustled with this animal's every breath.

I was being fanciful, ridiculous – but that's what the night and fear and guilt can do to you. Where was she? Had my brother got to her before I could return? What if she'd tried to make it on her own and fallen and knocked herself out? Or worse? Or what if . . . ?

'Sephy?'

Oh, for God's sake! If I had any sense, I would take off whilst I still had the chance. But even as the thought entered my head, it left again, finding no room at the inn.

Abandon Sephy?

Yeah, right.

The grip on my gun tightened. Someone was watching me, I could feel it. I opened my mouth to call to Sephy, then thought better of it. The moonlight which had been my ally before was now the enemy. The moon might as well have been a spotlight. Yet directly overhead were silver-laced clouds which were thickening all the time. I edged closer to where the trees and shrubs were densest, the area in the immediate vicinity which had the most shadows. A splash of water hit my forehead – at least I hoped it was water. I wiped the back of my hand across my forehead, just as another drop touched my cheek. Great! That was all I needed. Rain!

I needed to call out for her again. I had to risk it.

'Sephy, p-please . . .' Oh, God! Was that really my voice, shaky with panic?

Where the hell was she?

'Callum, I'm here.'

The voice behind me had me whipping round, gun in hand. The moment I saw it was indeed Sephy and that she was alone, I lowered my gun.

'What the hell? Didn't you hear me calling you?'

'I heard.'

'Then why didn't you answer?'

No reply. She was holding a thick, stripped branch which she hadn't had before. What was the plan? To knock me out whilst my back was turned?

My eyes narrowed. 'Oh, I get it. You were waiting to see if I'd brought back reinforcements.'

'Why d'you do that?' asked Sephy sadly. 'Why d'you ascribe the worst possible motive to everything I say and do?'

'Ascribe? Is that a Chivers Boarding School word?' I mocked. 'You'll have to forgive me. My education didn't get me as far as words like "ascribe". You'll need to use words of one syllable when you talk to me.'

Sephy drew herself up to her full height, looking at me as if she'd never seen me before. She slowly shook her head before turning round and limping away from me, using her branch as a makeshift walking stick. The rain was beginning to make its presence felt now, like a manifestation of all the hurt between us. Sephy took a couple of steps before I ran after her.

'Where're you going?'

'Anywhere, as long as it's away from you, before the chip on your shoulder crushes me too.' Sephy kept moving. Every other step made her wince but she kept going. I moved in front of her. She hobbled around me.

Damn it! Every time I opened my mouth, I managed to make things that much worse between us.

'Sephy, wait.'

'Callum, just point me towards the road and I'll leave you in peace. OK?'

'Don't be stupid. You won't make more than twenty paces without my help.'

'I don't want your help. I don't like the price tag attached,' Sephy told me with a sudden burst of anger. 'You say you're helping me for what we once had and meant to each other, but that was then and this is now. You've gone out of your way to show me how much you despise me. Well, don't worry, I've got the message. So all you need to do is tell me if I'm heading in the right direction for the road, then you'll be rid of me for good.'

I brushed my wet hair off my forehead. 'You're going the wrong way.'

Sephy stopped walking and faced me. 'Well?'

'Well what?'

Sephy glared at me. 'Which way to the road, Callum? Is that succinct enough for you?'

She was talking to me like I was a moron – and I didn't like it. But I had to admit that I'd had it coming.

'Sephy, we can't make it to the road like this. It's too far and it's too dangerous to attempt in the dark, especially in this rain. We'll both break our necks if we try it.'

'We don't have any choice.'

'That's what I'm trying to tell you. I found the shack. We should spend the night there. Once I've strapped up your ankle and we've both rested, come dawn we'll make much better time and it'll be easier to escape.'

'How far away is this place then?'

I was careful to hide the relief whooshing through me. Sephy was prepared to listen to reason, in spite of the antipathy she felt towards me. 'Ten minutes, fifteen max,' I said, deliberately underestimating the actual time it would take.

'OK,' Sephy sighed. 'Lead the way.'

'Let me help you walk,' I said.

'No thanks. I can manage.'

'But you don't have to all by yourself,' I told her. 'I'm here.'

I reached out to put my arm round her waist so she could lean on me, but she vigorously pulled away.

'I said I can manage,' Sephy said, her tone so hostile I was in immediate need of an anti-venom jab. 'I don't want to be touched by someone who feels the need to take a shower immediately afterwards. So thanks, but no thanks.'

We stared at each other.

Just apologize, Callum. Just explain what's going on in this warped head of yours . . .

But I didn't. Somehow, the words just wouldn't come.

'It's this way,' I said at last.

I started walking. Sephy followed. At least we were both heading in the same direction. It was progress – of a sort.

eight. Shelter In The Storm

By the time we made it to the shack we were both drenched. In spite of my leather jacket, my T-shirt was soaked and my trousers felt like they'd been hosed down. My boxers were beyond soggy. They clung to my skin like they were glued. It was bloody unpleasant. I opened the door and let Sephy enter the shack first.

'Well, this was certainly worth waiting for,' Sephy said dryly.

After over twenty minutes of walking in silence, it was a relief to hear her voice again. Our journey to the shack had been achieved without either of us saying a word. Sephy had kept a step or two behind me so that I constantly had to keep turning round to make sure she was still with me, and she gave no sign that she had the slightest interest in anything I had to say. Every time I thought to pierce the uncomfortable quiet, my mouth snapped shut again without saying a word. And every time I slowed down to at least walk in step with her, she'd slow down too so that she stayed behind me. After ten minutes, the rain was pelting down so hard, I would've had to shout to make myself heard anyway.

Not fun.

But at last we'd made it.

Only now I wondered if I'd made the right decision. I watched as Sephy looked round, seeing it through her eyes.

It was a hovel.

A dank, dismal, smelly hovel.

During my previous visit, I'd stripped the leaves off numerous branches and piled them against one wall to make a bed – of sorts – for Sephy. But now that I looked at it again, it just looked embarrassingly pathetic.

I don't know what I was thinking.

'I know it's not much . . .' I began.

Sephy turned to me and actually smiled. 'It'll do. At least it's shelter out of the rain. I'm freezing. And at least I can rest my ankle for a while.'

'It's not exactly what you're used to,' I said.

'Believe me, I'll take this over the cabin with your brother and your friends any day,' Sephy said. 'Besides, it's not that bad. Fix the roof, a lick of paint, some bijou furniture and there'd be no place like home.'

I laughed, much to my surprise.

Sephy grinned at me.

'I should shut the door,' I said doubtfully, my smile fading. 'But once I do, it'll be pitch black in here.'

'Couldn't we start a fire?'

'There's no chimney. And if we start a fire in the middle of the room, it'll be like sending up a flare telling the others where we are – if we don't burn down this place with us inside first,' I replied.

'Can we at least open the shutters, then?'

I shook my head. 'The windows are too low. We could get all kinds of animals coming in whilst we're asleep. Plus, it would leave us too exposed if anyone were to stumble across us.'

'D'you think that's likely?'

'No. The others must believe that we're long gone by now, but there's no harm in being careful.'

Sephy nodded and headed for one corner of our dwelling.

'You can bunk down over there.' I pointed at the pile of leaves on the ground. 'They're dry at least.'

Sephy frowned. 'Hell, no! God only knows what they might contain. Rats or millions of creepy-crawlies – or worse.'

'There's nothing inside them.'

'How d'you know?'

'Because I checked out the pile when I first got here.'

'How much checking could you do in the dark?' Sephy argued.

'Sephy, I'm the one who put the leaves there in the first place so you'd have somewhere a bit softer than the ground to lie on. OK?' I admitted testily.

Sephy's eyes held stunned surprise as she stared at me. 'You did that for me?'

'Yeah. And it's not a big deal so don't turn it into something it isn't.'

Now why the hell did I say that? Damn it!

Sephy smiled faintly. 'Thank you.'

'What's so funny?' I asked, my eyebrows practically knitting together.

'Nothing.' Sephy turned away from me to head for the leaves, but not before I saw the smile on her face broaden.

She struggled to sit down so that she didn't injure her

ankle further. I took a step forward to help, but remembered what had happened the last time and froze. Sephy sat with her back to the wall, facing the front door and just to one side of the room's shutters.

'OK,' she said. 'I'm ready now. You can shut the door.'

'I'll strap up your ankle first,' I told her.

'With what?'

'I'll use my socks,' I told her.

'Are they smelly?'

'Probably. Actually, change that to definitely.'

'So you've decided to kill me slowly by degrees instead,' said Sephy.

My heart hitched at that. She couldn't still believe . . . ?

No. It'd been a joke, that's all. I needed to chill.

'It's a reflection on the nefarious way my mind works,' I told her, attempting to reflect some of her teasing tone.

'Nefarious?' Sephy raised an eyebrow. 'Now that's a university word if ever I heard one.'

'You're not going to let me forget that, are you?' I sighed.

'Nope. Never,' Sephy replied.

'Not that you bear grudges or anything.'

Sephy's smile faded. 'I try not to,' she told me pointedly.

We watched each other. I was the first to avert my gaze. I pulled off my trainers, then my socks, before slipping my shoes back on. I sniffed at my socks dubiously. They did whiff a bit – not surprisingly. I'd had them on all week.

'Oh. My. God! I can smell them from here.' Sephy gagged. She started to have a coughing fit.

'Funny, Sephy.'

Cough! 'I'm not . . .' Cough! '. . . joking!'

I glared at her, she scowled at me. Then we both spontaneously started laughing. When our laughter faded, we were still looking at each other. I broke the spell first.

'I'll just bandage up your ankle, then you can get some sleep.'

'What will you be doing?'

'I'll be keeping watch.'

'You don't have to do that . . .'

'Seph, I'm keeping watch and that's all there is to it. I'd never forgive myself if anything happened to you.'

'But you need to get some rest too,' Sephy protested. 'Why don't you keep watch for a couple of hours and then let me take over?'

'No.' I wasn't about to argue and I wasn't about to budge either.

Sephy's puzzled frown deepened by degrees as she looked at me. 'I'm damned if I understand your attitude. You hate my guts, you can't stand to touch me, you hated me kissing you, and yet you tell me that you won't let anything bad happen to me and you watch over me like a guard dog. I am officially confused.'

'I don't hate you, Sephy.'

Sephy turned her face away from mine. 'There's no need to lie about it, Callum. Actions speak louder than words and I'm a big girl now. I may not like it but I can take it.'

'Sephy, I don't hate you.'

'Yeah, right,' Sephy scoffed. 'So can you bear to touch my skin to strap up my ankle, or should I do it?' She held out her hand for my socks as if my answer was a foregone conclusion.

I sat back on my heels, ignoring her hand, and reached

out to place her injured foot in my lap. Sephy inhaled with a hiss.

'I'm sorry I hurt you,' I told her without looking at her. 'It wasn't intentional.'

Without waiting for a response, I eased Sephy's shoe off her foot. A cursory examination of her ankle revealed that her Achilles tendon was enlarged and swollen, but I didn't think anything was broken. I tried to be as gentle as possible whilst checking it, but she still ended up gasping in pain once or twice. Each time I apologized and tried to be gentler, but it still did no good. I still hurt her.

Knotting my socks together, I started to wrap them round Sephy's ankle and instep before tying the ends together to hold the socks tight and secure. When I'd finished, I risked a glance at Sephy. Her eyes sparkled with unshed tears.

'I'm sorry, Sephy. I tried to be as gentle as I could.'

Sephy shrugged and wiped a quick hand over her eyes. 'It's done now. Thanks for your help. I suppose you'd better shut the door.'

I got to my feet and adjusted the door so that it covered most of the entrance. Kicking it in earlier hadn't helped much with its alignment, but even a door half-hanging off its hinges was better than no door at all.

'At least the rain's easing off now,' I told Sephy.

The moment I propped the door over the entrance, the shadows in our room instantly took over. The roof was missing in one corner so some moonlight managed to seep into the room that way, but it was nowhere near as light as outside. I stood by the door, unsure what to do next. The dark didn't bother me. It usually didn't bother

Sephy either. But her breathing was rapid and audible – almost like she was on the verge of hyperventilating. Though she was trying her best to hide it, she was terrified.

That's when it hit me.

We'd done this to her.

I'd done this to her.

She'd thought she could trust me and I'd betrayed her. When we kidnapped her, we'd placed a bag over her head and kept her in the dark in the back of our stolen van as we made our getaway. Then we dumped the van and set fire to it, before manhandling Sephy into our car and making for the cabin. And what then? We'd locked her in a pit of a room with no windows and a locked door and a low-wattage light bulb that was off most of the time. Jude had physically assaulted her. I'd deliberately cut her finger as well as lacerating her with words to make her feel worthless.

I'd done this to her.

No wonder she was so fearful.

I took a step towards her, then stopped. I'd made so many mistakes, I was desperate not to make another. Maybe it would be better to tell her what I intended to do first? The last thing I wanted to do was scare her even more.

'Seph, I'm going to sit with you a while. OK?'

Sephy whispered, 'Why?'

'You're cold. I'll sit with you until you warm up. And I . . . I don't want you to feel like you're alone. I'm here and I'm not going anywhere, not without you.'

I made my way over to her, moving slowly and carefully. I pulled off my leather jacket, then sat down next to Sephy, my back against the wall.

'Here, wear my jacket. It'll help to warm you up.'

'But what about you?' Sephy asked.

'I'm fine,' I assured her. 'Lean forward.'

After a moment, Sephy did as I asked. I pulled my jacket over her shoulders but as she was leaning back, I slipped my arm round her as well and moved in closer.

'Callum, you don't have to do this,' said Sephy, trying to pull away.

But this time I wouldn't let her.

'I know I don't have to, but I want to,' I replied, kissing her forehead.

Sephy was suddenly still. Puzzled, she turned to look at me, but in the half-light of the shack it was hard to decipher her expression.

'Try and get some sleep, Seph. I'll be here when you wake up.'

Sephy sighed. 'I wish I could figure you out.'

'I'm easy to read, like an open book,' I told her.

'Yeah, but written in an obscure alien language where the characters and symbols keep changing on the page,' said Sephy.

'OK then. Let's play a game. Ask me anything and I'll answer honestly.' The moment the words left my mouth, I wondered if that was such a good idea. 'I mean . . . ask me any three questions and I'll answer honestly!'

I felt rather than saw Sephy's smile. 'Could you beep when you back up fast like that?! You rethought that one sharpish.'

'I think I should change it to one question, instead of three,' I said ruefully.

'No way. Too late. You said three questions and I'm going to hold you to that. But I'll tell you what, you can ask me any three questions too. That's fair,' said Sephy.

I could feel her begin to relax against me, in spite of my arm round her.

'And you'll answer them truthfully?' I asked.

'Always,' Sephy replied. 'So who's going first?'

'I'll go first,' I said quickly. 'OK . . .' My arm tightened marginally round Sephy's shoulders. At first I stared out into the semi-darkness, trying to dredge up the courage to look at her. I turned and scrutinized Sephy, bracing myself for what I was sure I'd see once I asked my question. 'Do you . . . do you think you'll ever be able to forgive me?'

Silence.

I was asking a lot.

I was asking too much.

'You can say no,' I told her softly. 'I'll still help you to get back home. I just . . . need to know.'

'Callum, I've already forgiven you. I just wish . . .' Sephy's words trailed off into silence.

'What d'you wish?'

'That things were different between us.'

I expelled the breath I hadn't realized until that moment that I was holding. Different . . . Different how? I was too wary of the answer to probe further.

'My turn,' said Sephy. 'That's two questions you've asked me, by the way. You've got one left.'

I frowned. 'Just a second, that's not fair.'

'You made the rules, not me.'

Damn it! Sephy was always tricky like that. Not much had changed there then. 'Go on then,' I said with bad grace. 'What's your first question?'

'You do realize you've now asked me all three of your questions, don't you?' Sephy grinned at me.

'Huh? Wait a minute. Asking you "what's your first question?" doesn't count!'

'I think you'll find it does,' said Sephy. 'A question is a question. You never said anything about the required subject matter.'

'Jeez,' I scowled. 'You should be a lawyer.'

'The benefits of a Chivers Boarding School education,' Sephy said.

'Funny, Sephy! Funny.' I was being bulldozed!

'My turn.' There was a significant pause. 'Callum, what do I need to do or say to stop you . . . h-hating me so much?'

I placed my hand under Sephy's chin to turn her face towards mine. Brushing my lips against hers, I asked, 'Does this feel like I hate you?'

Sephy's fingers crept to my lips and, before I realized what she was about to do, she started to wipe my mouth.

I pulled my face away from her hand. 'Don't.'

'You did it,' said Sephy. 'I'm just saving you the trouble. I don't want or need your pity, Callum.'

I had really hurt her by wiping my mouth, much more than I'd realized at the time. Time to be honest.

'I wiped my mouth because I thought you were about to do the same,' I admitted. 'It was a stupid gesture meant to save my stupid pride, nothing else.'

Sephy tilted her head. 'So you don't hate me?'

'Talk sense, Sephy. Would I be doing all this if I hated you?'

'I don't know. I wondered if maybe you were helping me escape as a result of a guilty conscience?'

I took a deep breath and allowed what was left of my pride to dive out of the shutters and scarper.

'Sephy, I'm doing this because I love you. You went away to Chivers and I promised myself I'd get over you, but I never did. I joined the LM, but being with you is the real and only cause worth fighting for.'

Sephy inhaled sharply.

Silence.

'You really love me?' she said at last.

'Yes, really! And I'm sure that's a lot more than three questions. Seems like neither of us can count.'

Sephy sighed. Did she believe me? God only knows, I meant every word.

Love . . . That was such a small word for what I felt. She had me so wrapped up, I couldn't even think straight. It didn't matter how far apart we were, in distance or time, I was hers. No one else's.

There was a lull where she leaned her head on my shoulder and I held her tighter. 'Callum, what's going to happen to us?'

'I don't know,' I admitted. 'What d'you want to happen?'

'Couldn't . . . couldn't we go away somewhere, just the two of us?' Sephy whispered. 'I have some money saved.'

'What about your family?'

'I'll let them know I'm safe, but I want to be with you. You've always meant far more to me than anyone else.'

Oh, God! 'Sephy, don't say things like that. You don't know what it does to me when you say things like that.'

'But it's the truth,' Sephy replied. 'I want to be with you. Don't you want the same?'

I needed to be with Sephy more than I needed my next breath, but how on earth was this going to work?

'You're thinking too much,' Sephy told me. 'Don't over-analyse it, just answer. D'you want to be with me?'

'Yes.'

Sephy's arms snaked round my waist. 'I love you, Callum. Tonight is the start of the rest of our lives. And in the morning, where you go, I go.'

'You make it sound so simple . . .'

'That's because it is,' said Sephy. 'Because you and I have never belonged anywhere except with each other.'

I'd never thought that words could set anything on fire before, but that's what Sephy's words were doing to me. I was burning up. Time to move. I shifted, pulling my arm away from her shoulder as I attempted to stand up.

'What're you doing?' asked Sephy.

'I'm moving to the other side of the room,' I told her.

'Why?' Pause. 'Didn't you mean any of the things you said?'

I immediately hugged Sephy to me, hating the uncertainty I heard in her voice.

'Seph, I meant every word, but you've got to give me a break here. I'm not made of stone and being this close to you, knowing that you don't hate me . . .'

'I love you,' Sephy interjected. 'Always have, always will.'

I groaned. 'Damn it, Sephy. You're not making it easy to walk away from you . . .'

'Then don't. Kiss me instead.'

'Seph, if I kiss you, it won't stop there.'

Sephy nuzzled my jaw, planting kisses as she went. 'Good, because I don't want it to stop there.'

'Do you know what you're saying yes to?' I had to be absolutely sure. 'I want to make love to you, Sephy.'

'Jeez, Callum!' Sephy huffed. 'I had kinda worked that out. And am I pushing you away?'

All my birthdays and Crossmases had come at once. I wanted to whoop for joy, but then reality intruded, just a bit, and my smile faded.

'Sephy, if we're going to be together, I want you to promise me something first.'

'Anything.' Sephy resumed nuzzling me.

I pulled my head away. 'Persephone, this is serious.'

Sephy became still in my arms. 'What is it?'

'If at any point we come across anyone from the LM and I tell you to run, I want you to promise that you'll do as I say. You'll run as fast as you can and not look back.'

'But Callum, how can I just . . . ?'

'I mean it, Sephy. I need you to give me your word. If we're going to have any kind of life together, I need to know that you'll do this.'

'You're asking me to just abandon you?'

'I'm asking you to survive.'

Silence.

'And if I say no?' asked Sephy.

'Then I move to the other side of the room for the night and in the morning I deliver you to your mother's door.'

'But Callum, how can you ask me to do that?' Sephy didn't sound at all happy, but she wasn't the only one with a stubborn streak.

'Sephy, this isn't a debate. Either I get your promise or after tomorrow we never see each other again.'

'You're serious, aren't you?' Sephy's voice barely rose above a whisper.

I didn't answer. I didn't need to. Sephy always knew when I was playing – and when I wasn't.

'OK. I . . . I promise,' said Sephy reluctantly.

'And I'll hold you to it,' I told her, my tone gruff.

'I promise,' Sephy repeated with a sigh.

We held on to each other whilst unwelcome thoughts crowded around us. Sephy took an audible deep breath.

'You're probably worrying about nothing,' said Sephy. 'This time tomorrow, we'll both be so far away from here that no one in the LM will ever find us. You can dye your hair and I'll grow a beard and no one will see through our disguises.'

I laughed, just as she'd intended that I should.

'Callum, you and I are going to have the rest of our lives together.'

I smiled and forced myself to relax. 'I know. I'm counting on it.'

'Now what happened to the kiss you promised me?'

I kissed her.

nine. Maybe Tomorrow

I awoke slowly, basking in a contentment I don't think I'd ever felt before. I glanced down at Sephy who was still asleep with my arm round her, her head on my shoulder, her arm round my waist, her thigh resting over mine. Pure happiness replaced my blood and raced through every part of my body.

I was happy.

God, it felt strange, alien – but so good.

I could definitely get used to this.

Sephy was mine. She loved me.

During the night, after we'd made love, we both got dressed again and held each other whilst we talked and kissed and erased our years apart, until finally we'd both fallen asleep, wrapped round each other. And we'd woken up in the same position. No matter what happened now, no one could take that away from me.

But so much for keeping watch!

Thoughts of the night I'd just shared with Sephy filled my head and healed my heart. I kissed the top of Sephy's head, unable to keep the grin off my face. At that moment, I was so happy, I might self-combust with it.

'Shame on you, little brother. I thought I'd taught you better than that.'

Jude's voice was like a bucket of ice-water thrown over me. I sat bolt upright, dislodging Sephy in the process. My brother was leaning against the opposite wall, next to the now-open door, the gun in his hand pointing straight at my head. I felt round surreptitiously for mine.

'If you're looking for this, then don't bother,' said Jude, tapping my gun which was half hidden beneath the waist-band of his trousers.

Shit! I'd really messed up.

Sephy was awake and sitting up beside me by this time. Jude cast her a look of acid hatred. We were in big trouble.

'Like I said, little brother. I thought I'd taught you better.'

'Sod you, Jude.' I got to my feet, reaching out to help Sephy do the same.

I glanced at Sephy. Her eyes were wide with fright and something else, something worse. Resignation. I slipped on my shoes, desperately trying to think whilst I never took my eyes off my brother.

'Jude, let Sephy go. It's me you want.'

Jude looked me up and down, his gaze dripping with complete contempt. 'Was screwing this dagger whore really worth betraying your cause, your race, your own flesh and blood?'

Oh, God . . . a little help, please . . .

If you're up there . . .

What was I going to do?

Some way, somehow, I had to get Sephy out of here and to safety. But even if I fought Jude for the gun and I won, how far would either of us get before he came after us again? The only way to stop him from pursuing us was to kill him.

But Jude was my brother . . .

But Sephy was my lover . . .

Oh, God.

'How did you find us?' I asked, slowly moving to stand between Jude and Sephy.

'An elephant stampeding through the forest would've left less of a trail to follow than you two,' Jude informed me with derision. 'You screwed up – on so many levels.'

'Jude, please let Sephy leave. This is between you and me.'

'No, it isn't. You brought her into this. She's not going anywhere,' my brother replied.

'Don't make it sound like Sephy stood some kind of chance if she'd stayed in the cabin with you and the others,' I said with scorn. 'We both know the truth behind that one.'

'Yes, but now you've let her drag you down with her,' Jude told me. 'And that was your decision, no one else's.'

'Then why didn't you just shoot us both when we were asleep?' I asked bitterly.

'And miss the look on both your faces when you saw me?' Jude mocked.

That's when I knew that between me and Jude, only one of us would leave this room alive.

'Jude, I don't care what you do to me, but please leave Callum alone,' said Sephy. She stepped out from behind me.

Jude turned his malevolent glare on Sephy. I took her hand in mine and gave it what I hoped was a reassuring squeeze.

'Whatever you may feel about me, Callum is your brother . . .' Sephy continued.

'Not any more,' Jude replied. 'Not when he chose you

over me.'

And Jude levelled his gun to aim straight at Sephy's heart. I stepped in front of her.

'Callum, move,' Jude warned.

I stood absolutely still. Behind me, Sephy tried to side-step me again, but I moved in front of her again. Jude and I regarded each other. His finger began to squeeze the trigger.

I leaped forward. 'SEPHY, RUN!'

A loud retort echoed throughout the entire shack. A bolt of white hot lightning lanced straight through my right shoulder, so hot, so intense it sucked all the breath from my body. But only for a moment. With a yell of rage, I lunged at my brother, my heartbeat thunderous in my ears, my blood roaring.

'SEPHY, YOUR PROMISE. RUN!' I yelled.

I grabbed hold of Jude's gun hand, forcing it upwards as he pulled the trigger yet again. A blur took off past me through the open door.

Run, Persephone. Don't stop. Don't look back. Run.

I said the words over and over in my head as I wrestled Jude to the ground. But one of my arms was beyond use-less.

Please, God, let Sephy escape. Please. I won't ask for any-thing ever again, but just let her escape . . . If you're up there. Somewhere.

Jude punched my wounded shoulder.

'ARGGHHH!' I cried out in agony.

He started to level his gun at me again. I brought my knee up to his groin just as hard as I could. He howled, dropping his gun as he clutched between his legs. As he rolled on the floor, retching, I scrambled for the gun he'd now dropped. Jude quickly pulled out my gun from beneath the waistband of his trousers. I leaped up, his gun in my left hand. Jude struggled to his feet, my gun now in his right hand.

We stood facing each other, each gun pointed at the other brother's heart. My right shoulder was screaming at me in white hot fury. Blood poured down my arm and over my T-shirt. My right arm might be useless but my left still worked and what's more, Jude knew it.

'So what now, little brother?' asked Jude. 'You do remember that we are brothers? Blood? Blood should mean more to you than some Cross whore.'

'Brothers? That didn't stop you ventilating my shoulder.'

'It was meant to be your heart,' Jude told me, eyes narrowed.

'Then it's just as well my aim is better than yours,' I replied.

My head was beginning to swim. I was losing too much blood.

'I will catch up with that whore of yours. You do know that, don't you?' said Jude silkily.

Don't let him get inside your head, Callum. Don't play his game.

'Assuming that you leave this place alive,' I said.

'Even if I don't, even if you do kill me, Morgan or one of the others in the LM will get her. And you. You can't win, Callum.'

My arm, my whole body was so tired. Tired of the bloodshed, the hatred, the means which had grown so large and grotesque as to obscure the end. Tired. And my head felt like it weighed ten times more than usual.

'So what happens now?' I asked, already knowing the answer. My finger tightened on my gun's trigger.

'We both know this can only end one way,' said Jude.

I nodded. With Sephy's teasing, loving smile dancing through my head, I pulled my trigger, just as Jude pulled his.

CALLUM AND SEPHY'S STORY CONTINUES
IN MALORIE BLACKMAN'S POWERFUL,
AWARD-WINNING SEQUENCE . . .

9780552548922   9780552551946   9780552559607

Black and white. Right and wrong . . .

'Few writers can sustain a plot as well as Malorie Blackman' – *Sunday Telegraph*

'Inter-racial teenage love has never been more painful' – *The Times*

'Dramatic, moving and brave' – *Guardian*

'Blackman is a terrific thriller writer' – *Evening Standard*

Malorie Blackman's masterpiece is now available

in a new format – illustrated throughout

by rising star John Aggs

9780857531957

All the latest books, news, videos and podcasts

malorieblackman.co.uk

'Love, hate, fear, jealousy and more than a dash of betrayal.
It's a stylish tale and one ripe for a sequel' – *Telegraph*

'Goes boldly where few YA titles have gone before: never before have I
come across a book that's a combination of *Star Trek*, *Ten Things I Hate About You*
and a murder mystery. What's not to like?' – *Guardian*

9780857531414

What happens when love brings loss?
When love brings lies? When love brings hate?

Olivia and her twin brother Aidan are heading alone back to Earth
following the virus that wiped out the rest of their crew, and their family,
in its entirety. Nathan is part of a community heading in the opposite direction.
But on their journey, Nathan's ship is attacked and most of the community killed.
Only a few survive.

Their lives unexpectedly collide, and Nathan and Olivia are instantly
attracted to each other, deeply, head-over-heels – like nothing
they have ever experienced.

But not everyone is pleased. Surrounded by rumours, deception,
even murder, is it possible to live out a happy ever after . . . ?

'Blackman is a bold, engaging storyteller whose intellectual daring and clear prose reaches kids that other authors don't' – *Sunday Times*

9780552554626

9780552548625

9780552573979

9780552556002

9780552554633

ICE

A NOVEL

LINDA HOWARD

THORNDIKE
WINDSOR
PARAGON

LIBRARY OF CONGRESS CATALOGING-IN-PUBLICATION DATA

Howard, Linda, 1950–
   Ice / by Linda Howard. — Large print ed.
     p. cm. — (Thorndike Press large print basic)
   Originally published: New York : Ballantine Books, c2009.
   ISBN-13: 978-1-4104-2034-3 (alk. paper)
   ISBN-10: 1-4104-2034-5 (alk. paper)
   1. Ice storms — Fiction. 2. Large type books. I. Title.
PS3558.O88217I27 2009
813'.54—dc22
                               2009039653

BRITISH LIBRARY CATALOGUING-IN-PUBLICATION DATA AVAILABLE

Published in the U.S. in 2009 by arrangement with The Ballantine Publishing Group, a division of Random House, Inc.

Published in the U.K. in 2010 by arrangement with Little, Brown Book Group.

U.K. Hardcover: 978 1 408 46022 1 (Windsor Large Print)

U.K. Softcover: 978 1 408 46023 8 (Paragon Large Print)

Printed in the United States of America
1 2 3 4 5 6 7 13 12 11 10 09

ICE

CHAPTER ONE

The place never changed.

Gabriel McQueen actually liked that about his hometown, Wilson Creek, Maine. He liked the continuity of it, the security, the solidarity. He liked that his seven-year-old son, Sam, was seeing the town almost exactly as Gabriel himself had seen it growing up. He liked that Sam was building some of the same memories he had.

He liked the little town as it looked during the march of seasons: the budding of spring, the green of summer, the rioting colors of autumn when the twin white steeples pierced a deep blue sky, but his favorite time of the year was right now. The last few weeks leading up to Christmas were special, when excitement and anticipation seemed to grip everyone and the little kids were almost giddy from it all. He could barely wait to see Sam enjoying the same things he'd enjoyed at that age.

He drove his black four-wheel-drive Ford F-250 through the town square, smiling as he saw that every storefront was decorated with tinsel and twinkling multicolored lights, that the big fir tree in front of the courthouse was festooned with so many lights that it looked like a solid blaze that even the cold, steady, miserable mist of rain dripping from the ugly leaden sky couldn't dim.

There was an empty parking space at the end of the metered row in front of the courthouse, and he squeezed the big pickup between the white lines. Jamming his weatherproof cap on his head, he got out and fed enough change into the old-fashioned meter to buy him two hours. He wouldn't be there that long, but he erred on the side of caution because it would be embarrassing as hell for the sheriff's son to get a parking ticket in front of the courthouse on his first day home — not to him, but to his father. Not embarrassing his father was well worth a couple of quarters.

The mist of rain blew in his face; the last weather report he'd checked predicted snow later on tonight when the temperature dropped. Ducking his head against the wind, he quicktimed up the courthouse steps, opened the double glass doors, then took the stairs on the right down to the basement. The sheriff's department still occupied the basement of the courthouse even though the jail was on the top floor and the arrangement was damned inconvenient, but that was how things had always been and Gabriel figured they would still be that way when he died.

The sheriff's department was the first door on the left. The door opened into an area filled with four desks, three women, and a lot of attitude. Behind them was another door, and stenciled on it was *Harlan McQueen, Sheriff.* The stencil had been done almost thirty years before, and in some places the lettering was almost gone, but Gabriel knew his dad was thinking of retiring — had been for the past five or ten years — so, as a thrifty Mainer, he didn't see any sense in having the doors relettered.

All three women looked up when Gabriel entered, their faces immediately wreathing in smiles. All three jumped up with disconcertingly girlish squeals, considering the youngest was a good fifteen years older than he was, and rushed at him; you'd think he hadn't seen any of them in a year, instead of just two months. Somehow he managed to almost get his arms around them all; he was a big guy, but three women were a lot for any man, especially when one of the women was pleasantly hefty.

Two of the women wore brown sheriff's department uniforms; Judith Fournier and Evelyn Thomas were sisters, and their resemblance was strong enough that when they were in uniform and their hair was pulled back and secured per regulations, they were almost indistinguishable. Patsy Hutt, the queen of the outer office, was soft and round and crowned with snow-white hair. Today she wore thick-soled boots, jeans, and a wool sweater decorated with sequined snowflakes. She looked like the most benign woman in the world, but Gabriel had a very clear memory of her swatting his ass when he was about seven and full of self-importance because his dad was the sheriff.

Among the three women, they controlled the outer office and access to the sheriff, ran most of the department, and knew everything there was to know about everyone in the county.

"It's about time you got here," Patsy scolded. "I was getting worried, with you driving in and meeting this storm head-on."

"Storm?" He went on alert, adrenaline surging. "I checked the weather forecast before I headed out; the rain was supposed to turn to snow tonight, but that was all." That had been this morning, at a motel in Pennsylvania. Before leaving North Carolina he'd put snow tires on his truck because, hell, December in Maine meant snow. That was a no-brainer. Since leaving, though, he'd been listening to XM, so he wasn't up to the minute on the weather forecast.

Patsy's concern meant something, however. Mainers were accustomed to winter weather and knew how to handle it, so any looming storm severe

13

enough to get their attention told him a lot about the potential for danger.

Before she could answer, the door behind them opened and all four looked around. "Gabe," said his father, a wealth of affection and something close to relief in his lined face, and Gabriel tore himself from the clutches of the outer-office tyrants to stride across the floor. He exchanged a brief bear hug with his dad, they clapped each other on the back, then Harlan said, "I'm glad you made it. The weather is turning nasty in a hurry and I need help."

Gabriel's level of alertness ratcheted upward several more degrees. If Harlan McQueen was admitting he needed help, then something serious was going on.

"You got it," he said as they moved

on into Harlan's office, which tended more toward cramped than spacious. The county hadn't splurged on the department's offices, that was for damn certain. "What's up?"

His father's sharp gaze showed appreciation for Gabriel's unhesitating support and willingness to act. When he'd been younger, that natural inclination toward action — any action — had sometimes landed his ass in hot water, but as a sergeant in the military police, he'd been able to channel that aggression and decisiveness into the job, which was good for both him and the army.

"This damn weather system is dipping our way," Harlan said tersely. "We were supposed to get snow, with the ice staying northeast, but now the weather service is saying we're going to get hammered by the ice. They issued the storm warning just a little over an hour ago, and we're scrambling to get ready, plus there's an accident tying up three deputies when I can't spare even one."

Shit, an ice storm. Gabriel was on full alert now, his eyes narrowing, his stance subtly shifting as if he could take on the storm in a bare-knuckle brawl. Ice was ten times worse than a blizzard, in terms of damage. Maine had taken two hits from ice in the past ten or twelve years, but both times the storm had missed this area. That was good then, but bad now, because it meant there was a lot of weakened timber that had been spared before but would now be coming down under the weight of the ice, crushing cars and houses, taking down power lines and leaving hundreds of square miles in the cold and dark. Ice was like a crystal hurricane, destroying everything it touched.

"What can I do?"

"Drive out to the old Helton place and check on Lolly. I haven't been able to get her on her cell phone, and she may not know this weather system has shifted our way."

Lolly Helton? Gabriel almost groaned aloud. Of all the people —

"What's she doing here?" he asked, trying to disguise his sudden hostility, which was the way Lolly Helton had always affected him. "I thought the whole family had moved away."

"They did, but they kept the house for summer vacations. Now they're thinking about selling it, and Lolly's here to check things out and, hell, what difference does it make? She's out there by herself, with no way of calling for help if she gets hurt."

Despite his reluctance to put himself out for Lolly Helton, Gabriel immediately grasped the logistics of what his father was saying. Anyone who wasn't from Maine might not be able to read between the lines, but he could. Cell service was spotty at best; if she'd been safely here in town, Harlan would have been able to reach her on her cell phone, but out by the Helton place a cell phone was useless for anything except throwing. And because no one lived in the old house now, the land-line phone service had long ago been disconnected. Probably there wouldn't be any televisions in the place either, for the same reason. Unless Lolly happened to drive into town and was listening to her car radio, she'd be unaware of looming disaster.

Fuck. There was no way out of it. He had to go after her.

"I'll take care of it," he said, striding to the door. "How much time do I have?"

"I don't know. That's a higher elevation, the icing will start sooner than it does here. The weather service is saying it could begin here as soon as sundown."

Gabriel glanced at his watch. Three p.m. This far north, sunset was around four p.m., which didn't give him much time. "Shit," he said. "I won't have time to see Sam."

"You will if you hurry. The kids were let out of school as soon as the weather service changed the forecast,

19

so your mom has already picked him up. I'll call her to get some coffee and food ready for you, stop by there on the way, then haul ass."

He was out the door, moving fast, before Harlan had stopped talking. The coffee and food were more of a necessity than a comfort. He'd been driving all day, he was tired, and in severe weather conditions having something to eat and drink could make the difference between living and dying. He didn't know what kind of situation he'd be in, once he left the main road and started the long, winding climb toward the Helton place, so it was better to have the provisions and not need them than it was to not have them and maybe die because of it.

The wind slapped him in the face as soon as he opened the courthouse door and stepped out. That wasn't good. The air had been fairly calm when he went inside, but now, barely ten or fifteen minutes later, it was really blowing. Wind made the tree limbs and power lines come down faster, besides sapping the body heat of every poor fool who was outside, or who was being sent to rescue some bad-tempered bitch with a snotty attitude who was as likely to tell him to go to hell as she was to park her dainty ass in his truck.

Nevertheless, an unholy grin split his face as he sprinted for his truck, unlocking it with the remote while he was still about ten feet away. He wrenched the door open and vaulted inside. Lolly Helton! Damn, nobody else had ever locked horns with him the way Lolly had, or got on his wrong side so easily. He probably owed his success in the army to the early training she had given him; after all, how much trouble could the most fractious recruit be compared to Miss Hoity-Toity Helton?

Lollipop! Want me to lick you, Lollipop?

Putting the gear in reverse, he powered out of the parking space in an arc that left him facing the direction he wanted. His grin grew wider as he shifted into drive and put his boot down on the accelerator. The memory echoed in his head, the taunt that he'd known would drive her over the edge, the laughter of his buddies, the way her tight, unfriendly expression had gotten even tighter as she stared at him as if he were an insect she'd stepped on and smashed flat.

That was the thing about Lolly Helton. Even as a little girl, she'd been so convinced that she was so much better than everyone else in town that nothing he or anyone else had said to her had put a dent in that superiority. Her father was the mayor, and she never forgot it, or let anyone else forget it. If she'd been especially pretty, or especially smart, or anything else out of the ordinary maybe she'd have been more popular in school, but there hadn't been anything special about her. He remembered her frizzy brown hair, and that nothing she wore had ever looked very good on her, and that was it. Well, except for the way her expression had said *Eat shit and die, peasant.*

There had to be something wrong with him to actually feel a sort of anticipation at seeing her — and probably arguing with her — again.

Keeping a steady hand on the wheel, he switched the radio from XM to a local station so he could catch any weather updates. Within a few minutes he left the city limits of Wilson Creek behind, speeding up to gain whatever extra seconds he could. Another kind of anticipation built inside him, sharp and strong. Sam. He was going to see his kid again in just a few minutes, and his heart began pounding with joy.

Four miles down the road he turned between two huge spruce trees onto a concrete driveway. Behind the spruce trees was a sprawling white house with neat black shutters and a three-car detached garage. The back door was already slamming open as he lurched to a stop, a small, dark-haired dynamo erupting from the house yelling, "Dad! *Dad!*"

Gabriel left the truck running and leapt out, barely in time because Sam launched himself upward. He grabbed the kid out of midair, and skinny arms wrapped around his neck so tightly he could barely breathe. He didn't need to breathe. He just needed to hold his son.

"We got out of school early!" Sam said, beaming at him. "There's going to be an ice storm. Gran's making plenty of soup, because she said we'd probably need it."

"That's good to hear," Gabriel said. Sam was wearing a coat but it wasn't zipped, and the hood had fallen back so the cold rain was falling on his bare head. Gabriel pulled the hood up, then opened the truck's back door to grab his duffel, shouldering the door shut. Holding his son in one arm and the duffel with the other, he ran through the rain to the back porch. His mother was standing there, trim and capable-looking in her jeans and boots, the wide smile on her face not quite disguising the concern in her green eyes.

"He wouldn't wait," she said, throwing her arms around Gabriel and hugging him, then planting a swift kiss on Sam's cheek as well.

"Ah, Gran," he said, squirming, but he didn't wipe his cheek. Gabriel grinned, remembering how mortifying it had been at that age for his mother to kiss him. Sam might as well get used to it, because nothing stopped Valerie McQueen from kissing the people she loved.

He dropped his duffel, set Sam on his feet, then squatted and began rifling through the duffel for his knife and flashlight. "The coffee's almost ready," his mom said. "I already have one thermos filled with soup, and here's one of your father's insulated rain ponchos." She gave him the poncho, then turned and hurried back into the kitchen.

"Thanks," he said, hoping he wouldn't need it. His boots were all-weather and insulated, so his feet should stay warm and dry, but he tucked an extra pair of socks in his coat pocket, just in case. His coat was thick and heavy and he had gloves in the truck, as well as a blanket that Sam had shoved under the backseat over a year ago and which he'd never gotten around to dragging out. He figured he was as ready for a quick trip up the mountain as he was going to get.

"Where are you going?" Sam asked as he watched the preparations. "You just got here." Disappointment laced his tone, edging into sulky.

"I have to rescue a woman from her house on a mountain," Gabriel replied, keeping his own tone brisk so Sam would know this wasn't the time for an argument, but he put his arm around him for a quick, hard hug. "I don't want to leave either, but when something needs doing, someone has to step up and do it."

Sam mulled that over. With Gabriel being career army and his grandfather a sheriff, in his short life he'd heard a lot about responsibility, and seen it in action. He might not like it, but he understood it. "Is she hurt?"

"I don't think so, but your grandpa wants me to get her before the ice storm leaves her stranded."

Sam gave a solemn nod. "Okay," he finally said. "If you have to. But be careful."

"I will," Gabriel promised, wanting to grin but keeping his expression grave. His little guy was learning how to step up to the plate himself.

Valerie returned, and he stood to take the two big thermos bottles from her. "Be careful," she said needlessly, echoing Sam, but now that he was a parent himself he understood that the worry never stopped, no matter how old or how capable he was.

"Aren't I always?" he asked, knowing that would make her roll her eyes, which it did. He kissed her cheek, then knelt to give Sam another, extra-big hug. "I'll be back as soon as I can. Can you take care of Gran until then?"

Sam nodded solemnly, and he squared his thin shoulders. "I'll do my best," he replied, though the look he gave his grandmother said that he doubted he could control her. Gabriel bit the inside of his cheek to hold back a grin.

"Bring Lolly here," Valerie said briskly. "Don't try to take her into town and then make it back. We have plenty of room and plenty of food, so there's no point in pushing your luck with this weather."

"Yes, ma'am," he said obediently, but inside he was thinking: *Oh, shit, I'll be stranded with Lolly Helton.*

Maybe she wouldn't be there. Maybe she was somewhere safe in town, and had simply turned off her cell phone. Maybe he'd slide off the road and have to walk back, and wouldn't be able to make it up the mountain to the Helton place. Maybe, even if she was there, she'd refuse to go anywhere with him. Yeah, he could see that.

Then that weird sense of anticipation rose in him again, the antsy feeling he got when he knew he was going to be in a fight and was actually looking forward to it. He'd been in a lot worse situations than this, he thought. He'd waded into brawls with nothing but his fists, kicking ass and breaking heads, and come out of it okay. Lolly had a tongue like a scorpion, but that was about it. He could handle her and anything she dished out. "Thanks," he said to his mother. "I'll see you in about an hour." Then he dashed back out into the cold rain and the deepening gloom, off to fetch the spoiled princess from her mountain.

CHAPTER TWO

Earlier that afternoon

The old white Blazer, crusted with grime and salt, turned into the small parking lot of the local grocery store. A skinny, ill-kempt man with straggly, dirty-blond hair pulled the Blazer so it was facing the road and put the gear in park. "Ready," he said, drumming his fingers rapidly on the steering wheel. "I'm ready. Ready to go." The words were fast and abrupt. "You got the gun?"

"Right here," the woman beside him

said, shoving a pistol into her stained, red canvas tote bag. She was as skinny and straggly as he was, her eyes and cheeks sunken, her long, dark hair plastered to her head so that her ears stuck out through the strands. Her gaze roved restlessly around the parking lot, darted to the front of the grocery store, back to the parking lot. She put her hand on the door handle and shoved the door open, then quickly closed it again when another vehicle turned into the parking lot and drove past. She watched as a black Mercedes SUV, driven by a lone woman, went past them with tires hissing on the wet pavement and parked in a slot close to the store door.

"What're you waiting for?" the man asked, still drumming his fingers. He shifted restlessly in the seat. His name was Darwin Girard, and he hadn't slept in three or four days, maybe even longer. Despite that, he felt as if he might explode with energy, and just sitting there was almost more than he could handle.

"That woman looked at me." Niki Vann indicated the driver of the black Mercedes as the woman got out of the small SUV and pointed a remote at it. The lights blinked, signaling that the vehicle was locked, and the woman hurried through the rain into the little grocery store.

"She did?" Darwin asked, his attention zeroing in on the woman like a laser. No one was supposed to notice them. That was the plan, and he didn't like people messing with his plans. Feral hostility glowed in his sunken eyes as he glared at the door through which she'd passed.

"Yeah. Bitch," Niki growled, for no reason other than that the other woman was driving a Mercedes. Then an idea began to squirm in her brain. "I bet she's got a lot of money in her purse. Look at what she's driving. I bet she's got more than that rinky-dink little grocery, and she's by herself."

Darwin drummed his fingers faster, faster. "What're you thinking?" he asked, as if he didn't know, grinning at her. Niki was even better than he was at seeing an opportunity and not hesitating to act on it. Because of her, their supply of meth was fairly steady. She was always looking for a way to get more money.

She shoved the Blazer door open again, and got out. "Be back in a minute," she said before closing the door, then she darted through the rain, her thin body almost dwarfed by the huge green jacket she wore.

Inside the store, Lolly Helton grabbed a cart and headed down the first aisle. She didn't need much, just some cans of soup and a couple of sandwich items, maybe a couple of magazines to read, and she wanted to be home before dark so she was in a hurry. Because she was in a hurry, of course, she was stopped almost immediately.

"Lolly!" said a woman wearing a bright red apron that covered her from neck to knees, looking around from where she was neatening the stacks of produce that had been disordered by customers picking through them for a perfect head of cabbage, or apples that were either firm or soft according to their individual tastes. "I heard you were back. You're looking well."

"Thank you," said Lolly, good manners making her pause. "You, too. How have you been?" Mr. and Mrs. Richard had owned the little grocery store for as long as she could remember, and she'd always liked Mrs. Richard, who loved to joke and gossip and never had anything negative to say about anyone. The door opened behind her and a gust of cold air swept in. She didn't look around, but moved her cart to the side so the newcomer could pass by.

"Well. Busy, this time of year, with all the holiday cooking." She wiped her hands on the apron, her gaze moving beyond Lolly to whoever had entered the store behind her. She gave a brief nod of acknowledgment, then turned her attention back to Lolly. "Where are you staying tonight?"

"At home," said Lolly, a little startled. Where else would she be?

"Goodness, child, haven't you been listening to the radio? They're predicting ice for tonight."

An ice storm! As if she could see the approaching storm, Lolly turned and looked out the window, her gaze sliding past the woman who had entered behind her. It wasn't anyone she knew — didn't look like anyone she'd *want* to know — so she didn't make eye contact. "I haven't had the radio on," she admitted. She seldom listened to the radio anyway, preferring her own CD collection for music.

"You can't stay way out there by yourself. If you don't have anyone you could stay with, Joseph and I have an extra bedroom — two of them, in fact, now that the boys are married and gone."

Lolly's mind raced. She didn't have any old school friends she could stay with for the duration of the storm, mainly because she hadn't really been friends with anyone. Her school years hadn't been good ones. She was much better at making friends now, but that meant all of them were back in Portland. She didn't like the idea of staying with Mr. and Mrs. Richard — she liked them, but she wasn't close to them — but with an ice storm looming she had to make some fast decisions.

"Thank you, I'll take you up on that offer, at least for tonight," she said, lifting her purse from the cart. She wouldn't need any groceries, after all. "I need to go home and get some of my things. How much time do I have?"

"The weather service said it should start around dark. Don't tarry."

Lolly checked the time. She had a few hours, but the icing could start sooner than that at home because the house was at a higher elevation. "I'll be back as soon as I can," she said. "I can't tell you how much I appreciate the offer."

Mrs. Richard made a shooing motion with her hand. "Go on, hurry!"

Lolly did, though she took the time to return the cart to the small corral, pushing it past the woman wearing an oversized green jacket and carrying a dirty red canvas tote, as if that was her nod to the Christmas season. A sense of urgency drove her to almost run back to her vehicle; an ice storm was nothing to dismiss. Snow was nothing, at least to a native Mainer, but ice was unbelievably destructive. She could have been stranded for days, even weeks, if she hadn't happened to stop by the grocery store and talked to Mrs. Richard.

So much for her plans, she thought ruefully as she wheeled out of the parking lot, but a looming ice storm trumped packing. There weren't even that many personal items left to pack up, so it wasn't as if she had to get everything done right now. The house had been used so seldom in the past several years, there was just the bare minimum of furniture and some odds and ends left, anyway. She had intended to take her time packing — in fact, her actual plans for the night had been to heat some soup, turn on the gas fireplace, and read, leaving packing for tomorrow morning. She enjoyed the peace and quiet, and there was something about being snug in a warm house on a snowy night that deeply appealed to her.

She had come here this week wanting to enjoy a few leisurely days in the house where she'd grown up, wallowing in warm fuzzy memories and, in her own way, saying good-bye to the house and to Wilson Creek. With her parents in Florida and her job keeping her busy in Portland, there was no need for a vacation home that was so rarely used.

The Helton house had once been the finest in the county, a large and somewhat extravagant — for the area

— two-story house on the mountain-side, just outside of town. For a lot of years all the important local political meetings and parties had been held there, which Lolly found slightly ironic, as she was the only family member left in Maine and she had no interest in politics and even less in partying. She'd outgrown some of her youthful awkward shyness, but she'd never be outgoing. She much preferred an evening at home to a night on the town.

She didn't look forward to staying with the Richards, preferring to be on her own, but she'd deal. She worked for an insurance company and had learned, out of necessity, how to interact with people. As a child and, even worse, a teenager, she'd always hung back, never knowing exactly what to

44

say and certain no one wanted to talk to her anyway. She'd hidden all those painful insecurities behind a wall of hostility, so it wasn't surprising she hadn't had any real friends here. She didn't know why she kept coming back, but she managed at least one trip almost every year. She wished she could afford to live here, in the house where she'd grown up, but Wilson Creek simply didn't have much in the way of job opportunities, and she didn't have the money to open her own small business.

The windshield wipers swished back and forth, clearing away the light rain that hadn't varied in intensity all day. There was something unnerving about the sheer unchanging relentlessness of the rain, as if the very lightness of it was proof that Mother

Nature didn't need to make a dramatic statement to squash civilization like a bug. All it took was a rain not much heavier than a mist, and some cold air in the right position, to wreak havoc. She felt a chill run up her spine; even though it was hours yet until nightfall, the gloom was deepening, and she had to turn on her headlights. She hadn't met any traffic since turning on this road, and that in itself was kind of spooky. For a moment she felt the urge to turn around, buy some pajamas and underwear in town, and dart for the safety of the Richards' house.

Then she saw the blur of a vehicle behind her, too far for her to make out any details, but just knowing she wasn't alone on the road was enough to settle her nerves. She'd allow herself fifteen minutes, no more, to gather what she needed and head back to town. She should be safe and secure well ahead of the storm's arrival.

Within minutes she had turned off the main road and was carefully navigating the narrower road that wound up the side of the mountain toward the house. She still knew every curve, every tree and rock, of this road, because she had driven it so often after she'd gotten her driver's license. Even before that, her mother had taken her to school every day, and picked her up in the afternoons, so for almost her entire life she'd had at least two trips a day up and down this mountain. The road held no surprises for her, no fears; it was the weather that made her anxious.

Her sure-footed SUV, bought used

three years ago because she'd needed a dependable four-wheel-drive vehicle, climbed steadily. Visibility dropped as the mist grew heavier. She took a quick glance at the outside temperature gauge and saw that the temp was just a couple of degrees above freezing. The trees had a faint silvery cast to them; was ice already beginning to form?

Then she turned into the driveway, powering up the long slope toward home. It wouldn't be "home" much longer, she thought, but right now it still looked welcoming and somehow just right. Never mind that the house was almost sixty years old, had faded a bit, and sagged here and there; it was still large and solid, offering a warm, safe refuge on a wintry night. Too bad she couldn't stay here, but if she got iced in it would be a couple of weeks before she could get off the mountain, depending on how bad the damage was and how many trees came down.

Much as she loved this place, she knew it was time for the house she'd grown up in to be home to a family again, as it had been home to her. Once the few remaining personal effects here were packed away, sold, or stored, her childhood home would go on the market, and it would no longer be hers in any way. Too bad she wouldn't have the few days of escaping into the past that she'd wanted, but the weather had other plans.

She didn't bother with parking in the detached garage, just pulled up close to the front porch. Keys in hand, she hurried up the steps and unlocked the front door. As soon as she let herself in she shed her heavy, hooded winter coat, tossing it over the newel post and dropping her purse on the bottom step. Detouring to the back, she grabbed her snow boots from the mud room and brought them to join her coat and purse.

She didn't know when she'd be able to come back, she thought as she started up the stairs. Was there anything in the refrigerator she needed to clean out? No, she didn't think so. She'd been eating granola bars for breakfast, not bothering even with milk for cereal, and at night she'd either had peanut butter and jelly sandwiches or picked up a sandwich in town. She knew how to turn off the water at the valve, and turn off the gas to the water heater; other than locking the door, that was all she could do to get the house ready to withstand the coming storm.

She was halfway up the stairs when she heard the rumble of a vehicle. She stopped, then reversed her path. Knowing the people here as she did, she wouldn't be at all surprised if someone had heard about the storm, realized she was here with no television or phone, and come to collect her. This had always been the kind of community where neighbors looked after neighbors, and she missed that — some days. She was both glad for the company and concerned at the delay.

Crossing her fingers that she wouldn't have any trouble getting down the hill, Lolly opened the front door. She expected to find someone she knew, an old friend of her parents or the closest thing she had to a neighbor, and a welcoming smile was on her face. The smile froze when she realized she didn't know the rough-looking couple coming up the porch steps, though the woman looked vaguely familiar. Then Lolly remembered seeing her in the grocery store earlier, recognized her even though the stringy dark hair was now partially covered by a knit cap, and a thick coat disguised her thinness.

A couple of possibilities rapidly crossed her mind. Were they lost? Looking for shelter? Maybe they were unfamiliar with the area and didn't know that they did *not* want to be stuck here on the mountain if the ice was as bad as predicted.

"I'm just on my way out . . ."

Lolly began.

The man right behind the stringy-haired woman pulled a gun from his parka pocket. Shock hit Lolly like a slap in the face; she gaped at the gun, barely comprehending what she saw, then she sucked in a quick breath and instinctively stepped back. The man and woman both rushed at her, shoving her back inside so roughly that she slammed hard into the newel post, staggered, saved herself from falling with a desperate grab at the wood.

The man shoved the door shut behind them. The woman glanced around, at the living room on the left, the flight of stairs straight ahead, the dining room on the right. She smiled, showing discolored and rotten teeth. "See, baby, I told you she was alone."

Lolly clung to the newel post, literally frozen under the sudden lash of terror, her brain numb, coherent thoughts scattered before they could even form. She groped for understanding, and finally, like a switch being flipped, her sluggish brain began to function. Home invasion — *here,* in Wilson Creek! It was so wrong, that something like this could happen here, that sheer indignation abruptly shoved terror aside and suddenly she could move, was already moving even before she realized. She ran, ran for her life.

The man shouted, "You bitch! *Fuck!*" as Lolly darted through the dining room, dodging around the table, grabbing one of the heavy chairs and slinging it in his path then racing into the kitchen. Footsteps thudded behind her but she didn't look, didn't spare even a split second, just ran for her life. If she could just get outside —

She grabbed for the doorknob, and a hand grabbed her hair. Pain laced her scalp; her head jerked back and she was sent spinning away from the door. Her feet went out from under her and she fell to the floor, the man's grip cruelly tight on her hair. He shoved her down and she hit the cold, hard linoleum face-first.

Lolly screamed, then caught her breath and held it. She grabbed for her hair, trying to pry his hands away. The sudden weight of his body on hers was heavy and hot. He pressed her into the floor, forcing her breath out, and she couldn't take another.

"Now you got me all excited," he

whispered in her ear, grinding himself against her bottom. His breath was hot and fetid, and a rough stubble scratched her cheek. She turned her head away from the stink and roughness, but she couldn't move far. Her fingers scrabbled at the linoleum, trying to find purchase, trying to find something, anything —

There was nothing. A kitchen was full of weapons, but none of them were on the floor.

He began tugging at her jeans, trying to pull them down.

Damn it, *no!* Both panicked and enraged, she instinctively fought back, slinging her elbows back as far as they would go, trying to hit him. She wiggled and bucked and squirmed, trying to throw him off, but he was too heavy and she was in a helpless position, flat on her stomach on the floor.

He couldn't get her jeans down. He shoved his hand under her and fumbled with the button and zipper, grunting like an animal. Lolly pressed her hips harder to the floor, trying to mash his hand so he couldn't get the zipper down, but he jerked her head up and slammed it down on the floor again and white spots swam in her vision. Dazed with pain, she went limp for a second and he shoved his rough hand inside her jeans, against her bare belly.

She was going to die. He was going to rape her, and kill her. Her last minutes alive would be filled with unspeakable terror.

Tears filled her eyes, and she screamed. The sound was rough and raw, like an animal's, the noise tearing from her throat. She didn't want to die; she didn't want her last memory made in this house to be a nightmare. She screamed again and again, unable to stop herself.

He shifted upward, lifting his weight from her. She gulped in a deep breath and tried to gather her strength, then he rolled her over and started yanking again at her jeans.

"Don't," she said, sobbing. "Please. Please don't." She hated to beg but she couldn't seem to stop herself, and what did pride matter anyway? She'd do anything to get him to stop. Desperately she searched for some reason she could give him, something that would appeal to him. "I can pay you. I can give you all the money I have."

He didn't seem to hear her at all.

The kitchen was dim, with only the scant light from the window, but she could see that he was almost as thin as the woman, most of his teeth were dark with rot, and his eyes . . . they were strangely wide open and feral, glittering with something that was inhuman.

Drugs. He had to be on drugs, both of them did. There wouldn't be any reasoning with him, so she stopped trying. He continued jerking at her clothes and she kicked, she screamed, she clawed at any patch of skin on him she could reach, but his coat was heavy and protected him from her nails, so she went for his face. He couldn't hold both her hands and undress her at the same time, so she punched and clawed at him with every ounce of strength she had, but the blows didn't seem to affect him at all.

He got her jeans halfway down and reared back to unzip his own pants. Laughing, he clamped one hand around her throat and leaned his weight on it. She couldn't breathe, couldn't reach him . . . her vision grayed, and she couldn't see anything except his grinning face above hers. *Tunnel vision,* she thought vaguely, and knew she was about to pass out. If she did, she'd be entirely helpless, and his maniacal face with the rotten teeth would be the last thing she ever saw.

Desperate, on the verge of unconsciousness, she tried to jerk her knee up. He shifted, blocking the movement, and laughed.

"Darwin, you son of a bitch!" the woman yelled in a grating tone.

The overhead light came on, the lights shining right in Lolly's eyes and blinding her. The weight on her throat eased and she coughed, sucking in air. Darwin was very still. "I was just having a little fun," he said sulkily.

The woman with the stringy hair stood over them both, and with blurred vision Lolly looked up at her. There was no sympathy in the woman's face, no woman-to-woman empathy, nothing but fury. She had a gun, too, and she had it pointed at Darwin's head. "Get up."

"Now, Niki," he began, belatedly placating as he realized where the pistol was pointing. "Baby, I —"

"Don't 'baby' me, you two-timing son of a bitch."

Darwin's gaze shifted from Niki,

back to Lolly. She saw the animal in his eyes, saw him weighing his options. He smiled a little, and then he forced Lolly's thighs farther apart.

Niki swung her pistol and hit Darwin on the side of the head with it. He yelped, and finally . . . *finally* . . . moved off of Lolly. "Fuck, Niki, you could've killed me!" he shouted, getting to his feet and pulling up his pants from where they'd drooped over his skinny ass. "Are you fucking crazy?" He grabbed a dish towel and pressed it to the bleeding wound on the side of his head, where the pistol had split the skin.

Lolly struggled to pull her jeans up, scooting across the floor as she did, toward the back door and icy freedom. Maybe these two bags of shit would kill each other. She was dimly shocked by the violence of her own thoughts, but if she could just get away, she didn't care what happened to them.

Niki's gaze swiveled from Darwin to Lolly, and so did the pistol barrel. "Where the hell do you think you're going?" she spat, then glanced at something in her hand. Lolly froze, blinking. "Lorelei Helton. Portland," Niki said, and Lolly realized the something was her own driver's license. Niki had apparently been going through Lolly's purse while Darwin had been trying to rape her. "What the hell kind of name is 'Lorelei'? It sounds like a hooker."

Lolly didn't bother arguing, just nodded her head in agreement.

"Get up," Niki said, and Lolly obeyed, using the motion to take another step back, toward the door. Could she beat both of them, and a bullet? They were druggies, they were likely high right now . . . their eyes were wide, the pupils shrunk down to tiny dots. How clearly could they think?

Clearly enough. Darwin suddenly said, "Whoa there, bitch," and lunged across the kitchen to place himself between her and the back door. He shoved her forward.

Niki shook her head and stuck the driver's license in the front pocket of her baggy jeans. "For a woman driving a Mercedes, you don't have much money on you," she growled. "Where's the rest?"

Lolly tried to think, to reason. Her heart was pounding, she was shaking from head to toe and nausea roiled her stomach, but she could still think. Right now, her brain was the only weapon she had. "In the bank. We can go to town and I'll give it all to you, I swear I will, just . . . don't kill me." She shot a glance toward Darwin. "And don't let him near me." If she could actually get to town with these druggies, she'd find a way to escape . . . to get help.

"They'd be closed now, right?" Niki asked, looking at the last gleam of light that pressed against the windows.

Dear God, she couldn't spend the night in the house with these two. Her stomach lurched, and she barely controlled the urge to vomit. "Yes, but I know the bank manager," she lied. She had no idea who the manager was now, and she had never banked here anyway. The first and only account she'd ever opened was in Portland. Would they realize that, if she lived in Portland, she wasn't likely to have an account here? Desperately she plunged ahead. "He'll open up for me. We can leave right now."

Niki considered it, her head tilted to the side and her feral, too-wide gaze locked on Lolly, but after a couple of seconds she shook her head. "No, he'd get suspicious if you did that. We'll wait until morning."

Lolly's heart lurched, just like her stomach. She felt the hard beats hammering inside her chest. The ice was coming; by morning there would be no way down the hill. The road would be a sheet of ice, and she'd be stuck here with these two. She heard what sounded like frozen rain hitting the kitchen windows; maybe it was already too late.

Niki gestured with the gun, waving Lolly forward. Lolly followed the silent direction, passing the woman with the gun more closely than she liked, exiting the kitchen and walking through the dining room with Niki directly behind. When they reached the living room, Lolly saw the contents of her purse scattered across the couch and floor. Her key ring, with the key to the Mercedes between the key to this house and the one to her apartment door, was resting between two cushions. If she could get to the Mercedes, she'd take her chances driving on ice. Even if she slid off the side of the mountain, that was better than being stranded with these two. She needed those keys . . .

Niki gave Lolly a shove toward the

staircase. "Go on," she said, jabbing the pistol barrel hard into Lolly's spine. Lolly took the stairs, her knees shaking so badly she half-expected to fall at any moment. Niki led her to the bedroom closest to the head of the stairs, which happened to be Lolly's own room. "Any guns in the house?" Niki asked brusquely as she switched on the lights and looked around the neat, sparsely furnished room. "And don't lie, because if you say no and we find some, I'll shoot you in the face. Got it?"

"No, no guns," Lolly said, her voice shaking so much her words were barely understandable.

Niki opened all the drawers, gave the contents of the closet a cursory glance, and was satisfied. There wasn't much here, so searching wasn't exactly a chore. There was Lolly's underwear in the top drawer of the chest, some pajamas, and four clean changes of clothing hanging in the closet. Niki looked out the dark window, noting the two-story distance between the window and the ground with some satisfaction. Lolly looked, too, but at the window. Was that a film of ice already forming on the glass?

Niki's crossed the room, and Lolly stepped out of her way. "I'll be watching this door from downstairs," she snarled. "If it opens even a crack, I'm going to send Darwin up here to deal with you." She glanced at the simple lock on the doorknob, and smiled. "And don't think that flimsy lock will do you any good, not when we have these *keys*." She indicated the pistol in her hand and took imaginary aim at the lock, making a shooting noise, then she grinned.

The sight of those rotten teeth made Lolly shudder, but suddenly something she'd heard, or read, clicked in her brain, and she realized what drug these two were likely on:

It was meth — another type of ice, and just as deadly.

CHAPTER THREE

Dazed, Lolly listened to Niki's footsteps as the woman descended the
stairs. Voices drifted up from the
living room, angry at first, and then
softer. Darwin laughed. The sound
sent a shudder rolling through her
body, which seemed to be the signal
that now her brain could allow her
body to feel again because she suddenly felt like one huge, head-to-toe
ache.

She began trembling. Her shoulder
and side hurt from being shoved into
the newel post, her scalp ached from

her hair being pulled so viciously, and her cheek and one side of her head throbbed from being slammed into the linoleum. Her heart was pounding so hard she thought she might yet be sick, and she felt both sweaty and icy cold at the same time.

Shock, she thought, just before her knees wobbled and she collapsed on the side of the bed. That didn't help much; her vision tilted, as if the world was turning over, and she toppled to the side. She lay there panting, trying to control her breathing, but the raw, ragged sound of her gasps filled the quiet room.

Knowing what was wrong didn't make her feel any better. If Darwin had come through the door right then, she'd have been completely helpless.

Dear God. What should she do?

What *could* she do?

She didn't know what she could do, but one thing she did know: she'd rather die than let Darwin touch her again.

The thought propelled her to a sitting position, and though her head swam she forced herself to stay erect. There was a very strong probability she was going to die anyway, but she'd be damned if she'd huddle there, sniveling, waiting for them to do whatever they wanted with her. She'd rather freeze to death in the ice storm than just sit here like a helpless idiot.

One thing she wouldn't do was make things easy for them. Moving as cautiously as she could, both because she was still dizzy and because she didn't want them to hear her moving around, she eased over to the door and turned the lock. Niki was right: the lock was too insubstantial to stop them for long, but at least she'd have a moment of warning before they walked in on her.

With any luck she wouldn't be here when they decided to return, because she'd rather take her chances with the ice than with them. She took a deep breath, willing her head to stop spinning, and went to the window to look out. Yes, there was definitely ice on the window, and very little light left as the pressing clouds brought a premature twilight. She didn't have much time, because conditions were only going to get worse.

The ground below looked so far away that her instincts screamed she'd kill herself if she jumped, but she didn't intend to *jump.* It was a straight drop from her window to the ground below, with no roofline or eave to assist her, but there were sheets and a couple of thin blankets on the bed. The down comforter was probably too thick and bulky to be useful, but if she tied the bottom sheet to the top sheet to the blanket and then tied the makeshift rope off well, she'd be able to get close enough to the ground to drop down safely.

Swiftly she ripped all the covers from the bed and began tying her make-shift rope. The sheets were easiest, because they were the thinnest. She knotted the first corner to the foot of the bed, tugging hard to make certain the knot would hold; she'd never been a Girl Scout, wasn't a sailor, didn't know a damn thing about knots be-yond tying her shoes. She just hoped a regular old knot would be sufficient.

After the sheets came the two thin wool blankets. She would love to have one of the blankets to huddle in as she made her escape, but she needed both of them for length, since the best place to tie off the rope was the end of the bed and it was eight, maybe ten feet from the window. She had always loved the spaciousness of the house, but now that space was working against her. She couldn't move the bed, not without attracting more attention than she wanted. She had to get out, and she had to do it quietly.

When that task was finished, she forced herself to sit quietly for a minute, to give her racing heart time to slow. She was sweating a little, and that wasn't good. One of the first rules of surviving in the cold was not to overexert yourself, because that caused sweating, which would freeze on the body and cause hypothermia to set in even faster.

Then she shook her head at herself. Hell, it was raining; she was going to get wet, anyway. How was a little sweat going to make things worse? She must still be a little shocky, addled but functioning. She just needed to function a little faster, because at any time they might come up those stairs to check on her.

She took every piece of clothing available out of the closet and the chest of drawers, tossing them onto the bed. Before she went out the window, she needed to get as many clothes on her body as possible. Her big, heavy, weatherproof coat and boots were downstairs, so her only chance of surviving the cold rain and ice was to keep dry as long as possible, and that meant layers . . . a lot of them.

Quickly she kicked off her shoes, then stripped off her jeans and sweatshirt and began pulling on thin layers. She'd brought a pair of insulated long underwear and she put that on first, then began pulling on T-shirts, the thinnest first, the looser ones on top. One flannel shirt, the one she wore while lazing about, she laid aside to tie over her head. There was one pair of old sweats, as well as the sweatshirt she'd been wearing, but before putting on the bulky stuff she stopped to tug on as many pairs of socks as she could fit on her feet.

Her shoes weren't waterproof; her feet *would* get wet, no way around it.

The only question was whether she'd be able to get down the mountain before hypothermia killed her. If she managed that, then she'd worry about losing her feet to frostbite.

Then an idea occurred to her, and as quietly as possible she hauled her suitcase out of the closet. She had brought a jar of Vaseline, which she used to remove mascara. She hadn't bothered with any makeup since she'd been here, so she hadn't even gotten the Vaseline out of the suitcase. Thank goodness she hadn't, or it would now be in the bathroom down the hall with her other toiletries.

Vaseline was waterproof, wasn't it? It was at least water *resistant,* and might be just the edge she needed. It wouldn't keep out the cold, but every little bit helped.

She pulled off her socks and coated her feet with the Vaseline, especially her toes, then put her socks back on, and another pair on top of that. Two pairs of socks was all she could manage and still get her feet in her shoes, so that would have to do.

Next came her jeans, then a pair of old sweatpants. Once her pants were on, she coated the outside of the socks with Vaseline, put on her shoes, then smeared the remainder of the stuff on the leather. That was as waterproof as she could make her feet; maybe, just maybe, the multiple layers would do the trick. After pulling on the two sweatshirts, she felt like the Michelin Man, but she was as ready as she could get.

Lolly tiptoed to the door, pressing her ear to the wood, holding her breath as she listened. The intruders seemed to be right at the foot of the stairs, but from years of living in this house she knew that sounds from both the living room on one side and the dining room on the other carried right up the stairs, because when she was young she'd often listened to the parties downstairs.

The argument over Darwin's attack hadn't lasted long. The voices were lower now, and the occasional bout of laughter sent chills down her spine. She didn't think for one minute she'd survive until morning. Right now Niki planned to take her to the bank tomorrow morning for a big withdrawal, but that plan wasn't going to last. One of them would come to their senses and realize it wasn't going to work, or they'd realize they were iced in. One of them would get carried away, and Lolly would end up dead long before morning.

The voices and laughter stopped. She strained her ears and after a moment she caught some grunting and the occasional moan. Her stomach heaved, but thank God they were otherwise occupied. Now would be the best time to make her escape.

She took one quick look around the room, to see if there was anything else she could use. Only the pillowcases were left, but any covering was better than none, so she stripped them from the pillows and tied them over her head. Her pajama shirt doubled as a muffler. Over that she tied the remaining flannel shirt, and she was as ready as she could get.

Grasping her makeshift rope, once

more she tugged on the knot securing it to the bed. Walking backward to the window, she tested the other knots as well. They seemed solid enough; they would have to do.

It was now or never. She unlocked the window and pulled upward on the handle. Nothing happened. She pulled again, putting more muscle into it. Still nothing. The bottom dropped out of her stomach. The stupid damn window was stuck, and if she couldn't somehow get it open, then she was stuck, too. Desperately she gripped the handle with both hands, bending her knees and putting her leg muscles into the effort too, and with what sounded like a deafening noise the window rose a scant inch before stopping again.

She leaned her head against the cold

glass, only vaguely noticing how good the chill felt against her forehead. She could do this. She *had* to do this. If necessary, she'd break the glass and take her chances that the noise would be heard. One way or another, she was getting out of this house.

Something thunked against the side of the house, just below the window, and she almost jumped out of her skin. She didn't know what had made the sound, but what if Niki and Darwin had heard it, and came to investigate? She turned her head to stare in frozen agony at the door, trying to hear if they were coming up the stairs, but this far from the door she couldn't hear anything. Frantic, almost sobbing, she grabbed the window handle and began tugging viciously.

A man's head suddenly appeared on

the other side of the window. A squeal almost popped out and she choked, slapping a hand over her mouth. She stared, so frightened she could barely move, and abruptly she recognized him. Her heart leapt, and her knees almost buckled. The relief that washed through her was as warm as the sun she longed for at this moment.

Gabriel McQueen.

CHAPTER FOUR

By the time Gabriel reached the turn off the main road, the combination of rain and low clouds had deepened to the point that he needed his headlights on to see. The wind had picked up, too, tossing the trees and whistling around the truck. Wind was bad; it would make the limbs and trees begin coming down just that much sooner.

He would much rather have been with Sam, but he never once thought of turning around and simply telling his dad that he hadn't been able to make it up the mountain. Giving up wasn't in his DNA; he'd fetch Lolly off the mountain if he had to drag her down by the hair, which probably wasn't what his father had had in mind when he sent Gabriel on this mission, but then the sheriff didn't know Lolly the way Gabriel knew Lolly.

She'd always been a spoiled brat, nose in the air, convinced she was better than anyone else. Some kids took teasing well; Lolly wasn't one of them. Hostility had rolled off her in waves. Once she'd looked at him with complete disdain and said, "Worm!" He'd hidden his reaction, but inside he'd been furious that she'd dismissed him so completely with that one word. He was the sheriff's son, he was popular and athletic and invited everywhere, and she thought he was a *worm?* Who the hell did she think she was? Oh, right, she was a *Helton,* and she didn't associate with people like him.

She had held herself separate from everyone else, not part of a crowd, never at any of the parties. Looking back, Gabriel wondered now if she'd ever been invited to any of the parties. Probably — but only because she was the mayor's daughter. None of the kids had liked her, and wouldn't have willingly invited her anywhere. He didn't know if that had bothered her, because she certainly hadn't been a joiner. The only school activity she'd been involved in was keeping her nose buried in a book, if that counted.

He wondered if she was still that way — different, and alone. From the distance of years, he could now also wonder which had come first: her attitude, or the teasing. His own parents seemed to like her well enough. Would his dad have bothered to send him on this errand if it had been anyone other than Lolly Helton who was out of cell range and possibly unaware of what was coming? Harlan McQueen had been lifelong friends with the Heltons, and that hadn't changed just because the Heltons had moved to Florida, trading ice storms and snow for the occasional hurricane.

Meeting up with her again after all these years should be interesting. He just hoped she wouldn't give him any grief about coming back to town with him.

A new weather bulletin came on the radio, and he turned up the volume to listen; evidently it looked as if the storm was going to take a turn for the worst, and faster than expected. He slowed down, looking at the trees, checking for icing. Surely even Lolly would see the wisdom of getting off this mountain before she got stuck here for possibly weeks, without electricity. Unless she had laid in a lot of provisions, she'd be out of food, too. If enough ice coated the trees some of them would come down, blocking the road. Clearing this road wouldn't be a high priority for the county, because the Helton house was the only one on it. Once there had been a couple of other houses, but one of them had burned years ago, and the other had been so neglected the county had condemned it and had it torn down.

One way or another, he didn't want to waste even an extra minute of time on this assignment. He was going to do as he'd been told, then get his ass off the mountain while he could. He missed Sam every day, but at the base he could bury himself in work. Now, with the kid so close, being away from him was an almost physical pain.

The road took a sharp curve, and curled upward in a steep grade. His tires skidded on the pavement and he took his foot off the gas pedal, letting the truck slow to a crawl. Was the road icy already, or had he skidded simply because of the steepness of the wet pavement? His snow tires weren't worth a damn on ice; nothing was, except chains, but even here in Maine not many people had chains. If the weather was that bad, the smart thing to do was park your ass and wait it out, not go out for a Sunday drive.

Damn her, why couldn't she stay

in a house that was more accessible? This damn road wasn't much wider than his truck, and trees overhung the pavement in a way that made him wary as he eyed them. Not only would they be deadly if the ice got bad, but they made the road even darker by blocking out whatever light was left.

The temperature gauge on his truck said the outside temp was thirty-two degrees now. Great. Just fucking great. Even as he watched, the digital readout changed to thirty-one. As the road climbed higher, the temp was dropping like a rock. That was ice on the road, all right. He slowed down even more, letting the weight of the truck provide what traction it could.

Turning around wasn't even an option; his truck was too big, the road was too narrow, and the left side was nothing but a steep drop-off. The first place where he'd be able to turn around was at Lolly's house. He was as stuck as a rat on a treadmill, with no way to get off.

His frustration and temper ratcheted up a few notches. If he got up there and no one was home, if Lolly had left town that afternoon and the sheriff just hadn't realized it, Gabriel was going to be royally pissed. He couldn't be mad at his dad, but Lolly was another matter. He might even make a point of hunting her down to tell her what a thoughtless bitch she was.

Odds were he'd find her right where she was supposed to be, though, as cool and detached as always, surprised that he'd show up at her door in the middle of a fucking ice storm when he could be sitting at home with his kid. Hell, he was risking his life to get to her, and that made him even angrier, because he had to stay alive for Sam; his little boy had already lost his mother, and that had been a lot for a four-year-old to get through. Thank God they'd had each other when Mariane died; he couldn't imagine how he'd have made it without Sam. What would Sam do if something happened to him, now? Gabriel couldn't make his mind go there.

The truck powered slowly up the hilly road, but he could feel the tires spinning some, feel the truck sliding to the right as the surface became slicker. The higher he got, the worse it was going to be.

That thought had just formed when he eased into a right-hand curve and suddenly the truck began sliding to the right. This wasn't just the tires skidding; the entire truck moved sideways, the banking in the road, as slight as it was, taking him toward the inside of the curve. As soon as his right tires left the asphalt and hit the shoulder they grabbed traction and began slewing him around, throwing him toward the outside edge where there was nothing but a long drop.

Gabriel shoved the gear into neutral, stopping the tires from grabbing, and let the truck slide back toward the inside. He had no traction, so braking wasn't an option; instead he worked with the truck's momentum and steered away from the edge, toward the mountain side. With a thump, the right front tire crossed the shallow ditch that ran along the inside of the road and his bumper dug into the soft dirt of the bank, bringing him to a stop.

Swearing a blue streak, he stared through the icy windshield at the road ahead.

No way was his truck going to make it up that hill, and no way was he even going to try it. The rain was still falling, a wickedly gentle rain that wasn't heavy enough to run off, which would at least reduce the amount of ice that could form on the trees. No, this was the worst possible rain, a slow, light rain that the cold air would freeze before it could slide off the leaves and branches, and had now made the road impossible to drive. With a sinking feeling in his gut, he looked over his shoulder at the road behind him, remembering some of the hills and curves he'd already maneuvered.

Damn it, fuck, and son of a bitch! If he'd arrived in town an hour earlier, he would've been able to make it to the Helton house and back with no problem. If he'd arrived an hour later, it would've already been impossible to make it even this far. Instead he'd arrived just in time to get his ass stuck a little more than halfway up the mountain.

Shit. He'd have to walk the rest of the way.

He switched his all-weather cap for a knit cap that he could pull down over his ears, wrestled himself into the hooded poncho his mother had given him — the Ford was a big truck, but he was a big guy, and he needed a lot of room — then tugged on his gloves. His boots were waterproof and warm, too, so at least he was dressed okay for the weather.

He grabbed the flashlight and got out of the truck, slamming the door with a vengeance, still swearing. He used all the words and variations he'd learned during his years in the army, which was a lot. Why not? No one could hear him, because everyone in their right minds was indoors, preparing for the storm. Not him. No, he had to be out in the damn storm, playing Dudley Fucking Do-Right.

He put his head down, pulled his knit cap down low to protect his ears, and tightened the drawstring of the poncho hood so the wind wouldn't blow it back. The last thing he needed was for his head to get wet. Moving to the side of the road where the narrow, weedy shoulder gave him a better surface for walking than the slick road, he plodded forward, realizing with a boulder in his gut that he was going to have to spend the night at the Helton house. No way was he getting down the mountain now, not unless he decided to walk it — and walking back to town in an ice storm would be damn near suicidal, at least right now. After the rain stopped, walking would be more feasible. Spending the night with Lolly Helton, who would probably be blindly ungrateful, was the better option . . . barely. Even then, only the thought of Sam tipped the balance toward staying.

The footing, even on the shoulder, was more precarious than he'd realized. Hell, how had he made it as far as he had without going off the road? Several times, when his feet slipped, he had to grab one of the overhanging tree limbs to keep himself upright. A sense of foreboding seized him when he played the flashlight beam along the branches and saw the layer of ice that already coated them.

At last he made it to the top of the hill. The road dipped there, then curved once again, but when he looked ahead he saw the lights of the Helton house. So, she was there after all, and hadn't made an escape earlier in the day. He didn't know if he was glad his fool's trip hadn't been in vain, or angry that he'd had to make it at all. Both, probably. He was pissed, and he intended to stay pissed.

Even though he could see the lights, the house was still almost two hundred yards away, sitting on the right in a clearing that was surrounded on three sides by the woods. Now that he was at the top, almost, he realized how much the mountain itself had been shielding him from the icy blast of wind, because it hammered at him with such force he almost staggered back. Then it eased, before another gust pounded him. Despite his layers of clothing and the poncho that kept him dry, the wind leached his body heat away and he shivered.

He'd left the two thermos bottles in the truck. Great. He'd give a lot for a cup of coffee pretty damn soon, but no way was he going back for it. He wiped the wind-blown ice crystals from his face. Maybe Lollipop would have coffee. If she did, it would probably be some flavored shit, but if it was hot he'd drink it.

That's assuming she'd let him inside.

As Gabriel neared the house he pulled his anger in, a little. A lot of years had passed since Lolly had been the spoiled stuck-up brat teenager he remembered. He wasn't the same, and she probably wouldn't be either. It wasn't her fault the sheriff was a control freak where his people were concerned. Most lawmen would've been content to assume his constituents could take care of themselves, until informed otherwise. Not Harlan McQueen.

All the lights in the downstairs appeared to be on, as was one light upstairs, in the front room on the right. There was a Mercedes SUV parked beside the front porch, and behind was an old, beat-up Blazer. He could see Lolly driving the Mercedes, but who the hell did the Blazer belong to?

Shit, maybe she had some kind of romantic rendezvous going on. What was he supposed to do now? She wouldn't want to be interrupted, and he sure as hell didn't want to do any interrupting. His only other option, though, was to walk back to the truck and spend the night there, hoping that there was enough gas in the tank to keep the truck running most of the night so he wouldn't freeze to death, at the same time praying that he — and the truck — didn't get crushed by a falling tree limb. So he guessed Lollipop would have to be pissed.

Tough shit.

Then he frowned at the two vehicles. That was weird. Why was the Mercedes parked out in an ice storm, when the garage was right there at the rear of the house? Why hadn't she parked in there, to protect her vehicle?

Instinctively he switched off his flashlight.

Before he stepped onto the porch steps, Gabriel slipped into a deep shadow and came to a dead stop. Ice danced around him, peppered his face, stuck to his coat and boots and gloves. Something wasn't right. He'd spent a long time in law enforcement, albeit the military version, and he'd learned to listen to his instincts. Right now, everything in him was telling him to approach with caution. Maybe there was nothing going on other than some screwing, but he wanted to make certain before he knocked on that door. At the very least, his dad had been wrong about Lolly being up here all alone.

Keeping to the shadows, Gabriel moved to the end of the porch and up the steps. It was an old wooden porch, and he stepped carefully, keeping to the edge of the planks where it was less likely there would be any squeaks. He didn't approach any of the windows, but shifted around until he could look past the partially open curtains into the living room where several lights burned, illuminating the man and the woman there.

The man looked as if he belonged to the truck. He was scruffy, thin, rough-looking, and dressed in clothes that bagged on him, as if he'd lost weight — either that, or they weren't his.

The woman, who Gabriel could only see from behind, was painfully thin herself. Stringy dark hair fell down her back. Faded jeans bagged where her ass should be.

Lolly's hair was brown, but had she lost forty pounds, and taken up with a loser? Gabriel surveyed the rest of the room, and his gaze fell on the paraphernalia that was spread across the coffee table. *Shit!* He knew what he was looking at, and his gut tightened. If that was her, she'd started using meth, as well. No wonder she was so painfully thin.

No way in hell. His dad would have noticed something like that, known if Lolly had gotten into meth. The drug was wreaking havoc all over the country, and even in the military he had to deal with the shit. It turned users into physical wrecks, rotted their teeth out, took over their lives, and a lot of time killed them.

The man reached out to grab the woman where her ass should be, and instead of being insulted by the move, she laughed. Gabriel heard her too-loud rough laugh, as she fell back and into her companion. A hand came up and he saw the pistol she carried; it was a revolver, a big one, a .357 or even a .44. Adrenaline spurted through his veins, drastically intensifying his alertness. He didn't have a weapon with him; it hadn't even occurred to him that he'd need to come here armed.

The armed woman turned, and he stepped back enough that she wouldn't be able to see him through the window. A rush of relief filled him. The

thin, wasted, angular face didn't belong to anyone he knew. Maybe it had
been years since he'd seen Lolly, but
no one could change that much, even
on meth. That wasn't Lolly.

That didn't mean she was in the
clear. Were these friends of hers? Had
Lolly Helton changed in other ways,
maybe not physically, but in the type
of person she was? If she'd become a
dealer and was caught up in this shit,
he would turn around and take his
chances in the truck. What else could
he do? Somehow he didn't think the
couple in the living room would take
kindly to being interrupted. Meth
users were violent, unpredictable.
They'd probably shoot at him as soon
as he knocked.

But where was Lolly? He couldn't
leave without seeing for himself if

she was okay. The Mercedes left out in the storm made him uneasy. Had these two broken in, killed her? With meth users, anything was possible, and none of it was good.

Remembering the reflected light from upstairs, he left the porch as silently as he'd stepped up, and moved back until he could see the windows. The curtains were drawn over the front window, so he circled to the side of the house. At least the curtains on that window were open. He had to move well out into the yard in order to see through the second-story window . . . and there she was.

Lolly was moving around the room, passing by the window now and then. Her face wasn't thin and wasted, like the couple downstairs, and even from here he could see that she was intent on . . . something. She pulled on a sweatshirt, even though she already wore something that looked strangely misshapen and lumpy.

As if she'd put on every piece of clothing she could find.

As if she were preparing for escape.

Gabriel took a deep breath, ignoring the cold in his lungs and the chill that surrounded him. Shit, his dad had been right. Again. Lolly *did* need rescuing.

He looked toward the detached garage. Maybe he could find a ladder in there.

CHAPTER FIVE

Every household needed a ladder, he thought, even if the house was used only a few times a year. Surely there was one around somewhere; his dad had always said Mr. Helton was a careful man, and a careful man would have a ladder. The most logical place where a careful man would put a ladder was in the garage, right? Cautiously he opened the side door into the garage, turning on the flashlight so he could see. The garage was fairly small, built in a time when most families owned only one car, and mostly empty. There were some odds and ends, some folding lawn chairs, and — *yes!* — a ladder.

He dragged it out from behind the lawn chairs, and his heart sank. This wasn't much of a ladder. For one thing, it wouldn't reach all the way to Lolly's window. For another, it was wooden, and it was old. The rungs weren't in good shape; two were broken, and he wasn't at all sure any of the others would hold his weight. But Lolly didn't weigh as much as he did and she was the one who'd be on it, so maybe it would hold together long enough for her to climb down. If not . . . then he hoped she'd bounce. No, hell, he'd have to catch her, he thought sourly. The way his luck was running, if he didn't catch her she'd probably fall on him and break his leg, or a few ribs.

Maybe Lolly had some other way of climbing down — the old sheets-tied-together rope, for instance. If she was making preparations to escape, then she definitely had something in mind. Maybe the ladder wouldn't be needed. He sure as hell hoped not, because it was a half-rotten death trap.

But as he was hauling the ladder from the garage to the house, he looked up at the window again and saw Lolly tugging on the window frame with all her might, trying to wrest it open. She stopped, got another grip, and tried again. From what he could see the window hadn't budged an inch.

Swearing again, but this time silently, he revised his plan. He'd have to go up and raise the damn window. No matter how she'd planned to get to the ground, she wasn't going anywhere unless she could get out the window. He sent up a silent prayer. Maybe the ladder would hold together.

He had to look up to position the ladder and the icy rain felt directly on his face, in his eyes. A sudden gust of wind caught the ladder, almost tearing it from his grip. Getting the ladder propped against the house without making any noise was going to be tricky. Just in case, he mentally ran through the operation: the objective was to get up the ladder without falling and breaking his neck, open the window, get down the ladder without falling and breaking his neck, and position himself beneath the ladder so he could catch Lolly if she fell, so she wouldn't break *her* neck. Simple enough.

Oh, yeah: he had to do all that in something like five seconds flat without making any noise and alerting the two meth addicts in the living room.

No problem, he thought sarcastically. Piece of cake.

He stood the ladder up, holding it steady with both hands as he let it drop closer and closer to the house, until it settled below the window with a barely audible thunk. It must have sounded louder inside the house, though, because he saw Lolly jump back from the window as if someone had just smacked the glass. Damn it, the ladder ended a good three feet below the window casing, which meant he'd have to climb all the way to the top to have any leverage opening the window.

There was no point in delaying, so he firmly gripped the outside of the ladder and began climbing, placing his boots on the outside edges of the rungs, where they were nailed to the frame and less likely to crumble under his weight. In just a few seconds he was standing precariously on the top rung, praying like hell, and staring through the glass at Lolly Helton, who stared at him as if she couldn't decide whether to scream or faint.

She didn't do either, thank God. Instead he saw her lips move, framing his name, then she closed her eyes for a brief second before gathering herself.

When she opened her eyes again, Gabriel held a finger to his lips, signaling her to be quiet. She nodded, an obvious and telling relief washing across her face.

She'd managed to raise the window a little, after all. He worked his gloved fingers into the gap and tried to lift upward, but there was only the slightest bit of movement. The window hadn't been painted stuck, and it wasn't locked, but the old wood had warped to the point where it might as well have been. Tensing his muscles, he tried again, putting everything he had into the effort and hoping that the howl of the wind would cover the noise he made. The ladder wobbled but he ignored the precariousness of his perch and wrenched at the window again. He had to get Lolly out of the house; if he fell, then he fell. He'd deal with that when it happened.

On the third try, the window popped free and slid upward with a creaking sound. He shoved and wiggled the frame, gaining another few inches of clearance. The window wasn't all the way up, but maybe this was enough.

In a quick glance he took in the room behind her; the bed was stripped, and sure enough one end of a sheet was knotted around the leg. Then he looked at her, and for the first time saw that one side of her face was bruised and swollen. Fury roared through him, swift and deep and startlingly savage. Some asshole abusing a woman pushed all his buttons, but somehow the fact that this was Lolly hit him particularly hard. He reined in his anger, because this wasn't the time to lose control. He had to get her safely away from here; that was his primary goal. Much as he'd love to take on the jerks downstairs, they were armed and he wasn't . . . and right now the weather was damn near as dangerous as two armed, high druggies. His only concern had to be getting Lolly and himself off the mountain. Everything else could wait.

Besides, he wasn't going to recklessly put his life in danger when he had a little boy expecting his father to come home. They were probably already missing him, wondering what was taking so long.

"I saw two in the living room," he said, keeping his voice low. "Are there more?"

She shook her head. "Just those two." Her voice was as low as his.

He reached through the open window and cupped her bruised cheek in his hand; his glove was cold and wet, and it must have felt good on her face because she made a soft little moan and tilted her head against the leather. "Are you hurt anywhere else?" he asked, needing to know if she could make it down the ladder by herself. She'd been getting around okay, but adrenaline could be driving her; he'd seen people do some amazing things when they were riding an adrenaline high.

"My shoulder and side are bruised, but I'm okay," she replied in a whisper, squaring her shoulders. She added fiercely, "Let's get out of here."

She had covered as much skin as possible, he saw; even her head and her ears were lightly protected with some folded material, and a flannel shirt tied over that. She'd layered her clothing and judging by the length of sheet in her hand she was making a pretty well-planned escape. If the window hadn't been stuck, she might've been on the ground and well on her way to town by the time he'd found her.

She dropped the rope of sheets and blankets and started to put one leg out the window. "Wait," he said, thinking fast. If she tossed the rope out the window and left it hanging, and he put the ladder away after she was down, the assholes downstairs would believe she'd made it out on her own. That way if they were stupid enough to get out in the storm and come after her, they'd be caught by surprise if — or when — they discovered that she was not alone. Just as swiftly he disregarded the plan, because the bottom sheet would be flapping right in front of the dining room window, and might alert them sooner than necessary. He was holding his breath hoping they didn't see the ladder through the window; at least the aged wood was dark, and not as easily made out as a white sheet would be.

He surveyed Lolly once more. She'd done the best she could to dress warmly, but the rain would seep right through all those layers, and then she'd be in deep trouble.

Moving carefully, the rickety ladder wobbling under him, Gabriel removed his poncho and handed it through the window. Lolly took it, then gave him a sharp look. "What about you?"

"You need it more. At least my coat is weatherproof." The poncho was covered with ice crystals, but provided much better protection against the rain than what she was wearing.

His coat was heavy, he had gloves, and his feet were protected by warm, waterproof boots. The only problem was that the knit cap he wore wasn't waterproof, like the cap he'd discarded in the truck, but he hadn't known then he'd be giving the hooded poncho to Lolly. The knit would repel the rain for a while, but eventually his head was going to get wet, and that wasn't good. When they got to the truck he'd retrieve his cap; he could make it that far without too much risk of hypothermia.

"I'm going back down," he whispered. "This ladder is half rotten, and it won't hold both of us at the same time." He wasn't certain it would stay together long enough for him to get down, but if it didn't, they'd go back to plan A and the tied-together sheets.

"There are two broken rungs. One is halfway down, the other is three below it. Put your feet on the outside of the rungs, not in the middle."

Lolly nodded, and began pulling on the poncho over her layers of clothing. Gabriel carefully backed down the ladder, not taking a deep breath until his boots were safely on the icy ground again. He turned up the collar of his jacket to protect his neck from the wind, and positioned himself so he could brace the ladder. She stuck her head out to make certain he was on the ground, then quickly drew it back in and stuck one leg out the window, feeling with her foot for the top rung. She couldn't reach it, of course, because the ladder wasn't tall enough. Finally she sat on the windowsill, put both legs out, and turned until she was on her stomach. She found the ladder, set both feet on it, and cautiously moved down the creaking wood. She was favoring her right side, he noticed, and wondered how she'd hold up for the long hike off the mountain.

The walk, which would be treacherous because of the ice, would take hours. In normal circumstances he wouldn't even attempt it, but the circumstances weren't normal and the only other choice they had was to simply hide and wait . . . but wait for what? The meth addicts in the living room were stuck, too; they weren't going anywhere, and at least they were in a warm house. He and Lolly couldn't wait for the ice to melt, because that could take a week or more. Their best bet, and it wasn't a good one, but it was better than their other options, was to get off the mountain as fast as they could, before the weight of the ice started snapping tree limbs like toothpicks. They'd be warmer if they were moving, too.

"Watch for that missing rung," he warned in an urgent whisper just before she reached it, and her step faltered. She hesitated, then changed her rhythm and instead used her right foot to step past the missing rung, so she could bear most of her weight with her left shoulder instead of the bruised right one.

A splintering sound was the only warning he had, before the next rung gave way, too, and she came tumbling down.

It wasn't a long drop, but in these conditions and with the hike they had ahead of them, a sprained ankle was as good as a broken leg. Instinctively Gabriel let go of the ladder and grabbed Lolly in a bear hug before she could hit the ground. The ladder clattered and banged against the side of the house.

"Shit!" he said, setting Lolly on her feet and grabbing her wrist. There was almost no chance the two inside hadn't heard the ladder slamming against the house. They needed to move — *now.*

"Let's go," he said, and started across the icy yard at a fast clip, towing her behind him. She didn't make a sound of protest, just put her head down and did her best to keep up. They slipped and slid, but he kept his feet; once Lolly started sliding, but she regained her balance, aided by his grip on her wrist. If they could just make the tree line . . .

There was a shout behind them, and a shot rang out.

Double shit.

CHAPTER SIX

Lolly went down with a cry of pain, and for one stark split-second time froze as Gabriel thought she'd been shot. Then she was scrambling to her feet, muttering "Damn it!" with muffled fury before grabbing his hand and taking off again. She fell again, almost immediately; the thick treads on his boots didn't afford him a lot of traction, but her sneakers had almost none.

Gabriel hauled her to her feet once more; she stifled another cry of pain, and too late he realized he'd pulled on her right arm, and her injured right shoulder. To keep her upright, he wrapped his arm around her and held her, his grip so hard he expected her to protest, but she didn't make a peep. Running in that locked-together position was impossible, unless they wanted to end up facedown on the ground while the two meth-heads took potshots at them. Their best bet was to keep moving, no matter how agonizingly slow their progress seemed to be.

At least it was dark up here, away from the lights of town and other houses; hiding would be easier. Of course, that meant they had to be extra cautious themselves, because he couldn't turn on the flashlight without pinning a bull's-eye on their backs. All he could do was keep moving, get them into the trees, and hope for the best.

Even though she'd spent the last hour — two hours? She had no idea how much time had passed — in terror, expecting to be killed, somehow the first explosive crack of a gunshot still caught Lolly by surprise; her entire body lurched, and her heart jumped so hard it felt as if it would come out of her chest. She stumbled, lost her balance on the icy grass, and went down. Cold immediately seared her legs. The poncho somewhat protected her, but from mid-thigh down her pants were wet. After all the effort she'd made to stay dry, what did she do but fall on the wet ground the very first thing? Furious with herself, she scrambled up, grabbed Gabriel's hand, and took off running again.

And immediately fell again.

This time Gabriel jerked her to her feet, and the pressure on her bruised shoulder and side wrenched a cry from her before she stubbornly shut her mouth. What was a little pain in her shoulder compared to maybe getting shot? Gabriel clamped his arm around her waist and set off again, all but dragging her along with him.

Behind them, the porch light flared on, and the front door opened with a pop and a slam; the first shot must have been through the dining room window if they were just now making it out on the porch. Niki and Darwin began firing from the porch; their aim was off, but every cell in her spinal cord seemed to shrivel as she waited for a lucky shot to find her. Again, time seemed to have lost its meaning; logically only ten or fifteen seconds could have passed, because how long could it have taken them to get to the porch? It felt as if she and Gabriel had been running for the woods for a lifetime, but they were still several yards away. Lolly was afraid to turn and look at the porch, afraid to do anything except try to keep her feet under her and make as much progress as she could.

Don't fall, don't fall. Instinct screamed at her to run, but even with Gabriel's support it was all she could do to keep her feet under her. They were still on grass, which wasn't nearly as slick as the driveway would be, but every step sent her feet slipping and skating in various directions. Gabriel fared better, maybe because of his boots, maybe because he was heavier and crunched through the layer of ice to the ground. *Don't fall.* She clutched the back of his coat in a death grip, hanging on for dear life.

Then they reached the tree line and Gabriel whirled, shoving her behind one of the larger trees and pressing himself full against her as if he were trying to push her into the rough bark. Lolly clung to him, her head buried against his shoulder as she sucked in huge, rapid gulps of air. Random shots splintered the air, the sound curiously flat and muffled, as if it was absorbed by the ice instead of echoing back. Her heart still pounded like something wild, even though they were significantly safer behind this tree trunk than they had been before. But what now? If they ran, they'd be exposed again, at least sporadically. If they didn't run, then all Niki and Darwin had to do was walk across the yard to shoot them at close range.

Gabriel incrementally leaned to the left, until he could see the house but still presented almost no target, given they were in the darkness of the tree line and Niki and Darwin were hampered by standing on a lighted porch. Even knowing they likely couldn't see a thing, Lolly's hands involuntarily tightened on Gabriel's coat as she tried to wrench him back to safety. She couldn't move him at all, not even a fraction of an inch.

His right hand patted her shoulder, the movement so absent she knew the reassuring gesture was pure reflex. He was concentrating on the situation, on the two murderous idiots on the front porch. Feeling slightly ashamed for being such a wuss, Lolly forced herself to release him. She'd gotten this far without turning into a spineless blob; she'd make it the rest of the way, or die trying . . . literally.

"How many weapons did you see?" He breathed the words, the sound barely existent.

"Two." That didn't mean there weren't more, though. For all she knew, there was a cache of weapons in their old Blazer.

"Do you know guns?" he asked.

She shook her head. She knew what a shotgun looked like, because her dad had gone skeet shooting, but her experience was limited to that and whatever she'd seen on television or in a movie.

"Can you tell the difference between

a revolver and an automatic?"

That much she did know. "They were both automatics . . . I think. I didn't get a good look at the one he had." Darwin had pulled it from his pocket, but she'd barely had time to register the fact before he'd shoved her against the newel post.

"I don't suppose you could tell me how many bullets they had in each gun," he said wryly.

Lolly just shook her head, even though the question had been rhetorical. Had he actually been *counting* the number of shots? She'd barely been able to think at all, much less keep track of how many shots were being fired.

Then the gunshots stopped, and that was almost more frightening than being shot at. What was happening? Were Niki and Darwin coming after them? She could hear the two of them yelling at each other. She could also hear her own heartbeat, Gabriel's breathing, and the wind. At this moment, there was nothing else.

"What are we going to do now?" she whispered. Her voice was all but lost against his thick coat, but Gabriel heard her and gave her another of those absent pats.

"We're going down the mountain. There's nothing else we can do, no other option." He didn't sound happy about that, but she couldn't think of anything else they could do, either. She'd been prepared to make her way down the mountain alone, anyway, so she wasn't going to complain.

Gabriel looked toward the house, took Lolly's hand again, and together they eased away from their protected position behind the tree to move deeper into the woods. His step was quick but sure, and she had to struggle a little to keep pace. Her legs weren't as long as his, and hiking through the woods wasn't exactly her thing. She didn't have many "things," she realized. She was excruciatingly normal, lived a normal life, worked at a normal job. She liked books and movies, forced herself to exercise, but despite growing up in Maine, she didn't care for roughing it or any winter sports at all, so she was definitely out of her element right now.

The trees had sheltered the ground beneath them, so there was less ice here, though their feet still made crunching sounds. That meant ice was building on the limbs and branches overhead, and she knew how dangerous that could be; working for an insurance company had given her insight into all sorts of situations, because she'd seen the claims.

Gabriel led her at an angle that generally followed the long driveway toward the narrow secondary road, stepping over fallen dead branches, maneuvering around clumps of wild growth. A couple of times he looked back at her. She felt like a tethered balloon, being tugged along in his wake. Her breath huffed out in rapid gasps. He must have realized that she was struggling to keep up with him because he shortened his stride, but not by much. "It'll be a bit easier when we can leave the woods," he said once, as he helped her around an overgrown, brambly bush. "I have soup and coffee in my truck."

"Dangling a carrot, eh?"

That might've been a smile, but it was so dark she couldn't be sure. "Whatever works."

"Um . . . exactly where *is* your truck?" The shock had worn off enough now that she could think a little. Obviously Gabriel hadn't flown there, so he had to have wheels somewhere.

"About half a mile farther. The ice was so bad I had to stop."

Questions tumbled in her mind, questions like: why was he here? It wasn't as if she and Gabriel McQueen were close friends — or even *friends,* come to that. Of all the people in the world, what was *he* doing at her house? None of this felt real, and somehow his presence was the most unreal part of it all. Being knocked around, terrorized, almost raped, and held captive were all shocking enough in their own right, but the fact that he, of all people, had appeared out of the night to help her escape was simply dumbfounding — either that, she thought wryly, or this was her brain's way of helping her cope by shoving all that other stuff to the side until she could cope.

If concentrating on Gabriel Mc-Queen was a coping mechanism, then she'd go along with the game plan; that was much better than thinking of the violence, of everything that could go wrong, of how dangerous walking for miles in weather like this could be. The odds were so heavy against them surviving the night that only sheer desperation made her willing to try.

The darkness in the woods was almost complete; they both stumbled over obstacles, feeling their way along. Her eyes had adjusted somewhat, and still she could barely see. If Gabriel had a flashlight he didn't produce it, and she didn't ask; much as she wanted to see where she was going, she seriously didn't want the equivalent of a spotlight pinpointing their position for Niki and Darwin.

In spite of the poncho Gabriel had given her, before long the cold cut through all the layers of clothing she wore. Her jeans and sweatpants were wet from falling on the ice, and the wind went right through to her skin. She would have liked nothing better than to stop and hunker down so the poncho draped around her and blocked the wind, but if she stopped moving she was afraid she wouldn't be able to start up again. Knowing what waited behind her, in the warmth of her own home, spurred her to keep up. She'd walk all the way to Portland if that was what it took to get away from those two.

She'd even put her life in the hands of Gabriel McQueen, who had been the bane of her teenage years. He'd been everything she wasn't: popular, outgoing, self-assured. And she'd had the most horribly painful crush on him all through junior high and high school. The flip side of that was she'd hated him, too, for all the times he'd made fun of her, all the times he'd taunted her and laughed at her, and she'd never passed up an opportunity to slip a verbal knife between his ribs. When he'd graduated two years ahead of her, she'd been relieved, yet she'd still caught herself watching the hallways for that proudly held dark head.

She should probably count herself lucky he'd bothered rescuing her. The teenage Gabriel wouldn't have bothered — though, to be fair, if she'd still been a teenager she'd probably have slammed the window on his hands anyway.

Thinking about the past could occupy her mind only so long before her physical misery began to push its way to the forefront. The rain was coming down harder now, coating the trees, the underbrush, even them. She couldn't see it, but she could feel the weight of it crusting her wet pants and shoes. At least her feet didn't seem to be quite as wet as her legs, thanks to the Vaseline . . . either that, or they were so cold she couldn't feel the moisture. The wind soughed through the tree limbs, making them rattle like bones in their ice-coffins. The sound was eerie, ghostly, and she was glad for the big, hard hand that gripped hers.

Then Gabriel pushed through some particularly heavy undergrowth and halted so abruptly she plowed into his back. "Finally," he said, reaching back to steady her. "Here's the road. There's about a three-foot drop down to it, so be careful."

He bent down, gripped a sapling, and used it to steady himself as he jumped down the low embankment. His feet skidded on the ice, but with the aid of the sapling he stayed upright. Gingerly he turned, reached up, and grasped Lolly around the waist, then lowered her to the road with easy strength. "Watch your step," he warned. "There's a shallow ditch here. Walk on the weedy strip between the ditch and the pavement; it's better footing."

Head down, Lolly concentrated on putting one foot in front of the other. Surely they had gone more than a half mile; shouldn't they have reached his truck by now? She had grown up on this mountain, knew it like the back of her hand, most of the time, but the darkness, the cold, the unrelenting series of shocks, had all left her disoriented and she had no real idea where they were. Her hands and feet hurt so much from the cold she felt as if she could barely shuffle forward. She couldn't do anything about her feet, and Gabriel gripped one of her hands so she couldn't do anything about it, either, but her other hand she wormed under the poncho and several other layers of clothing to reach the bare skin of her warm belly. She could barely feel the warmth on her fingers, but her belly could definitely feel the cold of her hand. There, that was a little better.

Now and then she darted a glance at the man who was leading her, though in the darkness she couldn't make out much more than his height and the width of his shoulders — that, and the determination with which he faced the storm head-on. She remembered the way he'd looked when he'd popped up in her window, though. He was older, obviously; so was she. A lot of years had passed since he'd graduated — fifteen of them! — and they'd both changed.

He was no longer a cocky teenager with the world at his feet; he was a grown man, a widower with a son, as she'd heard during one of her trips to Wilson Creek. Becoming a father and losing his wife were life-changing events; no way could he be the same person he was when they were in school. She wasn't, and she hadn't been through anything as traumatic as losing a spouse. There was nothing traumatic in her life at all. Instead she'd quietly made her way, made a settled life for herself, shed a lot of her insecurities and shyness.

She had butted heads with him for as long as she could remember, and right now . . . she wasn't sure why. Was it because she'd always had such a ferocious crush on him, and never expected him to like her in any way, so she'd protected herself by developing a shield of hostility? Teenagers were such tangled pits of angst and emotion, anything was possible. Looking back, she felt slightly bemused by their teenage selves.

If there would ever be any time for putting the past behind them, that time was now. She leaned slightly toward him and said, "Thank you," her voice raised so he could hear her over the rain and the wind.

"Thank me if those psychos don't come after us and we get off the mountain before the trees start to fall," he said without looking at her.

Okay, that sounded a little abrupt, but she did something that, fifteen years ago, she could never have done: she mentally shrugged and let it go.

Under the circumstances, he was allowed to feel testy.

They were walking right into the wind now, which gave her some bearings. Lolly glanced up, but not for long; the rain stung her face like icy pellets, the wind stole her breath with its chill. The wind was from the north, so if it was in her face then they were walking north, which meant they were on the long slope before a very sharp curve that would take them southeast.

They weren't that far from the house at all.

They had some time before the ice that coated everything was so heavy these old trees started to come down . . . she hoped. How long would the dead trees hold up with this wind and ice? she wondered. Their fragile limbs would come down first. The side of the road was littered with limbs that had fallen in one storm or another and been left to lie, giving her a hint as to the length and breadth of what might come crashing down.

The wind picked up a bit just then and the trees creaked, literally, as if their very fabric was groaning. Lolly shuddered. They had one option, and it wasn't a good one. Darwin and Niki were behind them, ice-covered limbs hovered above their heads and could come crashing down at any time, and the ground was increasingly slick beneath her feet. There was no place to go except forward, toward the safety and warmth that seemed so very far away.

She slipped, her sneakers giving her no purchase at all. The Vaseline definitely helped, but some moisture had seeped into her shoes and socks and her feet were painfully numb. She'd grown up in Maine; she knew the dangers of frostbite. She knew what the outcome of the night was likely to be, and a sense of fatalism seized her. Better to lose her toes than let herself get caught by Darwin again.

She adjusted the sleeves of the flannel shirt tied over her head, pulling them over her nose and mouth, but the sleeves were wet and icy and she didn't know if that would do much good. Thank goodness Gabriel was there, steady as a rock, plowing forward with the determination of a pit bull. His grip was solid, a comfort in a decidedly uncomfortable world. He was that kind of man, she supposed, the kind who would go out in an ice storm to make sure a neighbor was all right, a man who would throw himself between danger and a woman even if she was nothing to him, even if she was a girl he'd once known and hadn't liked.

She hadn't had a chance to tell him everything that had happened back at the house and after a moment of reflection she decided she wouldn't. Not only did she not want to talk about Darwin's attempted rape, she wasn't sure how Gabriel would react to the news. Would he feel as if he had to turn back? Would he care at all? She suspected he would care, just because of who he was, and she didn't want to go back to the house. She didn't want Gabriel going back there either, and for now she was sticking by his side. Her sights were set firmly away from the house and the nightmare there. No matter what the conditions, she was moving forward.

There was silence behind them — at least human silence. Mother Nature was making a racket, with the patter of falling rain, the wind, the ghostly rustling and creaking of the trees. Maybe they'd given up. Maybe they hadn't given chase at all. Maybe Niki and Darwin were unwilling to leave a nice warm house in this weather, just to chase her and Gabriel.

She glanced up once more, at the tall man towing her along. "So . . . how've you been?" she asked.

Gabriel snorted. "You want to chit-chat now?"

"Maybe talking will keep my face from freezing."

He nodded once. "I've been okay. You?"

So much for dragging him into conversation. "Fine." What else could she say? *Still single. Job's good, if unexciting. Mom and Dad are in good health, but they lost a good bit of their retirement money in the latest financial disaster, so keeping a house they no longer use is ridiculous. I didn't want to sell it, but I can't afford to buy it from them, and now I don't want to. I loved that house, and now I don't care if I never see it again.* The sense of loss was surprisingly sharp; she took it in, accepted that she would never again feel the same about the house, then she resolutely put the house in the past where it belonged and mentally faced forward.

She should have been paying attention to what she was doing, rather than wool-gathering. She slipped again, and once more Gabriel caught her.

"We need to get you out of this ice," he said, his tone concerned. She had to admit, getting out of the weather was a good idea. The best, in fact. But there wasn't a neighbor for miles, and town was even farther.

"My truck isn't far," he added encouragingly.

Lolly knew very well that these roads were now impassable. Nasty as it was, dangerous as it was, she'd rather walk down the steep road than get in a vehicle and take the chance of slipping and sliding over the side of the mountain. There were some wicked curves and steep drop-offs between here and Wilson Creek. But they could stop at Gabriel's truck, get inside and get warm, maybe break out the soup and coffee. With that thought in mind, she had a reasonable destination in mind and that kept her moving forward, putting one foot in front of the other. If she had to think of walking all the way down the mountain she'd probably drop here and now, certain she couldn't make it.

None of this was real. It couldn't be. Her life was unexciting, boring, ordinary. To fight off an attack, escape through a second-story window, get shot at and fight against a storm as dangerous as what she'd left behind — these were things she'd never thought to do. Lolly decided she liked unexciting. At the moment, she craved it. She'd never again complain about being bored. This . . . this was all like a bad dream.

Every step now was a struggle. The cold cut through her clothes, slowing her down. Her instincts screamed at her to stop, rest, give in, but she knew if she stopped here, she'd die. Freezing to death couldn't be a pleasant way to go, and even if it was, she wasn't ready to go.

"Soup," Lolly said with all-but-frozen lips, throwing the word out like a talisman, something to keep her going. Suddenly she realized she was starving. The thought of the soup warming her from the inside out encouraged her to keep moving, even when the ground beneath her turned sharply down and each step became even more precarious.

"Yes, there's soup." His arm was tighter around her now; he was all but carrying her. Lolly gathered her strength, focused on what she was doing.

If she could just get some soup — and coffee! He'd said he had coffee! — she'd be able to make it. They could rest for a few minutes, turn the truck heater on full blast and thaw out a little, have some soup and coffee, and be on their way. With a little fortification, she'd be good to go.

Then there was an enraged shout from above, followed by a gunshot, and terror blasted its way through every fiber of her body. Darwin was coming for her after all.

CHAPTER SEVEN

Darwin followed Niki out onto the porch, reluctant to leave the comfort of the house. The wind was brutal out here, and . . . hell, was that *ice?* The shit covered everything, even the Blazer. He hadn't noticed any ice when they'd been out here just a little while ago, after the Lorelei bitch went out the second-story window and escaped. He blamed Niki for that. If she'd just left them alone, everything would have been okay. He'd have had some fun, and Lorelei wouldn't have been in any shape to go out the win-

161

dow. Now that strange dude who'd showed up out of nowhere would be the one having the fun.

Man, that ice was unreal. He thought it might have been sleeting before, but to come outside and find everything coated with ice was fucking weird.

He scratched at his face, and thought he needed another hit of meth. They still had plenty inside, unless that bitch Niki had used it all. She was using more than her fair share, he thought resentfully. She was always doing that, and he was tired of it. Yeah, she was good about coming up with ideas for getting more money, but then she used up the shit so it was her fault they had to have more money, anyway.

"It's your fault," he said, because he was tired of her bitching and complaining and the way she wanted to make all the decisions. He stared at the icicles hanging from the eaves of the porch. This was her fault, too, because she'd come up with the bright idea of following Lorelei home, when they could have taken her money in town and wouldn't be stuck on this fucking mountain now. "If you hadn't left her alone upstairs, she wouldn't have got away."

Niki erupted in rage. "That bitch!" she screamed, and fired a shot at Lorelei's Mercedes, which might have made her feel better but was a waste of a bullet, as far as Darwin was concerned. Was the stupid car going to feel anything? They didn't have many bullets left, he figured, after all the shooting they'd done earlier. They'd gone back inside and Niki had spent the time working herself into a fit, but neither of them had checked how many rounds were left in the guns. Then Niki decided they had to go look for Lorelei and insisted they come outside, made him put on his coat and get a flashlight, but Darwin had lost all his enthusiasm for that. Niki could go out in this shit if she wanted to; he was going back inside.

"You'll pay for this!" Niki screeched into the night, as if Lorelei was standing around out there listening to her. She turned to face Darwin, her face twisted and distorted, her sunken eyes glaring at him. "When we find Lorelei and kill the bastard with her, I'm going to let you have her. That'll teach the bitch to play games with me!"

Now, that sounded interesting. Darwin's spirits lifted as he regained his enthusiasm. "Really?"

"As long as you let me watch and you make it hurt, why not? Teach her to fuck with me," Niki added beneath her breath.

Okay, maybe that was worth going out in the weather for. Lorelei . . . women like her looked down their noses at him. It would be nice to have someone like her to do what he wanted to, to treat any way he liked. Yeah, that would be fun. Maybe he'd keep her. Maybe he'd get rid of Niki and train Lorelei right. A dose or two of meth and she'd be begging for it, willing to do anything he told her so long as he kept giving the ice to her.

They had found several flashlights in the house and each carried one: a gun in one hand, a flashlight in the other. Carefully they made their way down the steps, and Darwin grabbed the door handle of the Blazer.

"Don't be stupid, Stupid," Niki snapped. "If they're hiding in the woods and we're driving along in the Blazer, how the hell we gonna see them? Unless they're dumb enough to be standing in the middle of the road, we won't. They're on foot, so we have to be on foot."

She called *him* stupid? he thought, the resentment bubbling again. He wasn't the one who let Lorelei get away in the first place.

He trained the beam of his flashlight down the driveway. The ray of light cut the darkness, but didn't exactly illuminate the area for them. It was too dark and the flashlights weren't all that great; they'd be fine for finding his way around a house if the power went out, but they weren't a whole lot of good for a manhunt. Still, they were better than nothing. Lorelei and her pal had to be down there somewhere, and they weren't armed. If they had been they would've fired back as they'd been making their escape. They were probably hiding, waiting until they thought he and Niki had gone to sleep before they snuck back into the house. Only reason anyone would stay out in this mess was if they had no choice.

He'd shoot the guy on sight, get him out of the way, then there wouldn't be any way for Lorelei to escape. His imagination took over, and he remembered how pretty and soft she was, how good she felt. Without watching what he was doing, Darwin took a step and his foot shot out from under him. He hit the ground ass first and the flashlight went flying, but he managed to hold on to his gun. The impact rattled his bones, stole his breath. Niki, damn her, bent over laughing.

"Get on the side of the road, you moron," she said, shining the beam from her flashlight into his face and effectively blinding him. Great. Now he wouldn't be able to see anything at all for a while.

Darwin slowly rose to his feet, edging off the driveway and onto the grassy shoulder. Once he was there, he retrieved his flashlight and a portion of his dignity. He looked down the slope, imagining the woman he craved to the bone hiding there, somewhere. He'd make her pay for this. He didn't let Niki know how much his ass hurt, because he knew she'd make fun of him if she knew. Niki had a mean streak in her, and she didn't care who she turned it on.

Well, fuck her. No, forget that. He'd rather fuck Lorelei. Get rid of Niki, take Lorelei instead.

"Oh, Lorelei," he called in a sing-song voice. "Where are you, Lorelei? Come 'ere, baby, come to daddy."

Niki laughed again. She was easily amused tonight, flipping from rage to laughter at the slightest reason. They eased down the slope. The icy wind blew the stinging rain into his eyes. His ass hurt. They were chasing after two people who had a head start, in the dark, but at the moment he didn't much care about any of that. Lorelei was going to pay for running away from them.

He remembered her expression of terror when he'd had her down on the kitchen floor. He'd liked that, liked the feeling of power, of knowing he could make her so scared she'd been about to pass out. Yeah, he'd like having her around for a while. He'd like showing her how ice could make her feel, like having her beg him for it — and for anything else he wanted to give her. "I think I want her high this time," he said as he took careful steps down the hill. If she was high she'd like what he gave her, whether she wanted to or not.

"You hold her down, I'll shoot her up," Niki said, then, like a light switch flipping, went straight into anger again. "The damn bitch!"

"Works for me." Reckless with anticipation, Darwin tried to hurry. His foot slipped again and his arms wind-milled until he got his balance. Cursing, he slowed down. He'd better not fall; he might break something he'd need later. Snickering, he called out again. "Lorelei! Ready or not, here I come." He laughed at his own pun — and Niki thought he was stupid.

Gabriel reacted immediately at the flat crack of the gunshot, pushing Lolly up the embankment, back into the woods. A quick glance showed the flashlight beams dancing as the druggies came down the hill, not nearly as far away as he'd like. They hadn't been forced to cut through the woods but had gone straight from the house to the driveway, which had saved them time. They weren't more than fifty yards away.

Fortunately, they couldn't move any faster than he and Lolly could. Unfortunately, they could use their flashlights and they were armed. If they shone their lights into the woods at the right place at the right time, and they were halfway decent shots, he and Lolly would be sitting ducks.

In this weather, hunkering down in the woods wasn't a great idea. They needed to keep moving so they didn't get too cold, but at the same time movement would give away their location. He just hoped tree limbs didn't start snapping.

He found a big pine and positioned Lolly behind it, concealing her as best he could between his body and the tree trunk. He bent his head so his mouth was close to her ear. "After they go past, we're going to backtrack.

They won't expect it, and we can hide in the garage until morning."

She nodded, her head moving against his shoulder. Gabriel hoped he wasn't making a mistake. He'd have liked to get to the truck, get some hot coffee, get this frozen knit cap off his head. He was losing so much body heat through his head that he wasn't certain how much longer he could keep going, but he didn't want to say anything to Lolly. He didn't want her feeling guilty because she had his poncho. It wasn't her fault two brain-fried meth addicts were hunting them down; none of this was her fault.

"If we're lucky, they'll break their fool necks long before then." He wouldn't mind at all. He'd leave their bodies where they lay, and get himself and Lolly back to the house as fast as they could move.

Again, Lolly nodded.

Of course, they hadn't had a lot of luck so far tonight; what were the odds they'd get lucky now?

In the wood behind them, he heard the crackle of wood straining to resist the weight of the ice, and the sound sent a shiver down his back that had nothing to do with the cold and everything to do with dread. Lolly heard it, too. Her head lifted, and he felt the stillness in her body as she listened, waiting. It was early in the storm for limbs to start falling, but when he took into account the number of dead trees in these woods and the wind that would make the limbs fall sooner, he knew they didn't have long. The question was, how soon would limbs start to drop, and how widespread would the fall be?

Dead limbs first; healthy limbs later. Then treetops would be splintering and falling; by morning entire trees would be coming down. If they didn't get off the mountain soon, they weren't going anywhere for a while.

"Lorelei! Ready or not, here I come!"

Lolly shuddered in his arms as she heard the lilting, savagely amused voice of the man who'd invaded her home. Gabriel didn't like the way the man called her name, didn't like the way Lolly trembled. She hadn't given him any details about what had happened before he'd arrived — there hadn't been time — but he knew how violent meth addicts could be. Whatever had happened — and he'd find out later, *if* they survived — she was handling it.

He'd never thought he would be admiring of Lolly Helton, but damn if he wasn't. Not only had she showed plenty of spunk and common sense, not once had she complained, though he knew her feet had to be excruciatingly cold in those inadequate sneakers. A lot of people, with perfect justification, would have been ready to sit down and give up, but Lolly just put her head down and kept going. Given that determination, *something* had to have happened to make her react to the meth-head like this.

He tightened his arms around her, offering her both protection and comfort. "I won't let him hurt you," he breathed, because the two addicts were closer now and even a low tone would be too loud. That was a promise he intended to keep, come hell or high water, unless he was dead. Grimly he assessed the situation. If the two would pass by, keep going, and get far enough away that he and Lolly could make it back up the hill again without drawing attention to themselves . . . there had to be something in the garage he could use as a weapon, if it came to a confrontation.

Lolly leaned forward, fell into him. Her arms went around his waist, held him tight. They had on too many clothes to share any body heat, but the contact was nice. Gabriel gently cupped the back of her head, held her to his shoulder. All they had to do now was be very still and very quiet, and pray they weren't seen. If they could just stay here a while longer, if they could melt into the darkness and be invisible . . .

Soon the druggies were too close for even an exchange of a whisper. He felt tension coiling in her muscles, but she didn't move an inch. Even over the wind, he could hear the two talking as they picked their way down the hill, occasionally shining their flashlights into the woods. The flashlights were standard household models, the beams weak compared to what he used, but he and Lolly were just barely inside the tree line and the lights easily penetrated that far. He kept his face tucked down, because the relative paleness of bare skin was almost like a beacon in the dark.

The change from just a couple of hours ago was staggering. When he'd left his parents' house Gabriel had expected to do battle with the weather and with Lolly, but this . . . this had never crossed his mind.

A beam of light flashed just a few feet to his right. The tree they stood behind gave them some cover, but not enough, not with light coming in from an angle. If they moved in order to keep the tree between them and the druggies, they'd make too much noise. There were twigs, untended undergrowth, and even dead leaves left to rot from the autumn fall — not to mention the ice — all at their feet. Even with the wind howling, it was more likely that movement would alert the hunters to their hiding place than their intermittent flashlight beams would find them.

Lolly stopped breathing. So did he. And as luck — very bad luck — would have it, a beam of light caught his sleeve. He watched it from the corner of his eye, watched it move away, then suddenly return and settle on his face. A woman's voice yelled, "I got 'em! Darwin! Over here!"

No point in keeping quiet now. Gabriel shoved Lolly away from the tree, away from the flashlight, and lunged for deeper cover. "Run," he said, grabbing her arm, and they both ran like hell as a gunshot exploded behind them.

Niki aimed into the woods where she'd seen the man, his face a startling bit of white in the darkness, and fired, but she was too slow. The two disappeared, but she could hear them crashing deeper into the woods. She'd lose them in there, and she didn't like letting anyone get away from her, especially some hoity-toity rich bitch like Lorelei. She fired again, her aim following the sound they made as they ran. This was like hunting, she thought in pleased excitement as she followed them into the woods. Lorelei Helton and her friend were just like deer, a doe and a buck, running from danger, running from her gun. She liked thinking they were frantic with fear, and completely defenseless.

"Don't shoot the woman!" Darwin shouted with what seemed to be real concern in his voice.

"Like I can see what I'm shooting at," Niki screamed. The bastard, all he wanted was the woman. He was really good at just sitting on his ass and letting her do all the work, then telling her how to do it. She'd do better without him, and maybe, just maybe, the day was coming when she'd do something about that. Right now, though, she had to track some deer. She moved forward, her footing sturdier once she was entirely under the trees. She picked up the pace then, continuing in the direction she'd heard her deer take, sweeping her hand from side to side and pulling the trigger until the hammer just made a clicking sound and there were no more bullets left. On her right, Darwin was shooting, too, finally more concerned about not letting the two get away than he was about wounding or killing his prize.

Neither of them were trained shooters. Even on a good day, all they could do was point and pull the trigger; it wasn't like they usually cared if they hit anything or not. Just the fear of a weapon, the fear of getting shot, was usually enough to make people do what they wanted, and when they did shoot someone it was always up close where there was no question of missing. They'd never before needed more than a bullet or two, maybe three, to get what they wanted.

Within seconds, Darwin was out of ammunition himself. They stopped, unsure what to do now. They flicked their flashlight beams around, but couldn't see anything other than black tree trunks, underbrush, and ice. Well, wasn't this great? Here they were, standing in the woods, cold, angry, and effectively disarmed. To top it off, that bitch Lorelei had gotten away again. While there were plenty of sounds in the forest, none seemed to be coming from the human deer.

A tickle of warning crawled up Niki's spine. Without bullets she didn't feel nearly as confident as she had just moments ago. Maybe this hadn't been such a good idea. Besides, she was coming down from the last hit, and she needed another one pretty soon. She'd feel better then.

"Forget it," she said angrily. "We'll go back to the house and get warm, and in the morning when the sun comes up and melts the ice on the road, we can get out of here."

"But what about Lorelei?" Darwin asked, whining like a kid who'd just dropped his ice-cream cone in the sand.

Niki tamped down her surge of jealousy. "Your bitch Lorelei and her friend are going to freeze to death out there." With her useless gun, she gestured into the depths of the forest.

It was so dark, and shit, now that the hunt had lost its appeal, the cold was starting to really seep through her coat.

"But . . ."

"You want to keep looking? Fine. Go right ahead. I'm going back to the house and I'm going to enjoy myself."

"Just five more minutes of looking around and —" There was a faint rustle behind them. Darwin went still. The beam from his flashlight danced across the dark forest floor. "Did you hear that?"

Too late, Niki said, "Turn off that light!" She fumbled with cold gloved hands to press the switch on the one she carried to the off position, but it was too late. In the beam of Darwin's flashlight, she saw the long, thick tree

limb that came swinging from behind, like a baseball bat aimed at the
side of his head.

CHAPTER EIGHT

Gabriel pulled them to a halt behind yet another big tree. "Stay here, and don't move a muscle," he whispered.

He moved away from her and she almost lunged to grab his jacket and hold him back. She didn't deliberately go toward danger, she ran away from it; that's what made sense to her. But Gabriel was military, and his training was not only to go to the danger, but to neutralize it. Her heart jumped into her throat and lodged there, knowing he was risking his life. Every instinct in her screamed for her to stop him, beg him not to leave her, to hold him there and keep him as safe as possible.

She bit her lip until the sharp coppery taste of blood touched her tongue. She had to do exactly as he said, or she'd be endangering him even more.

Gabriel stooped slowly and silently, his hands sweeping the ground around him. He picked up an old fallen limb that was about three feet long and hefted it, then silently discarded it and began feeling for another one. Lolly tried to keep an eye on Darwin and Niki for him, so she could warn him if they got closer. They had stopped, and from the sharpness of their voices, appeared to be arguing, though she couldn't make out any individual words. She glanced back at Gabriel, and he was gone.

In a panic she looked in all directions, but she couldn't see him. He had disappeared into the rain and darkness.

But if she couldn't see him, then likely Darwin and Niki wouldn't be able to either . . . except for those damn flashlights. Maybe she could draw their attention her way — No. She discarded the idea as soon as it formed. Gabriel had told her not to move. If she did, not only would he not have any idea where she was, in the darkness he wouldn't be able to tell her from the bad guys. Gabriel McQueen was hunting, and she didn't want to get in his way.

The shadows were deep there under the trees, but the icy coating on the trees and bushes seemed to give off a faint glitter, reflecting back the light from the flashlights that Niki and Darwin were waving around. The flashlights pinpointed their positions as exactly as if they were caught on stage by spotlights. There was a glow all around them, as if the air was full of tiny particles of ice. The scene would have been breathtakingly pretty if it wasn't so breathtakingly cold, and she wasn't so damn scared.

Then she caught sight of Gabriel, easing up behind Darwin, every step as slow and careful as that of a big cat stalking an antelope. Lolly remained frozen to the spot, afraid to move, afraid she'd make a noise that would distract him.

Gabriel lifted his makeshift club like a baseball bat. He was still well back, out of the circle of light, but if either Darwin or Niki looked around they'd surely see him. The stance he took reminded her of watching him play baseball in high school, all those years ago when he'd been young and skinny and arrogant as all hell. He'd hit more than one home run in the old days; he looked poised to hit one now.

Lolly's heart pounded. She was tempted to cover her eyes with her hands, to hide from reality like a two-year-old playing hide-and-seek, but she had to watch. She had to know what was happening. If she was a betting woman she'd put everything she had on Gabriel. But nothing in life was certain, not even Gabriel Mc-Queen, and tonight their lives hung in the balance.

Abruptly Niki screamed something and turned off her flashlight. Darwin wasn't as fast, and Gabriel stepped forward, swinging away, his muscular arms bringing the limb around so fast it made a whistling sound. Darwin dropped his flashlight and ducked. Instead of a solid blow, the limb glanced off his head, and with a growl like an animal, Darwin whirled and leapt on Gabriel.

Gabriel couldn't swing again because Darwin was inside his reach, so he shifted his hands apart on the limb and used it like a bar, making short, hard jabs with the ends and lightning-fast moves to block the wild punches Darwin was throwing, beating at Gabriel with the pistol. The flashlight Darwin had dropped had rolled to the side, pointing away from them, so they weren't much more than a massive shadow. Gabriel was taller, more muscular, but Darwin was still riding a meth high and was impervious to pain. He landed a solid kick behind Gabriel's knee and Gabriel went down, but he dragged Darwin with him.

Where was Niki? Lolly realized she could no longer see the woman and she looked around wildly, half-expecting Niki to leap out of the darkness at her, or rush to Darwin's defense, but . . . no Niki. Either she'd seized the opportunity to run, or she was biding her time, looking for an opening to either shoot Gabriel or bash him in the head. Lolly couldn't tell which of the rolling, cursing, grunting men on the ground was Gabriel and which was Darwin, so likely Niki couldn't either.

Abruptly Lolly realized that she was too far away to help Gabriel if Niki attacked. Without letting herself think about how likely she was to get hurt or killed for her efforts, she copied Gabriel and felt around on the ground until she found a stick of her own, a broken limb that had fallen recently enough that it hadn't rotted yet. It wasn't as hefty as Gabriel's limb, but it was better than nothing. No longer worried about remaining quiet, Lolly rushed toward the fight.

Where was Niki?

Lolly grabbed the fallen flashlight and frantically shone it around, trying to spot the woman. If she was there, she was hidden behind a tree or a bush. She could be behind them, to the left, the right, anywhere . . . even on the way back to the house. Lolly had seen only the two weapons, but that didn't mean there weren't more

— belatedly she realized that the fact that Darwin was trying to hit Gabriel with the pistol instead of just shooting him meant that he'd fired all the bullets in the gun and didn't have any more, at least not with him.

Was Niki out of bullets, too? Was she running after more, or simply running? No way to tell. Lolly darted a quick glance at the fight. Darwin had torn Gabriel's knit cap off and was trying to head butt him in the face. Quick as lightning, she darted in and slapped Darwin in the face with her stick, which wasn't big enough to stop him but did briefly pull his attention to her. Gabriel seized that brief moment of inattention to punch Darwin in the face with his gloved fist. The sound was sickening, but Darwin didn't seem to even notice.

Gabriel was bigger, more muscular; he should have been able to take Darwin down in a matter of seconds, Lolly thought, then remembered how crazed meth could make people. She'd read reports of meth users who had been shot several times by the police and who not only didn't go down, but kept attacking. Darwin fought like a man possessed, sounds of maniacal rage growling in his throat like an animal.

She had never seen a real fight before, just the Hollywood staged version, never realized how much dirtier and noisier it was. This wasn't standing toe-to-toe and slugging it out, this was kicking and punching and gouging and anything else the two combatants could do to hurt each other. There were grunts and curses, the sickening thuds of gloved fists against flesh, the icy ground crunching beneath them. Their heavy winter coats prevented any significant damage to their bodies, prolonging the fight and increasing the odds that Darwin might land a lucky punch.

Maybe she could help. Lolly eased closer, raising her stick so she was ready to strike if the chance presented itself, but holding on to the flashlight handicapped her because she had only one free hand to hold the stick. She couldn't worry about Niki; the woman was either there or she wasn't. All she could do now, Lolly thought, was help Gabriel in any way she could.

The grappling men rolled almost out of the light, and when they stopped Darwin was on top. He drew back his hand and something was in it. Lolly didn't hesitate, didn't try to identify what he held; she simply leapt forward, swinging the stick with all her might, and began trying to beat the hell out of the man who'd tried to rape her. She dropped the flashlight, gripped the stick with both hands, and hit him again and again, on the head, the shoulders, anywhere she could reach.

With a howl he launched himself off Gabriel, straight for her. She staggered back, sick terror blooming in her stomach, her chest. Her feet went out from under her and she went down, Darwin on top of her and his hands fumbling for her throat. He began squeezing.

Then he was gone, lifted off her as if he were a child. Gabriel's expression was cold and fierce as he hammered his big right fist over and over into Darwin's face. Darwin was too stunned by the blows to fight back; he threw his arms across his face to protect himself and began sobbing. "Don't hurt me, man, don't hurt me," he pleaded. "I ain't done nothing to you, have I? Huh? What'd I do?"

Lolly struggled to a sitting position, staring at him in disbelief. He'd changed from enraged animal to pathetic loser in the space of a few seconds.

"Shut the fuck up," Gabriel snarled, breathing hard. He wrenched Darwin's arms behind his back, shoving them high, and looked around for something to secure them. "Get the laces from his boots," he said to Lolly.

She didn't want to get anywhere

near Darwin, didn't want to touch him in any way, but she made herself half-crawl to where Gabriel held him, taking care to stay to the side so he couldn't kick her in the face. Gingerly she began picking at the leather lacings. They were wet and hard to handle, and she had to use both hands.

Gabriel's head swiveled as he looked around. He was still breathing hard and fast, and his expression . . . he was really pissed, to put it mildly. "Where did the other one go?" he asked Lolly. There was a savage note in his tone.

"I don't know," she replied. She was doing some hard breathing herself, and she paused a moment to take a few deep breaths. "She turned off her flashlight, and I guess she ran. I haven't seen her since then."

Gabriel turned his attention back

to a weeping Darwin. He wrenched Darwin's arms harder and higher, putting agonizing strain on the shoulder sockets. "Do you have more ammo or weapons back at the house?"

"No," Darwin said, shaking his head. "I swear, we don't. Buddy, please, you're tearing my arms out of my shoulders!"

"I'm not your fucking buddy," Gabriel said. "And if you lie to me, I *will* tear your arms off and beat you to death with them, got it?"

"I'm not lying!" Darwin shrieked. Snot was running from both sides of his nose, dripping in his mouth. "Niki and me, we just have the two guns and what bullets are in them. That's usually enough. Ow! Ow! Stop, please stop!"

Usually enough. Lolly wondered how

many other homes he and Niki had invaded, how many women he'd hurt, raped, murdered.

Deep in the forest, there was a sudden crack as sharp as a gunshot, followed by a crash and a thud. For a moment of sheer panic Lolly thought Darwin had been lying and Niki *did* have another weapon, but then she realized what had happened: limbs were beginning to give way under the weight of the ice.

"What the hell was that?" Darwin asked, a new fear in his quavering voice.

Neither Lolly nor Gabriel bothered to tell him what was happening.

"Now what?" she asked, looking up at Gabriel before returning her attention to Darwin's boot laces. They didn't know where Niki was;

Darwin was unarmed, would shortly be secured, but it wasn't as if they could call the sheriff and have their prisoner collected and jailed within a matter of minutes. She didn't want to spend the night in the same house with him, not even if Gabriel hog-tied and gagged him, and she didn't think they could manage to get him down the mountain tonight. With limbs already beginning to come down, it was too dangerous to go anywhere tonight.

Gabriel opened his mouth to answer and Darwin suddenly threw himself backward in a convulsive movement that knocked Gabriel off balance, and wrenched his arms free from Gabriel's grasp.

With an inhuman roar he went for Lolly. Crouched down the way she was, she didn't have a chance to run. He knocked her flat; she was hit with a force that knocked the breath out of her, and banged her head hard on the frozen earth. She heard a ripping sound as she slid across the rough, icy ground, then he was on her and trying for her throat again.

Gabriel recovered his balance and launched himself forward, both hands grabbing Darwin by his coat collar and slinging him off Lolly. Darwin surged to his feet, came at them again. Gabriel pivoted, planted his foot, and smashed his elbow backward into Darwin's face. There was a sickening crunch, and Darwin was suddenly boneless, his body oddly slack as he slumped to the ground. His eyes were open and staring, and twin black trickles of blood leaked from his nostrils.

Gabriel spared him only the briefest glance. "He's dead." His tone didn't reveal a shred of regret. The elbow to the nose, smashing it and driving bone fragments into the brain, hadn't been an accident.

Deep in the forest, another limb gave up its life with a sharp crack, and crashed down. Hard on the heels of it came another one, this one much closer.

Lolly was still on the ground, her eyes huge dark pools in a stark white face as she stared up at him. He leaned down and caught her arm, pulled her to her feet. "We have to go back to the house," he said. "We can't walk out now, not with limbs already coming down."

Solemnly she nodded, but she asked, "What about Niki? That's her name," she explained in a vague tone. She gestured at the body on the ground. "His name is Darwin. *Was* Darwin." A faint note of satisfaction leaked into her voice. Looking around, as if searching for the missing woman, she added, "She might be at the house."

"Maybe," Gabriel said grimly. "If she is, I'll handle it. From what this asshole said, they're out of ammo. If she didn't go back to the house, if she's out here somewhere . . . she can freeze to death, for all I care."

Still Lolly just stood there, and he gentled his tone. "Lolly, we don't have a choice." He bent and collected the flashlight Lolly had dropped, as well as Darwin's empty pistol. The pistol he slipped into his front pants pocket.

His own flashlight was still secured in his coat pocket; he'd use the other one as long as the battery held out, because who knew how long they'd be in the house before the road was clear? If the electricity at the house hadn't already gone out, it would soon.

"I know," she said, her voice subdued.

God, he was cold. His knit cap was gone and the damn miserable rain had formed ice crystals in his hair. Not even his good cold weather gear could keep his body warm when he was losing so much heat through his uncovered head. He shivered convulsively, but forced himself to concentrate. He could see that Lolly's pants were dark with moisture from mid-thigh down, moisture that would leach all of her body heat away, too.

They had to get dry. They had to get warm. The exertion of the fight had warmed him while it was happening, but now the letdown was leaving him even colder, and Lolly would be in worse shape because she had neither his muscle mass nor the experience in handling the aftermath of an adrenaline burn.

He turned her toward the house, his arm behind her back, urging her forward. "Are you cold?" he asked, though of course she was.

"I was," she said. She sounded exhausted. He'd expected that; it was normal. "I don't think I am now, though. But I can't feel my feet."

He shuddered again, his body trying to generate some heat, and suddenly he noticed that Lolly wasn't shivering. Shit, that wasn't good. She was hanging in there now, but he had to get her to the house in a hurry.

He left Darwin's body where it was; the only other option was to carry it out, and he had to devote what energy he had left to getting himself and Lolly out of these damn woods and back up the mountain to the house.

Cautiously they worked their way back to the pavement. They'd have to stay on the weedy edge where they'd have at least marginal footing, which meant they would be beneath the dangerous and increasingly ice-coated trees that leaned over the road, but they really had no choice because the road was the fastest way up. Whether they stayed in the woods or went by the road, they had to face the possibility of being crushed by a falling limb, so the less time they spent under the trees, the better. He kept his arm around Lolly, pushing himself as well as her. She didn't know how close to the edge he was skating, how much of an effort it was for him to walk, and he wanted to keep it that way. She'd been a trouper so far, but who knew where her breaking point was? He didn't think she'd give up, but now wasn't the time to find out.

He made his voice purposely steady and without emotion. "Earlier today, before I got to the house . . . did Darwin hurt you?"

He expected an immediate "No" that he wouldn't believe, or a painful "Yes" that would make him want to go back to the body and kill the man all over again, but Lolly hesitated before answering. "He tried. He almost —" Her voice broke and she stumbled.

Gabriel stopped, pulling her to a halt, and he turned the flashlight so he could see her expression. Her face was white and pinched with cold. The poncho had torn, and ice crystals had formed on her hair, just as they had on his. But her gaze was steadier now, even if her lips were blue. He cupped her face in the gloved hand that wasn't holding the flashlight. "He won't hurt you now."

Her answer was a nod, and in spite of the dire circumstances, it was relief that changed her expression. "Yeah, I know. You killed his ass." She paused, then added, "Thanks. Good job."

He almost laughed. Reassured, he started them walking again. She was going to be okay. Lollipop was turning out to be a pretty tough cookie. He continued to steady her as they walked up the hill, one slow, cautious step at a time. He stayed alert, watching and listening for the woman — Niki — but all he could hear was wind and the straining limbs of old, ice-covered trees.

CHAPTER NINE

Niki struggled to her feet. When that man had just appeared out of the darkness like a demon or something and attacked Darwin, her instinct for self-preservation had kicked in and she'd run like hell, without even a single thought about helping Darwin. She'd been looking over her shoulder instead of paying attention to where she was going, and she'd stepped in a shallow dip. Her feet had immediately gone out from under her, and she fell hard on her back, hard enough that she had lain there for a minute, too stunned to move.

When she'd been able to roll to a sitting position she'd just sat there on the frozen ground, watching Darwin and the man as they fought. She was out of bullets, so she couldn't do shit to help Darwin. The best thing she could do, she thought, was take care of number one; it wasn't as if Darwin would have been rushing to *her* aid, if the situation were reversed.

She couldn't see all that much, because of the trees and the way the flashlight had rolled when Darwin dropped it, but as she watched the fight she thought maybe Darwin would get hurt. The son of a bitch who'd rescued Lorelei was a big guy. She also thought that maybe Darwin would win the fight, because he was a lot stronger than he looked and he fought dirty. This was one of those wait-and-see situations, though she didn't want to wait too long. If things started looking bad for Darwin, she'd be better off taking care of herself. She had to get back to the house, get the ice they'd left on the coffee table . . . she needed some now, *right now.* It would make her feel a lot better, get rid of this crawling, antsy feeling.

But she must have knocked herself silly when she fell, because she was a little dizzy. It wouldn't be smart to head out too soon and fall again, really hurt herself. She'd sit there for another minute or so, see what happened to Darwin. Maybe she'd get to watch him kill the big dude.

So she sat very still, even though the ground was so cold the sensation went through her clothes like a sharp knife, even though her ass got wet, and she watched as Lorelei Helton came rushing out of the darkness, a stick raised high, and hit Darwin in the head with it. It didn't slow him down much, but it distracted him, and suddenly Niki knew this wasn't going to end well for Darwin. Two against one just wasn't fair.

Then Lorelei began beating at Darwin with the stick, over and over, *whap whap whap.* He'd had the big man down, but he let Lorelei get to him, and he rushed at her. Niki closed her eyes in disgust. Darwin never could plan worth a damn. That left the big man free, which was so damn stupid, and then of course the fight was over and Darwin was whining in that way that got on her nerves so bad. All she could do was shake her head. She couldn't help him, she had nothing except an empty pistol. Darwin was on his own in this, the stupid shit.

Her head felt better, the dizziness had subsided. Silently, while they were preoccupied with Darwin, she got to her feet and began easing away. The sound of renewed struggle made her stop and look again, and she saw the big man smash his elbow into Darwin's face, saw the way Darwin just sort of went down like an empty skin sack, and she knew he was dead. She'd seen enough dead people to recognize how they flopped, as if their bones had all of a sudden turned mushy.

She never had been able to depend on the dick-head, and now he'd gone and gotten himself killed.

Carefully, as silently as possible, she

worked her way out of the woods. Twice there were really loud cracks and it scared the crap out of her until she figured out what had happened. Limbs were breaking off the damn trees. All around her, tree limbs were drooping under the weight of the ice; one of them could come down on her, at any time. This shit was creepy.

When she reached the road, she was so relieved to be out of those damn woods that she forgot about the ice and tried to run. Her feet immediately went out from under her and she went down hard on her knees. The pain was excruciating. Niki ground out a few cuss words as she slowly stood. She remained bent over for a moment, rubbing her knees, until she thought she could walk again. This time she eased to the shoulder —

what there was of it — where she had better traction, and continued uphill at a much slower pace.

The cold, the darkness, the keening wind, the creepy ice . . . all of it surrounded her, and she realized how alone she was, how horribly alone, with no one to turn to. Darwin hadn't been much, but at least he'd been there. Now he was dead, because that big man was a murdering bastard. He was dead, she was alone, and she was outnumbered. On the up side, the Blazer belonged to her now. It wasn't as if Darwin would be needing it again.

As she walked, Niki got more and more pissed. If it hadn't been for that bitch Lorelei, Darwin might've won the fight, and instead of walking back to the house alone, she'd have Darwin beside her now. They'd get warm, do some meth to celebrate their victory, and maybe screw in Lorelei's bed.

Ice pelted her face, and she didn't like it. It was too fucking cold out here, and everything had gone wrong. Everything! They should've just robbed the grocery store this afternoon and gotten the hell out of town. Nothing had gone right from the minute she'd seen Miss Lorelei Bitch in her fancy Mercedes.

She caught a wisp of a voice on the wind and turned around to look down the long, winding driveway. Lorelei and the big guy were behind her, walking back to what they probably thought was safety. For a moment she saw a flash of light, and then it was gone. Like her, they were keeping to the side of the road and staying in the dark.

An idea came to her, and slowly she began to smile, even as a gust of stinging wind caught her full in the face. If things turned out right, when she left here she'd be driving that Mercedes instead of Darwin's piece-of-shit old Blazer, and those two would wish they'd never tangled with her . . . for a little while, anyway, then they'd never wish for anything again.

"As soon as we're around this curve, we should see the lights," Lolly said. Gabriel didn't know if she was encouraging him, or herself. Laboriously they plodded forward, rounded the curve, and she stopped as she searched the darkness for the beacon of the porch light that would encourage them to keep going, to reach the warmth and safety of the house.

There was nothing. The darkness was absolute. "The power's out," she said thinly.

"Yeah." Gabriel urged her forward, his arm literally propelling her. He wasn't surprised by the loss of electricity, though he wished they'd at least made it back before the lines went down. Going toward a warm, brightly lit house was more of a psychological lift than seeing nothing but darkness at the end of the road. He needed something besides his own strength to keep them going, because he was fast running out of it.

Lolly was slowing down, her steps becoming heavier and more laborious; both of them had lost enough coordination that he was concerned. The cold was sapping her strength.

She was about to give out, but he couldn't allow her to stop, not when they were so close to shelter. Shelter meant survival, and he couldn't afford to think of anything else.

He steadied Lolly, made sure they continued to move forward, and at the same time kept an eye out for Niki, who from all he could tell was no less deadly than her friend had been. Without a gun, would she even try to take him on? Experience with meth addicts said she would. She might try to get past him, get to Lolly. Even an empty pistol could kill, if you hit someone in the vulnerable temple area with it. Lolly was protected by all the stuff she'd tied over her head, but that was no guarantee she couldn't be hurt or killed.

Logically, Niki would realize she

needed shelter just as much as they did. She might already be at the house, waiting for them. The electricity might not be off; she might have turned off the lights herself, so she'd have the advantage of surprise. He couldn't afford to assume she was either out in the cold, or inside the house; he had to expect anything, everything, and make no assumptions that could prove out wrong and catch him unprepared. Until Niki was accounted for, he couldn't let his guard down.

The night continued to be punctuated by the sharp retorts of limbs and trees snapping. The sound wasn't constant, but neither did it end. None of the trees closest to the road had fallen, not yet, but they would, and soon. For now the worst of the fall was deeper in the woods, where trees had been left untended for an eternity. At least the ones bordering the road had occasionally been trimmed.

"I don't suppose there's cut wood for the fireplace stacked by the back door," he said, trying to distract Lolly, trying to encourage her to imagine the comfort that waited ahead.

"No wood," she said, panting with the effort to keep going. He winced, kissing the dream of a fire good-bye, then she continued, "We converted to gas years ago."

Even better. "Hallelujah. Gas stove, too?"

"Yes."

"Water heater?"

"Uh-huh."

That was a relief, a huge one. They'd have some means of getting warm, and could spend the night in relative comfort. "Not much farther to go, Lolly, and we'll have a roof over our heads, heat, even some food."

"What if she's there?" Lolly asked, terror in her voice. Obviously her thoughts had been running along the same lines as his.

Gabriel shrugged. He was outwardly calm, inwardly concerned. "If Niki's there, I'll handle it. I promise."

She nodded in agreement, but didn't seem to be entirely convinced. Who could blame her? Their situation wasn't a good one, between the weather, the dark, and the nut-job who could come bursting without warning from out of the forest, or out of any closet or from under any bed.

Above them, a big engine abruptly roared to life.

Gabriel lifted his head at the sound. "Well, we know where Niki is," he murmured.

Lolly drew closer to him. "Yeah." She sounded nervous and wary.

Was Niki really stupid enough, or strung out enough, to try to drive down this hill? She wouldn't be starting the Blazer just to get warm, when all she had to do was go in the house. Why give her position away like that?

The sound of the engine changed, and gears shifted. Headlamps came to life, cutting through the darkness, catching in its beams the almost ethereal mist and making it glow.

Niki smiled. The Blazer was coated with ice and just getting the door open had been a bitch, but she'd managed it. She was alone, she was out of bullets, but Lorelei Helton and her big guy with his stick didn't stand a chance against her Blazer. She'd run them down like the dogs they were.

"For Darwin," she said, getting teary at the memory of the miles they'd covered in this Blazer. Maybe he hadn't been perfect; maybe he had cheated on her a few times. But through it all he'd been *hers*, and now he was gone. Darwin, gone. She couldn't believe it.

She gunned the engine and headed toward the hill and the center of the narrow drive. The rear end of the Blazer immediately started sliding around and she fought with the wheel for control, which she gained, and lost, and gained again. At least she was headed in the right direction. She was barely out of the yard when the headlights picked out her targets, there on the side of the road. The two murderers stood side by side, close together, stupidly looking up the hill, looking at her. They didn't realize what she had planned. They probably thought she was running away, that she was a coward who would give up and let them win, a coward who wouldn't make them pay for what they'd done.

Then the big guy seemed to realize what she planned to do, because he bodily lifted Lorelei and leapt into the tree line with her. A bloody haze of rage rose in Niki's vision. No fucking way was she going to miss them now, like a few trees could stop her. They had to pay. They had to pay for killing Darwin; Lorelei had to pay for making a fool of her by going out a second-story window; she had to pay for leading Darwin on until he couldn't think about anything except getting in her pants. She'd catch them and ram them up against a tree, pinning their bodies there, and she'd laugh while they died in agony. She wanted that. She wanted it as much as she wanted her next hit. She'd have her hit soon, in just a few minutes, as soon as she'd taken care of this little chore.

The slope of the driveway increased, going down to the first sharp curve. Niki barely glanced at the pavement; her attention was on the spot where the big guy had gone into the woods. She spun the wheel to the left, and the entire Blazer began sliding sideways to the right. Swearing, she turned back to the right, trying to straighten the vehicle. The old Blazer responded, then the rear end swung around and damn if she wasn't sliding to the left now. Furiously she fought the vehicle. How in hell was she supposed to do what she wanted if the damn truck wouldn't go straight? What good was four-wheel drive if it didn't work on ice?

She jerked the wheel to the left, and both right wheels of the Blazer came off the ground. "Shit!" she yelped, suddenly realizing how close she was getting to the bottom, and the steep drop-off on the other side of the driveway. *"Shit!"* The Blazer settled back onto all four wheels; the big tires tried to grab traction but spun uselessly on the ice. The Blazer slid backward, then slowly began a sickening spin, around and around, gaining speed as it whirled toward the looming drop-off. She had the totally inane thought that it was almost like riding the tea-cups at Disneyland.

Niki screamed once, in rage and fear at the injustice of this stupid ice, then the Blazer's wheels lost contact with the ground and she plummeted over the side.

Lolly clung to Gabriel's wet coat, watching as the Blazer abruptly dropped out of sight. There was a brief moment of silence, then a horrible screech of metal being crushed and torn.

"Oh my God," she said in shock, then added, "Good!" She didn't think it made her a bad person that her first instinct was one of relief. Darwin was dead and Niki had just driven herself off the side of the mountain. For the first time in hours that had seemed as long as days, Lolly suddenly realized the terror was over. She was safe; cold to the bone, shivering, shaken in a way she hadn't known was possible . . . but safe.

"Stay here," Gabriel ordered, as he took a much larger flashlight from his coat pocket, turned it on, and stepped cautiously onto the road.

He had been her rock for the past couple of hours. Everything in her protested at being separated from him for even a few seconds, but she did as he instructed. There was no point in both of them going to look. Besides, she could barely walk, she was so cold. All she wanted was to sit down and close her eyes.

The sloping pavement was treacherous with ice. Gabriel slipped a couple of times, but both times managed to catch his balance and stay upright. Lolly breathed a sigh of relief as he reached the other side of the road and shone his light down the mountain-side.

After a long moment, he made his way back across the driveway to Lolly. Turning off his powerful flashlight, he once more stowed it in his coat pocket and took out the much weaker flashlight Darwin had dropped. "The Blazer's about a hundred and fifty feet down. It met a tree head-on. The tree won. If Niki isn't dead she's seriously hurt, but I can't get down there to see." He frowned, because he didn't like not knowing for certain.

Lolly wouldn't have thought it was in her nature to be relieved at the news that someone, *anyone,* had died; it certainly wasn't like her to be willing to leave an injured woman in a wrecked car to freeze or bleed to death — or at least she hadn't thought it was like her. Darwin and Niki had changed her mind about several things. "Thank God," she whispered. She felt as if the world around her had warmed a little. Her fear of finding Niki waiting in the house, of the strung-out woman jumping out from behind a tree or springing out of a dark corner, was gone. She wanted to drop to the ground and sob in sheer relief, but she settled for a deep breath instead. It was too soon to declare victory, because she and Gabriel weren't home free. They still had to battle the ice, and the ice wouldn't make any stupid decisions, like trying to drive down a mountain in weather like this. The ice wouldn't do anything, other than exist, but its very existence reshaped the world.

"Come on," he said, "let's go get warm." He slid his arm around her, holding her upright as he propelled her forward. Without his aid, she couldn't have moved. The first few steps were an exercise in pain and lack of coordination; she could barely slide one foot in front of the other. She felt as if she had frozen to the spot, as if she could do nothing other than just stop. Gabriel was shivering violently against her; he was in better shape than she was, but that wasn't saying a lot.

"Do you need me to carry you?" Gabriel asked.

She was horrified at the idea. He could barely walk, and he thought he could *carry* her? "No, I'm fine," she said.

He made a gruff noise that made it clear he didn't think she was at all fine, but he didn't forcefully lift her and throw her over his shoulder.

In the total darkness, with only an increasingly weak flashlight beam lighting their way, they gingerly made their way across the icy yard. What had never seemed like much distance at all now seemed almost insurmountable, but they were barely shuffling along and every inch gained was paid for in agony. Finally she could very faintly make out the dark house looming just ahead of them, and only then did she really believe they could make it. "I'm sorry," she said softly, wondering if Gabriel would even hear her, with the wind howling as it was.

He glanced down at her. "Sorry for what?" he asked matter of factly as they negotiated the last few yards, maneuvering around her ice-coated Mercedes. The steps loomed like Mount Everest. She honestly wasn't certain she could go up them. "Sorry you got caught up in this mess. Sorry you had to kill a man. Sorry you're stuck here with me when I know you'd much rather be at your parents' house, with your son."

"You know about Sam?" he asked, surprised. His voice was breathless. Somehow he hadn't expected her to know anything about his life after he'd graduated from high school and joined the military.

"I've kept up with the news from here."

They reached the steps, and Gabriel gripped the railing with his left hand. His right arm tightened around her, and he physically hauled her up the steps, groaning in pain as he did. Then they were on the porch, but the howling wind was still blowing the rain in on them so there wasn't much improvement.

"I'm not sorry," he said, releasing her to bend over and catch his breath, gather his strength.

Without his support Lolly almost collapsed on the porch, but she wrapped one arm around a column and forced herself to remain upright. "I don't believe you." She even managed a credible snort.

"Seriously, Lollipop, do you think I'd be happy sitting in a nice warm house with my kid, eating soup and drinking coffee by the fire, when I could be up here freezing to death with you while we run from two crazy-ass meth addicts? Where's your sense of adventure?"

"I don't have one," she said, suddenly wheezing with laughter. She felt giddy, and she wasn't certain how much longer she could keep standing, but right now what he'd said was one of the most hilarious things she'd ever heard. "And do *not* call me Lollipop." If he'd forgotten anything at all about her, why couldn't it have been that horrid nickname?

"Lollipop," he promptly returned, just as he'd done in high school. He straightened, grunting with the effort, and said, "We're idiots to be standing out here. Let's go inside."

"Easier said than done," she said, and abruptly her legs gave way and she sat down hard on the ice-crusted porch.

"Don't you fucking give up on me now, Lollipop," he grunted as he lurched toward the door. "I didn't haul you all this way to let you freeze to death on the porch."

It scared her that the concept wasn't all that far-fetched. It would be so easy just to curl up on the porch and relax, but she knew if she did she'd never make it inside. Fear drove her to roll onto her hands and knees, but that was as far as she could get. No way could she stand up. Laboriously she began crawling toward the door. "You just get the door open, hero," she said, "and I'll make it the rest of the way."

There was a horrible, gunshot of a sound at the edge of the woods, and a sixty-foot-tall tree snapped at the base, the entire thing crashing to the ground with a force that seemed to rattle the entire world. They both went motionless for a brief second, then Gabriel turned back to fumble with the doorknob and Lolly resumed her slow, clumsy crawl.

She wouldn't have survived tonight if it hadn't been for Gabriel. She would already be dead, shot or frozen or crushed beneath an ice-covered tree. She would have died a violent death, her last few hours spent in terror and pain, her last thoughts that of a horrible man attempting to rape her, and maybe succeeding. And wouldn't you know it, as soon as the danger had passed, they'd started arguing. Some things never changed. The *feel* of their squabble had changed, though.

She wasn't angry, wasn't upset. Arguing with Gabriel had a comfortable feel to it, almost like coming home.

Home. She really *was* home. All she had to do was get inside, and she'd be safe. She wasn't shivering anymore, hadn't for . . . how long now? She was a native Mainer, she knew that wasn't a good sign. She could still think, hadn't suffered any of the disorientation that came with severe hypothermia, so she thought she'd be all right. But then again, if her thinking was impaired, would she even realize it?

Gabriel tried to open the door, but his ice-coated gloves couldn't grasp the doorknob. Swearing under his breath, he used his teeth to tug off the glove; the doorknob turned, and the door swung open to warmth and sanctuary. Turning back, he grasped Lolly's arm and half-dragged her over the threshold, far enough inside that he could shove the door closed. Then she fell over on her side on the floor and the strength left his legs and he fell beside her. He swore some more, struggling to his hands and knees, then he grabbed the newel post of the stairs and pulled himself to a mostly upright position. Lolly closed her eyes. She just wanted to lie here on the floor . . .

"Get up," Gabriel ordered, his voice commanding and harsh.

She cracked her eyelids open a little. "I don't want to get up."

"Too bad."

He clumsily swiped his hand over his head, and shards of ice flew from his hair. He shucked off the jacket and gloves, then leaned down and grabbed her arm again. She couldn't get her feet under her, so he dragged her to the first step of the stairs.

"I just need a minute —" Lolly began.

"You have to get dry and warm," he said, jerking at her first layer of clothes. He whipped off the ripped poncho and ice crystals flew, hitting the floor and a nearby table and instantly melting.

"Leave me alone," she said fretfully, slapping at his hands. "We're inside now. Just let me rest for a little while."

"Not until you're warm." He continued to peel away clothes, and she let him. A part of her wanted to fight, just on principle, but she was so tired and moving was so difficult that fighting him was impossible. He pulled her to her feet and she closed her eyes and just stood there, swaying. It was wonderful to be out of the ice, out of the cold. She could sense the warmth around her, lingering heat from before the power had gone out, but she couldn't really feel it.

"Open your eyes, Lollipop," Gabriel barked.

With an effort she opened her eyes and scowled at him. "Why can't I just sleep?"

By the light of the flashlight he'd placed on the floor, pointed upward to reflect off the ceiling, she saw the worry on his face, the anger. "Not yet."

And suddenly she knew what he'd been doing, calling her Lollipop, all but picking a fight. He'd been trying to get her angry, keep her going.

Touched, feeling her insides turning to mush, she reached up and laid her cold hand along his rough cheek. "I'm sorry I snapped at you," she said.

"Did you snap? I didn't notice. You must be out of practice. Now stop apologizing and get out of those clothes," he ordered. "All of them."

CHAPTER TEN

Niki slowly lifted her head, not quite sure where she was or what had happened. She stared around her, trying to make sense of her surroundings, but the effort was too much and she closed her eyes, let her head rest against something cold and hard. She felt . . . she felt as if a giant had picked her up and thrown her down on the ground, as if her entire body had been stunned. Had she fallen out of bed? No, she wasn't in a bedroom, she was in . . . what was she in? She didn't know where she was. Nothing looked right.

Then, like a light switch being flipped, her memory clicked and it all came back in a rush. Darwin. The Helton woman and that big dude. The storm, the ice, and the edge of the world.

The dashboard lights glowed softly, even though the engine was dead. One headlight shone, marking her spot in the night. All she could see through the shattered windshield was the tree that had stopped her descent down the mountainside. The entire front end of the Blazer was crumpled, the dash twisted and crushed and caved in on itself. Slowly she turned her head, because she felt as if it wasn't securely attached to her neck. What a weird feeling; she didn't like it. But her neck worked, and that was good.

A big limb had crashed through the window, impaling the passenger seat. Broken glass was strewn about the front seat, and cold wind whipped into the cab from all the broken windows.

Niki touched a hand to her head, felt the sticky blood there. Her entire scalp throbbed, and she was shaking from head to foot, one big convulsive shudder. She couldn't stop shaking, couldn't make her muscles stop quivering. Damn it, she could've been killed, she could be dead right now, like Darwin. And it was all their fault!

A part of her wanted to stay right where she was. She was so tired, so cold. Moving would take more energy than she had. After a few minutes, though, her survival instinct kicked in. Ordering her thoughts was difficult, but determinedly she set about getting them all lined up. She couldn't stay here. Once the battery wore down, she wouldn't have even the little bit of light she now had. She'd freeze to death here, in the dark and cold, if she didn't bleed to death first. Again she gingerly touched her head. The cut there was bleeding, but wasn't as bad as it could have been. Hell, she was alive, and she didn't seem to be missing any body pieces, so she'd already come out ahead. She listened, wondering if Lorelei and the big guy were working their way down the mountain looking for her, to come help . . . but there weren't any voices. There was wind, there was ice, and the creaking of the tree. That was it. Those bastards had left her here to die. What kind of people would do something like that?

She stared at the limb that had come through the windshield, imagined what would've happened if it had been just a foot or so to the left, and shuddered.

The driver's side window had broken out, too, and Niki turned her head in that direction as she attempted to orient herself. Most of the light from the one remaining headlight was blocked by something, maybe the bumper, but some leaked out to show her where she was.

On the side of a freakin' mountain, perched on an old, creaky, badly damaged tree that was coated with ice. If the tree went, if it snapped and gave way, the Blazer would go the rest of the way down. She doubted she'd be so lucky the next time some obstacle stopped what was left of the truck.

Niki pulled the door handle and pushed. When nothing happened she pushed again, putting all her weight, such as it was, into the task of opening the door. The Blazer creaked and rocked and she stopped for a moment. Anger flared up inside her, making her forget her physical pain. Everything that had happened so far — the storm, Darwin's death, the destruction of the Blazer, and Niki's injuries, even the fact that the damn door wouldn't open — it was all Lorelei Helton's fault. That bitch, look what she'd done. If she'd just stayed where she'd been told to stay, none of this would've happened.

Where was her flashlight? She felt around for it but couldn't find it, and she didn't have time to look for it. There was just enough light from the truck to show her the way. The door wasn't going to open, she finally decided, so she heaved herself up and crawled through the broken window, her movements cautious so as not to rock the Blazer. As she crawled out into the cold wind, she decided the vehicle was pretty firmly caught against the tree.

The slope was so steep she couldn't stand upright. Clinging to the wrecked truck, Niki looked down at herself. She hadn't escaped the wreck entirely unscathed. Her head was bleeding, there was a huge rip in the right thigh of her jeans and blood was seeping from it, and her shoulder hurt. It wasn't broken, but it might've been. Still, as she looked up to the top of the slope, she felt pretty damn lucky, and she knew there had to be a reason for her survival.

She had survived so she could take revenge on those who'd done her and Darwin wrong.

She had survived so she could do what was right.

With ice covering everything, the only way up the steep hill before her was to crawl, so that's what she did. With every inch she moved forward, she was more and more certain of her purpose. She wasn't going to run. She wasn't going to find a warm spot and cower until morning. She was going to kill Lorelei Helton and the man who murdered Darwin. After all, it was justice, plain and simple.

"How many damn clothes do you

have on?" Gabriel growled, pulling at yet another shirt.

"Enough!" she said, slapping at his hands. "Stop that! I can get my own clothes off."

"Then do it." He couldn't carry her, but he could bully her and half-drag her and push her up the stairs, with only the bobbing light from one increasingly dim flashlight to show him the way. In a newer house maybe there would be a full bath downstairs, but the only downstairs bathroom in the Helton house was a half bath that had been added on years earlier.

A hot shower would warm Lolly up. Shower, dry clothes, warm food. It was a simple plan, a necessary plan, if she'd just cooperate.

"I can walk, you know," she said, sounding grumpy but also more tired than he was comfortable with. He didn't think she was so far gone that she needed hospitalization — not that he could've gotten her to a hospital if she did — but she was on the edge. Another half hour outside, and a hot shower wouldn't have been such a great idea.

"Yeah, sure. If you can walk, then do it. You need to get in the shower as fast as you can."

"All right, all right." She began struggling up the stairs, so he didn't have to do all the work. "When I'm warm," she added with a sigh, "I'm going to wrap myself in the comforter and sleep for days." She stopped abruptly. "Wait. Did you lock the front door?"

"Yes." He had, out of sheer reflex. On the very slim chance that Niki had survived the crash and somehow managed to make it back to the house, a locked door wasn't a bad idea. It was unlikely that anyone could've been mobile after a crash like that one, but stranger things had happened. Why was it a drunk always walked away from a bad accident, leaving his victims dead while he shook his head and wondered what had happened? It was much the same for people strung out on drugs; he'd seen it many times over the years. God watched over fools and drunks, he'd heard. Didn't make much sense to him, but some days it proved to be true.

"Bathroom?" he asked as he reached the top of the stairs.

"This way." Lolly pointed, and he followed her lead to a door that opened onto a long, narrow bathroom that contained both a tub — standard issue, not a whirlpool — and a separate shower. These days it would be considered crowded and on the small side, but for its time this bath was quite a luxury. Gabriel didn't care how small or large the room was, he only cared that there was a shower and plenty of hot water — as well as, hallelujah, a radiant gas heater built into the wall. He couldn't think of many things that would be more welcome right now than that heater.

"We're going to get you warm," he said as he closed the toilet lid and sat Lolly on it. He placed the flashlight on the back of the toilet tank, standing it up so the light would reflect off the white ceiling. He reached into the shower to turn on the water and let it get warm. He just hoped he didn't get the temperature too hot, because even though he'd been wearing gloves his hands were so cold he couldn't really judge how warm the water was.

He turned around and saw that Lolly had closed her eyes again. "Wake up!" he snapped. "Lolly! Get your clothes off!"

She jumped like a startled deer, her eyes popping open. "Jeez," she muttered. "All right. All I did was close my eyes for a second."

"You can close them later, after you're warm." As she struggled out of her clothes he turned and lit the gas heater, turned it on as high as it would go, then held his hands before the flames to soak up the heat. Ah, God, that felt so good it hurt. He held them there for just a minute before turning his efforts to stripping out of his own clothes. "Stripping" was the wrong word, because it implied speed. He struggled out of them, just as Lolly was doing. The fabric was cold and uncooperative, his hands were cold and uncooperative, and his jeans were cold, uncooperative, *and* wet, which greatly upped the unco-operative factor. He could barely keep his balance, and finally he propped himself against the sink so he could finish. He'd have liked to sit down and close his eyes, too, but he was afraid if he did he wouldn't be able to start moving again.

He half-expected Lolly to protest but she didn't, either at taking her clothes off in front of him or him getting naked, too. He was trying to keep her alive and stay alive himself, and she was either practical enough to shove other concerns to the side, or she knew how close she was to being in real trouble. She was also human enough to dart a quick, troubled glance at his genitals.

"Don't worry," he reassured her in a growl. "It's drawn up so far I couldn't find it with both hands and a flashlight."

"Then I hope you don't need to pee any time soon," she retorted, and if he hadn't been so cold he would have laughed at that. As it was, he couldn't even manage a smile.

Before they got in the shower he checked out her fingers, stooped to look at her toes. They were blue with cold, but didn't yet show any signs of the white that signaled frostbite. Then he pulled her from her seat on the toilet, clamped his arm around her waist again, and hauled her into the shower.

Lolly whimpered as the warm water sluiced over her. He couldn't tell if the whimper was from pain or pleasure; she was so cold, either was possible.

Thank God the showerhead was set high on the wall, so he could get completely under the spray. He stepped under it, letting the water beat down on his head and melt the ice that crusted his hair. The water hit his cold skin like pellets; it was both pleasure and pain, and he all but whimpered, too.

"You're hogging the water," Lolly complained, and he solved that problem by wrapping his arms around her and pulling her against him, so the warm shower rained down on both of them. With a shuddering little sigh,

Lolly put her arms around his waist, nestled her head on his chest, and closed her eyes again.

Now that they were actually in the shower, closing their eyes seemed like a damn good idea, so he propped his chin on top of her head and let his own eyelids drift down.

"God, this feels so good," she whispered.

He wasn't sure if she was talking about the heat or him, and he sure as hell wasn't going to ask. He didn't care. He could feel the cold leaving him, draining away under the driving water pressure. He could feel his head warming, feel the pain receding.

A part of his brain — a dangerously small part — remained on alert, listening for anything he might hear over the sound of the shower. He hadn't been able to go down the mountain and make certain Niki was dead, and as long as that uncertainty remained he couldn't completely relax. He and Lolly were vulnerable here in the shower, but they had to get warm, and when he weighed the two factors against each other getting warm trumped everything else. He'd been so cold he was almost beyond functioning, beyond helping either Lolly or himself, and if Niki had come at them again he wasn't certain he could have managed much in the way of a reaction.

Two things weighed in their favor. One, even if Niki was still alive he saw no way she wouldn't be injured, probably too severely to be able to move. Two, if by some perverse miracle she *was* able to move, she had to be as cold as they were — unless she'd been using meth for so long she'd gone into hyperthermia, which would be doubly dangerous in this weather because she wouldn't feel the cold, wouldn't properly protect herself from it.

When he was recovered and dry, he'd bundle up and go back outside, check out the crash scene again. From a different angle he might be able to see if Niki was still in the mangled Blazer. Until then, all he could do was handle one problem at a time and stay alert for any strange sounds.

Then another problem presented itself.

As he'd gotten warmer he'd become aware of how good Lolly felt pressed against him, soft and shapely, with very nice curves that had been hidden beneath all those layers of clothes she'd been wearing. The spray of water hit her and ran down perfect, smooth flesh. She was wet and soft and naked . . .

Gabriel ran his hands up and down Lolly's back, trying to create heat with friction as well as with the hot water. He could feel the change in her as she warmed; she relaxed, her breathing became more normal and her stance became stronger, steadier. She was going to be okay. They'd made it, survived a hellish situation, and for the first time in hours he let himself relax from a state of high alert.

He almost went to sleep there, standing in the hot shower with Lolly wrapped in his arms. Maybe he did doze, for just a second. Maybe she did, too, because other than the rise and fall of her chest she didn't move.

Gradually he surfaced from that almost-sleep. The ice storm continued its deadly accumulation outside, but he and Lolly were safe inside, warm, protected, free to simply feel and react. As his body absorbed the heat of the water he felt as if he, too, were melting, until there was nothing left in the world but his body and hers.

It was easy to stand beneath the spray and hold on to Gabriel and let everything else go. No more fear, no more cold. Just this.

Gradually she became aware that he no longer had any problem finding his penis. It swelled between them, long and thick and rock hard. Vaguely startled — Gabriel McQueen was turned on by *her?* — and yet completely accepting, Lolly opened her eyes and looked up to find him staring down at her with the set, intent expression of a man who wanted sex and knew he was about to get it. Even in the dim, fading light of the flashlight, she could see the glitter in his eyes.

He smoothed her wet hair back from her face, cupped her bruised cheek with one big hand, then his mouth was on hers.

His hand was gentle. His mouth wasn't. He kissed like a marauder, hungry and fierce, demanding and taking surrender. Without thought or hesitation she gave him what he wanted. Nothing mattered beyond this moment, beyond the sudden reckless fever that flared to life between them. They could both be dead, so easily. They weren't; they were here, alive, warm, and they came together in a frenzy.

He lifted her, crushed her against the tiled wall under the showerhead so the water continued to beat down on them. Instinctively she wound her legs around his hips, the position opening her to him. Reaching down, he positioned his penis; the thick head brushed against her soft flesh, barely entered, and that was enough to make her whimper in need. She writhed, searching for more, and he gave it to her. With a groan he pushed deep, stealing her breath, both easing and increasing the sharp need. She groaned, too, at the taking of him, at the sensation of being stretched by the heavy fullness already pumping back and forth inside her. Lolly closed her eyes and tightened the grip of her legs around him, riding out the storm.

She came hard and fast, crying out, trembling and arching under the onslaught of sheer pleasure. He gripped her ass and moved her back and forth on him, short, fast strokes that intensified her orgasm and was almost too much to bear. Moaning, she dug her fingernails into his shoulders as the sensation peaked, subsided, then abruptly peaked again. She couldn't bear it, couldn't stand any more, and tears suddenly flooded her eyes. "Please," she said, and with a shudder and a deep groan he buried himself to the hilt and came, too, pumping hard and fast and gradually changing his rhythm to slow and rolling as he drew out his own pleasure.

In the aftermath there was silence, but a silence in which they clung together, gulping in air and trying to regain some strength in legs that had none. His heavy weight crushed her into the wall; if it hadn't been for the support of that wall, she suspected they would be on the floor of the shower. Her arms were wound around him, and absently she stroked the back of his neck, absorbing the feel of him naked against her. He was all hard muscle, every inch of him, and everything in her that was woman delighted in being pinned there with his penis still heavy inside her.

He roused up enough to reach out and turn off the shower with a snap of his wrist. The water was cooling anyway, and the efficient gas heater had already warmed the bathroom to pleasantly toasty.

Neither of them said anything. There

would be a time for talking, but that time wasn't now. For now, they just *were,* adrift in the moment.

Gently he cupped one breast with his big, hard hand. His rough thumb brushed back and forth over her nipple and she felt that touch everywhere, tingling along nerve endings that hadn't yet quieted. She pressed her lips to his wet shoulder, then with a soft sigh let her head rest there.

Her thoughts drifted as relaxation spread through her bones. She loved this house, she thought drowsily, always had: the smells, the large rooms, the old furniture. Until tonight, all her memories in this place had been good ones. She didn't want her last memory made in this house to have anything to do with Darwin and Niki. When she walked away, when she said goodbye, she wanted her final memories to be good ones. Gabriel had given her that, replaced horror with pleasure, bad with good.

Lolly moved her mouth, tasted the wet skin of his neck and inhaled his heat. His breathing changed; his body shifted, but not away from her. He moved closer, deeper into her, and nothing had ever felt so right.

"How do you feel?" he asked, his voice gruff and steady and soothing.

"Better." She was wonderfully warm, wonderfully lethargic. They did need to get dried and dressed, but not just yet. She kissed his neck again. "You?"

"Yeah. Better." He paused. "Uh — Lollipop . . ."

She smiled, hidden against his shoulder. "I'm on to you, now. You're just trying to make me mad, calling me that," she said without heat.

"Well, yeah. That was always the point," he said, as if that were obvious.

"I had a terrible crush on you." She would never have admitted that before, she would have been mortified if he'd ever suspected . . . and now it didn't matter.

He pulled his head back a little, looking down at her. "No shit?" He sounded pleased. "You didn't act like it."

"Of course not. I was a teenage girl. I'd have died rather than let you know." Thank God those years were behind her; no way would she ever want to relive the angst and raging hormones, the excruciating insecurity.

"I liked fighting with you," he admitted, his own mouth quirking in a little smile. "It got me going."

Men, she thought. They couldn't be the same species. She sighed, so content she could barely move. In that moment, everything was all right; with Gabriel inside her, with the flush of pleasure still fresh, she was content.

He stirred, reluctantly separating their bodies, and she let him. Her legs unlocked from around him, her thighs sliding down his until her feet once more touched the floor. He tilted her chin up so their eyes met. "Are you on the pill?" His voice rumbled in his chest, deep and gruff.

She couldn't help smiling. "It's a little late for that question, isn't it? But the answer is, yes, I am."

"That's good." He rubbed his thumb

over her lower lip. "We can do this again."

"Right now?" she asked, startled, and he laughed.

"Fifteen years ago, yeah, but now it'll take me a couple of hours to recover. Come on, let's get dry."

Her legs weren't quite steady, but she felt much better, almost normal. She felt a bit self-conscious at being naked in front of him, which was a little silly at this point, but her cheeks heated as she stepped out of the shower and quickly headed for the linen closet, where she grabbed two towels. She tossed one to him and briskly began drying herself, standing close by the wall heater.

"I have a few cans of soup in the kitchen," she said, trying to sound as normal as possible.

"Sounds good to me." Gabriel scrubbed the towel over his hair, then paused to glance at the cold, wet clothes on the floor. "I don't suppose your dad left any clothes behind."

"No," she said. "They cleared all their personal items out a couple of years ago." Then she laughed. "He's six inches shorter than you, and his waist is probably ten inches thicker. I don't think any of his clothes would have fit you, anyway. We'll hang your clothes in front of one of the fireplaces; they should be dry by morning."

"Great." His voice rumbled. "Guess I'll be bare-assed naked until then."

"I don't mind," she said, and smiled at him. "But we have blankets, several wall heaters, a couple of gas fireplaces, plenty of candles, and those cans of soup I told you about. I have some instant coffee, too."

His eyes lit at the mention of coffee, even instant coffee. "That'll do."

"I'm starving," Lolly said, realizing as she spoke how true those words were. She also realized that she wouldn't mind if she and Gabriel were stuck here for a few days. After what had just happened in the shower, so quickly and naturally that she'd barely had time to think, she didn't wonder at all how they'd pass the time.

Life took some astonishing turns, she thought. She never could have anticipated this, never thought she'd be so comfortable with him, or that making love with him, of all people, would feel so right.

Good Lord. *Gabriel McQueen.*

CHAPTER ELEVEN

Niki huddled on the floor in a dark corner of the kitchen, listening to the water running upstairs as she tried to force herself to throw off the chill. She strained to hear more. It wasn't certain that Lorelei and the big guy would be together, though it was likely. One of them might be in the living room, in another room upstairs . . . right around the corner.

Did they know she was here? Had they heard her?

In their earlier exploration of the house, before everything had gone to shit, Darwin had checked out the mud room and the back porch for portable stuff they could pawn, when the money they got from the Helton woman ran low. He hadn't found shit, naturally, but at the moment that didn't matter. What mattered, what she'd counted on as she'd crawled up an icy slope and made feverish plans for the night, was that he hadn't bothered to relock the door when he'd come back in. She'd entered the dark house through the back door, into the mud room, into the kitchen, cold and shaking and hurting all over. She'd felt her way to this corner, cowering and listening. That's when she'd first heard the water running and realized that at least one of them was upstairs.

The water stopped, and a moment

later she heard faint voices, two of them. She couldn't tell what they were saying, but those voices assured her that no one was waiting around the corner; they were both upstairs. Relief washed through her; she could breathe again. She could think.

There wasn't much of anything in the house that could be used as a weapon, now that all the ammunition was gone, but what better place to find a weapon than the kitchen? Niki forced herself to stand, pushing past her pain and the lingering chill. Her hands were so cold, her entire body was so cold she could barely move. Now that she was inside that iciness would fade, but it wasn't happening fast. Once she had the place to herself she'd light a fire, kick back, take a hit, and relax. She'd earned it tonight.

Slowly she opened a drawer, then another, cautiously feeling around and not bothering to close them since that might make too much noise and she wasn't yet ready to face her enemies. She couldn't see much, but her eyes had adjusted to the dark and there was a touch of light, reflecting off the ice, coming through the kitchen window. There was just enough for her to see shadows and shapes as she felt around inside the drawers, finding nothing suitable. There was only the bare minimum in the way of utensils. After searching four drawers, she silently huffed in frustration, then she scanned the countertop and smiled at the dark shape she saw there.

A touch confirmed that the dark shape was a butcher block of knives. She grabbed the handle of the largest knife, and was horrified to find that her hands were so cold she couldn't properly grip it. What good was a knife if she couldn't hold it? She carefully placed the knife on the counter within easy reach, then removed her gloves and rubbed her hands together, bringing blood flow and warmth back. She would have liked to turn on the faucet and run warm water over her hands, but the sound of running water would alert the two upstairs, just as it had alerted her, so she didn't dare. She had to make do. After rubbing her hands for a minute she stuck them under her arms to absorb what body heat she had left.

With the return of warmth came a rush of pain. She was hurt, she didn't know how bad, but she thought about Darwin and how those two jerks had killed him, and she pushed the pain away. She'd deal with that later, after they were dead. The big dude would go first, because he was the most dangerous. He'd killed Darwin with his fucking *elbow*. One quick pop and that was it, no more Darwin. Lorelei was nothing. Niki knew she could take her with no problem, after the big dude was out of the way.

When she picked up the knife again, she was pleased with her grip. She could hold it properly now. She concentrated on listening again. For a moment there was nothing, then a board overhead creaked. There was a footstep, then another.

At first she'd been pissed because the power was out, but now she thought that would work in her favor. There were shadows and dark corners where she could hide, where she could wait and catch them by surprise. She had an advantage, a big one. She knew where they were; they thought she was helpless, dead, out of their lives.

They were wrong. She was like a ghost, a very dangerous ghost who intended to make sure they were both dead before the light of day gave them a chance to find her.

She remembered seeing a few candles and a couple more flashlights lying around, but searching for them would make too much noise, and any light she made would give her position away. That could wait. They'd know she was here soon enough, but not yet.

She was a part of the night, she thought, at once giddy and yet strangely detached, as if a part of her was floating along unconnected to her body. She was a shadow. She was death. With the knife gripped in her hand she listened, then took a few careful steps forward. She didn't need to see.

And they would never see her coming.

God, he hated pulling on his wet jeans, but Gabriel fought his way into them anyway. They'd started to dry, thanks to the gas heater in the bathroom, but were still unpleasantly damp and clammy. After everything he'd been through tonight, he could handle unpleasant for a while. Besides, once they got downstairs and started the fireplace, the jeans wouldn't be damp for long. His coat had kept his shirt dry, and his boots had protected his feet. Once the fireplace had the living room warmer, he'd strip off the jeans and drape them over a chair or something, shoved close to the fireplace so they'd dry faster.

Lolly had some clothes in her bedroom, which surprised him because she'd been wearing so damn many he thought for sure she'd had them all on. Her bedroom door, however, was locked from the inside. He'd be able to pop the lock with no problem, with a straight pin or a paper clip, neither of which he happened to have on him.

"There are both downstairs," she replied, when he said as much. She could have put her own wet clothes back on, as he had, but she couldn't stand the thought and instead got a thin blanket from the linen closet and wrapped it around her. "I'll wait until you can get my bedroom door open."

That suited him, he thought. Yeah, it was a real hardship, spending the night with a woman wearing nothing but a blanket, when he remembered *exactly* what she looked like and felt like underneath the cloth.

He hadn't intended to have sex with Lolly in the shower, but he sure as hell couldn't say he was sorry. He'd be lying if he said he hadn't wanted it, that he regretted what had happened. Whether or not it happened again . . . shit, if she touched him and smiled, if she put her mouth on him again, he likely wouldn't have any more control than he'd had the first time around.

It occurred to him that he didn't know if she was married or ever had been, if she had a husband or a boyfriend back home. Knowing Lolly, he suspected not. She wasn't the kind of woman who'd screw around on a man.

Then again, could he really say he knew her? People changed in fifteen years. Sometimes they changed a lot. And yet he felt as if he knew her, felt as if the fifteen years were maybe fifteen months instead, that the interval had given him time to see her in a different light and appreciate the differences. Maturity was a wonderful thing.

"You know," he said, as casually as he could manage, "we're probably going to have to walk out of here."

Lolly hugged the blanket closer and grimaced. "You're kidding me, right?"

"How much food and propane do

you have handy?"

She sighed. "Enough for a couple of days, max."

"That's what I figured. We'll get warm, eat, sleep, wait for the sun to come up and listen for the tree fall to ease up a bit. By tomorrow afternoon, at the latest, the road crews should be out working. The road up the mountain is low priority, probably at the bottom of the list, but if we can make it down the hill we'll probably meet up with someone long before we reach town."

"And if we don't?"

He smiled at her. "Then we'll walk the rest of the way to town." After tonight, a long, difficult walk in the cold seemed like a cakewalk.

"I need something hot to eat before I even think about walking out of here." Bundled up in her blanket, Lolly headed into the hallway, and toward the stairs.

Lolly hated, hated, *hated* to go back into the kitchen. Because she hated it so much, she forced herself to keep going, to not hesitate. The memory of what had happened here remained too strong, even though so many other memories — good and bad — had been made tonight. But she wanted and needed warm food in her belly, and she refused to allow a dead man to keep her from it. He was dead; she wasn't. She'd won.

With the power out the electronic ignition on the stove wouldn't work, so she found the matches and lit a burner on the stove; the flame gave off heat and a little bit of light, enough for her to look for some candles and the oil lamps she knew were still here, somewhere. She turned, and stopped dead in her tracks, hugging the blanket closer to her. Several drawers were standing open, and her heart lurched at the sight.

She took a deep breath and slowly let it out. Darwin and Niki must have been looking for something, but what? Anything that could be sold, she imagined. She wondered if she'd ever again be not afraid. From here on out was she going to jump at the sound of every ring of the doorbell or creak of the house? Would she be suspicious of every stranger?

Gabriel was in the living room, lighting the gas fireplace, laying their clothes out to dry. She wouldn't think about Darwin; she'd think about Gabriel. She would concentrate on finding the candles, getting some soup heated, then they'd settle down in front of the fire.

It hadn't bothered her before, but she suddenly realized how lumpy she'd looked in all those clothes, layer upon layer. How mortifying, no matter how necessary it had been. She wanted to look good for Gabriel, and wasn't that a kick in the pants? She'd never cared very much what anyone thought of her appearance, much less Gabriel, but now . . . now she wished she had the blue sweater that her friends said made her eyes shine, and those really expensive snug jeans that made her butt look fantastic. She touched her wet hair. She could really use a hair dryer, too.

With one hand holding the blanket,

which was wrapped tightly around her, Lolly collected a sauce pan from the cabinet, then grabbed a can of soup from the pantry. She set the can on the counter, reached into an open drawer for the can opener . . . and froze.

When she'd last been in this kitchen, she'd been trying to fight off Darwin, and she had instinctively scanned the room for weapons. At that time, the block of knives had been full — out of reach, but full. Now, the largest knife in the collection was gone.

Why would they have taken a knife when they both had guns?

A chill ran up her spine. Niki could've survived the crash and come back. They hadn't heard her breaking through a window, and Gabriel had locked the front door. But her keys had been in her purse, and Niki had had the purse.

Lolly could barely breathe. She'd been so intent on getting warm, so sure Niki was either dead or down for the count, she hadn't even thought about the keys.

The nightmare came roaring back. The fear and the cold gripped her.

"Gabriel!" she screamed, whirling to run, and she came face-to-face with the nightmare.

Niki — bleeding, limping, holding the missing knife in her raised hand — lurched toward Lolly.

Lolly threw herself backward until she slammed into the cabinet, and then she had no place to go. She grabbed the can of soup and threw it; it bounced off Niki's shoulder. "Fuck!" Niki said furiously. "That hurt, bitch!"

Lolly grabbed the saucepan and threw it, and when Niki ducked she seized the chance to dart to the side, away from the cabinets. There was a small dried floral arrangement on the kitchen table; she threw that, too. Niki ducked again, and kept coming.

Then Gabriel was there, fast and silent on his bare feet, looming out of the darkness. He hit Niki from behind, the impact sending her crashing into the cabinets. She screamed with pain, tumbled to the floor. Gabriel pounced, grabbed the hand that held the knife, and slammed it against the floor over and over again until she lost her grip and the knife clattered to the floor.

Immediately, Niki began to wail. "Stop! I'm hurt! My arm . . . I think my arm is broken." She began to sob. "What was I supposed to do? You killed Darwin and then you left me out in the cold to *die.* How could you?"

Easy, thought Lolly. She didn't feel sorry for the woman at all, even though dried blood caked her face, her clothes. But Niki continued to whine; just like Darwin, she went from enraged attacker to pathetic beggar in a heartbeat. How many times had that act worked for them? Gabriel didn't buy it, though, and neither did Lolly.

"Shut up," he said brusquely, and reached for her other wrist to secure it.

Infuriated that her tactic hadn't worked, Niki screamed and swung the empty pistol that she'd pulled from her coat. Gabriel jerked his head back but the barrel caught him on the outside corner of his right eye and whipped his head around. She surged up, shoving him back, and the blow had stunned him enough that for a second he couldn't react fast enough. Niki scrambled up and away, scooping up the fallen knife and lunging for the back door.

Gabriel gave a quick shake of his head and launched himself in pursuit.

Her heart beating so hard she could barely breathe, Lolly jerked open the cabinet door under the sink, grabbed the hammer from the small open toolbox that had been there as long as she could remember, and followed them both.

CHAPTER TWELVE

Gabriel caught up with Niki on the back porch. The cold seared his bare skin. He had on nothing but a pair of wet jeans, not even a shirt he could pull off and use to snag the knife away from her. She whirled, lashing out with the knife, and he leapt back. She was nothing but a shadow in the darkness; only instinct, and experience gained by fighting with men who had been trained for combat, helped him avoid the blade. She was drug-crazed, unpredictable, and lethal as hell.

He wished he'd had time to grab something, anything, he could use as a weapon, or to block the slashing knife, but when Lolly had screamed his name he'd reacted instantly, without pausing to look around. He'd known, known without doubt, that somehow the homicidal bitch had not only survived the slide off the side of the mountain, but had managed to get out and make it back to the house. All hc'd thought about was getting to Lolly before Niki could.

Niki darted in, slashed at him, darted back. She missed, but not by much. She came at him again, and he saw the glint of the blade swiping at his stomach. He jerked back, grabbed for her arm, missed. From the corner of his eye he saw more movement at the door, and his heart almost stopped. Lolly!

"No!" he yelled. The last thing he wanted was her out here in the dark, where he wouldn't be able to tell her from Niki, but Niki would know exactly who Lolly was. Niki whirled toward the new threat and he heard her laugh as she surged forward. He knew he couldn't get to her in time to grab her arm, knew he couldn't move fast enough to knock Lolly out of the way, but he tried anyway, leaping for her even as his heart whispered that he was too late, too late . . .

Lolly swung the hammer. She could barely make out a dark shadow coming toward her, but Gabriel yelled from somewhere to the left and she knew it wasn't him. It was so dark she had no real way to judge distance, but she swung as hard as she could and was almost astonished when the hammer struck something with a sickening sound that was both a solid thunk and yet somehow squishy.

Then Gabriel was there, enveloping her in a body-slam of a rush that knocked her back into the mud room. She knew it was him, knew his scent, felt the bareness of his arms and chest. They crashed to the floor and the impact knocked the hammer free from her grip. He rolled off immediately, leaping to his feet and whirling to meet Niki's next attack, but . . . nothing happened. No drugged-out maniac came through the door. There was nothing but silence from the back porch.

"Get my flashlight," Gabriel said, breathing hard, and Lolly scrambled to her feet. The blanket . . . somehow she'd lost the blanket and she was completely naked, but she'd worry about that later. Frigid air swept through the open door, stinging her flesh as she raced to the stairs where Gabriel had dropped his coat when they first came in. The fireplace in the living room was lit, providing enough light that she found the coat with no problem, fumbled in the pocket, pulled out the big foot-long flashlight, turned it on, then ran out to the back porch again.

Gabriel took the flashlight from her and shone it on the heap that lay on the floor. Niki was collapsed on her stomach, breathing shallowly, her face turned away from them. The knife lay on the floor beside her hand. Gabriel moved forward, kicked the knife well out of her reach, and only then did he stoop to pick it up. The beam of the flashlight plainly showed the damage the hammer had done to her head.

And even as they watched, she tried to heave herself to her knees. What was she, the fucking Terminator?

"Why won't she die?" Lolly whispered, evidently thinking along the same lines. "What do we have to do, put her in a vat of molten steel?"

And then Niki died, after all, very quietly. The shallow breathing stopped.

Gabriel caught Lolly's arm, steered her back into the house. Bending down, he snapped up the blanket and wrapped it around her. She was trembling like a leaf, and though there was a lot he needed to do, at the moment holding Lolly was more important than anything else on that list. "Are you okay?"

"Peachy," she whispered.

"Seriously, look at me."

She looked up at him, and what he saw assured him that she was indeed okay, or at least as much as someone unaccustomed to violence could be in such a situation. She wasn't happy, but neither was she collapsing under a ton of misplaced guilt. She'd done what she had to do, and she accepted that.

He kissed her, then left her standing in the middle of the kitchen hugging the blanket to her shivering body, and went back out on the porch. He crouched beside Niki, reached out and touched her throat in search of a pulse. Nothing. He blew out a sigh of relief.

Some of the freezing rain blew onto the porch, settling on Niki's body and on his bare skin. His feet felt almost as frozen as they had been an hour ago. He wasn't dressed for this shit, so he left Niki where she was, and went back into the house.

When he closed the back door he took a moment to lock it. Couldn't hurt.

The seconds dragged on, and Lolly listened hard. She should move, do something, follow Gabriel or run away. She found she could do nothing but stand there, hold tightly on to the blanket, and listen to her own heartbeat as she waited. Was it over? Was Niki going to somehow get up again, ignoring death? Lolly wanted peace; she wanted this night to be over.

She heard the back door close, and her heart matched its thud. A moment later Gabriel walked into the kitchen, blessedly alone and unharmed.

"Is it really over?" Her voice shook.

"It's over. She's dead," Gabriel said as he came to her, tightened the blanket around her cold body, held her close.

"You're sure?"

"I'm sure."

Lolly hadn't thought she'd ever be glad to hear that anyone was dead, but pure relief washed through her. She rested her head on Gabriel's shoulder, wallowing in the strength and warmth of it. "I killed her," she whispered.

Gabriel stepped back, made her look him in the eye. How could he be so calm? So steady? The flame on the stove flickered, casting strange shadows over his face. "Good job," he said briefly, paying a very subtle compliment to her strength by not sugarcoating anything.

Lolly squared her shoulders. "I'm not sorry," she said. "She was coming after you with a knife. She would've killed us both."

Lolly took the few steps that separated her from the stove and turned the knob that killed the flame, plunging the room into darkness. "I don't want soup, I don't want anything that comes out of this damned kitchen," she muttered.

"We need to eat," he argued.

"I have breakfast bars," she said, hugging the blanket to her cold body and walking away. If she never set foot in this kitchen again she'd be perfectly happy.

Gabriel followed her out of the kitchen, so when she stumbled on the end of the blanket — halfway through the dining room — he was there to catch her, to keep her from falling on her face. After everything that had happened, to trip over the trailing end of a blanket shouldn't be traumatic, but tears welled up in her eyes. Gabriel heard them, saw them, maybe felt them, and lifted her into his arms. She let him, without a word of protest that she was perfectly capable of taking care of herself. At the moment she didn't feel capable at all. He whispered soothing words. She didn't pay any attention to what those words were, but she felt the intent, the comfort, to the pit of her soul.

The living room was like another

world: warm, lit by the fire, quiet. What was left of the storm raged on the other side of the window, beyond the sturdy walls, but for the first time tonight that storm was separate and unimportant. They were alive. They had survived a threat that was greater than the storm.

Gabriel lowered her to the sofa and sat beside her, continuing to hold her close. Lolly wanted to stop shaking, but couldn't. It wasn't the cold that made her tremble, not this time.

"I think I'll hire someone to come in and pack up everything that's left," she said, her gaze on the fire, her body fitting nicely against Gabriel's.

"Probably not a bad idea."

"If I thought we could make it safely to town tonight, I'd be out that door in five minutes. I can't come back here after this. I don't ever want to see this house again."

"Too bad." His voice was a rumbling whisper, as if he were simply thinking out loud.

Lolly lifted her head and looked at him. "What?" Surely she hadn't heard him correctly. "Seriously?" How could he think she could ever look at this house as home again? Why would anyone in their right mind want to return after a night like this one?

"Wilson Creek won't be the same without a Helton around, even if just part-time."

"Wilson Creek will survive," she argued.

Gabriel sighed. "I guess so, but how am I supposed to ask you out whenever I come back to visit if you're in Portland instead of here?"

She didn't know what shocked her most, that he'd consider asking her out, or that he knew details of her current living situation. "How do you know I live in Portland?"

He shrugged broad shoulders. "I must've heard someone mention it. Mom, probably. Which reminds me, you're invited to stay at the house until the roads are clear."

"That's very nice," she said, knowing without a doubt that the invitation had been Valerie McQueen's idea.

She turned toward the fire, finding Gabriel's solemn face somehow disturbing, and her gaze fell on the drugs and needles sitting on the coffee table. She all but jumped from the couch, reaching for the plastic bags, intending to toss everything into the fire. Gabriel grabbed her hand before she could touch anything.

"Evidence," he said simply. "Leave everything right where it is."

She turned on him, irrationally angry. "I'm supposed to leave this crap sitting on my mother's coffee table all night?"

"Yes."

"That's ridiculous. It's . . . it's obscene! If Niki had died in the kitchen, would you have just left her there all night?"

"Yep. I'm a cop, honey — a military cop, but still a cop. You don't disturb a scene until the investigation is finished."

It was good to feel something besides fear, so she fully embraced her annoyance. "So Niki and Darwin are both dead, and yet somehow they're still in charge."

Gabriel snorted, completely unflustered. "No, *I'm* in charge, and my dad will have my hide and yours if I fuck around with the evidence."

"So I have to sit here and look at *this* all night." She pointed to the coffee table, silently thanking her lucky stars that Niki had had the grace to die outside. If the body was in the kitchen, under her roof, she'd be trekking down the mountain tonight, ice or no ice.

Gabriel got to his feet. She expected him to take her in his arms again, but he didn't. He placed two steady hands on her shoulders and looked her directly in the eye. "I'm going upstairs to collect a sheet to cover the coffee table and a couple of blankets and pillows for us. You're going to pick out some dry clothes and get dressed.

Then I'm going to heat up some soup
. . ."

"I'm not going back in that kitchen
. . ." Lolly said forcefully.

". . . and bring a couple of bowls in
here," he continued without pausing,
"so we can get something hot into our
bellies. We'll save the breakfast bars
for the trip down the mountain."

"How can you be so calm?" she
asked, annoyed and grateful and mad
at herself because a part of her was
still scared.

"What choice do I have?" he responded.

Lolly felt a wave of release wash
through her. Naturally, he was right.
If they both panicked they'd simply
create yet another disaster, and God
knows she'd had enough disaster for
one night.

"I'll get dressed," she said in a more controlled voice. "You do what you have to do."

Gabriel leaned in then, and did what he'd neglected to do earlier. He kissed her. This wasn't a "let's get busy" kiss, it was a reassuring, warm, very pleasant connection that served to remind her that she was not alone, and at the same time very effectively took her mind off the night's horrors — for a few precious seconds.

She felt the kiss in her gut. Her earlier panic, which had fluttered inside her as if it were a physical thing trying to escape, faded.

She could do this. *They* could do this.

The kiss didn't last long enough, but it did the trick. She laid her hand on Gabriel's cheek, felt the rough stubble there. "All right," she said softly. "I'm okay now."

She turned to the fireplace and its welcome flame, listened as Gabriel rushed up the stairs.

Realistically, this adventure was far from over. The walk into town tomorrow would be dangerous and difficult. But it wasn't tomorrow yet, and tonight she was safe, warm, and sheltered.

She felt a bit Scarlett O'Hara-ish. She'd deal with tomorrow when it arrived.

CHAPTER THIRTEEN

Gabriel leaned his head back against the couch and closed his eyes. Chicken noodle soup out of a can had never tasted so good. The simple pleasure of not being out in the cold, of having a fire, of knowing he and Lolly were safe for the night — it was a fine feeling, one to be treasured even if just for a while.

The gas fireplace didn't crackle like a wood-burning stove, but he didn't have to worry about feeding it logs so that was a fair tradeoff. Lolly didn't know exactly how much propane was left in the tank, but she did tell him it hadn't been serviced for a while. She'd estimated that there would be enough for her stay, so they should be good for the night. A few hours more, that was all they needed.

"Tell me about your son." Lolly leaned against him, as she had since finishing her soup. Her body was finally warm — and clothed. The shared body heat was kind of a cliché, he supposed, but it was nice. With a dead meth freak on the back porch and another in the woods, and an arduous walk ahead of them, *nice* was a good thing. He might as well enjoy it while he could.

"What do you want to know?"

"Does he look like you or like his mother? Is he into baseball or art or music? Is he loud or quiet?" Her head rested comfortably against his shoulder. "Is it hard for you, having him live so far away?" This last question was delivered with a hesitation in her voice, as if she wasn't certain it was a question that should be asked.

Gabriel never minded talking about Sam. There were times when he'd realized that he'd said too much, that he was boring whoever was listening — though they were usually too polite to say so. Since she'd asked, he was glad to answer. "Sam looks like me, but he has Mariane's eyes. He's not big for his age but he's not too small, either. He's into baseball, definitely, and basketball. Believe it or not, he's also a whiz at math. Well, a whiz for a seven-year-old. I'm not sure where he got that from, since math was not my best subject in school, and it drove Mariane nuts to have to balance the checkbook." It was strange to talk about his late wife without the usual rush of grief. Strange, but right. "He's definitely not quiet. Have you ever spent any significant time with a seven-year-old?"

"No," she said softly.

"Well, they're bundles of energy, and Sam is no exception. He's either going full speed ahead or he's asleep." He took a deep breath before continuing. "And having him live so far away is more than hard, it's torture." He found himself explaining how Mariane's parents had stepped up to help after her death, how his father-in-law had been transferred to Texas, and though he'd tried to find another job, one that would keep him and his wife near to their grandson, in the end he'd had no choice but to move. It was that or be unemployed. Gabriel told Lolly how he'd tried to make the single dad thing work, something he'd never really talked about before in any but the simplest way, not even with his own parents.

"Babysitters, neighbors, Mariane's friends, my friends' wives . . . everyone did what they could to help, but in the end my schedule was so erratic it became a problem. Sam had no continuity. He never knew where he'd be, who would keep him when I was working night shift or was called away suddenly. Here he has stability. He knows where he's going to sleep at night."

"It's a high price to pay," Lolly said. "For both of you."

He'd been telling himself the situation was temporary, that he'd find a nanny he could afford so his son could be home at night, but with every week that passed there was a growing fear that he'd never be able to make the proper arrangements. He was a sergeant in the army, and though he made a decent living, he didn't make enough to pay someone twenty grand a year, which was the bare minimum for fulltime child care.

He didn't want his son to grow up with an absent father who visited when he could, but in his darkest moments he didn't see how he could avoid that, at least right now. Sam's grandparents would effectively become his parents, and his father would be an after-thought, an occasional visitor who disrupted the everyday routine. Lolly was right; the sacrifice was a high price to pay for stability.

"We'll make it work," he said. "Whatever's best for Sam, that's what I'll do." He was anxious to change the subject. "What about you? Married, engaged, divorced . . ."

"None of the above. I do date, on occasion, but there hasn't been anything serious in a long while."

"Why not?" She was pretty, smart, and if what had happened in the shower was any indication, a wildcat in the sack. She had taken him by surprise, but then just about everything she'd done since he'd climbed that rickety ladder a few hours ago had surprised him. Whoever would have thought that he'd come to admire Lolly Helton? She had been out of her element from the get-go, but she had toughed it out, and even come to his aid during both of his battles with Darwin and Niki. Her inner strength, especially concerning Niki, brought up a deep sense of respect. That couldn't have been easy for her, but she'd done what had to be done, and she hadn't collapsed afterward.

He wasn't about to admit that he'd expected less of her though, because the one thing he didn't want to do was hurt her feelings or get on her bad side. To his astonishment, he liked her too damn much, liked everything he'd learned about her tonight.

"Maybe I'm too picky." Her answer brought his attention back to the question he'd asked. She sighed. "Maybe I'm unlucky. I don't know. The simple answer is, it's just never happened for me. Love, that is," she said more softly. "I have certain expectations and I don't want to settle for just any halfway decent man because thirty crept up on me and desperation set in."

He couldn't see the Lolly he used to know or the woman he'd come to know tonight being desperate to land a man. She'd survived a tough situation without falling apart, and while she leaned on him — literally and figuratively — she was far from being fragile and needy.

And he'd forever remember the image of her rushing after Niki, coming to his defense even though she was scared half out of her wits — and naked, to boot.

"What about you?" she asked, as if an idea had just occurred to her. "Has there been anyone since your wife died?" He could hear the hint of discomfort in her voice, as she wondered if she'd had sex with a man who was committed to another.

"No."

He was certain Lolly didn't expect that her relief would be so evident to him, but her sigh and the way her body relaxed told it all. So, she was pretty, smart, not desperate, and she had morals. Otherwise the thought that she might've had impulsive sex with a man who was involved with another woman wouldn't have bothered her at all.

"Did you mean what you said earlier?" she asked. "About asking me out if you came home on leave and I was around."

"I wouldn't have said it if I didn't. Why? Would you say yes?"

"Maybe. But only if you promised

that our second date would be less exciting than the first."

He laughed, surprising her and himself. This wasn't a night for laughter — or hadn't been until now. "This is a date?"

"You saw me naked and you fed me dinner." There was a touch of humor in her voice. "Sounds like a bang-up date to me."

Gabriel had wondered a time or two what his first date after Mariane's death would be like, if he ever found the right woman — and the courage to move forward. He'd sure as hell never pictured anything like this, never by any stretch of the imagination thought it might be Lolly Helton, of all people, who for the first time in three years made him feel both physical and emotional attraction. He wanted to have sex with her again, he wanted to share mundane things with her, he wanted to find out what made her laugh, what made her cry, what colors she liked, her favorite flower. Lolly made him feel as if there might be a real life out there again, a life both full and ordinary. He'd had that with Mariane, and her sudden death had left him so empty that only having Sam had given him the strength to go on.

He and Lolly had been through a very stressful few hours that made their sense of intimacy, their connection, far more intense than if they'd met again under normal circumstances. But would they have given each other a chance if the circumstances had been normal? Had it taken a crisis to make them see each other as they were now, rather than how they'd been fifteen years ago?

But the connection was definitely there, and all of a sudden he felt the promise of his future rather than the loss of his past. They'd have to go slow, he figured, give themselves as well as Sam time to adjust to everything, give themselves time to see if things really would work out between them, instead of rushing in and maybe making a mistake that would upset Sam's world even more.

But they had time. He smiled, thinking about how much fun they'd have.

Lolly did her best to forget what had happened today, and she pushed her worry about tomorrow out of her head. The howling wind had stopped and icy rain no longer pelted the windows. But the roads would still be coated with ice, and she still heard the occasional crack and crash of a falling tree or heavy limb. There was no telling what she and Gabriel would encounter after they walked out her door tomorrow, headed for Wilson Creek and safety.

At the moment she was happy to be right here, warm and in Gabriel's loose but secure embrace.

As a teenager she'd had such a crush on him, and she'd been supremely annoyed with him for not returning, or even being aware of, her tender feelings. Looking back, she realized that there had been absolutely no reason for him to know what she'd been feeling. She hadn't told him, or anyone else. She hadn't even looked his way, unless he picked a fight with her and she responded. At fifteen, she hadn't been so logical. Though to be honest, what fifteen-year-old was well acquainted with logic?

There was something very appealing about a man who talked with such evident love about his son, who sacrificed everything so that his child could have a secure and happy home. She worried less about tomorrow's long walk to town than she would have otherwise, because she knew Gabriel would not only do everything in his power to get them there as soon as possible, he'd also be damn sure to get them there safely — if not for her, or for himself, then for Sam.

Sleep was creeping up on her fast. She could feel oblivion, welcome, certain. But she wasn't ready to fall just yet.

"I'll probably be back in Wilson Creek a time or two in the next few months," she said softly. "Even if I hire someone to pack up the house, there will be papers to sign to put it on the market, and then when it sells I'll have to come here to see to the legalities." She was almost positive she could handle the details long distance, but . . . maybe she didn't want to.

"I try to get back at least every other month," Gabriel said casually. "Sometimes it's just for a couple of days, but I have to see Sam whenever I get the chance."

Duh. All his talk of a date was just a way to kill time, maybe an attempt to make her forget what had happened tonight. When Gabriel came back to Wilson Creek he wanted to be with his family, most particularly his son, not a girl he barely remembered from high school.

And then he added, "You should meet Sam. When it warms up we can go fishing." She didn't immediately respond, so he added, "You don't fish, do you?"

"I'm world-class at reaching into the freezer and pulling out some filets," she said, smiling. "I could probably learn. From what I've seen it doesn't appear to be too demanding." She tried to picture a warm summer day, the lake, the three of them fishing and maybe picnicking on a large, checkered blanket . . . and she couldn't do it. The picture she tried to create in her mind didn't quite come together.

She didn't belong. Lolly realized she wasn't a part of the picture and never would be. Still, it was a nice illusion, a pleasant way to push aside reality for a while. "I make great chocolate chip cookies and a killer pasta salad. We could have a picnic, too." She closed her eyes, and for a moment she was there, she belonged in that picture. Maybe it wasn't real, maybe it would never be real, but as she drifted toward sleep she got caught up in the fantasy, then sleep overtook her and she went under fast and deep.

The sunlight sparkled like diamonds on the ice-coated trees; overhead, the sky was a pure, crisp blue. It would be a breathtaking scene, Lolly thought, if she was looking at it through a window with a blazing fire behind her, or maybe standing on a beach in Florida looking at a postcard. Instead she was part of the picture, which included cold air, a slick surface beneath her feet, and the occasional obstacle of a fallen limb or tree, for good measure — in case walking downhill on a sheet of ice wasn't challenge enough.

Not knowing when she'd be able to make it back, Lolly had stuffed what she needed in her pockets. Keys, driver's license, cash, credit cards, cell phone, which would be useless until they reached the highway. Everything else had been left behind. There was no telling when she'd be able to collect her Mercedes. She might have to arrange alternate transportation to Portland and come back for her vehicle once the roads were clear. That all depended on how bad things were in town, and how badly blocked the roads up the mountain were.

At least her clothing today was better suited to the weather. She had on her own thick, hooded coat, her boots, her gloves. At least the sun was shining, and they could see where they were going. At least they weren't being chased by homicidal drug addicts. All in all, today was much better than last night, even though the air was so cold she could barely breathe it and had to keep her nose and mouth covered with a scarf. The sunlight on the ice was almost blinding, and both she and Gabriel wore shades. Compared to last night, though, this was a walk in the park. It was cold, sure, but there was no cutting wind, no rain. All that was left were the remnants of the storm — the fallen trees, the icy ground, the crisp, cold air.

The weight of the ice was still a

burden for the trees, and that would be their greatest obstacle as they made their way down the mountain. Not long after leaving the house they heard the now-familiar crack, followed by a crash. Gabriel's head had snapped around at the sound and he'd stopped, listening hard as if he might be able to tell where that tree was, how close it might be. The fall was in the distance, in the woods that surrounded Lolly's childhood home, but it was telling — a warning, of sorts. They couldn't get off the mountain without walking beneath trees. None of the ice was melting, the air was still too cold, so any of the trees could go at any time. They would have to be on constant guard against the weighted, weakened limbs overhead.

This wasn't over, not by a long shot.

Gabriel stayed close, either right beside her or directly ahead of her, depending on the width of the grassy strip and the thickness of the vegetation, as they walked along the side of the driveway. Though he hadn't said much, he had to be as worried about the treefall as she was. That was why he often glanced overhead and, when possible, followed a path that didn't take them directly beneath the overhanging limbs.

They were halfway down the driveway when they came to a splintered, icy tree that had fallen crookedly across their path. Gabriel straddled the tree, offered Lolly a hand, and helped her up and over. Walking on an icy surface was tough enough, but maneuvering over obstacles only made things harder. If they'd had enough food and propane they would've been better off staying at the house until help arrived . . . at least in her opinion. Gabriel might've had other ideas, since he'd left his son behind to rescue her and was anxious to get home.

Hiking wasn't her thing. She wasn't into athletics at all, other than admiring the great physical condition of professional athletes; she was definitely a woman who admired a great tight end when she saw one. Her layers of clothing made her feel awkward and unwieldy, while Gabriel managed to remain his usual capable, annoyingly perfect self. He'd always been athletic, and, yes, he had a great tight end. If he hadn't been wearing his own heavy coat, she'd at least have been able to admire his personal scenery. Thank goodness he didn't know she was imagining his butt; he continued on, steadfast and skillful, leading the way with aplomb.

She didn't do anything with aplomb, even when she wasn't hampered by layer upon layer of clothing. At least if she fell she'd be well cushioned when she hit the ground.

Gabriel looked great. Good-looking, muscled . . . really great eyes, a blue-green hazel ringed by inky lashes. He was bigger than he'd been in high school, definitely older, but those eyes hadn't changed at all. Lolly had to forcibly stop herself from getting carried away. She tried to call upon reason, to think clearly. He'd saved her life, so there was probably some instinctive attraction going on that had absolutely nothing to do with who he was. Add the fact that they'd been skin to skin, that he'd been inside her, and she shouldn't expect anything less than total infatuation.

Oh, who was she kidding? She'd always had the hots for him — not to the point that she'd spent the last fifteen years pining over him, but enough so that when she saw him again that old interest immediately flared to life again.

When she was safely over the log that blocked her driveway, Gabriel held on to her for a moment longer than was necessary, making sure her footing was solid — not that she was in any hurry to move away.

"I have soup and coffee in the truck," he said. "We'll take a short break there, and if a tree hasn't fallen on it, we can get in the truck and get warm."

After the hours the truck had been sitting, she had no hope at all that either soup or coffee would be warm, but it was food and she'd take it. The breakfast bars weren't going to last nearly long enough. "Good idea." It was a long way to Wilson Creek, and the trip was best faced in small chunks. To the end of the driveway. To the curve where the old Morrison house used to be. To the hill where there was a break in the tree line, where the sun would surely shine. To the highway . . . and from there they'd start all over again, as they walked to the McQueen house.

Where she'd be a literal fifth wheel.

After taking several steps without any problem, without warning, Lolly's right foot flew out from under her. She instinctively flailed for a low lying limb, but as she grabbed it the thin, frozen twig snapped. Gabriel grabbed her, making sure she didn't land on her ass. He held her close, secure, and she took a moment to wallow in his body heat and solid build. Gabriel McQueen was like a rock. Without him, where would she be right now? She couldn't let her mind go there.

Lolly's heart pounded as she tried to catch her breath. She knew what a disaster a bad fall would be. She was already sore, bruised, and shaken. All she needed was to break a bone or sprain an ankle. If she thought she was a burden to Gabriel now . . .

"You okay?" he asked.

When she nodded her head he released her, and she moved forward.

One step at a time.

Gabriel had known the trek down the mountain would be a tough one, hour upon hour of watching every step and being alert to the dangers all around.

After stopping at the truck to get warm — no trees having fallen on the truck — to drink some lukewarm coffee and soup, and to retrieve his weatherproof hat, he and Lolly resumed their trek. Lolly didn't grumble, hadn't uttered a word of complaint, but she'd already started breathing harder and favoring her bruised right side.

He took her hand as they met a hill, knowing that on the other side of that rise was a sharp dip in the earth that would not be easy to take. They leaned into the climb, watching each step, breathing hard, not wasting precious energy by speaking.

Gabriel kept telling himself it could be worse. As far as mountains in this part of the country went, this was a small one, not high enough for good skiing. Some might even call it a big hill, instead of a mountain. Walking down was doable, and they should be thankful for that. The storm had stopped. If they'd had to walk out in the wind and falling rain, the walk would take twice as long and be ten times as dangerous. If either he or Lolly had been hurt last night, shot or slashed with a knife, then they'd be separated, the mobile one hiking alone to town for help, the other left behind. And if they'd both been hurt . . .

Would his dad figure that he'd been

347

stranded by the storm and that all was well, or would he be worried and doing what he could to get up this road? Lolly had said that when Darwin and Niki broke in, she was on her way out to stay with the Richards. Would Mrs. Richard be worried enough to call the sheriff's office and report that Lolly hadn't arrived? Or would she just assume that Lolly had wasted time and let the storm catch her on the mountain? Lots of possibilities, and he had no way of knowing what to expect. He might as well proceed as if he and Lolly were entirely on their own. For now, they were.

Halfway up the hill a patch of sun warmed the ground. That heat and light was a welcome relief — though he knew it wouldn't last. Where the sunshine touched the ground, the going was easier. They could even take a few steps on the roadway, when the shoulder was narrow and too close to a drop-off for comfort. He didn't bother to drop Lolly's hand, even when the walking was less slippery for a few precious steps.

"Not so bad, huh?" he asked.

Lolly was breathless when she answered, "Speak for yourself, Mc-Queen."

He would've turned to give her an encouraging smile, to tell her that they were making great time, but then he reached the top of the hill and got a good look at what lay ahead.

There weren't just one or two fallen trees across the road, there was one right after another for as far as he could see. Some lay there alone, with

349

stretches of blessedly untouched road-way on either side. Others criss-crossed, one trunk and another . . . and another . . . blocking their way. Some they could go over, as they'd gone over the one on the driveway. Others were too big, or the limbs were too tangled. They were going to have to go around some of the block-age, detouring into the woods, wast-ing precious minutes.

"Fuck," he muttered.

"Right now?" Lolly joked, but out of the corner of his eye he saw her straighten her spine and lift her chin. She looked a little ridiculous, the way she was bundled up, but she also looked strong. And kind of amazing. She pulled in a deep breath.

"I am *not* going to get away from Niki and Darwin and survive a cat-

and-mouse chase through the icy rain and in my own kitchen just to give up now," she said. Her eyes narrowed. "I'll be damned if I'm going to sit down and cry, even if that's the first impulse that comes to mind." She looked at him, and he saw the shine of tears in her eyes. "It's going to be a long day. Distract me." She moved to the side of the road and started her descent. "You must have hundreds of cute and funny stories about Sam. Tell me a few. Make me laugh."

Gabriel didn't feel much like laughing at the moment, but thinking about Sam waiting for his dad to come home drove him forward.

CHAPTER FOURTEEN

There were moments when Lolly didn't think she could take another step. Her feet hurt. Everything hurt. For a while Gabriel and his stories kept her moving, but now it was the sound of chain saws that kept her motivated. It was impossible to tell exactly where the sounds were coming from. Crews might be working in town, and the noise just carried. Then again, maybe the workers were on this very road. Maybe just over the next hill . . . or the next.

"When I buy a house in Portland,

it's going to be on completely flat land. With close neighbors. And constant five-bar cell service."

Gabriel looked over his shoulder. "You're planning on buying a house?"

"I've been thinking about it," she said. "I have a nice apartment, but rent is just money down the drain. They keep saying it's a good time to buy."

He made a sound, like a soft grunt from deep in his throat. "I didn't know you planned to put down roots in Portland."

"I have a good job there. Friends. I'm . . . comfortable."

Again he made that grunting noise.

At the moment *comfortable* seemed like a decidedly good thing to Lolly. She liked comfortable. She enjoyed a life where there were no surprises.

And then she got a surprise.

"Before you buy a house, you should come visit me in North Carolina. Maybe you'd like it better there."

The comment left her dumbfounded, but she didn't have time to read too much into the invitation, because Gabriel crested the hill they were climbing, and stopped. She was directly behind him, so close she almost crashed into his back. Instead she moved to stand beside him. There, in the distance — but blessedly not *too* far away — sat a massive truck with a crane built into the bed. A four-man crew was cutting limbs and tree trunks and moving them off the roadway with the crane. They'd already cut a swath from the highway.

Lolly was so relieved, her knees almost buckled out from under her. She leaned into Gabriel in sheer relief. He took her hand and squeezed. "Almost there, Lollipop."

She wanted to ask Gabriel more about his impromptu invitation, but the time for that question had come and gone in an instant, and she'd missed it.

Knowing that help was so close spurred them both forward. Gabriel continued to hold her hand. Whether to make sure she kept up or to maintain a connection she didn't know . . . and was afraid to ask. Every insecurity, the shyness she'd thought she'd defeated years ago, came rushing to the surface. Gabriel might ask her to visit him, when there was no one in the world but the two of them and the rush of survival was still warm within them. But now . . . what would happen now, with the real world intruding?

It seemed to take forever to reach the road crew, who spotted Gabriel and Lolly from a distance and waved enthusiastically. As they came nearer the one in the front — Justin Temple, who hadn't changed much since Lolly had moved away from Wilson Creek — called out in a booming, deep voice. "The sheriff said we might run into you two, but I didn't expect to see you so soon. We've got coffee and sandwiches," he added, and then he unclipped a radio from his belt and spoke to someone on the other end of the line.

This road should've been low priority, but thanks to the sheriff it hadn't been. Lolly knew there were other crews out there, clearing roads in town and in the neighborhoods just beyond, and she could only be grateful that she'd gotten herself stranded with the sheriff's son — and that Harlan McQueen carried a lot of weight around here.

The coffee was fairly fresh, fairly hot, and tasted better than any coffee she'd ever had. She was so exhausted she could only manage a few bites of the sandwich, but she ate what she could, then she and Gabriel sat on the back of the truck and waited for the sheriff, who Justin said was already on his way. Now that she wasn't moving the cold felt sharper, but at the same time it felt good to just *sit*. Gabriel put his arm around her, hugged her to him.

The crew continued to work, though

she suspected that since she and Gabriel had shown up, they might soon be sent to another, more heavily populated area. She still couldn't count on getting to her car anytime soon.

"I guess I could catch a bus back to Portland," she said. She wasn't sure when they'd be running again, but maybe it would be no more than a couple of days.

"What's the rush?" Gabriel asked casually.

"I can't do a thing with the house until the roads are cleared, I can't even get to my car. If it's like this all over town that could take days . . . even weeks. I can't stay here for weeks."

"Why not?"

Lolly opened her mouth to answer, but said nothing. She'd been invited to a friend's house for Christmas Eve, but on Christmas Day she'd be alone. The office wouldn't open until after New Year's, so she'd have that week to take care of a few chores around the house. She'd planned to clean her closets and go through the pantry getting rid of all the expired food she'd never used. Maybe watch some movies, organize her DVDs and CDs, try some new recipes. In other words, nothing of any importance.

Gabriel touched her cheek and gently forced her to look him in the eye. Without a word, he kissed her, the touch light and easy, familiar, as if they'd kissed a thousand times. When he pulled his mouth away he said, "Stay with us. I'd like you to get to know Sam. Mom would love to have you, and so would I."

"You've already had me." The words were out of her mouth before she could stop them.

Gabriel smiled. "So I have, and I've been thinking about a repeat. What about you?"

There was no ignoring what had happened in the shower, but at the same time she felt kind of clueless. Yes, she'd been icy cold, frightened, desperate . . . but she wouldn't have wanted just anyone the way she'd wanted Gabriel. She wasn't made that way.

"So, what is this, exactly?" she asked.

Her timing continued to be terrible. At that moment they heard the roar of an engine and the loud jangle of chains on tires making their way down the icy road. Gabriel grinned when he saw the sheriff's four-wheel drive, with his dad behind the wheel. He jumped off the truck and turned to slide his hands under Lolly's coat and grip her waist, then he lifted her down. Lolly smiled, too, but that smile was forced.

Because she knew from here on out she and Gabriel wouldn't be alone again. The adventure was over; she'd been rescued too soon.

Gabriel barely waited for the SUV to come to a stop at his parents' house before he opened the door and stepped carefully onto the salted driveway, new energy in his step in spite of his exhaustion. He and Lolly had to give official statements, but not even that was going to keep him from seeing Sam first. His dad had told him how worried Sam had been when Gabriel hadn't come home as promised last night. The storm had done nothing to ease the kid's fears.

When he reached the door, he met his mother — who was physically restraining Sam. She had him by the collar, the same way she'd corralled Gabriel a time or two. Valerie said, "See, I told you he was all right," and let Sam go.

"Dad!" Once he was free, Sam burst forward and up, into Gabriel's arms. Gabriel held on tight, and so did Sam.

"I thought you weren't coming back," Sam said, his head buried in Gabriel's shoulder. He began sobbing. "I thought you had a wreck, or got frozen, or a tree fell on your truck. Gran said you were fine, she said you knew how to take care of yourself, but I dreamed you weren't ever coming back."

Gabriel's heart constricted. A child shouldn't have such fears, but loss wasn't new to Sam. He patted Sam's narrow back, instinctively rocking his child from side to side in the universal comforting motion. "It wasn't that bad. I just got stuck at Lolly's house because the roads froze sooner than I expected."

Sam lifted his head and looked directly at Gabriel. His tear-wet eyes narrowed. "Lolly. That's the stupidest name I ever heard."

"It's short for Lorelei."

Gabriel half turned to see that Lolly and his dad had entered the kitchen behind him. He'd been so caught up in his reunion with Sam, he hadn't heard them come in. Lolly, who had offered the explanation for her name, smiled gently, showing no outward sign of the trauma she'd experienced. For Sam's sake, he knew, and for that he was grateful.

Sam was not appeased. He'd been terrified, and obviously Lolly was to blame. "If my name was Lorelei I'd make people call me something else, too. That's even stupider than *Lolly*."

"Sam," Gabriel chided gently. "That's rude. Apologize."

He ducked his head, his small jaw set. "Sorry," he mumbled, spitting out the word without an ounce of real regret. He wouldn't overtly disobey, but that was about as far as he was willing to go.

Lolly took no offense — or at least, she didn't appear to. She took a step forward, moving closer. "I imagine you're pretty mad at me for dragging your dad out of the house in a storm."

A sullen Sam nodded. "You shoulda left before the storm got here."

"I understand that," Lolly said. "Ah . . . something happened, and I couldn't leave." She reached out to tuck a wayward strand of hair away from Sam's face. "And I'm sure you understand that your daddy is a real, live, honest-to-goodness hero, in a world that needs all the heroes it can get."

"Well, *yeah,*" Sam agreed. "Duh."

Gabriel watched Lolly bite back a laugh. She was doing this right, not coming on too strong, not trying to act like Sam's best friend when they'd just met. "You look very much like him. Are you a hero, too?"

At that, Sam's spine straightened. With Gabriel holding him, he was able to look Lolly in the eye for a moment, before he nodded.

"I'm so glad to hear that," Lolly said with a friendly smile. "The world needs heroes like you and your dad."

Sam looked closely at Lolly's bruised face. "What happened to you?" He pointed to her cheek, and Gabriel held his breath. He couldn't protect Sam from all the ugliness in the world, but the kid didn't need to know that it had all but landed on his doorstep.

Lolly gently placed a hand over her cheek. "I fell," she said simply. "That was before your dad arrived, and I have to tell you, he saved me from falling several times."

"The ice is slippery," Sam said in

an almost grown-up voice. "Gran wouldn't let me go outside, even to meet Dad."

"Your Gran is a very smart woman," Lolly said sincerely.

Gabriel could see the wheels in his son's head turning, as he sized up the situation and the woman before him. "Sorry I made fun of your name," he said, more sincerely this time.

"You're not the first," she said in a confidential tone, as if there weren't three other adults listening in. "Your father used to call me . . ." She glanced around, then leaned in and whispered in Sam's ear. "Lollipop."

Sam started to giggle, and Gabriel put the kid on his feet. He didn't go far, though. Sam stayed close, leaning into Gabriel, occasionally grabbing on to his clothing, or his hand, to make sure he didn't go away again.

Valerie McQueen, always prepared, had a spread ready for them. Soup, sandwiches, coffee, cookies. Gabriel and Lolly sat at the kitchen table, Sam perched on Gabriel's knee, and ate until they couldn't get another bite down. It didn't take Sam long to relax with Lolly, or to release the remnants of his fear that his dad wasn't coming home. "Relaxed" didn't mean exactly friendly, but even as an infant Sam had always taken a while to warm up to strange adults.

For someone who didn't have kids, Lolly was good with Sam. Before he'd moved Sam to Maine, the friends — his and Mariane's — who'd spent time with Sam tended to smother him with sympathy. That sympathy was deserved, but after a while it didn't do the kid any good. Lolly talked to Sam almost like he was an adult, and the kid responded.

When she started telling Sam stories about his dad as a child, though, Gabriel had to interfere. He didn't want his kid — or his parents — hearing how he'd tormented Lolly. He called time-out and Lolly laughed — a real, honest laugh that warmed him to his bones.

Sam only called her Lollipop once, and they both immediately fell into a fit of laughter while Gabriel and his folks looked on, bemused and surprised. And Gabriel realized that at some point in the last twenty-four hours, his world had shifted.

Lolly leaned her head back and closed her eyes, letting the hot water do its work on her tired, overworked, once-frozen muscles. Usually she jumped in the shower, got clean, and got out. It had been a long while since she'd indulged in a real, soaking bath.

The McQueen bathroom was larger than the one at the old house, built years later when so much space was no longer a luxury but a necessity. The bathtub was wide and deep; the counter on the other side of the square room was long and crowded with soaps, towels, shampoos, and two flickering candles. This house still had electricity, though much of Wilson Creek did not. Lolly wasn't taking any chances, though, hence the candles. If there was a disruption in the power, she wasn't going to be plunged into darkness — not tonight.

After Sam had gone to bed, she and

Gabriel had given their statements to Sheriff McQueen. Gabriel's dad was glad that they were both safe, and at the same time incensed that meth addicts had invaded his county. As soon as it was practicable, road and power crews would make their way up the mountain to the house. And still it would be days, maybe weeks, before they reached what was left of Darwin and Niki.

Which meant Lolly was going to be without her car for a while. That was the least of her worries . . .

She was roused out of a near sleep by a soft knock, following by the rattling of the doorknob, which she'd locked behind her.

"I'll be right out," she called, gathering the strength to rise from the still-warm water.

"Don't move," a familiar deep voice called. The doorknob rattled again, the lock set in the knob popped, and the door swung open. Lolly grabbed a wet washcloth and positioned it across her chest in a poor, last second attempt at modesty.

Gabriel slid into the room and closed — and locked — the door behind him.

"You've just proven to me that the lock on that door is useless," she said. Maybe she should be more shocked, more shy. But she wasn't.

He held aloft a bent paper clip. "I grew up in this house. All the interior locks do is warn someone who tries to get in that the room is occupied."

"And yet you didn't take the hint."

He smiled down at her, and she wished she had a couple more washcloths handy. "Want me to leave?"

She knew if she said yes, he'd go. "No."

Gabriel turned off the harsh overhead light, plunging the room into near darkness. The candles provided flickering light. He unbuttoned his shirt and slid it off, then unfastened and unzipped his jeans and stepped out of them. Socks and underwear followed. Heaven above, he was gorgeous and tempting.

"Your folks . . ."

"Are asleep," he said as he stepped into the water. "Dead to the world, just like Sam. I don't think any of them got much sleep last night."

"Neither did you," Lolly said as she scooted back, making a place for Gabriel to sit, facing her. He sat down slowly, and the level of water in the tub rose almost to the edge. The slightest movement would send water sloshing onto the floor. "Why aren't you asleep?"

"Same reason you're here instead of tucked into a warm bed, I imagine."

Her mind wouldn't stop spinning. She didn't know what tomorrow would bring. Her world had been turned upside down. Of course she couldn't sleep!

Gabriel looked her in the eye. They were naked, wet, face-to-face. She wanted nothing more than to reach out and hold him, but she didn't make that move. "Why are you here?" Maybe it should have been obvious, but she was asking more than about just the sex.

He reached out and touched her bruised cheek with strong and surprisingly gentle hands. "I have a favor to ask."

"You did save my life," she said, wondering what kind of favor it might be. Since they were both naked, she had a clue . . .

"Don't go back to Portland just yet."

Even though he'd mentioned that this afternoon, as they'd made their way down the mountain, it wasn't exactly what she'd been expecting. Reality had descended with a bang, and even though she loved this house, this home, this family . . . she didn't belong here. "Why not?"

"Stay here, spend Christmas with us." Gabriel stopped and took a deep breath. "Let's see where this goes."

Her insides leapt and danced.

"Let's see where *we* go," he clarified, though no clarification was necessary.

"I can do that," she whispered.

He leaned toward her, peeled the washcloth from her breasts and tossed it aside, kissed her, and sent a bit of water over the lip of the tub. She barely noticed.

"And stop talking about buying a house in Portland. At least until you've visited North Carolina a time or two. It's much warmer there."

"And you're there."

He made an affirmative humming sound as he continued to move forward.

Lolly felt all her cares, all her worries, unwinding, fading away. "That doesn't seem at all like too much to ask, all things considered."

He put his mouth on hers again, and

the kiss quickly took on a rhythm. Lolly wallowed in Gabriel's heat and hardness, she welcomed the kiss, the connection, the warmth they generated . . . a warmth that transformed her from the inside out.

Gabriel took his mouth from hers, but he didn't move far. His nose touched hers; he was a breath away. "Lollipop, can I lick you?"

"Yes," she said, wrapping her arms around Gabriel's neck and surging into him to send more water onto the floor. "Yes, you can."

ABOUT THE AUTHOR

Linda Howard is the award-winning author of many *New York Times* best-sellers, including *Burn, Death Angel, Up Close and Dangerous, Drop Dead Gorgeous, Cover of Night, Killing Time, To Die For, Kiss Me While I Sleep, Cry No More, Dying to Please, Open Season, Mr. Perfect, All the Queen's Men, Now You See Her, Kill and Tell,* and *Son of the Morning.* She lives in Alabama with her husband and a golden retriever.

We hope you have enjoyed this Large Print book. Other Thorndike, Wheeler, Kennebec, and Chivers Press Large Print books are available at your library or directly from the publishers.

For information about current and upcoming titles, please call or write, without obligaton, to:

Publisher
Thorndike Press
295 Kennedy Memorial Drive
Waterville, ME 04901
Tel. (800) 223-1244

or visit our Web site at:

http://gale.cengage.com/thorndike

OR

Chivers Large Print
published by BBC Audiobooks Ltd
St. James House, The Square
Lower Bristol Road
Bath BA2 3SB
England
Tel. +44(0) 800 136919
email: bbcaudiobooksbbc.co.uk
www.bbcaudiobooks.co.uk

All our Large Print titles are designed for easy reading, and all our books are made to last.